PRAISE FOR ZYGMUNT MIŁOSZEWSKI

"Polish mystery writer Miłoszewski's first novel, *Entanglement* (2010), earned the High Calibre Award and was made into a movie . . . Miłoszewski's compelling mystery offers a revealing glimpse of life in modern Poland, a country still dealing with its complicated past."
—Barbara Bibel, *Booklist*

"Miłoszewski takes an engaging look at modern Polish society in this stellar first in a new series starring Warsaw prosecutor Teodor Szacki . . . Readers will want to see more of the complex, sympathetic Szacki."
—*Publishers Weekly*

"*Entanglement* has all we require from a thriller. It opens with a murder and quickly develops into a fast-moving and tightly plotted whodunnit with a host of colourful characters . . . Ultimately it is the descriptions of Szacki's personal life and his emotional turmoil which transcend our expectations of the genre."
—*Oxford Times*

RAGE

ALSO BY ZYGMUNT MIŁOSZEWSKI

Entanglement (Polish State Prosecutor Szacki Investigates)

A Grain of Truth (Polish State Prosecutor Szacki Investigates)

RAGE

ZYGMUNT MIŁOSZEWSKI

TRANSLATED BY ANTONIA LLOYD-JONES

WITHDRAWN

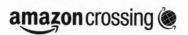

This is a work of fiction. Names, characters, organizations, places, events, and incidents are either products of the author's imagination or are used fictitiously.

Text copyright © 2014 Zygmunt Miłoszewski
Translation copyright © 2016 Antonia Lloyd-Jones
All rights reserved.

No part of this book may be reproduced, or stored in a retrieval system, or transmitted in any form or by any means, electronic, mechanical, photocopying, recording, or otherwise, without express written permission of the publisher.

Previously published as *Gniew* by W.A.B. in Poland in 2014. Translated from Polish by Antonia Lloyd-Jones. First published in English by AmazonCrossing in 2016.

Published by AmazonCrossing, Seattle

www.apub.com

Amazon, the Amazon logo, and AmazonCrossing are trademarks of Amazon.com, Inc., or its affiliates.

ISBN-13: 9781503935860
ISBN-10: 1503935868

Cover design by M. S. Corley

Printed in the United States of America

For Marta

NOW

Imagine a child who has to hide from those he loves. He does everything other children do. He makes towers out of building blocks, crashes toy cars together, has his teddy bears hold conversations, and paints houses under a smiling sun. A kid like any other. But fear makes everything look different. The towers never tumble. The car crashes are more like gentle bumps than major collisions. The teddy bears converse in whispers. And the water in the paint jar rapidly turns to dirty gray sludge. The child is afraid to go change the water, and eventually all the paints are smeared with sludge. Every little house, every smiling sun, and every little tree comes out the same nasty black and blue.

Out in the Polish provinces, that's the color of the Warmian landscape tonight.

The fading December light is too weak to pick out distinct shades. The sky, a wall of trees, a house at the edge of the woods, and a muddy meadow only differ by their depth of blackness. With each passing minute they progressively merge together, until finally the separate elements can no longer be seen.

It's a monochromatic nocturne, bitterly cold and desolate.

It's hard to believe that in this lifeless landscape, inside the black house, two people are alive—one of them only just, but the other so sharply and intensely that it's agonizing. Sweating, panting, deafened by the thudding of his own blood pulsating in his ears, he is trying to overcome the pain in his muscles to finish the job as fast as possible.

He cannot ward off the thought that in the movies it always looks different, and that after the opening credits they should give a warning: "Ladies and gentlemen, be advised that in reality, committing murder demands bestial strength, physical coordination, and above all, perfect fitness. Don't try this at home."

Just holding on to the victim is a major feat. The body defends itself against death in all sorts of ways. It's hard to call it a fight; it's more like something in between convulsions and an epileptic fit—every muscle tenses, and it's not at all the way they describe it in novels, where the victim gradually weakens. The nearer the end, the more forcefully the muscle cells try to use the last remnants of oxygen to liberate the body.

Which means you can't let them have that oxygen, or it'll start all over again. Which means it's not enough to just hold on to the victim so they won't break free; you've also got to choke them effectively. And hope the next jolting kick will be the last, and there'll be no strength left for more.

But the victim seems to have an endless supply of strength. For the killer it's the opposite—the sharp pain of his overstretched muscles is rising in his arms, his fingers are stiffening, starting to rebel. He can see them slowly slipping, second by second, from the sweat-soaked neck.

He's sure he can't do it. But just when he's about to give up, the body suddenly stops moving in his hands. The victim's eyes become the eyes of a corpse. He has seen too many of them in his life not to recognize that.

And yet he can't remove his hands—he goes on strangling the dead body with all his might for a while longer. He knows he's in the grip of hysteria, but he goes on squeezing, harder and harder, ignoring the pain in his hands and arms. Suddenly the larynx caves in disturbingly under his thumbs. Terrified, he loosens his grip.

He stands back and stares at the corpse lying at his feet. Seconds pass, then minutes. The longer he stands there, the more incapable he is of moving. Finally, he forces himself to pick up his coat from the back of a chair and pulls it over his shoulders. He keeps telling himself that if he doesn't act quickly, his own corpse will soon be lying beside his victim's on the floor. He's surprised it hasn't happened yet.

But on the other hand, isn't that Prosecutor Teodor Szacki's greatest wish right now?

TEN DAYS EARLIER

CHAPTER ONE

Monday, November 25, 2013

Scientists experimenting on mice prove that it is possible to eliminate the male Y chromosome entirely without any harm to the mouse's procreative abilities. A world without men is actually becoming technically possible. The world has its eyes on Ukraine, whose rulers have lately refused to sign an association agreement with the European Union. One hundred thousand people come out onto the streets of Kiev. It's International Day for the Elimination of Violence Against Women. According to statistics, 60 percent of Poles know at least one family where a woman is the victim of violence, and 45 percent live or have lived in a family where violence has occurred. Nineteen percent believe that there is no such thing as rape within marriage, and 11 percent do not agree that hitting your wife or female partner counts as abuse. During trials, the Italian-made high-speed train Pendolino beats the record for rail travel in Poland by reaching a velocity of 182 miles per hour. Kraków, the third most polluted city in Europe, makes it illegal to burn coal. The citizens of Olsztyn express their views on what their city needs most: bike paths, a sports arena, and a major festival. And new roads, to deal with the plague of traffic jams. There is surprisingly little support for the streetcar network that's meant to be the flagship urban investment project. As the deputy mayor explains, "I think a lot of the people out there have never ridden a modern streetcar." The Warmian fall continues—it's gray and ugly, and whatever the thermometer may say, everyone can tell that it's damned cold outside. There's fog in the air, and freezing drizzle.

1

Prosecutor Teodor Szacki was convinced that nobody deserved death. Not ever. Nobody, regardless of the circumstances, should take another person's life, neither in defiance of the law nor following it to the letter. He had firmly believed this for as long as he could remember, but now, as he waited at the lights at the junction of Żołnierska and Dworcowa Streets, he felt his deeply rooted faith begin to waver for the very first time.

On one side there were apartment buildings, on the other a hospital, and facing the hospital were pavilions, with a huge banner advertising a "Leather and Skins Fair." Szacki wondered if that sounded ambiguous only to his prosecutor's mind. It was a typical junction in a provincial town, where two streets bisect simply because they have to do it somewhere; nobody ever slows down to admire the view—instead they just drive on.

Though actually they don't—they drive up, come to a halt, and sit there like sheep, waiting for the green light while their feet merge with the pedals, and they grow long white beards that reach their knees, and clawlike nails on their fingertips.

Just after moving to this city, he had read in the *Olsztyn Gazette* that the city's traffic operations designer doesn't believe in the "green wave"—because it makes people drive too fast, and thus presents a danger for road traffic—and at first thought it quite a funny joke. But it wasn't a joke. He soon discovered that in this not very large city, which you could walk across in half an hour, and where the vehicles moved down wide streets, everyone was always getting stuck in traffic jams. And, to give the traffic designer his due, they really were at risk—of having an apoplectic fit, but at least they didn't present a danger to other road users.

On top of that, the traffic designer didn't believe that the citizens of Olsztyn were capable of turning left in the usual way, after first letting the cars pass from the opposite direction. And so, out of concern for their safety, at almost every junction it simply couldn't be done. Each stream of cars approaching the intersection from each street that led to it was given its own green light, one after another, while the rest sat and politely waited for their turn.

Which was why Szacki cursed aloud when on Dworcowa Street, two hundred yards ahead of his Citroën, the light went yellow. He had no chance of getting through. So he stopped, put the car in neutral, and sighed heavily.

Some sort of Warmian crap was coming out of the sky, neither rain, nor snow, nor hail. The stuff froze as soon as it hit the windshield, and even on the fastest setting the wipers couldn't scrape off this mysterious substance. The windshield washer fluid did nothing but smear it around. Szacki couldn't believe he was living in a town where such atmospheric phenomena were possible.

He was sorry Poland didn't have any overseas colonies—otherwise he'd have had himself assigned to some paradise island, where he'd have prosecuted old ladies for trying to persuade waiters and rumba instructors to submit to more advanced erotic activities. Although, knowing his luck, the only Polish overseas colony would have been an island in the Barents Sea, where there aren't any old ladies because nobody makes it to forty.

For entertainment he started imagining what he would do to Olsztyn's traffic operations designer—all the ways he'd punish him, and what sort of pain he'd inflict. That was the moment when his belief in not killing began to waver, for the more refined the tortures he devised, the greater joy and satisfaction he felt.

He would have just gone through on red, if not for the fact that as a state prosecutor he couldn't simply get a ticket, pay up, and forget about it. If he were caught by the traffic cops, he'd have to declare his profession, and then the cops would have to inform his boss of the incident and ask for the delinquent sheriff to be punished. It usually ended in a warning, but it remained on file, leaving a black mark on his service history, and depending how malevolent his boss was feeling, it could have an effect on his salary. And as Szacki was already getting the feeling that there was no love lost for him at his new job, he preferred not to expose himself. Finally he began moving again, drove past the hospital, the brothel, and the old water tower, and then—after serving his time at the lights again—he took a gentle curve onto Kościuszko Street. Here there was finally something worth looking at, first and foremost the Administrative Court. A huge edifice that demanded respect, it had originally been built as the headquarters of the Allenstein regional administration in the days when the city was part of Germany. It was a wonderful building—a stately, majestic five-story sea of redbrick rising from a ground floor made of stone blocks. If it had been up to Szacki, he'd have housed all three of Olsztyn's prosecution services in this building. He thought it would mean something to witnesses to be escorted up the wide steps into a great big building like this one, rather than into the miserable little 1970s box where his own local office was situated. The public should know that the state meant dignity and strength built on a solid foundation, not penny-pinching, stopgaps, terrazzo tiles, and gloss paint on the walls.

The Germans had known what they were doing. Szacki was born in Warsaw, and at first he'd found the Olsztyn citizens' deference toward the builders of their little homeland irritating. To him, the Germans had never done any building—on the contrary, they had reduced Warsaw to a heap of rubble, thanks to which his native town was a pitiful caricature of a capital city. He had never liked the Germans, but he had to give them credit: everything attractive in Olsztyn—everything that gave the city its character, or made it interesting with the not-so-obvious charm of a thick-skinned woman of the North—had been built by them. Everything else was bland at best, but usually hideous. And in numerous cases so ugly that time and again the capital of Warmia was held up as the laughingstock of Poland, thanks to the architectural horrors adorning it with a persistence worthy of a better cause.

It didn't really bother him, but if he'd been an old German on a sentimental journey to the land of his childhood, he'd probably have wept.

The school he was heading for was called Adam Mickiewicz High School, in honor of Poland's greatest poet. Yet the first kids to go to school here hadn't studied the Polish bard, but rather Goethe and Schiller. Again it occurred to him that location has significance, as he gazed up at the large, gloomy nineteenth-century redbrick block. It would have been a regular, large German-era school, if not for its neo-Gothic design features—pointed gables, a small round skylight, and huge windows in the central part of the building. This gave it an austere, churchlike quality, suggesting the set for a horror movie about a didactic experiment that has gone awry. Nuns with clenched lips, children sitting in silence in identical uniforms, all pretending they can't hear the bestial screams of their fellow student who hasn't done his assignment for the third time in a row. Nobody's hitting him, oh no. He just has to spend one hour alone in a small room in the attic. Nothing has ever been done to anyone there yet. But no one has ever come back the same. The nuns call it "private tuition."

"Prosecutor Szacki?"

For a couple of seconds he stared blankly at the woman standing before him in the school doorway.

He nodded and shook her outstretched hand.

The teacher led him down the hallways. There was nothing special about the interior. You could probably have smelled the odor of old brick walls in here, if not for the nose-tickling mixture of hormones, deodorant, and floor polish.

Before he even had time to wonder if he missed his school days and if he'd like to go through the hell of youth again, they entered the auditorium, where the assembled students were applauding three women of various ages, who had just finished a debate on the stage and were standing there smiling.

"Have you got a short speech ready?" whispered the teacher. "The kids are very much counting on it."

He said yes, he had, while thinking that even the penal code lets you tell lies if it's for your own cause.

2

Meanwhile, in a nondescript house on Równa Street in the suburbs of Olsztyn—neither very near, nor very far away—an ordinary woman, so ordinary she could be counted as a statistic, was sinking into unhappy thoughts about herself. She had just reached the conclusion that she'd been wretched and worthless from the moment she was born. She must have spent the nine months before birth drifting away from her perfect self. That's how she imagined it—at the moment of conception, the needle on the pressure gauge of God's control panel was in the middle of the green field, then suddenly it shifted in completely the wrong direction. Not enough to mean she was sick, disabled, or stupid—nothing of the kind. The needle had simply shifted from green to orange. And when the first cell—who knows, it could have been a really great one—divided into two, those were the first two parts of her imperfect self. After that, things just continued downhill, and by the time she was born she consisted of such a huge number of lousy cells that the harm was irreversible.

The list of her imperfections was infinite; paradoxically, she found it easier to bear the psychological ones because only she was aware of them. Lack of patience. Lack of logic. Lack of concentration. Lack of empathy. Lack of maternal instinct—that one probably hurt the most.

She was always telling her friends there was nothing she could do about it—the one child she could stand was her own, her kid was the only one who didn't get on her nerves. They always laughed, and so did she, though not at what she'd said, but at the fact that it was total crap—her own child got on her nerves most of all. Even when she was nowhere near a mirror, she only had to glance at that square-shaped brat with the tiny little eyes to see herself, all her crap-shit genes, produced by her crap-shit cells.

Well, yeah—her own eyes were just the same. She found them hard to conceal. Her hair could at least be dyed and styled, her narrow lips could be enhanced, her pointed ears covered up. But her tiny eyes? There was no kind of makeup that could change those peepers, sunk deep in their sockets, into lovely almond-shaped eyes. The kind of eyes that would have saved her, so that people could have said, *She's nothing special, but those eyes—she must have been at the front of the line when God was handing them out.* Well, she hadn't been.

Her eyes couldn't be concealed, and nor could her figure—you can't put dark glasses on your figure. Her figure gave her the most grief of all. There was nothing distinctive about her. If only she were very thin—girls like that have their admirers. Or very well endowed—that works, too. With huge breasts—hordes of men would have looked at her. And her man would be able to say, *Those tits are mine, those are my lovely tits.* But no, she was square, or rather rectangular. No hips or waist, the legs of a peasant woman, the kind you can stand on all day long. She wasn't entirely flat-chested, but there was nothing to grab hold of either—obese guys sometimes have tits like hers. And as for her shoulders—they looked as if she were always wearing a padded blouse, the kind that was fashionable in the '80s.

She was trying to choose a long skirt and sweater to make it look as if she had a waist and hips. She was really determined to look nicer than usual today. To give him something special, so he'd know he hadn't made a mistake.

She heard a plaintive wail from the living room. What else did she expect? She'd been ignoring him for a whole fifteen minutes—if he'd known how, he would surely have called ChildLine by now. She tossed the sweater on a shelf under the mirror and ran to the child. He was kneeling by the couch, crying with his head buried in the cushions.

"What's up?"

"Don't want it."

"What don't you want?"

"No." He pointed at the TV.

"You don't want that cartoon?"

"No."

"Do you want another one?"

"No."

"Bob?"

"No."

"Franklin?"

"No, no, no!"

By now he was laughing—he found it an excellent game. And the tears weren't yet dry on his cheeks. Apparently kids are like that—they can forget negative emotions in a split second. She didn't know what hormone was responsible for that, but thought they really should isolate it and sell it in tablet form. She'd buy a bucketload.

"Zebra?"

"No."

"Blue teddy?"

"No."

"Fucking dick with mint jelly?" The tone of her voice hadn't changed a bit.

"No. Ubbies."

He burst into giggles as sweetly as if he understood what she was talking about. She wiped his face with her hands. What a great mother she was. Finally she switched on whatever, because she couldn't remember where the *Teletubbies* DVD had gone; luckily the ads were running, which have the same effect on a small child as a shot of heroin. The kid froze with his mouth half-open, while she glanced at her watch and went to throw some cottage cheese–filled pancakes into the microwave.

She felt as if something had gone wrong with time—the kid should have had his dinner an hour ago. And she ought to be doing something. She'd been home all day, but when her husband got home she'd have nothing but microwaved two-day-old pancakes to offer him. Even if she whipped up some cream to go with them and defrosted some raspberries, they'd still be two-day-old pancakes.

What could she say? "I'm sorry, honey, I spent all day trying to choose the right clothes so you wouldn't realize your wife has no waist."

She could feel the panic rising in her throat like a third tonsil. She swallowed hard. Why wasn't she doing anything? Why was she totally worthless, so—he was really good at putting it into words—apathetic? That was spot-on, *apathetic*—every syllable in that word sounded like a slap: ap-a-thet-ic. The first was stinging, a surprise, the last was just a halfhearted click.

Why didn't she do something? She had a great little boy, a great husband, a house near the woods, she didn't have to work—the only thing missing was a maid. Pull yourself together, woman. Go fetch the child, drive to Lidl's, and make a proper dinner. Right on!

She took the pancake out of the microwave and put her son in his plastic high chair. He instantly began to cry because he didn't like abrupt movements. She kissed him on the forehead and positioned the chair to face the TV. There was no time for proper child-rearing if she was going to get everything done. She sliced up the pancake and raced to the mirror—he'd spend five minutes eating, and she'd get dressed and put on some makeup.

"Don't want it!" she heard him shout.

"Yes, you do, yummy pancake. Eat it by yourself like a big boy, and then we'll go for a walk."

She made a shopping list in her head. Simple, efficient, and quick. Grilled beef with a blue cheese sauce. And potato puree to go with it. Actually, boiled potatoes put through the blender, but it could be served nicely, the way it looked at a restaurant. She'd make each person's initials out of puree on their plate. The kid was sure to be happy to eat it too—it's simple, every guy likes potatoes. Some greens—not salad out of a bag, he couldn't stand that. Peas, peas and mayo. She'd reserve some of the peas to make a pattern on the puree.

Once she'd put on her shoes she raced into the dining room, taking the kid's overalls with her to save time.

What she found in there was hard to put into words.

Her son had managed to squeeze the cottage cheese out of the entire pancake, and then smear it all over himself, his chair, the table, and worse yet, the remote. The super-awesome remote, the Christmas gift that could be programmed to work the TV, the digital decoder, the DVD, and the hi-fi. The black designer object with a touch screen now looked as if it were molded from cottage cheese. The kid was aiming it at the TV.

"Ubbies."

Her head began to spin. As she knelt down by his chair, her knee landed on a piece of pancake.

"Listen up, kid, I've got something important to tell you," she began calmly. "You're a fucking spiteful, evil little brat. And I hate you. I hate you so bad I feel like ripping off your hairless head and sticking it on the shelf with your toys, next to your asshole Stinky-Winky. Get it?"

"Ubbies?"

She gave him a long stare, then snorted with laughter. He got the message, no doubt about it. She picked him up and cuddled him, thinking how her special "waist-giving" sweater was now only fit for the laundry. Tough.

3

He didn't want to be here; he hated this sort of event. The prosecutor's place was in his office, in the courtroom, or at the scene of a crime. Any other activity was a waste of the taxpayers' money, which the prosecutors were paid for being guardians of the law. Not for cutting ribbons or showing off in front of students. But somebody must have thought the image of the prosecutor needed improving, so the local high school's request for someone to hand out a prize for the best project on the prevention of violence had been enthusiastically accepted, and he had been singled out to represent the office. He hadn't had a chance to protest before his female boss had preempted his question by saying, "Because you're the only one who looks like a prosecutor."

She hadn't mentioned any speech.

"Thank you for all the work you've done," said the teacher, addressing the students in the usual schoolmarm tone, "and for the effort you've put into it. I admire your commitment and altruism, because of course I don't believe the malicious rumors that a good many of you only did it to get a better conduct grade."

A burst of laughter.

"I hope my class has informed the rest of you that what counts toward this grade is the whole three-year period, not just one-off spurts of activity."

A theatrical groan of disappointment.

Szacki looked around the hall and felt a pang of nostalgia. Not necessarily for the days of his youth, more for the days when he didn't feel embittered. He had started posing as an abrasive cynic in middle school, but everyone who knew him then was totally aware it was an act. The girls stood in line for the sensitive intellectual who hid from the world behind his armor of detachment and cynicism. So it was in high school, so it had been in college. Even when he was a junior prosecutor and in the first few years of his professional life, there was a general conviction that hiding beneath his gown, his immaculate suit, and the legal code there was a good and sensitive man. It was ancient history. He had changed jobs once, twice, a third time, grown older, and finally parted ways with everyone who had known him as a young man and a young prosecutor. The only people left were those who had no reason to suspect that his coolness and distance were masking something. And lately, even he had had to admit that he'd missed the moment for his last chance, when the armor ceased to be protective clothing and became an integral part of Teodor Szacki. Before then he could take it off and hang it on a peg. But now, like a cyborg from a sci-fi novel, he'd have died if his artificial parts were removed.

Here in this hall he felt for the first time just how much his own outer shell was chafing him; if he could choose over again, he'd make the same choices, but without adopting a facade.

"The job market is tough, and I think this piece of work will have gained some brownie points for many of you if you ever seek employment at the ministry of justice or home affairs."

"At the police academy!" someone shouted from the audience.

A burst of laughter.

"More like the detention center for you, Muniek!"

Wild hilarity.

"Now I have the honor of welcoming a man for whom justice is not just a profession but, hopefully, also a vocation. Prosecutor Teodor Szacki."

He stood up.

A sluggish round of applause. Sure, who'd clap for the prosecutor? The representative of a profession that's mainly occupied with crawling up politicians' asses, releasing bad guys who've been caught by the good old cops, or botching legal proceedings and indictments. If he only knew his sector from the media, he'd go to court in his spare time to spit on the prosecutors' gowns.

He did up the top button of his jacket and crossed the hall to the three steps leading onto the stage, moving at a confident pace. The stage didn't even come up to his knee, and he could have mounted it in a single step. But he had no desire to jump about like an ape, and he wanted to stride across the room to let the audience see how a guardian of the law presents himself.

He was wearing what he called his "Bond getup": a British classic that never let him down when he wanted to make an impression. A gray suit the color of the sky before a storm, with almost invisible pale pinstripes, a sky-blue shirt, and a skinny graphite tie with a subtle pattern. A handkerchief made of raw linen, protruding half an inch from his jacket pocket. Cuff links, and a watch of matte surgical steel—in the same shade as his thick, all-white hair. He was the perfect image of the strength and stability of the Polish Republic.

He could feel the gaze of the girls on him—girls who were just transforming into women; most of them had only recently discovered that male style did not end in their school friends' T-shirts, their fathers' crumpled jackets, and their grandfathers' pullovers. That there was such a thing as classic elegance, which meant a male declaration of calm and self-confidence. A way of saying, *Fashion doesn't interest me. I always have been, am now, and always will be fashionable.*

Now he was being followed by hundreds of pairs of eyes, incredulous that this guy, on whom the clothes sat better than on Daniel Craig, was a state employee. Conscious of the impression he made, Szacki walked past a dull painting of a scene from antiquity, and stood at the microphone.

He felt he should say something upbeat—he sensed that was what everyone was expecting: the students, the teachers, and the boy with dreads filming the ceremony for the school. His boss would want to see him on YouTube as well, lightly and zestfully representing the prosecution, finally a real man instead of a stuffed shirt reciting articles of law to the cameras. And he, too, wanted to feel like one of the audience for a while, to remember that once upon a time he had been . . . not so much young—he didn't miss that at all—but fresh. Or, to put it another way, not yet past his prime.

He scoured his mind for a school joke as an opening gambit but realized he couldn't replace one style with another.

As the silence dragged on, a murmur ran through the hall, a number of people whispering to their neighbors: "What's going on?" The teacher shuffled her feet, as if wanting to stand up and save the situation.

"The statistics are against you," said Szacki coldly. A strong voice, well rehearsed at hundreds of trials and closing statements, boomed over the heads of the assembled company too loud, before somebody turned down the volume. "Each year more than a million crimes are committed in Poland. Half a million people are charged with offenses. Which means that in the course of your life some of you are sure to commit an illegal act. Most probably you'll steal something, or get in a car accident. Maybe you'll cheat someone, or beat them up. One of you might murder someone. Of course, right now you can't possibly accept such a dreadful idea, but most murderers never imagine they're going to kill. Just like normal people, they wake up, brush their teeth, and make breakfast. And then something happens, an unfortunate tangle of events, circumstances, and emotions. And that night they go to bed as murderers. It could happen to one of you, too."

He spoke calmly, convincingly, as he did in the courtroom.

"But the statistics are lying." He smiled subtly, as if he had good news to tell them. "They only cover the crimes that come to light. In fact, there are far more crimes and felonies. Sometimes they're never exposed, because perfect crimes are committed every day. Sometimes they're too minor to be reported. But most often they remain hidden behind a double curtain of fear and shame. That includes domestic violence. Bullying at school. Bullying in the workplace. Rape. Sexual harassment. A vast number of unreported injuries that can't possibly be counted. It'll happen to you too. One in five of the girls sitting here will be the victim of rape, or attempted rape. You'll emotionally abuse your partners, steal money from your decrepit parents. Your children will curl up in their beds when they hear your footsteps in the hall. You'll beat your wives, calling it your right. Or you'll pretend the screams of someone being hit or raped on the other side of the wall are none of your concern, and that you shouldn't get mixed up in other people's business."

He paused.

"I'm not familiar with your projects, and I don't know how you imagine violence can be prevented. As a prosecutor I'm only aware of one way to do that."

The teacher gave Szacki an imploring look.

"If you want to prevent violence, don't do wrong."

He took a step back from the lectern, to indicate that he had finished. The teacher seized the opportunity, swiftly stepped onto the stage, and summoned the student who had won the competition. Wiktoria Sendrowska, class 2E. For an essay titled "How to Survive in the Family."

Applause.

A girl hopped up onto the stage. She looked no different from all the other clones Szacki passed every day in the street—he even had a clone of the same kind living at home with him. Neither tall nor small, neither fat nor thin, neither beautiful nor ugly. Pretty, inasmuch as all eighteen-year-old girls are pretty, whose facial flaws can, at best, be described as cute. Hair gathered back in a ponytail, glasses. A thin white turtleneck. The only thing to distinguish her was a flowing floor-length skirt, black as lava.

First the teacher made a move, as if she were about to hand Szacki the diploma to present, but she changed her mind, gave him a glare, and handed the framed certificate to the girl herself. Wiktoria nodded politely to her and to Szacki, then went back to her seat.

Seeing that it was a good moment to disappear, Szacki nodded too, then slipped into the hallway. He had just run past the scene from antiquity hanging above the main door—it showed a pensive, unhappy woman, surely the heroine of a tragedy—when his phone vibrated in his pocket.

From the office. The boss.

O Zeus, he thought, *give me a decent case.*

"Lessons over?"

"Uh-huh."

"Sorry to bother you, but would you go over to Mariańska Street? It won't take long. You just have to check off a German."

"Check off a German?"

"They've found an old cadaver while doing roadwork."

Szacki glanced at the ceiling and mentally cursed.

"Can't you send Falk?"

"Pinocchio? He's taking depositions at the penitentiary in Barczewo. Everyone else is in court or at the district office for training."

What sort of a boss explains herself?

"Is Mariańska the street where the morgue is located?"

"Yes. You'll see a patrol car there, at the bottom, near the hospital. You can always shift the bones across the river, then it'll be a case for South District."

Management through geniality, chumminess, and wisecracks always got on his nerves. He preferred to just get the case sorted. In Olsztyn it was especially bad—immediately on a first-name basis, funny little jokes, and the door to the boss's office was always so wide-open that her secretary must have been suffering from a chronic cold.

"I'm on my way," he said, and hung up.

He put on his coat and buttoned it. He hadn't parked far away, but the ice falling from the sky was like a biblical plague.

"Mr. Szacki?"

He turned around. Behind him stood Wiktoria Sendrowska, the student from class 2E, holding her diploma like a shield. He wasn't sure if she was expecting him to congratulate her or start a conversation. He had nothing to say. He took a closer look at her, but she still had no distinguishing features, just large pale-blue eyes, the color of a glacier. And they were very solemn. Perhaps she might have seemed interesting to him if he didn't have a sixteen-year-old daughter of his own. Long ago, life had flicked a switch in his head, and he had stopped taking notice of young women.

"The screams of someone being hit and raped on the other side of the wall," she said.

"Yes?"

"You were wrong. Not reporting a crime is punishable, but only in exceptional cases, such as murder or terrorism. You can commit rape at a sports stadium that's filled to capacity, and for the spectators it'll be, at most, morally reprehensible."

"Actually, in the case of rape you could concede that forty thousand spectators took part in sexual assault along with the perpetrator, and then you could slap gang rape on the whole lot of them. Even better, a higher sanction. Are you trying to test me on the penal code?"

She averted her gaze in confusion. He had reacted too sharply.

"I know you're familiar with the code. I was just curious why you said that."

"Let's call it casting a spell on reality. I believe Article 240 should be extended to include domestic violence. Anyway, that's how it works in the legislation in several other countries. I thought in this case a slight exaggeration would have educational value."

The girl nodded like a teacher who has heard out a good answer.

"Very well said."

Szacki bowed and walked away. Freezing drizzle hit him in the face like pellets from a shotgun.

4

From a distance it looked like the set for a fashion shoot, in industrial style. In the background the dark shape of the city hospital, built during the German era, emerged from the gloom. In the middle distance there was a yellow excavator leaning over a hole in the ground, as if peering into it out of curiosity, and close up was a patrol car. The streetlamps and the police vehicle's headlights carved tunnels into the thick Warmian fog, casting strange shadows. There were three men standing next to the car, all staring at the hero of the scene, an immaculately dressed man with white hair, standing by the open door of an angular Citroën.

Szacki knew what the engineer, the policeman, and the unfamiliar young CID officer were all waiting for—for the pretty little pencil pusher from the prosecutor's office to fall on his ass. He really was having a hard time keeping his balance on the cobblestones, which were coated, like everything else, in a thin layer of ice. The situation wasn't made any easier by the fact that Mariańska Street ran slightly uphill, and the loafers he'd worn, to make an impression on the high school kids, were now behaving like skates. He was afraid he'd take a tumble as soon as he let go of the car door.

His presence, like that of the police, was a formality. The prosecutor was called out to every death outside the hospital where there was a concern of foul play. And a decision had to be made whether or not to launch an investigation. This meant that sometimes they had to tramp around a road-construction site or a gravel pit, where bones from more than a hundred years ago were quite often found. In Olsztyn it was called "checking off a German." A thankless and time-consuming obligation, often involving an expedition to the other end of the province and wading up to your ankles in mud. Here, at least the German was lying in the center of town.

A formality. Szacki could call them over to have them tell him the facts, then fill out the forms in his nice warm office.

He could, but he never proceeded like that, and he realized he was too old to start changing his habits.

He spied some lumps of ice-coated mud on the ground, which should provide some grip. In four bizarre steps he reached the excavator and grabbed its muddy bucket, managing to restrain a smile of triumph.

"Where's the corpse?"

The young CID officer pointed at the hole in the ground. Szacki had been expecting to see bones sticking out of the mud, but instead there was a black pit gaping in the roadway, with the top of a small aluminum ladder protruding from it. Ice-coated like everything else. Without hesitating, he descended. Whatever lay in wait for him down there was sure to be better than the freezing rain.

He groped his way downward; in the hole it smelled of wet concrete, and after a few steps he was standing on a hard, wet floor. Freezing rain was lashing through the opening a couple of feet above him, and he could reach up and touch the ceiling. He took off his gloves and ran a hand over it. Cold concrete. A shelter? A bunker?

He stepped back to make room for the CID officer. The policeman switched on a flashlight, and handed a second one to Szacki. Szacki put on the LED light and looked at his companion. Young, about thirty, with sad eyes and a very out-of-date mustache. Handsome, with the provincial good looks of a healthy farmer's son who has done well for himself.

"Prosecutor Teodor Szacki."

"Deputy Commissioner Jan Paweł Bierut." The policeman made a gloomy face, surely expecting the joke he usually heard in this situation. It must have been hard sharing first names with the Pope and last names with an infamous Communist president.

"I don't know you, but then I've only been here two years," said Szacki.

"I was transferred recently from the traffic police."

The constant rotation of CID staff was the bane of Szacki's existence. No rookies ever turned up there, just officers who had already done their time, mostly in the operations department. Most of them soon found out that working in criminal investigation was nothing like being a detective in a Hollywood action movie, and they eagerly took advantage of early retirement. These days it was easier to find an experienced community cop than a CID officer.

Without a word, Bierut turned and set off down a regular concrete corridor that could have been the remains of anything—it didn't matter much to Szacki. After a dozen paces the side walls disappeared, and they found themselves in a vaulted hall, square in shape, over six feet high and about fifty feet long. In one corner towered some rusty junk, including hospital beds, tables, and chairs. Bierut went past the heap and approached the opposite wall. There was a bed there, white in several places where the enamel hadn't come off, elsewhere orange with rust. There was a piece of plywood lying on the frame, black with dampness, and on the plywood lay an old skeleton. Pretty much complete, as far as Szacki could tell, though the bones were partly mixed up, perhaps by rats, and some of them were lying on the floor. At any rate the skull was intact, with almost its entire dentition. The perfect German.

Szacki clamped his lips to avoid sighing. For months he'd been waiting for a decent case. It could be tough, or controversial, or not at all obvious. In any regard—investigative, evidential, or legislative. But there was nothing. Cases of a more serious nature had included two murders, one armed robbery, and a rape at the university campus. All the culprits had been caught the day after each incident. The murderers, because they were in the immediate family, the robber, because the street cameras had recorded him almost in HD quality, and the rapist, because his pals at the dorm had roughed him up, then taken him straight to the station—evidence that something was changing in this country after all. Not only were all the criminals detained the same day, they had all immediately confessed. They'd made detailed statements, and Szacki had been able to go home at four o'clock, without his blood pressure rising.

And now a German. For dessert, after the school gala.

Bierut cast him an inquiring glance. Szacki said nothing, because there was nothing to say. Bierut had such a sorrowful look on his face it was as if the bones belonged to a member of his family. If the policeman was like this all the time, his pals at the station were probably passing around the phone number of a therapist to get them out of their depression.

There was nothing to do here. Szacki swept the room with the flashlight, partly for the sake of routine, partly because he wanted to prolong the moment—it was far warmer down here, and he wasn't being assailed by any atmospheric phenomena.

Nothing interesting. Bare walls and the ends of a few corridors; judging by the architecture, the room was an old shelter, probably for hospital staff and patients. There must be some buried entrances somewhere, washing facilities, maybe a few more halls like this, or smaller rooms.

"Have you checked the rest of this space?"

"It's empty."

Szacki wondered how it had happened. Were the patients evacuated for the duration of some shelling at the end of the war, then this guy died, and the rest got out? Was there too much going on for them to remember a single corpse left underground? Or maybe someone hid down here when the war was already over, and his heart gave out?

Szacki went up to the remains and examined the skull. No visible injuries, characteristic depressions or holes from being struck by a blunt instrument, and nothing remotely resembling a gunshot wound. If someone had helped the German to the world beyond, there was no evidence of it. Whatever, death hadn't saved him from wartime or postwar looting.

"There were no clothes," said Bierut, reading his thoughts.

Szacki nodded. Even supposing rodents and worms had eaten what was left, there should still be some shreds of material—buckles, clasps, buttons. Someone must have helped themselves just after his death, before the clothing began to disintegrate.

"Secure these remains and have them taken to the university. I'll write an order for their transfer. We might as well find a use for the German."

Old Warsaw practice. No John Doe ever ended up in the ground. First, it was a waste of the taxpayers' money, and second, the medical schools were always happy to process the cadavers. Old bones were worth more to them than ivory.

5

He wasn't in a hurry to get home. He dropped by the office and quickly wrote out an order to transfer the remains for educational purposes. From his office in the regional Olsztyn-North prosecution-service building on Emilia Plater Street he could almost see the spot where half an hour earlier he had gone down into the old shelter.

In fact, he had a pretty good view from his office. The impersonal building stood at the top of an embankment, below which flowed the narrow River Łyna, from which Olsztyn took its name. Its former name, of course, when the river was called the Alle and the city was Allenstein. Wild undergrowth lined either side of the river—the people of Olsztyn, hopelessly in love with their own city, called it a park. Szacki called it a black-and-green hole. He wouldn't have gone down there after dark, not even with bodyguards, because he sensed that the black-and-green hole was inhabited by more than just thugs, muggers, and those eager to commit sexual assault. The one reason for something like that to be hidden away at the very center of the provincial capital was evil spirits.

Now bulldozers had forced them to retreat because the hole had just started to be revitalized. Bearing in mind that in Olsztyn the words *improvement project* sounded like a threat, they'd be sure to rip out the bushes, roots and all, replace them with a gigantic mosaic of pink paving bricks, and then boast that it was the only such structure visible to the naked eye from outer space.

As long as they didn't build any pink hotels and he still had his view. He got up, put on his coat, and switched off the light. Outside, the blackness of the green hole separated him from the city. Straight ahead, the brilliantly illuminated cathedral towered above the buildings of the Old Town, like a large mother hen gathering a brood of chicks. To the right, the keep of a Gothic castle and the Town Hall clock tower rose above the roofs. To the left, Olsztyn descended downhill, and it was there, just behind the green hole, that the old city hospital was located, and the shelter, which a short while ago had ceased to be the German's eternal resting place.

It had stopped raining, a thin mist had risen, and the little side street had become the dream site for a photographer working on an album depicting the melancholy of Warmia. Everything was black and gray, as usual in late November, and everything was covered in a thin layer of ice. On the sidewalk it was a danger, but on the leafless trees the effect was fabulous. Every last little twig had changed into an icicle that sparkled in the soft lamplight. He took a deep breath of cold, damp air and thought how his fondness for this great big village was always growing.

He cautiously crossed the street, thinking it was time to move house. It was truly perverse that he lived across from work. He had counted once—only thirty-nine steps away. He had no time to calm down on his way home, to settle his thoughts and switch into domestic mode. And he couldn't stand the gloomy formerly German villa, once home to the manager of the private gynecological clinic situated on the other side of the fence, now a youth club. Unfortunately the manager had wanted to be modern, and instead of a normal house he had put up a heavy block, a modernist monster, monumental, to the extent that a single-family home can be monumental. Suffice it to say that the traditional balustrade up the entrance steps had been replaced by a covered colonnade. Szacki had recently joked to himself, as he hung up a flag for Independence Day, that they ought to employ someone to stand guard holding a flaming torch.

On top of that, lately he really had needed a little time to prepare himself psychologically for what lay ahead at home. So he decided to give himself another minute, and instead of going straight into the house, he walked around it, crossed the icy garden, and peeped into the kitchen, trying to stand outside the pool of light coming from the window. With his overcoat and briefcase he looked like a perverted Peeping Tom from the '70s.

Of course the big sulky witch and the little sulky witch were having a great time together. The big witch was drawing something on a huge sheet of paper, most likely the seating plan for the guests at yet another wedding. The little witch was sitting on a high stool, swinging her legs and excitedly telling a story, gesticulating wildly. The big one looked up, intrigued, and finally burst out laughing.

"Goddamn man-eaters," whispered Szacki.

He had been living in Olsztyn for two years now and had met Żenia soon after he got here; they had been living together for more than a year. It was his first serious relationship since breaking up with Weronika over six years ago. And it was a good, successful relationship, really great. He wasn't afraid to use the word *happy*.

Despite various obstacles and minor spats, he had also made it up with his daughter, Hela, who had been to see them for shorter and longer stays. He had tentatively grown used to the idea that maybe he could still have a normal life, which for a good many years had not been so obvious.

So when the great scriptwriter in the sky had decided to add a new twist to the plot, he had felt more excitement than anxiety. Weronika's new husband had obtained a grant to do research at a technical university in Singapore, and she had decided to go on the adventure of a lifetime. She also realized that as her hormone-fueled daughter had just finished middle school, the new stage in her education could be combined with strengthening her relationship with her father. His response had been enthusiastic, to which his first wife had replied with a long silence, and then burst into the bitter laughter of an experienced woman.

And so, near the end of August he had brought a tearful, hysterical Helena Szacka to Olsztyn, to be educated at High School Number II, which didn't have as nice a building as Wiktoria Sendrowska's but took pride in its reputation as the best school in the province. Naturally Hela had spitefully dug up the national rankings to show him that coming first in the province of Warmia and Masuria meant coming in eighty-second in Poland, and twenty-five Warsaw schools were ranked ahead of the local pride and joy known as "Number Two."

After that it had only gotten worse.

The two women in his life had turned into the big sulky witch and the little sulky witch. Functioning quite normally until the second he appeared, when they began to fight for his attention. He realized he was the one doing something wrong, but he had no idea what. And in this emotional tangle he was totally helpless.

His foot had gone stiff. He changed position, and the inevitable happened—a few seconds dancing in place, and then he tumbled into the frozen rosebushes.

The kitchen window opened.

"Jerzy?" asked Żenia in terror.

Jerzy was Żenia's ex-husband, who had stalked her after their divorce and received a minor suspended sentence for it.

"It's me. I wanted to walk around the garden." Szacki scrambled up, hissing with pain because the rose thorns had scratched his hands.

"Aha." A chill replaced the fear in her voice. "I always thought Jerzy had a screw loose. But maybe I'm the one who's nuts, seeing that all my guys go hiding in the bushes."

"Give it a break. Look how nice it is out here. I just wanted to get some air."

"Dad?" He heard Hela's feeble voice coming from an upstairs window—she must have teleported herself up there, as she'd only just been sitting in the kitchen.

She had the face of a child from a documentary on third-world orphanages.

"Hey, darling. Everything all right?"

"I'm not feeling great. Dad, can we talk about something? Will you come up?"

Żenia shut the kitchen window.

Szacki hung up his coat and went into the kitchen to give Żenia a hug. She really was working on a guest list; judging by the layout of the tables, the wedding reception was going to be held in an unusual space.

"Where's that?"

"Floating platforms on Lake Ukiel. Combined wedding and solstice party. What a disaster—I keep imagining the dead bodies rising on the waves. I should put a proviso in the contract. Do you want your pasta from yesterday? It's matured well . . ." She hesitated, as if she were about to say they'd left him some, but that would mean admitting they'd had dinner together. "It's a bit too spicy for me."

"Put it out for me, I'm going up to see Hela."

"Uh-huh. Will you be back at any particular time, or can I go to the pool?"

Her tone left him in no doubt that she hadn't the slightest wish to go to the pool. She was just letting him know how hurt and disappointed she'd be if she spent another evening alone.

"I'll be right back."

Only the bedside light was on in Hela's room. She was lying on the bed in a thin jacket, as if that were the only cover available.

"Will you come sit with me?"

He sat down beside her.

"Is something wrong?"

"I've got a headache. I think it's the climate. Did you know the German soldiers stationed here got a bonus for working in tough conditions? The damp climate ruined their health. It's making it impossible for me to concentrate on my assignment."

He felt irritated. He was about to erupt and tell her the colorful anecdote was about another city, not Olsztyn. And then he would ask, What damn assignment? She had just been chatting away in the kitchen. But he avoided open conflict. He could never find a reasonable focal point for his conversations with his daughter when it came to disagreements, especially emotionally tricky ones, which demanded a frank and serious talk. Either he escaped into aggression, or he withdrew into formulaic chitchat about nothing, "How's school?—great—super."

"What's the assignment?"

"We've got to do a presentation on a world-famous Pole."

"Lech Wałęsa or John Paul II?"

She straightened up, quite briskly for someone whose health had been ruined by three months in Olsztyn.

"Well, actually I'd rather not do them. I found various things on the Internet, including a presentation about Aleksander Wolszczan. You know, the astronomer who . . ."

"I know."

"I'll show you."

She reached for her laptop.

"But I don't want to do Wolszczan. There's this article here, look . . ."

"The thing is . . . my pasta . . . ," he stammered. If anyone had recorded this and posted it on the Internet, plenty of Polish jailbirds locked up by Prosecutor Teodor Szacki would have rolled on the floor laughing.

She gave him a look, partly disbelief, partly inquiry. Her mother always used to look at him that way.

"Marie Curie?" he finally asked.

"She was a great scholar. A woman. A feminist. The first woman to win a Nobel Prize, and the only person to win it twice. I thought they could do with a little gender ideology out here in the sticks. I'll show you a clip from the documentary I found. I want to start with that. I'm so excited, but at the new school I've got to make a good impression right off the bat. You see?"

Downstairs the door slammed. It was going to be a long evening.

CHAPTER TWO

Tuesday, November 26, 2013

On the anniversary of Adam Mickiewicz's death, Tina Turner is celebrating her seventy-fourth birthday. Human Rights Network is warning about the scale of rape in Syria, where violence against women is being used as a weapon. As extramarital sex is prohibited there, a victim of rape is deemed guilty of breaking the law. Europe still has a faint hope that the Ukrainian authorities will change their minds about signing the association agreement. The deadline is Friday. Also, the Scottish First Minister officially announces a referendum in which the Scots will decide whether to leave the United Kingdom, and Pope Francis criticizes the cult of money. In Poland the debate continues on an act awaiting presidential signature, which is designed to send extremely dangerous criminals to special psychiatric institutions when they have completed their prison sentences. In Olsztyn, city of contrasts, the theme of the day is the remote past and the distant future.

Archaeologists have dug up a Gothic pillar beside the High Gate, the remains of a medieval bridge. It looks as if hundreds of years ago the River Łyna followed a different course than was previously assumed. The local authorities have signed an agreement to start building an international airport at Szymany in the spring; the rumor on the streets is that once the work is completed, secret CIA prisoners will finally be processed through the airport in a comfortable fashion. Throughout Poland the weather is quite good and sunny for this time of year, but in Warmia there is fog and freezing drizzle.

1

As he sat sipping a mug of coffee in his kitchen that was the size of a studio apartment, he pretended to be absorbed in the *Olsztyn Gazette* to avoid taking part in the conversation about emotions that was hanging in the air. His camouflage was extremely weak—no one on earth could possibly be so interested in the *Olsztyn Gazette*. Szacki had often wondered who kept an eye on the authorities around here, since the local media were busy—as in this edition—with public polls for Mailman of the Year. He skimmed over the typical article about domestic violence—three thousand new reported incidents in the region, and a sensible policeman was appealing for vigilance because the victims and offenders are very rarely from pathological families. His gaze was held for a while by a dramatic piece of photojournalism about the rescue of an elk that had gotten stuck in a mud-filled hole. He thought he'd better hide the paper from Hela, or else she'd roll her eyes again and insist she was being made to live in the backwoods. The elk had been rescued by some hunters, which prompted Szacki to suspect they had shoved the animal in there in the first place, to be able to say afterward on TV that they weren't just a bunch of testosterone-fueled maniacs who like to do a bit of killing over vodka and a bowl of bigos. Nothing of the kind—they go around saving animals.

"Is there something about you in there?"

He looked up in surprise.

"No, why do you ask?"

"Adela said you were on Channel One yesterday."

He shrugged, leafed through the rest of the paper, and tossed it aside theatrically.

"Somehow, from the outside world, this city looks more interesting than it really is. Women killing their children, bullies getting lynched, mayors shoving their hands into their secretaries' panties. Where's all that?"

Żenia cast him a look over her shoulder, raising an eyebrow. It was such a characteristic gesture that she should have had it printed on her business cards.

"Have you gone crazy? Do you want people to murder children?"

"Of course not. But if they must, let them do it on my watch. A little mob rule, for instance, like that case in Włodowo where the villagers took the law into their own hands. That would be good."

"You're sick."

"You're looking at it too emotionally. That was a fascinating case, as a story and in legal terms, and what happened? A boozed-up, violent ex-con who was terrorizing the whole neighborhood got killed. No great crime. The culprits spent a few months in jail, and then the president pardoned them, so they didn't exactly suffer much for their crime."

"And quite right, too."

"That's debatable. The public should be informed that they're not allowed to resolve conflicts by beating people to death with sticks."

"You're talking like a prosecutor."

"I wonder why."

Szacki got up, straightened his cuffs, and put on his jacket. It was three minutes to eight. He hugged Żenia and gave her an affectionate kiss on the lips. Even in her bare feet she was almost as tall as he was—he liked that.

"First of all, we need to have that talk. Do you realize that?"

He reluctantly nodded. He knew.

"Secondly, you remember the two-minute rule?" She pointed at his mess. Crumbs, spilled coffee, a plate and mug. It occurred to him that most of her statements changed into questions. In a person he was interrogating, he'd take that as a sign of uncertainty, but in her it was a communication technique that forced him to keep saying yes, which meant he ended up agreeing to something he didn't like.

So he didn't say yes.

"Any task that takes less than two minutes gets done right away, correct? Making life easier for everyone. Now I've got a question . . ."

What a surprise.

"How long does it take to wash a plate, a glass, and a mug? More than two minutes?"

"I've got a job to do." He pointed at the big station clock hanging above the door.

"Oh yes," she said, lowering her voice, "your real, masculine office job. You've even got a briefcase, my dear he-man. While I work barefoot at home—I've got such a funny girly job, just a hobby really, so I can clean up after you. Get real—we're not in the '70s."

He felt the bile rising in him. He'd had enough of being bossed around. He'd already put his jacket on. Now he'd have to take it off, remove his cuff links, roll up his sleeves, and wash the dishes. It would only take her a moment—she wouldn't even notice.

She glanced over her shoulder and through the window at the prosecution service building, and raised an eyebrow.

"Just tell me you've got to run because you're afraid of getting stuck in traffic."

For some reason that remark caused a red curtain of rage to fall before his eyes. Maybe it wasn't the '70s, but everyone deserves a bit of respect.

"I've got a job to do," he said coldly.

And left.

2

Edmund Falk was already waiting outside his office. As soon as he saw Szacki, he got up and held out a hand. He never said much; if asked a question, he replied politely and sparingly, as if they took a fee from his account with every syllable.

Szacki opened the door and let the junior prosecutor inside. Falk sat in the seat for clients, immediately took a file out of his briefcase, and silently waited for the signal to present his cases.

Szacki knew all of Olsztyn's legal service was laughing at the "King of the Stuffed Shirts" and the "Prince of the Starched Collars," as they were known. And indeed, there was some truth in it, because if Szacki had had a son, there was no way this son, his own flesh and blood, could have been more like him than Edmund Falk.

The young lawyer had graduated from the first year of students who must have really wanted and made an effort to become prosecutors. Before then it had been the other way around: the law graduates who went into the prosecution service were often the ones who had failed to get other apprenticeships or didn't have enough backing or families with the right connections. A few years ago, the prosecution and magistracy apprenticeship had been abolished, and an elite National School of Judiciary and Public Prosecution had been set up.

Anyone with a degree in law who dreamed of wearing a gown with red or purple trim—the prosecutor's and magistrate's court uniforms, respectively—now had to get into the school in Kraków and undergo an arduous three-year marathon of lectures, internships, and exams. But if they survived, they were guaranteed a post as a junior prosecutor. And it was worth the fight—as students they received a large monthly grant; a junior prosecutor's net salary was more than three thousand zloty per month, and a regional prosecutor's started at more than four. Maybe not a fortune, but in uncertain times it meant a job, and guaranteed employment in the public sector.

Two thousand people took the practical and theoretical entrance exams for the National School. Only three hundred were accepted for the first general year. Later on, one hundred and fifty were eliminated, and the rest were polished into legal diamonds. Falk was a representative of the first class to become junior prosecutors, not after three years of apprenticeship—in other words, making the coffee in a regional office—but after three years of hard work. He knew the codes and procedures thoroughly, had been taught to work with victims by the European NGOs and trained in interrogation techniques by instructors from the FBI academy in Quantico. He had done internships at forensic labs, morgues, police stations, prosecution services, and courts at all levels. He had a lifesaving diploma and a first-aid certificate. He knew English to a standard that qualified him to teach it, and he had studied Russian in college because he thought it was the logical choice: for employment at the prosecution service in Olsztyn, which bordered the Kaliningrad district and thus a part of Russia, that particular skill could come in useful. Their delighted boss had also informed Szacki that Falk had been the national junior champion ballroom dancer and was a qualified riding instructor. At the time, Szacki had thought that last item was purely to fulfill the image of a sheriff. He could probably spin a revolver on one finger, too.

Edmund Falk was a native of Olsztyn. He knew there was a junior prosecutor's post to be filled in his hometown. And he knew that the principles for assigning the posts were very simple, so he passed his final exams with the best scores in his class. Not because he wanted to come out on top—he just wanted to have first choice. It was a logical decision.

And then he had arrived in Olsztyn, met the boss, and instead of kissing her ring like she was the Queen Mother, he had set a condition:

he was ready to do them the honor of gracing them with his presence as a junior prosecutor, but only if his supervisor was Prosecutor Szacki.

And so for the first time in his career, Szacki had acquired an apprentice. He hadn't asked Falk why it mattered to him so much, figuring that Falk would tell him at some point. But he hadn't.

"I sorted out the case at Barczewo. They shouldn't be bothering us again," said Falk. He never talked about sports or the weather.

"I interviewed the inmate Grzegorz Jędras and realized his claim was part of a bigger problem that needed to be resolved."

Szacki gave him an inquiring look. Jędras's claim was typical humbug. The man had testified to having converted to Islam, and he claimed to have a deep faith, but the administration wouldn't accept that and was discriminating against him in terms of religion, refusing to take pork out of his meals or to assign him a cell with a window facing Mecca, or to adapt the daily timetable to the pattern of Islamic prayers. Lately conversions had been a fashionable form of amusement among prisoners—you could always rely on a change of cell or at least a few interviews, and then entertain your pals with the story of how you'd greeted the prosecutor with "Salaam alaikum!"

"So how did you resolve this problem?" Szacki was trying not to show surprise. He was legalistic himself, but he couldn't believe Falk had taken the matter seriously.

"I talked to the warden, and we jointly established that, unfortunately, the geographical position of the Barczewo facility does not allow for anyone to have a cell with a window facing Mecca. So out of concern for the prisoner's religious freedom, he'll be urgently transferred to the facility in Sztum. Although in his case, there are no grounds for applying Article 88 of the Executive Penal Code. The warden there was considerate enough to agree to accommodate him in the one block with cells facing Mecca. All meat products are to be eliminated from the prisoner's diet because we recognized that it's not possible to monitor the kitchen and the inmates working there closely enough to prevent them from harming Jędras, whether maliciously or accidentally, by including pork in his meals."

Szacki nodded his approval, though it cost him a lot to keep a straight face. Falk had torn Jędras to pieces. He had taken him away from his pals and sent him to a prison of ill repute in Sztum. On top of that, he had made him a vegetarian, and out of concern for his faith had placed him in a unit for dangerous criminals. It was an exceptionally dismal place, where they weren't allowed their own clothes, were forced to undergo a search every time they entered or exited a one-man cell, and defecation was performed under the watchful eye of a camera. Of course, Jędras would defend himself by lodging further appeals, but the wheels of justice turn slowly. In the meantime he was bound to become a militant atheist.

"Doesn't it bother you to be working on the edges of the law?" he asked Falk.

"On paper it all looks like an expression of the greatest concern for the prisoner. I looked for a solution that would not only satisfy Jędras, but also send an obvious signal to other inmates, and that will put an end to wasting the prosecution's time. The taxpayer has a right to demand that we keep things in order, not entertain inmates like Jędras. It was the logical solution."

Sometimes Szacki understood why the rest of the region called Falk "Pinocchio." He was really stiff, as if carved out of wood. Others were bothered by his attitude—unfortunately the natural human tendency was to fraternize, make friends, and close the distance. But Szacki was impressed by it.

"Anything else?"

"I dismissed the Kiwit case."

Szacki asked to be reminded of the details.

"The day before yesterday, the provincial hospital informed the police that an ambulance had brought in a man with injuries. He had called for help himself. The injuries weren't life-threatening, but they were serious enough to leave him permanently deaf in the left ear. Witold Kiwit, fifty-two years old, entrepreneur."

"What category is that?"

Falk didn't hesitate.

"One hundred and fifty-seven."

Szacki agreed. It had been a trick question—in theory, the preceding article, 156, directly mentioned depriving a person of "sight, hearing, speech, or the capacity to procreate," but from case law it emerged that it had to be total deprivation and not just damage. The difference was considerable—the penalty for 156 was from one to ten years, and for 157 from three months to five years.

"He refused to be interviewed, and kept insisting that he wasn't going to press charges."

"Scared?"

"Determined, more like. I explained that this isn't America, and that it's our job to prosecute people who stick sharp objects in other people's ears, because people like that are bad. And not because the injured party wants us to. Then he changed his tune and said it was an accident. He slipped on the ice on his way home and hit his ear on a sharp fence post. He can't remember where, he was in shock."

"Family?"

"Wife, two sons in high school and middle school."

"And what's his business? Boardinghouse? Café?"

"Tarpaulin."

Szacki nodded. It wasn't really the sort of activity that prompted the local hoods to insist on their share. But that possibility had to be considered when it came to strange injuries. Of course, the guy could be working on the black market; tarpaulin—what's in a name?—could be a cover. Having a family would then explain Kiwit's fear of involving the law.

"I had a quiet chat with him. I explained that if someone's threatening him, his family won't be any safer if he starts pretending there's no danger." Falk was proving that he was correctly following Szacki's line of reasoning. "I told him about victims' rights, and explained what measures we can apply with regard to a suspect. That an injury of that kind and threats were enough for an arrest, and that he wouldn't have to be afraid for his children. I was hoping to touch a nerve. But no such luck."

Szacki thought. Something was wrong here.

"What does he look like? Small and skinny?"

"Well built, broad shoulders, paunch."

"Any other injuries?"

"No."

The case should really be dismissed right away—there was no point conducting an investigation into a fight when the victim refused to make a statement. If it wasn't a fight, but the guy was involved in some shady business, with Russians for instance, he only had himself to blame. And Falk had taken a very practical, logical approach. Szacki would probably have done the same.

"Please postpone your decision for two more days," Szacki said. "If there aren't any other injuries, then Mr. Kiwit didn't fall onto anything, or take part in a drunken fight. There must have been at least three of them, to be able to overpower him and poke something in his ear. They may have blackmailed him with threats or physical abuse toward his family. Find out where the ambulance picked him up, put on a show of searching the house for traces of blood, interview the wife and sons, and then put pressure on him again. Best of all, at the central station. A room with a two-way mirror, cameras—let him think it's a serious matter."

Falk nodded, as if he understood he'd be making plenty of his own decisions in life. Now was the time for learning. He put away his papers and stood up. He was short, perhaps not unusually so, but noticeably, especially since he came from a generation of well-fed giants. It was either his genes, or his mother hadn't been able to lay off the sauce during pregnancy.

Short, slight, and thin, with the figure of a dancer. Suddenly Szacki regretted that in asking about Kiwit he'd used the words *small and skinny*. It was Falk who was small and skinny, on top of which he always dressed in black or dark gray, which caused him to appear smaller. He might have thought his own appearance had prompted Szacki to phrase his question like that.

"You made a fine speech at my old school, Prosecutor," Falk said on his way out.

"Did you hear it?"

"I saw it. It's the twenty-first century, you know." *Small and skinny* must have hurt him—he didn't usually take the liberty of making spiteful remarks.

Szacki's phone rang. Falk left the room.

"Szacki."

"Good morning, this is Dr. Frankenstein."

"Very funny."

"Professor Ludwik Frankenstein, D.Sc., from the university hospital on Warszawska Avenue. You signed an order for an unidentified corpse to be sent to us."

"Yes."

"Come see me right away. Anatomy department, square building on the left past the barrier."

3

For a while Szacki was lost. He remembered Olsztyn's Warszawska Avenue as a wide road leading out of town past the university, but it turned out to have an uglier sister—a short extension lined with scruffy little tenements right next to the Old Town. He had to turn left by Jan's

Bridge. The hospital was located opposite something that called itself the "regional beer center."

He showed the guard his ID and found a parking spot between the buildings. This had once been the German garrison hospital, probably of lesser importance, as the buildings of immortal red-brick looked much smaller and more modest than the neo-Gothic blocks of the city hospital. Part of it looked neglected, and part had been renovated, with a modern interior that was nicely integrated with the German architecture. The place had the atmosphere of a building site, arising from the fact that Olsztyn's university medical faculty had only been up and running for a few years. In a short time a squalid military hospital had been transformed into a clinical marvel. Szacki had been to see Żenia's mother here last year and had realized that on the whole it had quite a human dimension, compared with the various medical monstrosities he had seen in his career. That had been during a hot spring, when the chestnut trees were flowering among the buildings, and the old brick walls exuded a pleasant chill.

A chill was the last thing he needed now. He did up his coat and quickly walked across to the only square building, exceptionally coated in white plaster. It crossed his mind that if the man was called Frankenstein, he was sure to look normal and behave naturally. It would be a nice change after all the crazy pathologists he had met. Besides, he was a university lecturer, and not some weirdo cutting up corpses all day long. He had to be normal—he taught kids, didn't he?

A vain hope.

Professor Ludwik Frankenstein, D.Sc., was waiting for him at the top of the stairs, by the entrance to the anatomy department. Well, well—he'd done everything he possibly could to make himself look like a mad scientist. He stood straight as a reed, tall and thin, with the long, aristocratic, classically handsome face of the only good German officer in an American war movie. He had a steely gaze, a straight nose, as if drawn with a set square, a short, fair beard trimmed like Lenin's, round glasses in very thin wire frames, and a bizarre medical gown with a mandarin collar and a row of buttons down each side like an officer's greatcoat. To complete the image, all he needed was a pipe with a long stem and some amputated hands protruding from the pockets of his gown.

"Frankenstein," he said in greeting.

The only thing missing was a clap of thunder.

"Once this was the hospital canteen," he explained to Szacki, as he led the way through the lab.

"I see," said Szacki, noticing some small paper plates with the remains of cake and empty champagne bottles lined up against the wall. "So buildings don't change their habits."

Soon after, Frankenstein opened a door and they entered the dissection room, without doubt the most modern Szacki had ever seen. There was a chrome-plated table, equipped with all the essential instruments for dissection, as well as video cameras, lamps, and a powerful hoist. He probably couldn't deal with the smell of the corpse, but perhaps at least he wouldn't have to toss all his clothes in the washing machine after the autopsy.

There were several rows of high chairs towering around the table—this was not just a dissection room, but also a lecture hall.

"Here," said Frankenstein in a low voice, "we strip death of its mysteries."

The professor's solemn words would have sounded dignified, except that in this temple of death there were more empty champagne bottles standing on the windowsills, balloons were free floating against the ceiling, set in motion by the fan, and colored streamers were hanging from the surgical lights. Szacki passed no comment on this evidence of a party, or on the scientist's words. He looked at the bones of yesterday's German laid out on the table. At first glance the skeleton looked complete. Szacki stuck his hands in his coat pockets and tightly crossed his fingers. The scientist had a weird name and looked like a madman, but he might just be a normal guy with an unusual appearance. Down-to-earth, solid, pleasant.

"This table," said the professor, stroking the chrome surface, "is to a corpse what a Bugatti Veyron is to a seventy-year-old playboy. It's hard to imagine a better combination."

A vain hope.

Szacki uncrossed his fingers, swallowed a comment on whether in that case he should apologize for only providing old bones, and got to the point: "So what's the issue?"

"You, as a prosecutor, are sure to know the basics of biology, the pseudoscientific version of it that is enough for criminal investigation. How many years does it take for a man to become a skeleton?"

"About ten, depending on the circumstances," Szacki replied calmly, though he felt rising irritation. "But to be in this state, with no tissue, no cartilage, sinew, or hair, takes at least thirty. Even bearing in mind that corpses decompose faster in the open air than in water, and much faster than when buried."

"Very good. There are various minor factors, but in our climate, left to itself, a corpse needs a minimum of two or three decades to reach this state. That's what I was thinking as I laid our rascal out. I also thought the skeleton was complete enough for me to use it as a jigsaw puzzle: I toss various pieces into bags, and the students have to put them together against the clock. I was ready to make the missing pieces myself." He adjusted his glasses and smiled apologetically. "A little creative hobby of mine."

Szacki realized where this argument was leading.

"But there are no pieces missing."

"Exactly. That's what got me thinking—it's a mystery. This corpse has been lying there for dozens of years, but not a single bone has gone missing. No rat took even one?"

Szacki shrugged.

"In an enclosed structure made of reinforced concrete."

"That occurred to me, but I called some friends who take an interest in the history of Olsztyn . . . Are you from Olsztyn?"

"No."

"I thought not. We'll return to that. So I called my friends, and they told me it was an ordinary air-raid shelter, a cellar. So it wasn't hermetically sealed, it had washing facilities, plumbing, ventilation. You could say anything about it, but not that it was an enclosed structure. Which means that rats, fighting for food, should have scattered those remains into all four corners. Why didn't they?"

Szacki just stared.

"The body has its secrets." Frankenstein lowered his voice, so nobody could have been in any doubt that he was about to betray one of them. "Did you know that we have taste receptors in the lungs, as well as on the tongue?"

"I do now."

"And they're for bitter tastes! The alveoli react to bitter flavors. Which means that the ultimate remedy for asthma may not be some miraculously manufactured substance but something basic, as long as it's bitter. I don't envy the guy who discovered that. The pharmaceutical companies have probably put a price on his head by now."

"Professor, please . . ."

"To the point. But one more fact to take home with you: the cervix has taste receptors too. In its turn, it likes a sweet flavor. Do you think it has anything to do with the fact that to give them vitality, the spermatozoa travel along on a base of fructose?"

Szacki decided the best defense against a madman was attack.

"Curious," Szacki said, imitating Frankenstein's tone. "Maybe in that case you'd like to go into business producing huge chocolate vibrators? Your knowledge of human anatomy would be indispensable."

Frankenstein adjusted his glasses.

"I'll give it some thought. But let's get back to the bones." He folded his hands behind his back and strolled around the table. "Here was an enigma, the key to which was this very corpse. So I set about examining it. At first I hadn't noticed—"

"Is it a man or a woman?"

"A man, of course. I hadn't noticed, because sometimes even as a result of decomposition, the phalanges in the toes do not separate but remain stuck together by thin joint capsules and degeneration. Have a look." He picked up a single bone and tossed it in Szacki's direction.

Szacki caught it without a second thought; he had seen worse corpses than the professor had.

It was two small bones, one about two inches long, the other shorter, joined together by a thin layer of white transparent cartilage.

"Don't you see anything surprising?"

"The joint hasn't decomposed."

"Try moving those bones."

He tried, and to his amazement, he could bend them. There couldn't possibly be any working joints in a corpse that had been rotting for decades.

"And now try to separate them."

A gentle pull was all it took; in one hand he was holding the shorter bone, which ended in a small metal plate with a hole in it, like the washer that goes under a nut. The longer bone still had its cartilage, tipped with a half-inch square bolt.

"What is it?"

"It's a silicone endoprosthesis for a metatarsophalangeal joint, also known as a floating endoprosthesis, a modern solution in the field of joint prostheses. A surgical way of dealing with a condition known as stiff big toe. Extremely irritating for sportsmen. And for women, because they can't walk in high heels. Judging by his cranial sutures, this man was about fifty. So neither a woman nor a sportsman. He probably liked to look after himself."

Szacki's brain was working at full throttle.

"Does it have a serial number?"

"Normal ones, yes, silicone ones, no. But there's only one center in Warsaw where they make these things—they specialize in foot surgery. One of my former students is making a fortune there because there are women who are prepared to pay the price of a car for the perfect anatomical products to go with their high-heeled shoes. I called him out of curiosity."

"And?"

"So far he has only ever implanted one prosthesis of this kind and size. For a patient from Olsztyn. Who was very much counting on this operation because he loved going for long walks around his beloved Warmia. And how do you find life in Olsztyn?"

"It's a great place," muttered Szacki.

He needed names and details.

Frankenstein beamed and straightened up, as if about to get a medal from the Führer.

"I quite agree. Do you know that we have eleven lakes within the city limits? Eleven!"

"Did he say when the operation took place?" asked Szacki, thinking that if the corpse were five or seven years old, the case wouldn't be very fresh, but would still involve a mystery.

"Two weeks ago. Ten days ago the patient walked out of the clinic and drove home. November fifteenth, to be exact. He was greatly looking forward to his Saturday walk."

"That's impossible," said Szacki, staring at the bones he was holding, from a foot that had apparently been strolling around the Warmian forest just over a week ago. He joined them together and tried bending them again—the artificial joint worked perfectly.

Frankenstein handed him a small sheet of paper.

"The patient's details."

Piotr Najman, resident of Stawiguda. Born in 1963, turned fifty a week ago. Or would have.

"Thank you, Professor. Unfortunately I must complicate life for you. You cannot move these remains, and nobody may come in here or touch anything until the police take it to the lab for further analysis. We've already contaminated the evidence enough. Let's leave the room."

As he headed for the door, he was forming an action plan for the investigation. Of course, Najman might turn out to be watching TV in his slippers—there may have been a curious misunderstanding, or perhaps some bones had gotten mixed up during the party at the university. But he had to act as if that were the least likely possibility.

"Prosecutor . . . ," said Frankenstein, pointing a meaningful finger at him.

What kind of a goddamned professional did he look like? He returned to the dissection table and put the artificially connected bones back in place.

"I see you people spend your free time in here," Szacki said spitefully, pointing at the party debris.

"Don't you read the papers? We won the Grand Prix at the innovations fair in Brussels. For the first time since the days of Zbigniew Religa and his artificial heart. For a project allowing a 3-D view of models produced on the basis of combined MRI and CT scanning. A work of genius."

"And do you always celebrate in the dissection room?"

"Always," said the professor, as if nothing could be more ordinary. "We mustn't forget who's with us every step of the way."

"Who's that?" asked Szacki, once they had left the dissection room and were walking down the hallway toward the exit. In his thoughts he was miles away.

"Death."

Szacki stopped and looked at the professor.

"Can you explain how a corpse can become a skeleton in just a week?"

"Of course. I'm currently considering five different hypotheses."

"When will you be ready to talk about them?"

Frankenstein stared ahead, as if there were boundless space in front of him and not a lecture schedule hanging on the wall. It couldn't be a good sign. An expert pathologist would tell him to wait several months for a professional opinion. And a professor with a D.Sc.?

"Tomorrow, at eleven a.m. But you must leave the remains with me. Please don't worry. I taught most of Poland's pathologists, and I have equipment here to make the Olsztyn forensics lab look like a children's chemistry set."

"I'm not worried," said Szacki. "See you tomorrow."

Professor Ludwik Frankenstein, D.Sc., suddenly placed a hand on Szacki's shoulder and looked him deep in the eyes.

"I like you," he said.

Szacki didn't so much as smile. On the steps he took in a deep breath of November air. He felt faint and his head was spinning. Purely because, if not for old habits from his Warsaw days, he would probably have given routine orders for that corpse to be buried, and with it the proof of an unusual crime. Of course, he was mildly disturbed that in that case, justice wouldn't have been done. But at the thought that he might have deprived himself of the most promising case for years, his legs started to give way.

4

He must have been missing the action. He should go back to the office and tell the boss about this new, difficult, and soon sure-to-be-highly-publicized case. He should bring in the sad CID man, Bierut, and make an action plan. Instantly send someone to Najman's house and summon the family for questioning. Ask someone from Warsaw to question the foot doctor. Wait for the test results. All in all, an investigation. But instead of these routine measures, he told Bierut to find him Najman's address; fifteen minutes later he had spoken to Najman's wife on the phone and was driving down Warszawska Avenue—the real, broad one—toward Stawiguda. As he drove past the university, something began to fall from the sky. This time it wasn't freezing rain, just wet snow. The huge snowflakes looked as if someone had chewed them on their way down from the clouds, and then spat them out with hatred onto the Citroën's windshield.

In fact, it was a nice change from yesterday because at least the wipers could deal with this stuff.

Szacki passed the campus and was out of Olsztyn, with a wall of forest on either side of the road. He had never told anyone, but he loved the landscape of this road. Other major Polish cities were surrounded by a buffer of hideous suburban sprawl. After leaving the center, you drove through high-rise blocks, then a zone of stores, workshops, rusty signs, and yards full of plowed-up mud. In Olsztyn they had exit roads of that kind, too, mostly toward Masuria, but this one was different. Once out of the center, you came to the university campus, formerly a German psychiatric hospital. There were some old buildings shrouded in legend, then some modern ones financed by the EU. Then a gas station, and that was it. No more town. From here, the road ran in a gentle arc, and a few hundred yards beyond the sign announcing the Olsztyn city limits, there was no sign of civilization, just forest. What he loved about this place was that in only a few minutes you could find yourself in the middle of nowhere.

There wasn't much traffic. Szacki speeded up a bit as the road gently undulated, in tune with the rhythm of the hilly Warmian landscape. It was about twelve miles to Stawiguda.

He had always lived in the city. He had never had any other view than staring at apartments in neighboring buildings. For forty-four years. If right now this pile of junk had skidded on the slush, Szacki would have died without knowing what it felt like to stand at a bedroom window with a cup of coffee, gazing at a view that stops only at the horizon.

Three years ago, after a short time living in the provincial town of Sandomierz, he had gone back to Warsaw, merely to convince himself that he and his home city had already given each other everything they had to offer. He had been terribly tired and could feel that ugly leviathan crushing and depressing him. He had started looking out for recruitment offers before he even unpacked his clothes. And on a hunch, he had chosen this part of the country. Lakes, forests, and sunshine. Summer vacations. He had never been there and had always gone to the seaside, but that was how he imagined it. He would settle down, find a small cottage with a view of a pine copse, and he'd be happy, reading upbeat books in the evenings and tossing logs into a potbellied stove. There were no women inhabiting these visions—just him, peace, and quiet. At the time he ardently believed that only solitude could give a man a real sense of fulfillment.

Two years on, his reality in no way resembled his earlier imaginings. He was well into a relationship, still new, but no longer a passionate romance. And he had moved, of course, from a studio in a housing block to his girlfriend's apartment, so very much in the city that only a tent pitched on the town hall steps could have been more urban. It was in an old villa with a garden, but he could see his workplace from the kitchen window—such was the malevolence of fate.

Stawiguda was a large village, a messy sprawl, consisting mostly of modern single-family houses. There was no urban planning or architectural concept here that would have changed the area into a pleasant place. It was like an overview of projects from a catalog, separated from one another by various stone walls and fences. Disney castles alongside small-scale Polish manor houses, McMansions next to log cabins. On top of that, it was every neighbor's ambition to have walls of a distinctive color, as if the address alone were not enough to identify the property.

The Najmans' house was—as far as Szacki could see in the falling dusk—willow green. Apart from that, there was nothing distinctive about it. Fairly new, probably built in the last seven to ten years. Square plan, one story, with small windows and a huge roof, higher than the rest of the house. As if the attic were the most important space. There was a metal fence with solid stone pillars separating it from the neighboring properties, and a driveway made of paving bricks, now coated in melting snow.

Szacki parked in the mud outside the main gate and got out. Mrs. Najman was waiting by the side gate, wearing a long sweater. Her arms were folded, pressed tight to her body, and her hair was wet with snow. She might have been waiting for some time.

Szacki wondered if that meant anything.

Inside, the house was not unusual in any way. It was a large space, but had low ceilings and not many windows. The living room, kitchen, and dining room were combined into a single not very cozy space.

There was a blocked fireplace, a TV the size of a movie screen, and a large U-shaped leather couch with a split-level glass table in front of it. On the lower level were newspapers, and on the upper, a stack of remote controls. No books.

He kept quiet, waiting for the lady of the house to make coffee while he wondered what to say. If they had simply found Najman's body in the bushes, she'd have been the first suspect—the wife, who hadn't reported him missing for a week. But somebody had gone to a lot of trouble to kill him, reduce him to bare bones, and hide him in the city. And apart from all that, he wasn't 100-percent sure the skeleton was Najman's. When he'd called her to say he was coming, Szacki had only established that indeed, Najman hadn't been at home for over a week.

She set the coffee down in front of him, along with a small plate of cookies.

Szacki sipped the coffee. The woman sat opposite, nervously chewing her cuticles. He wanted her to speak first,

"So what's happened?" she asked.

"We're not entirely certain, but we suspect the worst."

"He's injured someone," she stated rather than asked. Her eyes widened.

That wasn't the answer he'd been expecting.

"On the contrary. We suspect your husband may be dead."

"What's that?"

He wasn't good at these conversations. Usually the people he interviewed had already been worked over by the police. Falk would have been useful—he was sure to have had some training.

"We suspect he's been killed."

"In an accident?"

"As the result of foul play."

"Does that mean someone else caused the accident?"

"It means someone else may have deprived him of his life."

"Murdered him?"

He nodded. Teresa Najman stood up and came back with a carton of vegetable juice. She poured herself a glass and drank half of it. She looked quite ordinary, like a teacher or an office worker. Average height, slender, with an unmemorable face, and ash-blonde shoulder-length hair. A suburban mother. He looked around, but he couldn't see any evidence of children. No streaks on the walls, scattered toys, or crayons in a mug. But Najman was fifty, she looked about thirty-five. Maybe a teenager?

"But who did it?"

"I'm sorry, but please would you try to focus? We've found a cadaver in Olsztyn, in a state that's not suitable for identification. We suspect it may be your husband's corpse." He felt he should say something like a normal person now. "I'm very sorry to be giving you this information. I must ask you a few questions, and then a policeman will come and ask you for something with your husband's DNA, hair from a comb, for instance. That will help us identify the body. I'd also like to get a picture of him, if possible."

She poured herself more juice and drank it in one go. It left a red ring around her mouth, as if she'd put on her lipstick without look-ing. For a short while she sat in silence, then got up and disappeared into another room. Szacki made a mental note that either she didn't keep a photo of her husband in her wallet, or she didn't want to hand over the most personal one. He also noted that Teresa Najman was not particularly talkative. The question was whether it was because she was in shock, or because she was being careful with her words. The prosecutor's experience was merciless: when it came to mysterious disappearances and murders, in four out of five instances, the spouse was to blame.

He decided to provoke her.

A few minutes went by before she came back and handed Szacki a print in postcard format.

"I had to print off an up-to-date one," she said. "They're all on the computer now."

He examined the picture. A portrait taken in summer, in bright sunlight, a smiling face against a brick wall. A handsome guy, masculine, distinctive, in the style of Telly Savalas. A bald, egg-shaped skull, thick black eyebrows, hazel eyes, a straight nose like a Roman general, full lips.

The macho type who's very attractive to women, even if their intuition tells them not to get involved.

The only flaw marring his manly image was a misshapen right ear as the result of some injury.

"Won't I recognize him?" she said, interrupting his contemplation of the photograph.

"The cadaver is not suitable for identification," he said, and seeing the blood drain from her face, he quickly added, "The DNA method is safer and will save you from distress. We generally try not to involve the relatives if the identification might be exceptionally traumatic."

"But what happened?"

Good question.

"Did somebody beat him up? Stab him? Shoot him?"

That was not just a good question, it was also a very difficult question.

"Unfortunately, at this stage we don't know."

She stared at him vacantly.

"Piotr's bald," she said, pointing at the photo.

"Sorry?"

"Piotr's bald. I can't give anyone hair from his comb."

"Please don't worry, the policeman will take care of that."

"Maybe from his electric razor, there's always some stubble dust. Do you think that'll do?"

He had no idea, but he nodded with the solemnity of a spiritual adviser.

"When did you last see your husband?"

"On Monday," she quickly said.

"In what circumstances?"

"He went off to work."

"Where?"

"He has a travel bureau in Jaroty. I mean an agency, not a bureau."

He has. Not "We have."

"And what do you do?"

"I work at the library in Kortowo."

"At the university?"

"Yes."

"Have you got any children?"

"A son, Piotruś, he's five."

He was amazed. A five-year-old who didn't turn the living room into a playground.

"Where is he now?"

"At my mother's place in Sząbruk."

He didn't entirely know where that was.

"For long?"

She stared at him as if he were transparent and she were watching a very interesting television program behind him. And froze.

"Has he been there for long?"

"Since last week. I wanted a rest, and Mom adores him."

"Since Friday last week, or since Monday last week?"

"I'm sorry, I'm totally wiped. Is this an interrogation?"

"No, we're just having a chat."

Something told him they would be having an interrogation, though.

"Did your husband say if he was going anywhere?"

"No, he didn't." She suddenly came to life and made a face as if that question had only just gotten her thinking.

"Had he ever gone off to work and disappeared for a week before?"

"He did a lot of traveling, you know. That's the tourist industry. The tour operators often organize trips for the salesmen so they can see what they're recommending. I went on one myself. The customers like it if you can tell them about it all."

"Did he just go off without warning? Do they take them away from one day to the next?"

"No, of course not. Why?"

"Weren't you surprised your husband hadn't come back from work and had vanished?"

She bit her lip.

"Sometimes he was secretive."

Szacki almost snorted with laughter. The woman was obviously lying in a way that made him want to leave right away. In a moment he'd ask her to establish a version and stick with it, otherwise he'd probably explode. It pained him to watch her thinking up lies—the only thing missing was for her to start mumbling to herself. On top of that, the whole situation seemed to defy logic. He had said he was coming in advance by phone, so if the woman had any connection with her husband's disappearance, or knew anything, she'd had enough time to sort out the facts in her mind. Meanwhile it looked as if the whole situation was a surprise to her. Except she was brazenly lying.

Why?

"Where did he get the scar from?" Szacki asked, changing the subject.

She gave him an inquiring look, as if he had addressed her in a foreign language.

"Where did he get the scar from?" he repeated.

He impatiently tapped a finger on the photograph. He'd decided to see if he could knock her off-balance.

"The scar. On his ear. Where did it come from?"

She spread her hands in a gesture of amazement, as if her husband had always gone about in a cap and only now, in that picture, had she finally learned the truth.

"Please, Mrs. Najman. This isn't a social chat. Your husband is dead. Do you understand? He's dead."

He was expecting her to burst into sobbing and hysteria, which was the usual reaction at these moments.

Teresa Najman squinted, trying to focus, chewed her lip, and finally said, "Yes, I do."

There was no hysteria; it was more like relief that she had actually managed an answer.

"He was murdered. I'm the prosecutor conducting the investigation. As the victim's wife, you're legally implicated. An important witness. At the very least an important witness."

He waited for righteous indignation and hand flapping.

"I understand . . . ," she said, in a hesitant tone.

"So please focus and answer the question. Where did he get the scar from?"

"From the past. We hadn't met then. I don't really know where he got it."

"Didn't you ever ask?"

"No, not really."

"Did you try calling him? At work? On his cell? Did you text him?"

There must have been a dramatic twist in the plot of the imaginary movie playing behind him, because Teresa Najman had completely tuned out.

"Did you call him?"

She wanted some more juice, but there were just a few drops left in the carton, which she spent ages carefully shaking out.

"It's funny you ask that, because I don't think I did call." She gave him an apologetic look. "I don't know why not."

5

He toiled away with Teresa Najman for a little longer, regretting that he wasn't interviewing her for a witness statement, and that it wasn't being recorded. If the woman had anything to do with her husband's disappearance, it would be persuasive in the case. He got her to provide some information about the foot operation, which confirmed what Frankenstein had said, including the long walks. He took the medical documentation with him, and on his way back he dropped it off at the hospital on Warszawska Avenue. He had to leave it with the watchman, though the lights were on in the anatomy department. "The professor has locked the door and doesn't want to be disturbed."

As Szacki was leaving the hospital grounds, he couldn't help imagining Frankenstein putting a stolen brain into the skull and attaching electrodes to it. His name obligated him to do it.

Szacki was sure the office would be empty at this time of day, but there was Falk in the hallway, filling out some documents. He was sitting at a small table on a little chair for visitors, twisted into an unnatural position. When he noticed Szacki, he stood up in a flash and put on his jacket.

"Haven't you got a better place to work?"

"I usually use a desk in the secretariat, but it's locked after hours."

So much for the boss's ever-open-door policy.

"Please come in my office. I'll leave instructions at reception to let them know you can make use of it whenever—I have a spare desk. Unless I ask to be on my own. All right?"

Falk did up the top button of his jacket and held out a hand in a stiff gesture, as if he really were made of pieces of wood tied together with string.

"Thank you very much."

He bowed comically, and Szacki suddenly realized who Falk resembled. He'd always sensed a likeness to someone, but he hadn't guessed who it was, because it had been ages since he'd last seen those movies. He looked exactly like Peter Sellers. He hadn't noticed it because, first of all, Falk was young, and second, he was deadly serious. Meanwhile, Szacki remembered the actor as older, with a permanent smile glued to his lips. But apart from that, Falk had the same slight figure, big schnozz, high forehead, and thick black eyebrows curving downward past his eyes.

"Yes?" asked Falk politely, because, thrilled with his discovery, Szacki was staring at him in an odd manner.

Szacki didn't answer, just opened the office door and let Falk in. Then he told Falk to listen, and recounted the story of the skeleton from Mariańska Street.

This profession can be thankless. Any prosecutor could reel off a hundred reasons why you shouldn't be a prosecutor—from the bureaucracy and the idiotic statistics, to the incompetent expert witnesses and the recalcitrant policemen, right through to the mental burden of being in permanent contact with evil and the public contempt that they encountered every step of the way. There was no prosecutor who hadn't sat at home and thought about becoming a defense attorney, or who hadn't been to a social gathering and decided to put on a counselor's gown, or who hadn't felt like packing the whole thing in after a drink or two. Curiously, surprisingly few people walked away from the profession.

Chiefly because being on the right side gave you unusual strength and confidence. In a world where most professions relied on tricking people into wanting objects and services they didn't need, where moral relativism and being prepared to be humiliated were often the pillars of a career, the prosecutors were on the side of the angels. Sometimes it worked out better for them, sometimes worse, but their profession involved administering justice, doing good, and making sure the world was a safer place. How many people could feel pride in their profession?

But it was also worth being a prosecutor for moments like this. The two men entered the office like actors in a pantomime. Stiff, straight as ramrods, dressed in their identical suits, rather aloof. To start, the younger one listened, then asked brief questions, but the further the account progressed, the more he lit up. In ten minutes they were both jacketless with their sleeves rolled up, sitting over two mugs of steaming coffee, coming up with numerous hypotheses.

It was great to be a champion of justice. But it was also great to be a detective out of an adventure story now and then. The older prosecutor loved that more than he was prepared to admit to anyone. The younger was only just falling madly in love.

"All this theatrical stuff will be their undoing," said Szacki, buttoning his cuffs—after their moment of excitement, each man was returning to his practiced persona.

"Why 'their'?"

"You've got to kidnap an adult male, kill him, reduce him to a skeleton, and drop it off in the city center. I'd be surprised if just one person did that."

"And why will the theatrical stuff be their undoing?" Falk finished his coffee and put on his jacket.

"I've been through this a few times. The really clever criminals, if they want to kill someone, get the guy drunk, strangle him, and bury him in a tough plastic bag somewhere in the middle of the forest. It's the perfect crime—one-third of this country is covered in forest. You've got to have really bad luck to get caught. But when someone starts to use theatrics, play games, stage corpses, they leave so many clues in the process, they're bound to get caught."

6

He exited onto Emilia Plater Street, which was covered with melting snow, and realized that he needed a good walk before returning to the realm of the two witches. He was too wound up and excited by the investigation, he might easily start a fight. He decided to take a stroll around the Administrative Court building—far enough to cool down a little.

He turned left. The wet snow had a strange consistency, like overcooked oatmeal. A quick march warmed him up and gradually took his mind off the case; finally he stopped seeing the skeleton before him, laid out on the chrome table. Beyond the lights, between the court building and the gallows—as everyone called the old "Gratitude to the Red Army" monument—his thoughts had already turned to what awaited him at home.

"We have to talk." Sure, they always had to talk. Best of all for hours and hours, best of all carry on an endless conversation that never led to any catharsis. Eventually they would fall asleep out of weariness, and the next day they wouldn't even remember what they'd been talking about. But he politely held these conversations, with a small part of his consciousness, devoting all the rest of it to not erupting, not tearing free, not banging his fist on the closet door, not running away. He knew that was necessary, that women demand it.

So he talked, negotiated, tried his best to be modern. He put a lot of effort into building a partnership. But goddammit, people are not identical. You can keep saying gender doesn't matter, but it will always matter. It's hormones, it's genetic memory, shaped by predefined social roles for centuries. They were building a partnership, but it was easier for Szacki—even if Żenia laughed at it—to go out to work with his briefcase. Of course, it wasn't mammoth hunting, but a symbolic gesture: I'm leaving the domestic hearth so we can have food on our plates and peace and quiet. On top of that, his profession meant, *I'm leaving the house so we can feel safe.* It would be interesting to know how many Wild West sheriffs came home from chasing bandits and shared the domestic chores with their wives.

He realized this wasn't America in the 1950s. He didn't expect to enter the house and have someone help him take off his shoes and put on his slippers, and then miraculously find a glass of bourbon and a newspaper in his hands after dinner. And only to take notice of his children once they came home from college, when he could decide if he wanted to befriend them or not.

He also realized this wasn't the '70s, which he remembered, the years of his happy Communist-era childhood. He knew he couldn't expect to return from the office to find a two-course dinner waiting for him—at worst to be heated up—and the delicious aroma of a freshly baked cake on Sundays.

He also realized this wasn't the '90s, that not every sexist joke was funny, and the length of a woman's skirt was something for her to decide, not her boss.

But goddammit, that business with the plate and two mugs was taking it too far. Today he'd had to stand beside a dissection table. He'd had to tell a strange woman her husband had been murdered. He'd gone down a hole in the ground to examine human remains. And for that he was due a little respect. Just a little fucking respect.

7

Meanwhile in the suburbs of Olsztyn, not very near and not very far away, toward the end of a road running from the city center to Równa Street, an ordinary man, so ordinary he counted as a statistic, was on his way home from work, listening to Samuel Barber's *Adagio for Strings.* He used to think it was by Georges Delerue because it was featured in *Platoon,* right in the middle, when Willem Defoe gets killed. He loved this music, and now as he drove along the winding road toward Gdańsk he was listening to it over and over. He'd had a good day, and he always listened to it on the way home after a good day.

Right on the curve at Giedajty there was a short lull in the music in the seventh minute, as if on request. After the bend he accelerated, raising his hand like a conductor, and letting it drop softly onto the steering wheel as the violins sang their mournful tune. Wonderful, today everything was wonderful. A long straight stretch and he'd be home—there should be just enough Barber left to get him to the gate.

There was. He kept the engine running a while longer, to avoid ruining the diesel turbine. Apparently you only had to do that after a long drive, but better play it safe. He looked at the house that he had built, and the tree by the terrace that he had planted, now charmingly coated in snow. At the lights in the windows, behind which his son was playing, and his wife was puttering in the kitchen. On the whole her culinary efforts didn't produce much, but he didn't complain. There are various types of women, and this one was his, the type he had chosen, and this was the type he cared for the best he could. He was a man, he had his job to do, and he did it. A modern man, who didn't demand reciprocity or gratitude for the care he devoted to his home and his family. He did it out of love, and—as he was prepared to admit—for the proud feeling that came with running the family.

8

He went into the house and hung up his coat, but unfortunately there was no aroma of a nice hot meal to greet him.

"Hela!" he shouted.

He took off his shoes and felt weary. It was ages since he'd had such a long day.

"What?" she shouted back from the depths of the big apartment, her voice echoing.

Sure, she'd sooner drop dead than come to him. He went into the kitchen—the house had the sort of layout where your natural instinct was to go past the hall and turn straight into the kitchen. Most of their guests never got as far as the rest of the apartment, all domestic and social life happened in the huge kitchen. He switched on the light. The plate, coffee mug, and empty glass were still in the exact spot where he'd left them. The crumbs too.

"Hela!" he yelled in a tone that made her come running. She gave him an annoyed look.

"What day is it?" he asked.

She raised an eyebrow, just like Żenia—surprising how people only have to live together for a short while to start being similar.

"I can explain . . ."

"Hela"—he interrupted her with a raised hand—"just one thing. Not a hundred, not ten, just one. You don't have to look after three younger siblings, or help me run the family business, you don't even have to wash your own panties or clean the tub, which miraculously cleans itself for you. Once a week, on Tuesdays, when you finish school at two, you have to fix the dinner. One thing a week. One, literally one. Which yet again has proved too difficult."

Of course she had tears in her eyes.

"You just don't understand my situation."

"Yeah, sure, a poor little kid from a broken family, raised by a psychopath father and a wicked stepmother. A fragile little flower, violently ripped from her Warsaw roots. Don't get on my nerves. We all walk around you on tiptoes, Princess Helena, and as a reward you spit in our soup. Oh, I'm sorry, of course you don't do that. You know why not? Because there is no goddamn soup!"

She was staring at him angrily, her mouth twitching, as if she didn't know which insult to choose.

"Go ahead and hit me!" she finally shouted tearfully.

He was dumbstruck with rage.

"Have you gone totally crazy? You've never had a smack in your life."

"I must have suppressed the memory. The teacher said that's possible. Suppressing trauma. God, what I've been through."

She hid her face in her hands.

He was trying to calm down, but he could feel his blood seething.

"I cannot believe it. Just get out of my sight before you earn yourself some real trauma. And I guarantee you won't be able to suppress it, not for the next seventeen years. Get out."

She turned and walked off, head held high. How proud, despite the injustice done to her. He couldn't stop himself from giving her the finger.

"And I'm subtracting the cost of a pizza from your allowance. I promise it'll be very expensive."

Worn out, he sat down on the counter, right on a blob of ketchup from breakfast. He felt a wet stain spread across his buttock.

He couldn't help laughing. He rolled up his sleeves, washed the breakfast items, and ordered a pizza. He was really in the mood for one. He was putting on the kettle for his sacred evening coffee when Żenia came home. And with her came the unexpected aroma of Chinese food.

He heard her taking off her boots in the hall, and then she came straight into the kitchen, tall, flushed from the cold, with a mega-long rainbow scarf around her neck. She looked lovely, like a teenager.

"I want coffee too. And if you heat up some milk, I'll . . ." She made a hand gesture implying a blow job.

He tapped his forehead. But he really liked this girl. Enough for the word *marriage* to have ceased to sound like a threat to him. Wouldn't it be great to put up with her earthy wisecracks for the rest of his life? He should give it some thought.

She put two big bags of Chinese food on the table.

He gave her a questioning look.

"Oh, I couldn't make up my mind, so I got more than we need—at worst there'll be some leftovers for tomorrow. Helena"—she always spoke of his daughter as Helena, which surprisingly enough, Hela really liked—"called me after school to apologize and say she couldn't fix dinner, because they had a charity project. She promised to make apple fritters tomorrow. Why are you staring at me like that?"

9

Meanwhile, on Równa Street, obscenely ordinary in its suburban way, in the house with nothing to distinguish it, as the man sat down to dinner, he cast his mind back a few months to the training course they'd had at a hotel near Łódź. The instructor had asked what they would compare their families to. They had laughed the most at a guy who'd said "a holiday on the Baltic Coast"—a vacation, kind of; something we wanted, kind of; and a whole pile of cash has gone into it, but where's the sunshine? He had told the truth, knowing that on a management training course it wouldn't sound too bad: his family was like a well-oiled machine.

It was good to be part of this machine. Well, maybe not so much part of it as the engineer. He was thinking about that as he sat down to eat. The meal looked delicious, beefsteak with a creamy sauce. And potato puree—each of them had their initial in potato puree on their plate. The kid was really thrilled, bouncing up and down in his high chair as if he knew what was written there, and he kept jabbing a finger at his letter, laughing out loud.

"You did that beautifully," he told his wife.

She smiled. She wasn't all that pretty or all that feminine, but she had her good days. This was one of them. And he was having a good day too. Really. A well-oiled machine.

"Mm, this sauce is yummy. What's in it?"

"Gorgonzola. Do you like it?"

"You don't have to ask. Isn't he having any?"

"Somewhere I read that blue cheese is only a good idea after they turn three. It's probably an exaggeration, but just in case."

"Did you take cash out from the ATM?"

"Oh, Christ, I'm sorry."

He shrugged. He knew his wife was sometimes like that. Even if she wrote something down or tattooed it on her hand, she'd either forget, or do the opposite.

"Never mind," he said reassuringly, because he could see she was upset, and stroked her hand. "It's just that if you pay by card it's easier to keep track of the expenses. Thanks to our notebook we know what we've spent in which store, and then we can decide if we need to cut back anywhere. And we can save up for a really cool vacation."

"I forgot, I shouldn't go to the local store."

"We don't do the shopping there, do we?"

"Yes, I know. I was trying to get to the supermarket, but somehow it just didn't work out, so I got cash from the ATM to shop at the local store."

"OK, I see, but you know what happens with cash."

"Yes." She repeated his words: "You break a hundred, and you no longer have a hundred."

He gestured to say, "I couldn't have put it better myself," and with the last bit of meat he wiped up the rest of the puree. He finished eating and started amusing the baby with some peas. Not that you should play with food, but the kid still had a while to learn that.

A well-oiled machine. He liked his career, his house, and his tree. But this family—this well-oiled machine—this was his greatest achievement in life. He'd never stop being proud of it.

10

Szacki tried to make up with Hela, but she wouldn't let him into her room. He'd just have to talk to her the next day when she'd gotten over it. Why couldn't she just say something now? Wouldn't that be easier? He knew he'd goofed, but he was still a little angry. With her, with himself, in general. Some kind of male PMS had come over him.

The good thing was that Żenia had taken pity on him and dropped the "we have to talk."

He was lying in bed reading Lemaitre. Although he usually avoided crime novels—not only were they far-fetched and predictable, they studiously avoided all mention of prosecutors—he had to admit that the Frenchman was really good.

Żenia came out of the bathroom in a long nightshirt, rubbing cream into her palms. She had stopped running around the house naked since Hela had come to live with them. He was grateful for that because before she had paraded her nakedness like a flag, and he realized it must have been a sacrifice for her to cover up for his child's sake.

She was one of those women who look older once they've wiped off their makeup, but without losing any charm. On the contrary, he liked her this way. Her features sharpened, and some might have found them masculine, but this raw look was to his taste. Strange how that works. Whenever he saw girls like her—tall, angular, androgynous, with sharp features, a small bust, and a husky laugh, he thought: *not my type.* But one look from Żenia and he'd been smitten. Now as he watched her buzzing through the bedroom, he was deriving immense pleasure from it.

"They spent three hours telling me about all their friends and relatives, who has what relationship with whom and why. Normally I'd take no notice, but I'm afraid if I get the seating plan wrong on those rafts and a fight breaks out, someone will drown. I did my best to draw it all out—that whole sheet of paper looks like a Soviet battle plan—but it's one hell of a brainteaser. The young people are seated together, but the young people from his work can't sit next to the young people from her family, because her father's firm once took a commission away from his firm. Are you listening to me?"

"Uh-huh," he said, pretending to be actively listening because during her diatribe he had gone back to his book.

"So what did I say?"

"Her father's firm took a commission away from his firm. Are you listening to me?"

She collapsed onto the bed beside him.

"I thought, what's the point of it all? I gave up medicine because I couldn't bear to be responsible for the fact that somebody's life would depend on my decisions. In that light it looked as if wedding planning was the safest business in the world. But what do you know? Fate has caught up with me. If I seat somebody wrong at the reception, I might have blood on my hands." She theatrically laid a hand on her breast—it looked quite sexy. "At any rate, I came back from that hellish meeting, drove to the gas station for a coffee, and ran into Agata. Remember? The one who used to go out with the guy who later married Agnieszka, whose uncle worked with my dad for a while at Michelin. I told you about the factory summer camp where I once got a tick, right? Not the Michelin camp, the one run by my mom's employers."

"I feel as if I spent my own childhood there."

"You moron. Agata told me an extraordinary story about her brother, Robert. They're these friends of mine. She said that 'when things go wrong, everything goes wrong,' but it reminded me more of that David Fincher movie where everything falls apart."

"*The Game.*"

"Exactly. A regular guy, wife, daughter, small house in Purda. Suddenly the bank withdraws his loan, an ordinary, personal loan.

They don't have to give a reason, that's in the contract. They can do that. So Robert thinks: *Screw you, I'll go get it somewhere else.* He has a full-time job. He goes to the HR department to get a form signed, and there's a termination letter waiting for him. They're cutting jobs. All in keeping with the law. It's in his contract, and so on. Guess what happened next."

"The tax man."

"How did you know?"

"Every story where 'when things go wrong, everything goes wrong' always involves the tax man. Simple."

"That's right. He used to run a firm, and they say they're doing an audit, there's been an incorrect calculation of VAT. Of course he quickly divided the assets, transferred it all to his wife's name, but even so it was pretty bad. Especially because the wife divorced him soon after. Not that I'd have complained—there was something wrong with that relationship. It was too sugarcoated somehow, like for show, as if there was something wrong under the icing. Everything seemed OK, but in reality—you get my drift."

She sighed and glanced at his book. He'd forgotten the title was all too meaningful in their situation. *The Wedding Gown.* He drummed his fingers on his crossed knee.

"How about a quickie?" she said.

"Do I have to put my book aside?"

"If I'm going to have a decent orgasm, then no."

He put it aside. Title facing downward, just in case.

11

Meanwhile, dusk had long since fallen on Równa Street, the children were asleep, the lights were out, and most of the homeowners had retired for the night. But not all. The man was still bursting with the energy he'd built up during the day. Sometimes he had a sense of such—what a dumb word—*potency*. As if he took up more space than usual. As if he could hear more clearly, see more sharply, feel everything more intensely. This day, the dinner, this family, this perfect home—he felt like a charged-up battery. All the needles were quivering in the red zone.

He went up to his wife as she made the bed, and ran a hand down her spine. He knew there are erogenous zones there, and women like it. But she did not arch her back like a cat, just froze, and gently withdrew from his touch. Gently, but he understood it wasn't the right day. He couldn't remember, but maybe it was her period. That would explain the ATM—hormones are thicker than water.

He was a modern man—it would never have crossed his mind to force his wife into sex when she didn't want it. Sure, sometimes he was sorry she wasn't as—another dumb word—*randy* as he was, and sometimes he dreamed of wild, demented sex. But whatever, in reality his wild sex would probably have ended in snoring after half an hour anyway. Nor would it have occurred to him to go looking for stupid adventures. And it wasn't just desperate women who had given him the come-on look at conferences. And not just the look. The memory alone was enough to boost his energy even more. But so what, nothing had ever happened. The family meant a lot, but the family also meant duties.

Luckily, long ago, right at the start of their relationship, they had found a way to cope with his excess energy. It meant he could calmly get to sleep, and she didn't have to perform her marital obligations if she didn't want to. In time, though he didn't admit it, it had started to suit him so well that oh, oh, oh—who knows—perhaps they were the Warmian record holders in this particular discipline?

He didn't even have to say anything—by now it was their little ritual, every relationship has them. She lay on her back on the bed, with her head hanging over the side of the frame. The bed was high enough for him not to have to kneel, just stand with his legs astride.

It wasn't so much a blow job as an Olympic sport. They had practiced for a long time so she could control the gag reflex, and they'd spent a long time looking for the right throat pastilles. So that he could enter her as deep as possible, so that her throat took in the whole length of his dick. Sometimes—like now—he could feel the pulse in her esophagus, as if she were trying to swallow him.

He watched her from above. She was lying with her legs and arms spread, her head suspended, her mouth wide-open, her eyes closed— like a corpse, like a drunk who has fallen asleep after collapsing on the bed. Only the violent trembling of her diaphragm—she used a special technique that stopped her from vomiting—betrayed that she wasn't asleep.

CHAPTER THREE

Wednesday, November 27, 2013

On his opposition rival Yulia Tymoshenko's fifty-third birthday, Ukrainian president Viktor Yanukovych confirms that in December he will know if Ukraine is going to sign the association agreement, but nobody takes this quasi-dictator seriously anymore. In Germany a major coalition of the CDU and the SPD is formed, in Italy Silvio Berlusconi loses his seat in the senate, and roars: "This is the death of democracy!" In Great Britain the prime minister announces cuts in benefits for immigrants. Five percent of Polish sixteen-year-olds admit to stripping in front of live cameras on the Internet, and the Polish TV news shows the seedy side of Warsaw, including a traumatized girl who has been the victim of attempted rape. After protests, the TV channel apologizes for its tactlessness. There's a scandal in Kraków: they call off the premiere of Krasiński's classic play *The Un-Divine Comedy* because it has leaked out of rehearsals that, in this production, the Polish national anthem is sung to the tune of the German one. In Olsztyn the police arrest a man who reported planting a bomb. He was so drunk that he told the policemen where he was calling from. The renovated exit road to Klewki and Szczytno is reopened, unfortunately without being finished, because there wasn't enough money for the last two hundred yards of asphalt. In the nationwide "Pearls of Medicine" competition the city hospital is judged best hospital in the under-four-hundred-beds category. The temperature is around 32 degrees, there's a dreadful wind, and there's fog. And freezing drizzle.

1

Pretty much every day there are people on television shouting that "you should go and complain to the prosecutor." Prosecutor Teodor Szacki knew from experience that shouting was rarely where it ended—these people really did come and complain to the prosecutor afterward. And he reckoned the worst nightmare of the profession was the opportunity granted to Joe Public to just come in off the street and report a crime, reducing the highly qualified guardian of the law to the role of a beat cop.

And so he found it hard to keep a professional look on his face when he saw a visitor at his door, picking at the handle of her purse. He wasn't on duty, but the desk clerk informed him that the duty officer would be late—she was stuck in a traffic jam, all because of the repairs at the junction of Warszawska Avenue and Tobruk Street, and besides, you know, typical Olsztyn. All Szacki's emotions must have been printed on his face, because the desk clerk leaned out of his little window and added as a consolation:

"But they'll have the streetcars up and running soon, and everything will be different, you'll see."

Szacki invited the woman into his room, smiling, and sincerely hoping it was just a trifling matter he could tell her to take to the police. Or even better: advise her to find herself a lawyer. He couldn't wait to get down to Warszawska Avenue to find out what Frankenstein had discovered.

"Yes?" He wanted to sound cold and professional.

"I'd like to report a crime," she said at once, as if she'd been practicing that sentence the whole way there.

"Of course."

As he took out the relevant form and a pen, he eyed the woman sitting opposite him, trying to guess what it was about. She wasn't on the margin, she was well dressed, tidy, with a neat, simple hairstyle. The sort of woman who prefers to go to the prosecutor than to the police because she feels better in this environment. About thirty, with the looks of a perfume store assistant: pretty enough to reflect well on the firm, but not pretty enough to make the female customers feel reluctant to shop there.

"Well, I wanted to report that my husband . . . that my husband, well, the thing is, I'm afraid of him."

Great, some paranoia to start the day. He spitefully imagined the content of the nonexistent law: "Anyone who, through persistent frightening of another person, prompts a sense of threat in them, is subject to a penalty of deprivation of sense of security for up to three years."

"Maybe you'd prefer to talk to my female colleague?" he said. He had an innocent lie on the tip of his tongue that, according to new directives for recording cases of domestic violence, women must report them to female officials. He swallowed it, partly out of shame, partly out of a sense of duty, and partly out of fear that he would give himself away.

The woman shook her head.

He took down her personal details. First name, last name, address. A village outside Olsztyn, on the road to Łukta as far as he remembered. Age thirty-two, a speech therapist by training, riding and sailing instructor by profession.

"That is until recently," she corrected herself. "Now I'm caring for a child."

"I'll cite you a regulation that might be relevant," he said. "Article 207 of the penal code concerns physical or mental harassment of a family member. The penalty for that is from three months to five years. Up to ten, if the prohibited act is combined with the use of particular cruelty. I understand you want to report a case of harassment."

"It's just that I'm afraid of him," she repeated.

"Do you have proof of physical abuse?" Szacki had no time to play psychoanalyst.

"Sorry?"

"A medical report after being hit, or at least the paperwork following treatment for breaks or injuries. If you don't have it, we can get the relevant details from the hospital."

"But he's never hit me," she was eager to say, as if she'd come here purely to defend her husband.

"So we're not talking about physical violence?"

She looked at him helplessly and licked her lips.

"Are we talking about physical abuse or not? Bodily injuries? Wounds? Bruises? Anything?"

"No, I said not."

He folded his hands and mentally counted to five, telling himself that this was the price for choosing a profession that involved serving the public. All of them, without exception. Even the ones who treated the prosecution service like divorce counseling.

"So it's mental abuse. Does he insult you? Or threaten to apply physical abuse?"

"Not directly, no."

"Do you have any children?"

"A son of almost three."

"Does he hit him? Shout at him? Neglect him?"

"Nothing of the kind, he's a great father, modern. He's really good with him."

"Ma'am," he began, wanting to say that she'd come to the wrong address—the *Olsztyn Gazette* was sure to be holding a poll for Husband and Father of the Year, but at the last moment he restrained himself. "I understand that your husband doesn't hit you or your child, doesn't insult you or shout at you. Does he keep you prisoner? Lock you in the house?"

"No, he doesn't."

"But you feel threatened."

She raised her trembling hands in a gesture of helplessness. Her cuticles were bitten to the quick. *Neurosis*, he figured. But neurosis doesn't amount to proof of a crime. He should have put his last remark in the form of a question, asked more questions, and given her time to say what she wanted to say. Outside, a world full of real crimes was waiting; he had no time to waste on imaginary problems.

"Because he controls everything so much, he doesn't give me any space," she finally said. "For instance, he tells me to pay for things with a credit card, because then it says on the statement where and how much I paid. And I have to put the receipts in a notebook recording expenses. They're all small things really. And everything has to be just the way he wants it, everything . . ." She paused, as if waiting for encouragement.

Szacki looked at her expectantly.

"But you know, it's also true that I'm a bit ditzy sometimes. With money, too, you know how it is. If you break a hundred, you no longer have a hundred." She laughed nervously. "I'm sorry, I got myself all psyched up, and here I am, wasting your time. I'm hopeless."

"That's what we're here for," he said in a sarcastic tone.

She nodded. He felt he should say something.

"Ma'am, I know these are delicate matters, but there are no public services that can help you make difficult decisions. I understand you're feeling very distressed in your marriage, otherwise you wouldn't have come here. But your . . ."—he searched for the right word—"your mental discomfort does not signify that your husband is going to commit a crime. It only testifies to the fact that perhaps you made the wrong choice. But then there's no law ordering anyone to live with a person with whom they don't feel happy."

She put her purse on her knees, tightly gripping the handle. She looked as if she knew she should leave, but was incapable of forcing herself to take that step.

"It's just that I'm very frightened."

Szacki glanced at his watch. He had to be at the hospital in an hour, and he still had a stack of paperwork to get through.

"I know," she said quietly, and got up. "There's no such service."

Shortly after, Szacki threw the uncompleted statement form away, and instantly forgot the matter.

2

Meanwhile his visitor left the prosecution building, and instead of turning right, to where she had parked her car at the bottom of Emilia Plater Street, she walked toward the shopping mall. An ordinary woman, neither chic nor unkempt, neither beautiful nor ugly. She melted into the crowd of other ordinary people. And that was a good thing; she always felt safer in the crowd. She sat down in one of the impersonal cafés and ordered an absurdly expensive coffee—she only had a little cash of her own. She had borrowed it from her mother on All Saints' Day, using some stupid excuse; her parents knew they were doing well. They always stressed how proud they were that she'd found such a fine husband. He'd built a house, planted a tree, fathered a son—a real man. Suitably traditional, and suitably modern.

As she drank the hot coffee, she winced—her throat still hurt from yesterday. She had fallen asleep so resolutely determined to go to the prosecutor and sort this out, to get herself out of this mess. Thinking that even if she was a hopeless, ungrateful, clumsy, messed-up bimbo, she didn't deserve this. She'd had a speech therapy practice and worked with young people. She'd loved the sailing camps, showing the teenagers the same knots over and over, making bonfires at the same sites each year, singing shanties off-key, and finding out, to her joy, that you never sail through the same inlet the same way.

That was how life had been less than three years ago, but now it seemed like ancient history. It was incredible to think how natural and harmless everything had seemed. She'd spent a lot of time with her husband because they hadn't been married for long. She'd stayed at the building site a lot because someone had to supervise the work. Then she'd spent a lot of time watching over the interior decorating, as it needed even more supervision. She'd spent a lot of time out in the boondocks because their dream house was out in the goddamn boondocks. She'd kept an eye on the expenses because a house consumes money, as everyone knows, and then there'd been a child on the way. And she couldn't go out to work, because someone had to see to the house, and then the kid. Anyway, the state of the job market meant that to earn enough to pay for a sitter and the commute to work and back, she would have had to be a speech therapist in Warsaw, or move to the Canary Islands, where the sailing season is year-round. There was a time when she really had dreamed of teaching sailing somewhere far away, like Croatia—the sailing was totally different on the open sea.

As well as the notebook for expenses, she should really have had a notebook for all the things she screwed up. Today she'd have included the visit to the prosecutor. On the one hand that white-haired flunky hadn't been very encouraging—he'd looked at her as if she were nuts and his only thought was how to get rid of her. On the other, what had she expected? That the prosecutor could read other people's minds? She should have pulled herself together and said, "My dear Mister Prosecutor, every day my husband sticks his dick so deep down my throat that I'm forced to swallow my own puke. Do you think there's a regulation for that?"

Would that have changed anything? Maybe. He would have asked if she had a medical report and bodily injuries, and advised her that, regretfully, there were no services to combat injuries sustained while performing oral sex. Or he'd have smiled dumbly, made a stupid joke, and told her that worse things can happen in a marriage. She had confided in a girlfriend right after it first began, because he'd developed a disgust for her pussy after the birth. Her friend had laughed, saying that she still had it easy. At least she could avoid the taste of sperm because it went straight down her throat.

As she drank the pricey coffee, it occurred to her that the white-haired flunky had been right about one thing. No public service was going to sort it out for her. Time to deal with it. Once and for all.

3

Szacki parked outside the regional beer center so he wouldn't forget to buy himself something for the evening on the way back. The Kormoran Brewery was a very nice discovery he'd made since he had migrated to Olsztyn. Some of their products were sweeter than an éclair, but some were first-rate. He'd always been a bit of a wine snob, but he realized that living in Olsztyn was a lot like being on vacation, and beer was more suited for that. He did worry about putting on weight, but every time he found himself standing at the checkout he swore to take up running again, and that was how he satisfied his conscience.

Of course he'd start running again, as soon as the weather got better. He buttoned up his coat. It was nearing eleven, but there was an icy fog, and dark clouds hanging so low that only a fraction of sunlight was getting through. It looked as if dusk were falling.

He went into the anatomy building, and suddenly had a strong and pleasant sense of being home—he felt a wave of nostalgia for the innocent years of his happy childhood, when his family lived in an apartment block in Warsaw's Powiśle district. The feeling was so over-powering that he stopped in his tracks. He looked around, but there was nothing eye-catching in the impersonal hospital hallway, with its fluorescent lighting and anatomical cross sections on the walls. It must have been the smell! A unique combination of floor polish and the wonderful aroma of beef stock—which he associated with childhood because on Saturdays there was always polishing, and on Sundays, beef soup. The minor rituals of traditional families in the days of the Polish People's Republic.

He was pleased to have recognized the source of his nostalgia. And then he was immensely surprised, because a morgue—even one where there'd been streamers hanging off the surgical lights a few hours ago—was hardly the place for beef soup.

He went into the dissection room. The skeleton was lying on the chrome table, with its skull tilted to one side, as if it were curiously watching what was going on in there. With his back to the skeleton, Professor Frankenstein was standing at a long table from which all the laboratory equipment had been removed and replaced with various containers. Frankenstein's assistant stood beside a large pot set on a gas burner, stirring its steaming contents. Seeing the bubbling liquid, Szacki imagined that any moment now eyeballs would come floating to the top. He coughed.

Frankenstein and his assistant turned around. Frankenstein looked the same as yesterday—like a mad scientist out of a German movie. The side-buttoning gown, the long face, the white-blond hair, and the gold-rimmed spectacles. Whereas his assistant looked as if she had just stepped off the set of a porno flick where they screw among laboratory equipment. She was gorgeous, with the natural beauty of the girl next door, black wavy hair and curves she couldn't have even hidden under a potato sack. Beneath her buttoned gown she wore black stockings, and she had on high heels so slender you could have pierced your ears with them. He tried not to think about the possibility that she had nothing on under the gown but her panty hose, but he couldn't resist it.

"Prosecutor Teodor Szacki, Miss Alicja Jagiełło," Professor Frankenstein said. "Once my most able student, now my assistant, working on her doctorate on how to determine the date of death. She's just back from an internship at one of the legendary body farms in the States. The experiments we're conducting here will be part of her doctoral work."

Szacki held out a hand to the woman, wondering if her ostentatious sex appeal had anything to do with her work with dead bodies. He knew a lot of pathologists, and they all had their eccentricities to save them from going crazy. The legendary head of the Department of Forensic Medicine in Gdańsk had opted for motherhood, for instance, and had a special room for feeding her babies right next door to the dissection room. Her husband, once a top prosecutor, did so much around the house that finally he'd penned some best-selling books about healthy meals for small children, and then dropped the legal profession.

Miss Jagiełło looked at Szacki with huge eyes, the pale-blue color of the sky on a very hot day. Her expression showed perspicacity and sharp intelligence. She made a major impression in every respect.

"Any news on my client's case?" He pointed at the skeleton.

"Plenty," she said, going over to the set of bones. She had evidently taken the initiative.

The old professor seemed pleased about it. He was watching Jagiełło with the affectionate gaze of a proud father.

"First I examined all the bones, looking for evidence that might point us toward the cause of death. Of course, they're just bones, but they could have been damaged by a bullet, a knife, or a blunt instrument. Any breaks or fractures would also give us some idea of what he experienced when he was alive."

She put on a pair of latex gloves, picked up the skull, and held it on her palm in a Hamlet-like pose.

"I found close to nothing. Definitely not the cause of death. On the occipital bone"—she turned the skull around to show him the back of it—"there's a star-shaped crack. We often see them on the frontal bone. It's the result of hitting the head against a flat surface, a wall, or a floor, and in people who suffer a fall, it's a standard injury. It's far less common on the back of the head. But something about it didn't seem right, so I looked at it under magnification. These cracks imply that it wasn't the result of a single blow, but lots of blows."

"As if someone had banged something flat against his head?" asked Szacki. "A snow shovel?"

"I thought about it, but it's hard to imagine anything quite like that. The victim must have been immobilized, with his head in the same position throughout, and someone must have hit him not just with something flat, a wide board for instance, but with precisely measured-out, identical force every single time."

"Not very likely."

"Right. Will you do the stirring, please, Professor?"

Frankenstein gave a dignified nod, and went up to the bubbling stainless steel vat.

"I thought it was more likely to be convulsions—spasms caused by an injury, poisoning, or a neurological disorder. I'm afraid I also have another theory, but I'll come to that in a second."

She leaned forward and carefully put the skull down. Szacki watched closely, trying to see the edge of a skirt or blouse, a button, a belt loop, or a bra strap poking from under her gown.

She went up to the cadaver and gently took hold of the middle finger of the right hand.

"There are strange injuries on some of the fingers and toes."

"Strange?"

"Unprecedented, or at least I've never come across anything like them, not in practice, nor in the literature. For want of a better term, the bones look filed down. As if someone had taken a blunt, old wood file and brutally filed the fingertip. Surgical precision doesn't come into play—the bone is broken and jagged. Please take a look."

She held the little finger under his nose. The thin bone really did end in splinters. Szacki felt a shudder at the thought of how anyone could have sustained such an injury.

"Interestingly, on the left hand the middle phalanges look like this, too, not just the outer ones."

"What does that mean?"

"If we stay with the file comparison, whoever was filing the finger didn't stop when part of it fell off, just went on filing."

"How could such injuries occur?"

She cast him the look of a woman who, despite her age, has already seen too much.

"I do have a theory on that subject, but I'll come to it later. Let's consider how a man who was walking around in the forest a week ago can possibly have ended up in a state where an experienced prosecutor took him for an old German skeleton."

She smiled at him to show that her sass was meant in a friendly way. Jagiełło went over to the long table. Apart from the vat of broth sitting on the gas burner, there were four other containers, two made of steel and two made of gray plastic. An open laptop with its screen turned off was lined up with the containers.

"The scientific truth is forged in the fire of experiments," said Frankenstein in a deep voice. "And lying behind them are not paper and pencil, but heated coals, the bellows, and the strength of a smith."

"And strength of mind, obviously," added Jagiełło, who had her back to Szacki, so unfortunately he couldn't see her expression.

She raised the lid of the steel vat.

"This is the object of our experiments," she said.

Szacki leaned forward, and inside he saw a lot of red meat and white bones. He cast her an inquiring look.

"My pugs and I are regular customers at the butcher's," said Frankenstein. "He immediately did as I wished. Shin of veal with the knee joints, meat, and skin, so we could have all the tissues for observation."

Frankenstein, his pugs, and their favorite butcher. Szacki thought it sounded like the title of a modern novel, in which literary form has a major role to play, and the author reinvents the Polish language.

"Do you know what body farms are?" asked Jagiełło.

"They leave cadavers in an enclosed area and observe the progress of decomposition, depending on latitude, temperature, weather, and season. Invaluable for later determining the time of death at the incident site."

She nodded her approval.

"'Body farm' is the colloquial term. Officially they're called 'anthropological research centers.' I worked for six months in Tennessee, where the oldest farm is. Curiously, they never complain of a lack of corpses. Most of them are donated by the families for research purposes, but here in Poland it's out of the question. Over there, plenty of people are willing to declare that they want their remains to be eaten by maggots under a bush for the good of science."

She tapped a finger on one of the pots; it was some sort of lab equipment, with a few cables and gauges sticking out of it. The lid was tightly shut with butterfly screws. The container was shaking slightly.

"And we're going to start with the maggots."

"Larvae," Frankenstein corrected.

"Larvae of *Lucilia caesar*, also known as the common greenbottle, a member of the blowfly family. You're probably familiar with this rather repulsive, buzzing beastie with a green abdomen. It's a very handy little cleaner, capable of consuming everything disfiguring the landscape at rapid speed—excrement, corpses, stinking organic remains. People should put up a monument to it instead of turning up their noses. It lays its eggs in the body, the larvae hatch out of the eggs, eat a big meal, and metamorphose into a chrysalis, from which the fly emerges. The larvae are what interest us most because they're the ones that feast on dead tissue. They're fabulous epicures." Jagiełło spoke with such rapture that for a while Szacki thought it was irony, but her glee was totally serious. "They'll eat anything that's dead and decaying, but they won't touch live, healthy tissue. That's why they're used to clean infected wounds."

"Are they capable of reducing a man to bare bones in a week?" he asked, afraid he'd be spending the rest of the day listening to a lecture on entomology.

"Theoretically yes, but you'd have to go to some trouble. Each *Lucilia* lays about a hundred eggs, from which the voracious larvae emerge several hours later. And then ten days go by before the larvae change into flies. So if we don't have much time, we've got to have a lot of insects to start with."

Szacki's imagination translated this into the language of criminology.

"So for example, a month earlier we toss a chunk of pig somewhere, wait until the flies come along, then lock up the whole company and wait until a generation or two has replaced them, adding more meat if need be," he said. "It's simple mathematics. Even assuming a mortality rate of 50 percent, you only need to start with ten flies to have five hundred in the next generation, and twenty-five thousand in the one after that."

"You've got it. If we throw a human corpse in there, it'll be consumed by tens of thousands of larvae, and it'll only take them a few days to deal with it. Yesterday," she said, laying a hand on the steel vat, "two pounds of veal on the bone was placed in this container with ten flies."

She broke off, noticing the look on Szacki's face. He was hoping her talents didn't extend to telepathy, because at that moment he was imagining her and the professor out catching blowflies in a parking lot in the woods, crawling about on their hands and knees around a huge turd left behind by some trucker nourished on pork neck.

"Let's suppose that if anyone did go to that much trouble, they also made sure to have the proper climate. The higher the humidity and temperature, the greater the chance of the eggs surviving, and the more energetic the larvae. That's why we've been maintaining favorable conditions in this pot. Please take a look at the result after just a few hours." She unscrewed the butterflies on the lid and nodded to him.

Szacki reluctantly approached the pot—he loathed maggots.

She opened the lid, and a fat, shiny green fly crawled out from inside, looking dopey. It tried to fly away but fell onto the table next to the pot as if it were drunk, and then sluggishly wandered off. Just then a rolled-up newspaper came down on it with full force. Szacki jumped—he wasn't expecting that.

"We won't be needing the queen mother anymore," said Frankenstein coldly, lifting the newspaper. There was a wet stain on the table.

Szacki leaned over the pot and held his breath, but he could still smell the terrible stench of rotten meat. His stomach churned. The inside of the pot was pulsating with life. Hundreds of grayish larvae were wiggling in a frenzy, as if fighting for access to the decay, making it look as if the white bones sticking out of the veal were shaking with convulsions. It was truly revolting.

As Jagiełło reached deep into the pot, the medical gown rode up her arm without exposing any other piece of clothing. With a flash of curiosity in her eye, she put her hand into the swarm of larvae and pulled out the veal, then used her other hand to brush the fat maggots off the meat. One of them landed on Szacki's jacket. He flicked it off.

"So what do you think?" she asked.

"If someone really did go to the trouble of breeding a swarm of flies in advance, which I doubt, then maybe so. For two pounds of veal, there's not much left." Indeed, there were just some scraps of meat hanging off the bone. "What do you think?"

"I think this experiment is useful for my work, but it won't help you."

"Why not?"

"Because *Lucilia* larvae are very good at gnawing off the flesh, but they leave the connective tissue. Which means that if they were responsible for dealing with our victim, the bones would still be connected by joints and tendons. Instead of a heap of dry bones, we'd have a complete skeleton, an exhibit for a freak show."

"By the way, we should do something like that next time we get a young corpse," said Frankenstein. "In an old one, the joints are already distorted; they're no good for anything. Some use they are to science!"

The assistant smiled radiantly at her mentor. What a delicious thought! said the look in her eyes.

Szacki didn't comment. The fact that the state entrusted the education of its youth to lunatics was disturbing, of course, but the penal code didn't provide any sanctions for it.

"Unfortunately the Australian experiment failed for the same reason," she said. She tossed the meat back into the pot, her gloves into the trash, and went up to the computer. "I asked a colleague in Sydney to drop a piece of veal into a nest of fire ants, in other words *Solenopsis invicta*. Quite a nasty, omnivorous insect. And not at all hard to obtain. I admit they disposed of their dinner much faster and more thoroughly than the larvae. Snip snap, it didn't even have time to stink. They ate the skin, too, and licked the bone clean." She pressed a key, and on the screen in a small window he could see a slightly pixelated image from an Internet camera, showing small red ants fussing around a piece of bone. "It'd be great, if not for the fact that once again the cartilage proved indigestible for our little guys."

She closed the computer, went up to the pot of broth, and stirred. "Hypothesis number three: *mos teutonicus*."

Szacki gave her a quizzical look.

"I thought lawyers knew Latin."

"They do." Szacki straightened up—he wanted to be the one making an impression too. "*Mos teutonicus* is the Latin for 'Teutonic custom.' But I don't understand what it has to do with the decomposition of a corpse."

"In this particular instance I would translate the word *mos* as 'ritual.' The Teutonic knights devised it during the Crusades, so they wouldn't have to bury their noblemen in the land of the infidel. When their commander died, they chopped him to pieces and boiled him until the flesh came away from the bones. Then they took the bones home to the North, where they held the burial."

"The chronicles don't say what happened to the flesh," said Frankenstein. "But perhaps they had a plentiful supper at the camp that day. It's worth remembering that the king of France himself Saint Louis IX was boiled after his death in Tunis, and what's more they boiled him in wine. You can still see some of his stewed bones in reliquaries, I can't remember where . . ."

"Unfortunately it's another blind alley," said Jagiełło, removing a white veal shin from the pot with a pair of tongs; there were some remains of boiled gray meat clinging to it. "For many reasons. Above all, the corpse wasn't cut up—it would have to be done by a skilled surgeon for no marks to be left on the bones. And it's hard to imagine a cauldron big enough to hold an entire adult male corpse, and then boil it for days on end."

"That long?"

"To dissolve the cartilage. Even so, I doubt it would be possible to dissolve it entirely. Maybe if the cauldron were hermetically sealed and if pressure increased the temperature."

"Too many ifs."

"Exactly. Apart from that, there would always be something left that would either have to be burned off or scraped away. Either way there would be traces. The remains of the brain would have to be scraped out of the skull. Sadly, we have to drop this elegant solution."

She gently put the bone back into the bubbling broth. Szacki thought the old professor should come out with the vegetables now.

"But do you have any other hypotheses?" he asked.

"Unfortunately, there is one theory."

"Why unfortunately?"

"Just a moment. In the meantime we can cross off a fourth hypothesis, which is acid. Have you seen the Borys Lankosz movie *Reverse*? The heroine's mother dissolves the secret policeman in hydrochloric acid, and then buries the bones in town. The screenwriters went to the usual trouble for a Polish movie because hydrochloric acid dissolves everything, including the bones."

"A pity," said Szacki. "Trade in hydrochloric acid is controlled because it can be used to produce narcotics, so it'd be easy to get a fix on a purchaser."

"That's why I'd use perchloric acid instead," said Frankenstein. "It's more caustic and has a stronger effect. The only problem is toxic fumes."

Szacki did not pass comment. He was starting to fear that eventually all he was going to find out was that, unfortunately, the nice, kind scientists had no idea how someone could possibly have transformed a guy who liked walking in the woods to a crumbling skeleton in a single week.

"Here you are," said Jagiełło, as she handed him a dry piece of old bone.

"What's this?" he asked.

"Two hours ago it was a lovely bit of veal," explained Frankenstein. "Pink and fragrant, maybe not good enough for a schnitzel, but you could have made goulash."

4

As Wojciech Falk watched his son across the table, he couldn't help being amazed that both genes and upbringing could have so little impact. Even if he had devoted his entire life to planning every element of Edmund's personality to make sure he turned out as his exact opposite, he could never have achieved such a thorough effect.

They were eating spit-roasted chicken, which he had fixed himself. Really tasty chicken, marinated all night in chili, cilantro, and lime juice. He liked to cook, and he had made Edmund promise to take a break from his work every other day and come here for dinner. He was concerned that his son would eat nothing but fast food in the city or sandwiches in cling wrap, when it was only ten minutes' drive to his father's house from the prosecution service.

And so they were eating together. As usual, Falk Senior was pretty hungry and eating sloppily, wiping his hands on his clothes, which were already filthy because he never bothered to change after coming home from his workshop. Sawdust and wood shavings littered the table and floor around his chair.

Whereas his son was behaving like a customer at a Parisian restaurant showered with Michelin stars. He had hung his jacket on a coat hanger (he never hung it over the back of a chair if he could help it), neatly rolled up his cuffs, and covered his lap with a clean napkin. And he was separating the meat from the bones with his knife and fork with the precision of a future jeweler or neurosurgeon, not a junior prosecutor.

Falk Senior sighed softly. There were two topics of importance to him that he wanted to bring up, but he knew that his son would not be pleased. He simply wanted what was best for him.

"You know, Tadek dropped by today. Partly to ask how much I'd charge to make his friend a dresser in the German style, but more art deco. Like I made for that doctor, you remember?"

Edmund gave him a searching look.

"Knowing Tadek, he came to ask if you'd do three weeks' work for his pal at cost. He's probably on the municipal or regional council."

"Tadek's almost like family, you know that."

"But his friend isn't. Dad, how many times do I have to tell you that you can't treat every client like your oldest friend? People take advantage of you."

Falk Senior shifted around. Suddenly his old armchair felt uncomfortable. He didn't want to explain himself, but he believed it was worth getting to know people, getting close to them. After all, he made the furniture they'd be looking at for decades.

"Somehow it came up in the conversation that they slapped that traffic fine on you the other day, and Tadek said that if you like, he'll get it thrown out for you. So you don't have trouble right at the start."

At these words, Edmund froze and put down his knife and fork.

"Dad, I've explained it to you already. The traffic cops have to inform the office, and I'll get reprimanded."

"You say that as if you were counting on getting reprimanded. Tadek simply won't have them issue the fine, and that'll be that."

"In a way I am counting on it. I broke the law, and like everyone I should be punished for it. As a prosecutor I should provide an example. Otherwise, what I do makes no sense. I think you'll agree with me."

He agreed—what else could he say? But he was more concerned about the other matter.

"Tadek said Wanda's back in Olsztyn. Apparently for good."

He did his best to make it come out naturally, but of course, Edmund smiled icily.

"Are you trying to set us up?"

The armchair became even more uncomfortable.

"What do you mean? I just thought you'd like to know. That's all."

They ate in silence. Falk Senior couldn't hold out for long.

"I'd like to see you happy. And fulfilled. Not just at work."

"Dad, I've told you before. Until I pass my exams and become a fully qualified prosecutor, there's no point in even dating, not to mention getting married. I might be staying here, or they might send me to the other end of Poland—I don't want to give myself any false hopes, let alone some girl."

Falk Senior gave his son such a pitiful look that it must have betrayed all the hopes and fears of a man who became a father at an advanced age, who longed for his one and only child to gift him with the wonderful family he had never had. And so Edmund decided to explain himself further.

"It's the logical choice," he said.

5

Szacki fixed his eyes on the bone being shown to him, like a paleontologist staring at the remains of a dinosaur previously unknown to science. And heard out Alicja Jagiełło's explanations.

"I repeated this experiment several times, and the result was always the same. I had to monitor the course of it carefully, because if the process is too short, there are bits of tendon and cartilage left, not many, but always some. If it goes on for too long, the bones don't actually disappear, but they become fragile and brittle."

"What is it? Some kind of acid?"

"It's an alkali, specifically sodium hydroxide, commonly known as lye. As caustic as acid, but at the opposite end of the pH scale. A simple compound, been around for centuries, very good at dissolving protein, but above all fats, which is why it's used in the manufacture of soap. It has a bigger problem with bones because of their calcium content. It manages eventually. It really is an aggressive agent, and yet it's easy to observe the moment when there's no more protein or fat left but the skeleton is still in good shape. I'll show you."

Next to the table was a plastic bag from which she took out a bottle of drain cleaner and a polystyrene tray with several chicken wings neatly lined up under cling wrap. She extracted one of the chicken wings and placed it in a surgical dish, next to a shiny stainless steel container.

"One thing about lye is that you only have to go to a dozen stores to obtain a sufficient amount to dissolve a horse. In fact, any substance for clearing drains with a fancy name and snazzy packaging is really just sodium hydroxide, usually in the form of granules. It's a fairly safe way to preserve it—you have to dissolve it in water for it to become a caustic alkali."

She poured the entire packet into the pot and mixed it for a while with a steel spatula. The solution hissed and fizzed like an Alka-Seltzer thrown into water, then it finally went quiet and changed into a liquid the color of highly diluted milk. Jagiełło picked up the chicken wing with a pair of tongs and carefully placed it in the solution. Szacki was expecting something big, but the chicken simply sank to the bottom.

"Nothing's happening," he said.

"Just give it a few minutes."

"The recent philosophy on sodium hydroxide has been undergoing some changes, not so much legal as ethical, perhaps," said the professor, smoothing his perfectly flat gown.

He said it in a tone that sadly left no room for doubt that he was about to embark on an anecdote. Szacki peered wistfully into the pot, but everything still looked ordinary, like Thai soup with a bit of raw chicken floating in it.

"We're afraid that having found out it dissolves fat, the female students could start drinking lye with their steamed vegetables. As you can imagine, that could have lamentable consequences."

Szacki said nothing. But Frankenstein needed no encouragement.

"It's an intriguing problem, the whole question of the diet pill, the Holy Grail of the pharmaceutical industry. There have been some interesting attempts to develop one. It didn't take long to discover the existence of a repletion hormone that's released when we've had enough to eat, to make us stop guzzling. In which case, what could be simpler than taking that hormone in pill form? The perfect, natural way to allay hunger. Unfortunately it turned out to have a list of side effects as long as the phone book, with infertility right at the top. Did they give up? You bet they didn't. Somebody noticed there are no fat drug addicts. Curious, isn't it?"

Szacki nodded, feigning interest—after all, he was in the man's debt for these experiments.

"You could say, What's so strange about that? Drug addicts are poor, they sleep under bridges, they spend the money they steal on drugs, not on food rich in nutrients. But drug addiction doesn't affect those on the margins of society. Quite the opposite—it's the white-collar workers who snort a line of coke, and they eat one-pound steaks with fries."

Szacki peeked into the vat again. The chicken wing hadn't changed an iota.

"That drain cleaner must be past its use-by date," he muttered.

"I don't think so," said Jagiełło, and picked out the wing with the tongs. She shook it a few times and the pale skin coating the piece of meat dissolved, leaving red, seared-looking flesh on the thin bones.

"Chicken skin is mainly fatty tissue, so it dissolves the fastest."

"Just imagine," Frankenstein continued, "during the research, which must have had plenty of volunteers, what stood out was the protein CART—cocaine- and amphetamine-regulated transcript—which is responsible for lowering stress and increasing euphoria, and above all, lowering the appetite. You realize what it would have meant to give people that sort of ambrosia without it leading to addiction?"

"So did they make a pill out of it?" asked Szacki, letting himself be sucked in.

"They tried. Too many side effects for the circulatory system, and it'd be hard to convince anyone that the best cure for obesity is coronary disease. That was the second factor. But the first was that people are weak. What would you do if you were given a pill that made you slender, relaxed, and happy? And that had no side effects?"

"I'd swallow them by the handful," said Szacki.

"Exactly. In theory, the substance didn't cause physical addiction. In practice, after two days people were walking up walls to get their next fix. Clearly mankind is not yet mature enough for modern medicine," said Frankenstein sententiously, fixing his gaze on the skeleton lying on the table, as if it alone could understand him.

Jagiełło took hold of the wing and gently stirred the liquid with it, helping the gloop that was gradually replacing the soft tissues to dissolve in the solution. Then she took out the wing—in under ten minutes all that was left of it were grayish bones with scraps of tissue attached to the thicker joints.

"Great. We've got a winner," said Szacki.

A new element appeared in the investigation, namely an industrial amount of drain cleaner. It was always a starting point. It had to be bought somewhere and transported, the crime site had to be prepared, and the corpse dissolved, then removed. The site had to be cleaned, the overalls thrown away. In short, plenty of opportunities for leaving evidence along the way.

Jagiełło didn't share his enthusiasm. She dropped the wing back into the solution.

"Unfortunately I'm not a chemist, just a forensic scientist. Which means I had to combine all this data to come up with an image of the victim's death."

The atmosphere became tense. Szacki drew his prosecutor's mask over his face and did up the top button of his jacket. He was ready.

"Go on," he said.

"The victim wasn't dissolved in lye after death but while he was still alive. The injuries on the bones testify to that. Wherever he was locked up, he tried to scratch his way out of there in a fit of pain and hysteria, ignoring that he was grating his finger bones to the second phalanx. When he realized it was in vain, he tried to commit suicide, or at least lose consciousness. Hence the cracks on the skull. That's why they're so even. Nobody hit him on the head—he did it himself, banging it against the floor on which he must have been lying tied up."

Szacki drove his emotions somewhere into his subconscious. He focused on imagining this scene in all sorts of different ways. Somewhere in there was evidence, proof. A great deal would depend on what questions he asked next.

"Do we know where it was? A bathtub? A factory vat? A concrete cellar?"

She turned off the light. There was no need to draw the blinds; the early November afternoon in Olsztyn was darker than a night in June.

"Take a look at the bones under UV light," said Jagiełło, switching on a lamp. The skull, the fingers, toes, and knees lit up blue, as if they'd been coated with fluorescent paint.

"Is that blood?" asked Szacki, who had seen this sort of image many times before at crime scenes.

"Not this time—all the organic evidence has been consumed by the lye. Blood glows under UV rays at the scene of a murder because it contains hemoglobin, and hemoglobin contains iron. These traces testify to the fact that the victim was enclosed in some sort of steel container, perhaps made of cast iron, which seems the logical choice. Lye doesn't react with iron. Besides, a piece of pipe would be easy to transfer or remove. A concrete cellar would be impossible to clean."

Szacki forced himself to examine this mental image in detail. An old barn in a formerly German settlement, perhaps? Or maybe an old collective farm storehouse, or a ruined mill in the middle of the woods. A piece of old cast-iron pipe a couple of feet in diameter and six and a half feet long. One end welded shut.

"How do you think it happened? Did someone pour the solution into a container with the victim inside it?"

She shook her head. Evidently, unlike Szacki, she was doing her best to push these images away from her.

"In that case, death would have been instant. An instant burning of the entire body and airways, a shock, more like fractions of a second than whole seconds."

"So how did it happen?"

Jagiełło was in no rush to reply. The old professor came to her aid.

"As you've seen, sodium hydroxide is preserved in a dry form. It's also easiest to buy it in this form. We suspect that the victim was gradually buried in granules. At first he wouldn't have known what was happening and probably would have figured it was mothballs or Styrofoam or stearin. Before any of the granules fell into his mouth or eyes, nothing would have happened."

"And then water was added?" asked Szacki.

"What for? The body of a man weighing 175 pounds contains about thirteen gallons of water. Plunged into the granules and trapped in a metal pipe, the terrified victim must have started to sweat instantly. The more he sweated, the more of the little white granules changed into caustic soda. His sweat was quickly replaced by blood, lymph, and other bodily fluids. The victim was eaten alive by lye. I imagine from the first burn until the moment he died must have taken about a quarter of an hour."

Szacki was trying to summon images of what had happened in those long fifteen minutes. He knew it was very important. But it was beyond his imagination.

6

Szacki arranged to meet Bierut at the Statoil station by Olsztyn's main crossroads, exactly halfway along the short stretch between the university hospital and the place where the corpse had been found. He planned to examine the German cellar again, but first he wanted to talk to the policeman. He'd had two cups of coffee, a hot dog, and an inferior croissant in the past half hour while waiting for Bierut to fight his way through traffic to get there. He'd have made it in fifteen minutes on foot.

Bierut gave him the results of the DNA tests. The lab had confirmed that the bones were definitely those of Piotr Najman. Szacki was extremely pleased with this information, as it gave the investigation a solid direction. He instructed Bierut to bring in Mrs. Najman for questioning to establish whether the victim worked on his own at his tourist agency and to find witnesses who could help establish when and where he had last been seen.

Then he gave Bierut a summary of the pathologists' findings, without sparing him the macabre details. At a certain point Bierut gestured for him to stop, then stood up. Szacki was sure he'd overdone the description, and the policeman needed a breather. But he merely went to get a slice of pizza, a raspberry croissant, and a hot chocolate. Then he sat calmly eating his meal, nodding to indicate that he got the idea, as Szacki conjured up the vision of a remote place and the horrible death of a man being slowly dissolved in lye.

"It looks as if he was conscious to the end," Szacki said.

Jan Paweł Bierut shook the crumbs off his fake leather jacket— he could just as well have been wearing a fluorescent vest marked "POLICE"—and went over to the coffee machine.

"Can I tempt you with a hot chocolate?" Bierut asked, pressing a button. "It's really good."

Szacki shook his head.

"Can you imagine anything like that?"

"Yes, of course, you described it in full Technicolor." Bierut tasted the hot chocolate, added two packets of sugar, took a little stir stick, and came back to their place by the window. He sipped the chocolate, which left a streak of brown foam on his outdated mustache. "What are the priorities?"

Outside, dusk had fallen, though it was only just past three. The fog had thickened, and the cars driving up to the gas pumps seemed to be emerging from another dimension. Szacki gazed at them absently, while sorting the various points in the investigation plan, rearranging them, and putting them in order of priority for action.

"Two things," Szacki finally said. "We've already talked about Najman's last day. I'll question the widow and his staff, if he had any. He probably did, as he was often away. Check for his car on the surveillance cameras—see if he got to work, when he left, and how far we can track him. Apart from that, check up on him the usual way—everything we have on him in the database, criminal record, tax returns, former employment, accounting books, clients. Search the house and the office."

Bierut diligently wrote it all down in a small homemade notebook, consisting of twenty-odd pieces of paper stapled together. Szacki thought it yet another eccentricity.

"What about the lye?" asked Bierut. "Check the stores?"

"Waste of time. You can't prepare for that sort of murder in a weekend. And if somebody were planning it, they'd only have to go to a few supermarkets twice a week for a month to collect the necessary amount of drain cleaner. Let's focus on people. And let's gather information on all the places associated with the victim. He liked going for long walks, he liked the forest, he liked Warmia. And somewhere in this freaking backwoods they dissolved him."

Bierut drew himself up proudly.

"You're not from Olsztyn, are you?"

"Eighth deadly sin, I know," Szacki said. He was starting to develop an allergy toward local patriots.

"More and more people are drawn here," Bierut said, unperturbed. "And I'm not at all surprised. Did you know there are eleven lakes within the city limits?"

"That's why rheumatism kills more people here than coronary disease. Let's go."

The fog must have been gifted with awareness, because rather than mindlessly enveloping him, it cunningly crept under his coat, pushing its way between the buttons of his jacket and shirt to wrap him in its cold, damp embrace. A shudder ran through him, as if he'd suddenly been thrown into icy water. He figured thermal shock would finish him off here long before the rheumatism.

They walked the short distance from the gas station to the city's main crossroads. Although it didn't seem possible, the traffic lights were even more of a pain for the pedestrians than the cars. Every vehicle that came through the junction was given the chance to drive off in any direction. So while the cars took their turns, the pedestrians waited, then had to sprint across because the green signal started to flash only seconds after it had come on. They'd just managed to reach the strip dividing the two streams of traffic when the light changed to red. Szacki merely continued at a faster pace, but Bierut grabbed his arm with an iron grip and held him back.

"It's red," he said, without even looking at the prosecutor.

Szacki realized there was no point in arguing.

Once they had finally crossed the street and were walking slightly uphill along Niepodległość Avenue, they passed a few prewar public-service buildings. First came a picturesque fire station, with the old garage doors painted red, and then a junior high made of the same redbrick. When they turned into Mariańska Street and reached the temporarily suspended roadwork, on the left were the scenic outbuildings of the old hospital, and on a hill to the right yet another post-German school, or at least that was how Szacki identified the architecture.

The entrance to the underground shelter had been painstakingly secured with plastic sheeting.

"Let's go in through the hospital," said Bierut.

He led them through a garden and on to a lab; it must have been one of the side entrances. Szacki was expecting an atmospheric neo-Gothic interior, but it was just a hospital with linoleum on the floor, suspended ceilings, and green walls with a wooden strip at waist height to prevent bed-wheel stoppers and stretchers from making holes in the plaster. They walked along part of a corridor and down some steps into the basement. It looked less neat, with a vaulted ceiling instead of the suspended kind, but it still wasn't the post-German dungeon he'd been expecting, which would have brick walls and the names of the rooms painted in Gothic script.

Bierut took down the police tape on an ordinary door and they entered the cellar.

"What did this place turn out to be?"

"An air-raid shelter, built during the war for patients at the hospital and the rest home."

"The rest home?"

"The building on the other side of the street is now a dorm for the nurses' academy, but a hundred years ago they built it as an *Armenhaus*, an almshouse for people who needed permanent assistance and had no family. A fine example of state care for social outcasts."

"So the Reich looked after its citizens."

They went inside. Bierut flicked a switch, and the harsh light of police lamps dispersed the darkness. Usually Szacki had seen them hooked up to whirring generators, but here they were connected to the hospital's electricity.

"In those days it was still the German Empire," Bierut corrected.

"Well, exactly, in other words, the so-called Second Reich." Szacki wasn't going to let the local patriot off lightly. "I thought you knew the history of your lesser homeland. The Lesser Reich, we could say."

The shelter wasn't huge, and just past the entrance were the sanitation facilities, then a large space identical to the one where they'd found the skeleton.

"Are there many of these halls?" asked Szacki.

"This one and the other one, where we were before. Four entrances. One in the hospital, one in the dorm, and two emergency ones, in case the buildings collapsed. Bricked up long ago."

"So they must have entered through the buildings."

"I know what you're thinking. Unfortunately there's only one security camera at the dorm, by the watchman's post, and in theory they'd have had to walk past it. But nobody in their right mind would go in through the dorm. There's someone there round the clock; sure, maybe in the dead of night, but we all know college kids are up at all hours." Bierut said this as if he himself had never been young. "The CCTV in the hospital is better, but it consists of several buildings from various periods, with about a dozen entrances, passages, and walkways—it's a labyrinth. And the place is always on the move, new faces every day. Not much harder than disappearing in the crowd at a train station."

It occurred to Szacki that it might not be so bad working with this rookie, who not so long ago had been booking drunk drivers and hunting down, no doubt doggedly, civil servants who crossed the road when the crosswalk lights were red.

They followed the familiar corridor, passing under the hole covered with plastic sheeting, from which the noises of the city were audible, and reached the hall where the bones had been found. Last time, by flashlight, this space had had a mysterious feel to it, a frisson of adventure, like something out of a young-adult novel. Now brilliantly lit, it looked typically gray and ugly; the police lamps had chased the mystery from the corners, replacing it with dust, mold, and rat droppings.

"Evidence?" asked Szacki.

"Gathered, but there's nothing really, except for the usual crap you find in this sort of junk room. There are no fingerprints in the area where the remains were found, and none on the door either. But it's the end of November, everyone's wearing gloves. A bit of mud brought in, but no footprints that would lead to any conclusions."

"A sack? A bag?"

"Whatever they dragged the bones in, they took with them."

Szacki thought for a while.

"Any mud from the direction of the hospital or the dorm?"

Bierut stroked his mustache. In a characteristic gesture, he ran his thumb and index finger from his nose to the corners of his mouth, ending by straightening his fingers abruptly, as if trying to shake something off. Szacki saw perplexity in this gesture.

"Prosecutor, none of us treated this as a crime scene at first. An old German, end of story. We came in, did a routine check of all the rooms, and the weather is as it is."

Szacki nodded. He wasn't going to start casting aspersions—he'd have behaved exactly the same way. He gazed at the rusted bed and thought about yesterday's conversation with Falk. Some lunatic had gone to all this trouble to make sure Najman died in agony, by dissolving him alive in a substance for cleaning drains.

And now for the first scenario: The guy's done his chemistry homework badly, and he's surprised to find he's left with a heap of bones. What can he do? Bury them, of course. Dig a five-foot pit, put the bones in a plastic bag, and toss them in—job done. Why hadn't he done that? Perhaps he couldn't. Because he committed the murder at some industrial site, where the ground was covered in asphalt or concrete. Or maybe because he didn't want to. He was scared somebody would dig it up. Either way, he removes the bones from the crime scene. Why does he leave them here? If he knows this place exists, then he also knows nobody ever comes down here. He's acting under pressure, in a state of stress, he's got a bag full of bones, proof a crime's been committed. He realizes the old shelter's a good place, until he can think of somewhere better. First he just tosses the bag in there, but at the last moment he decides to take the bones out. If by some miracle a kid from the dorm finds them while groping a nurse in the dark, everyone'll think it's an old German. That's almost what happened.

And scenario number two: The guy has done his chemistry homework well and was aiming to have nothing left of Najman but his bones. Maybe some Mafia ties would come to light, a gangster story—that would explain the wife's strange behavior. Perhaps it was meant to be a message for the competition: Take a look at this. We know how to turn a guy into a study aid for medical students in a matter of days. Don't get in our way. But then they'd have sent it to Najman's associates in a box with a ribbon, or dumped it in a funny place, in the castle dungeon for example, so the media would have a ball. Leaving the message in a place where nobody had a chance to read it made no sense.

So scenario number two was out. He shared his conclusions with Bierut.

"We're looking for someone from the hospital," he said. "Someone who works here, or has done some work here, carried out repairs or installed electrical fittings. Someone who had a professional reason for being in the hospital, knew about the old shelter, and could get inside."

"Set A."

"Exactly." Szacki liked Bierut's logical mind. "And set B are people from Najman's circle. Family, friends, colleagues, clients."

Bierut rubbed the end of his mustache. A contemplative gesture.

"Both sets are difficult to determine precisely, by definition they're incomplete, they may not have a common area. It would help to narrow things down somehow."

"First of all, let's do a profile. The crime is fanciful enough for a psychologist to have something to say. I know a crazy guy from Kraków who's helped me out before."

"We have a profiler on-site." There was a mild hint of the injured pride of a local patriot in Bierut's voice. *What was that? You might not want to employ the services of a Warmian expert?*

"I'd also like you guys to edit the press release. Remains found during roadwork were those of a resident of Olsztyn who recently went missing. The investigation is on track, luckily the perpetrator left plenty of forensic evidence at the crime scene, it's a matter of days before an arrest will be made, we're waiting for test results from the laboratory."

Bierut shook leftovers off his mustache again. In other words, he wanted to say he didn't agree, but he had a problem—he was a novice detective, and he knew about the prosecutor's reputation. That was why he felt awkward.

"Shouldn't we narrow down the range of suspects first?"

"We don't know how long that'll take, and the killer is under the greatest stress right now. I bet he's sitting somewhere glued to the local news channels. He'll hear that the case is being solved and the law's on his trail. What would you do?"

"Protect myself in some way."

"How?"

"Disappearing is always suspicious. Everyone will notice, everyone will remember during questioning that you suddenly weren't at work. I'd think up an excuse, a family illness, rather than a funeral, because that's too easy to check. I'd go to the boss and ask for a few days off, and then lie low. Then come back like normal if nothing happened. I'd realize the police were bluffing."

"Spot on. So we're not risking anything—that sort of information won't make the killer disappear. And tomorrow we'll check with the hospital personnel to see if anyone has asked for time off, or if anyone took a business trip to a conference they weren't supposed to go to. Intuition tells me it's someone who works here. You've got to know the building and its history. You've got to be up on anatomy, chemistry, and know something about the body, and about death."

"A doctor?"

"I'd be surprised if it was an orderly. Can we get out on the other side?"

Bierut nodded, and they walked in the opposite direction, away from the hospital. The corridor ended in a stairwell, and they went up a few dozen concrete steps before Bierut let Szacki through a massive door and into the dorm. He had to switch on a flashlight because the light switch was on the far side of a smallish space, which must have served as a junk room for years. The two men were separated from the exit into the corridor by a stack of chairs, some rolls of carpeting, boxes, old mattresses, and a dozen old toilets and sinks.

"Do you think it's a serial killer?" asked Bierut. "Like that pastor Pándy?"

András Pándy was a Belgian madman who had lived with his daughters, murdering the remaining members of the family, and then dissolving them in some sort of acid or lye. He was caught when his daughter finally blew the whistle after thirty years of an incestuous relationship.

"I have no idea. I hope not."

There was no path through the garbage heap, and the short walk across the room required balancing on piles of junk. At first Szacki was worried about his coat, but after two steps he couldn't have cared less about his wardrobe—his only concern was not to fall into one of the old crappers and break his leg. Finally, panting and cursing, he reached the other side of the room, only to realize that Bierut was still standing in the doorway where they'd come in.

"Everything OK?" asked Bierut in a tone devoid of concern.

Szacki calmed his breathing and said it was highly doubtful that anyone had entered the basement this way.

"Unless he was very fit," said Bierut.

He cast Szacki a serious look and disappeared into the darkness. Furious, Szacki brushed off his coat, exited into the basement corridor, and found his way up to the ground floor of the old rest home. The dorm lobby was almost identical to the one at the high school on Mickiewicz Street—either it was designed by the same architect, or the Germans had built everything according to the same plan. He made a brief stop at a display case with information about the history of the building. From it he learned that the Reich had indeed built it as a refuge for citizens used up by life, with a garden and a park, but mainly in order to placate the general public, enraged by the erection of the immense town hall with its tower more reminiscent of a palace.

State care, snorted Szacki. *Like hell.*

7

On his return to the office he had a chat with Falk, asking him to come up with some case hypotheses. Falk reeled off some potential theories: Mafia score settling, a Warmian version of Hannibal Lecter, and personal revenge.

As he listened, Szacki wondered how much you had to hate someone to dissolve them alive. It couldn't have been over a broken heart or an unpaid debt. How long would you have to nurture your hatred to inflict such an awful death on someone? There must be a very great injustice behind that sort of hatred. Had somebody lost everything they owned? Everything they loved? Everything that, from their point of view, constituted life? Lost it so totally and utterly that they had carried out this bizarre, violent revenge?

"All the answers are in Najman's past," said Szacki.

"Maybe not this time," said Falk. "I know it's a long shot, but the victim ran a travel agency—he sent people on vacation."

"Seriously? You think someone dissolved him in acid because they'd gone to Thailand and the hotel windows overlooked a trash heap rather than a pool full of teenage girls in bikinis?"

Falk sat up straight, clearly offended by the mocking tone.

"I think strange things can happen in exotic destinations. People fall sick with dangerous diseases, children get lost in the jungle, there are accidents just waiting to happen. I can imagine a situation where a child gets poisoned because the hotel turns out to be at the back of a fertilizer factory. When he gets home, the client demands compensation because he needs the money for the child's treatment in Switzerland. The agency refuses, the client loses his case because of Najman's testimony, and the child dies after a long illness. For example."

Szacki frowned.

"Far-fetched."

Falk adjusted his cuffs to make them stick out of his jacket sleeves the regulation half inch. The gesture had the same effect as yawning, so Szacki adjusted his cuffs, too, making them stick out half an inch more because they were fastened with cuff links. Frankly, as the King of the Stuffed Shirts and the Prince of the Starched Collars, they were a perfect match.

"Far-fetched," admitted Falk. "But his profession was unusual enough for it to be worth checking out. Exotic locations, trips away, plenty of contacts, lots of chance meetings."

Szacki shrugged and went back to work. Falk tapped away at his laptop nonstop, like a stenographer. Szacki filled out a few forms and waited for Mrs. Najman to arrive, killing time by thinking and staring at the black-and-green hole outside. He was surprised to find that he was feeling anxiety. Not just excitement brought on by an interesting investigation, but anxiety. Either the crap-shit local weather was affecting his mood, or else he'd made a mistake.

Everything seemed to match up, all their hypotheses appeared logical, and the killer had to fit one of them. So it would seem. Murder has its own inner workings, its own harmony, comparable to a well-composed symphony. The investigation was like finding each of the musicians and positioning them on the stage. To start with, there's just a single flute, sounding once every five minutes, and that leads nowhere. Then, let's say, a viola comes along, a bassoon, and a French horn. They play their parts, but for the longest time all you can hear is a cacophony. Finally something like a tune emerges, but only once you've discovered all the elements, found all one hundred musicians, and placed yourself in the role of conductor—only then does the truth ring out in a way that sends shivers down the audience's spine. Here there were only a few elements, a handful of musicians staring into space, but something already sounded wrong, as if the bassoon player was just pretending to play or he was out of tune. Presumably, at this stage it shouldn't really matter. It was just noise and nothing more, but despite that, there was something hard on the ears.

He suddenly felt terribly sleepy. It was happening to him more and more often at this time of day; with each passing birthday he felt sorrier that Poland had no tradition of taking siestas. The view from the window wasn't particularly stimulating. There was some construction equipment moving about in the fog at the bottom of the black-and-green hole, like monsters on the ocean bed, idly, regally, and with a very soporific effect on the spectator.

"What would you like to specialize in at the prosecution service?" he suddenly asked Falk, to wake himself up. He was surprised by his own question, but now it was too late to withdraw it.

The junior prosecutor froze with his hands on the keyboard. Rather than seeming surprised, he looked disappointed that Szacki wanted to chitchat like the office gossip.

They both seemed equally embarrassed by the situation. Szacki was waiting for Falk to say "organized crime," because every junior wanted to pursue the big, bad Mafia, whose members never carried suitcases full of underwear or wood for the fireplace in their trunks, just stiffs, machine guns, and drugs in wholesale quantities.

"Organized crime," said Falk as predicted.

Szacki was disappointed. He had hoped Falk was different—unique. That in some way he'd stand out from the crowd of young prosecutors. The disappointment was irrational; his junior—that was how he thought of Falk, as "his" junior—had summed up the possible investigation hypotheses well; they all came out of a commonsense evaluation of the situation and logical thinking. Maybe he should add another theory.

"It could also be that this whole performance is a smokescreen," said Szacki. "And as usual it's about money, or because somebody screwed another man's wife. Not very likely, but possible. People can be hypersensitive about their property."

Szacki instantly felt bad about describing people's wives as their *property*.

Falk stopped tapping the keyboard and cleared his throat.

"Perhaps I'm hypersensitive after my training courses at feminist NGOs on the issue of violence against women," he said. "But I believe we should avoid sexist comments even in private conversations. Language has meaning."

"Of course, you're right," said Szacki, though Falk's remark had raised the level of his irritation. "It's a pity you weren't here this morning. I had a pseudo panda in here who'd have been right up your alley."

"A pseudo panda?"

Szacki cursed mentally. First *property*, and now he'd used the sort of dumb cops' slang that he despised, but he'd heard it so often it was etched in his mind. He waited for Falk to get the idea, but he just went on staring at him with the dumbstruck dark eyes of Peter Sellers.

"The cops tend to call battered women 'pandas,'" Szacki explained. "You get it?" He drew a ring around his eye with a finger.

"So a pseudo panda," said Falk slowly. "That must be a victim of psychological abuse?"

Szacki nodded.

"It's interesting how much sexist contempt can be contained in a single word. It's pretty disappointing to be hearing something like that from you, of all people."

That rendered Szacki speechless. It was a long time since he had encountered such direct criticism, and he had no idea how to react. Edmund Falk wasn't a suspect, he wasn't a witness, nor was he his child or student. He was a colleague of lower rank, but not low enough that Szacki could take him to task. Szacki tensed; in his mind the words were forming into snappy comebacks and aggressive reactions.

He swallowed them all.

"I'm sorry, I shouldn't have said that."

Falk was nodding, with a look on his face clearly saying that in his view it was better to behave in a way that didn't mean having to apologize afterward. That was the logical choice.

"What was it about? If I may ask."

Szacki shrugged.

"Nothing, really. Work here for a while and you'll see that some people just come along looking for therapy. He hasn't done anything to her, or the kid, but she's afraid. But actually she just hasn't got a grip on herself. And he's a great guy. But he terrorizes her by telling her to keep a record of expenses. But she's scatterbrained, so maybe that's a good thing."

"That's typical." Falk was nodding.

"Unfortunately."

"That's the typical behavior of a victim of abuse. Either the woman reacted prematurely, or she's not saying everything. More likely the latter. Did you send her to the Sunbeam?"

"Where?"

"The family support center on Niepodległość Avenue, five hundred yards from here. It looks like a beautiful villa, as you drive by."

"No."

"So what did you do?"

"Nothing. I sent her home."

"You're joking?"

Szacki shrugged. He couldn't understand the problem. He'd never actually dealt with a harassment case in his professional life—he'd always managed to dump them onto someone else.

"Do you know, if all my training courses are to be believed, that's the typical behavior of a victim of domestic abuse? Not an unhappy wife, or a scatterbrained woman, but a victim of abuse. Desperate enough to come and see the prosecutor. But too ashamed to tell him the whole story. On the one hand she says something's wrong, but on the other she keeps saying it's her own fault. If she came in with a forensic report, screams on a voice recorder, and a journal with every instance of abuse written down in it, our red light would go on at once. But this is a clear-cut case."

"So what should I have done, in your view?"

"Behaved like a prosecutor, not a rigid misogynist from a bygone era."

"You know perfectly well that without a victim statement our hands are tied," said Szacki, finding it hard to keep his cool.

"Why? It's not a crime where a private individual has to bring the charge. Our task is to eliminate the criminal from society, even if his persecuted wife is going to clutch at our lapels and beg us not to do him any harm."

"Without a statement the body of evidence makes no sense."

"Of course it does. A good expert will recognize her attitude as typical of the psychological state of a victim."

"Your attitude is based on naive idealism devoid of reality."

"And yours is based on cynicism."

The phone on Szacki's desk rang. The police had brought in Teresa Najman. Falk got up, closed his laptop, and put it in a leather case.

"I'll have to inform our superiors of your conduct."

He didn't even add as a courtesy that he was sorry he'd have to do it.

"You're going to report me?"

"Of course. In this case the principle of general deterrence has relevance. We're trained lawyers, and if others find out that a star like you has been penalized for ignoring domestic abuse, that should give others something to think about. It's nothing personal, I assure you."

8

WITNESS INTERVIEW TRANSCRIPT. Teresa Najman, née Brode, d.o.b. March 25, 1975, place of birth Olsztyn, resident at 34 Irysowa Street, Stawiguda, university graduate (Polish philology), deputy director at the University Library, University of Warmia and Masuria in Olsztyn. Relationship to parties: wife of victim. No convictions for bearing false witness.

Cautioned with regard to criminal liability in accordance with Article 233 of the Penal Code, I testify as follows:

I met my husband, Piotr Najman, in February 2005, when I had just received an annual bonus from the university and decided to buy myself a trip to a sunny place. I had no other expenses, and the winter was particularly awful. Piotr was very kind and friendly, and he made an excellent impression on me. He was so convincing and gave me such good deals that although I'd been planning to go to Turkey, I ended up buying a trip to the Canary Islands—I'd always dreamed of going there. A month later he came to the library on my birthday with a bunch of flowers. He was very apologetic about the fact that he'd committed the date to memory after seeing it on my ID, and begged me not to report him. It was very funny, and of course I made a date with him, and we met up. In April I went on my trip, and there he was, waiting for me at the airport in Fuerteventura. That was when we started to date seriously. We got married in October 2006, and in December 2007 our son, Piotruś, was born, on Saint Nicholas's Day. We were living in an apartment and building a house on my lot in Stawiguda. We moved there early in 2009. We had a good life together.

The last time I saw my husband was on the morning of Monday, November 18, when he left for work. From there he was due to go straight to Warsaw, and then fly to Albania. And Macedonia, too, as far as I remember. Albania is being heavily promoted these days as a new destination, the country's getting back on its feet, the prices are low, and the Adriatic's lovely. Those trips are always made outside the season, when the tour operators show their best agents the new sites and hotels. The trip was supposed to be ten days, but I'm not sure, because they're often combined with briefings in Warsaw about other destinations.

I admit that Piotr's absence couldn't have come at a better time, for all sorts of reasons. We've spent a lot of time sorting the collections at the library, reorganizing the catalogs according to new EU rules, and even if we moved in there for the duration we'd never get it all done. On top of that the last few weeks before he left were exhausting. Piotr is a hypochondriac, and right through the operation on his toe he behaved like he was terminally ill. That day he went to work, and I took our son over to my parents in Szabruk. I was planning on spending the week working and watching TV in the evenings without having to take care of anything but myself.

Piotr and I exchanged a few short texts to say everything was all right. That was the only contact I had with him. Ten days went by in a flash.

There were various methods for taking a witness statement, and every prosecutor had his own approach. Some, for example, noted it down verbatim, every stutter and curse, transforming themselves into pen-wielding Dictaphones. Szacki very rarely used that method, only in dealing with the most aggressive suspects and witnesses. He knew from experience that later on in court, it gave the ideal impression when he calmly read out all the "fuckallyoucandotome's" and "I'llfuckingdestroyyou's," while on the other side, the defendant gradually shrank to three feet tall. But usually he listened and summarized, limiting the statement to the most important information and potentially significant details.

In the case of Teresa Najman, he didn't apply his summarizing method, because he didn't have to. The woman came in, sat down, and in a steady voice dictated it all to him—he didn't have to change a single comma. She was so well prepared that it was as if she had spent the week practicing her performance. Now she was looking at him, waiting to see what he'd do.

Szacki just clicked his pen and thought. Contrary to the fashionable theories, which Falk would probably give his right arm for, he regarded the modern methods of questioning as dumb shamanism, the only aim of which was to make the state budget cough up money for unnecessary training. They'd once forced him to go to one of those courses, and he'd almost died laughing. You were supposed to start with a conversation about meaningless crap as a way of checking how the witness behaved—this was called "tuning your inner lie detector"—then suddenly attack with a question relevant to the case and observe the reaction.

Over the lunch break he'd sat down with the course leader and chatted about the weather and politics, then debated which is better, an automatic or a stick shift. Suddenly Szacki had asked the man what had happened when he stuck a knife in his wife's ear and gave it a few hard twists. Did she scream? Try to defend herself? Was the blood on his hand warm?

The guy choked on his sandwich and Szacki had to give him the Heimlich maneuver.

Then he'd expelled Szacki from the course, but Szacki had proved his point. Anyone reacts when a conversation about the weather suddenly shifts to murdering your wife. Tuning your inner lie detector had nothing to do with it.

Nor did he believe in the good-cop, bad-cop method. All that soft-soaping and terrorizing seemed tacky—he felt embarrassed when he saw policemen behaving that way. People are vacuous, but not enough to say something they don't want to. Telling lies is not rocket science. If you're going to play games with them, you've got to have something up your sleeve. Something they want, or something they're afraid of.

Teresa Najman was telling so many lies that a lie detector—a normal one, not that inner one—would be shooting sparks in all directions and would eventually explode. But Szacki had absolutely nothing on her.

It didn't bother him. People are amateurs, think they're so sharp, but meanwhile the wheels of the investigation keep turning. He'd soon have the content of her texts, recordings from industrial cameras near her work, a list of times when her cell phone logged on to the network, statements from her colleagues at the library and from Piotr Najman's coworkers at the travel agency. He'd have another chance to talk to Teresa Najman once the files were a bit thicker; he didn't need tricks for an efficient investigation, just proof.

He looked at her. She was tense, all done up as if going to a job interview—neatly, modestly, office style, in a white blouse buttoned up to the neck, a dark jacket, and slip-ons with a low heel. Hair in a bun, contact lenses replaced by glasses. Good lawyers advise female defendants to look just like that in the courtroom.

He turned the transcript around and pointed to the spot where she was meant to sign.

She was surprised.

"Aren't you going to question me?"

"You've said it all already."

"You don't have any further questions?"

"Is there something you want to add?"

She thought so hard that he could hear the cogs going around in her brain.

"You don't believe me."

"If I say I don't, will you tell me the truth?"

She chewed her lip and gazed out at the November evening. For a brief moment she changed into the woman she'd been the day before.

"Will any further questioning be necessary?"

"I think we'll be seeing some more of each other."

"But do you suspect me of something?"

"Where do you get that idea?"

"Yesterday I wasn't myself at all."

It occurred to him that he really was unlucky where the women who came to his office were concerned. If not for the fact that a prosecutor isn't allowed to earn money on the side, he'd have had them pay him the standard eighty zloty an hour for all these confessions.

"I'm sorry, but do you want to add anything that might have a connection with your husband's disappearance and death?"

"Only that I had nothing to do with it."

"With what?"

"With it."

"Meaning?" He wanted her to say it.

"I didn't kill him."

"But are you pleased he's dead?"

She frowned, then looked shocked. She signed the transcript and got up to leave.

Next time he'd record her.

9

Szacki had no luck with his bosses. When he got to Olsztyn, at first he'd sighed with relief. Ewa Szarejna seemed a fairly typical product of the civil service. A good lawyer, not particularly interested in the front line, quickly got into the regional prosecution service, and from there, a few years later the supervisory board had sent her to be a district chief. Knowing the dynamics of a career in the prosecution service, she would either return to a higher post at the regional service or end up in appeals. He doubted the latter—like everyone here Szarejna was a psychopathic local patriot. She'd sooner drown herself in one of the eleven Olsztyn lakes than move to Białystok or Gdańsk, where the nearest appeal services were located.

Reliable, hardworking, decent, well organized, more of a specialist in theory than practice, but that had its pluses—everyone including Szacki treated her like a walking legislative database.

Around forty, a little younger than Szacki, slender and fit, she was into cross-country. Which was the source of plenty of workplace jokes because the walls of her office were decorated with competition photos in which, sweaty and mud stained, she hardly looked human.

But if anyone was ever asked about Ewa Szarejna, the first thing they mentioned was not her job, or her legal knowledge, or her eccentric hobby. They always said, "Ewa? She's a very good person."

The first time he heard that, he was worried. That was what they'd always said about his mother. But he knew better than anyone that his mother was not a good person. Behind her warm facade radiating empathy and understanding, there was an aggressive, bad-tempered bitch, putting up endless walls of goodness to conceal her rage and resentment toward the entire world. She was like an alligator in a velvet jumpsuit. Everyone wanted to cuddle up to her, but if anyone knew her as well as her own son, they understood she mainly consisted of claws and fangs.

Szarejna was identical. Szacki soon realized it, and she knew that he knew. For this reason they were not particularly fond of each other, hiding their dislike behind courtesy. His was minimalist and cool, hers was exaggeratedly friendly.

Szacki didn't even take his documents with him when she summoned him to her office; following the conversations with Bierut and Falk, he had the case all neatly sorted in his mind, like jigsaw puzzle pieces arranged by color, ready to be assembled.

Szarejna never received anyone from behind her desk, but at a small conference table where she could sit next to them, smile sympathetically, and create an atmosphere of friendship and trust. Now, too, she was sitting at the little table by the window, next to an unfamiliar man, who looked about thirty, a little pretentious in his casual Warsaw style. Szarejna jumped to her feet as if she'd seen a close relative who'd finally come home after years abroad.

"Mr. Teo!" she cried. "How wonderful you're here."

Totally wonderfularious. At the start of their acquaintance she had asked if she could call him Teodor, or maybe he preferred Teo, or Teddy. Szacki, who on principle was never informal with anyone at work, replied that he would prefer to stick to the standard Polish polite form of address, "Mr. or Ms. plus first name." Szarejna had exploded with such inner rage that her velvet jumpsuit had almost split. And she'd assured him that of course she understood, and then started to call him "Mr. Teo," uttering it without a pause, as "Misterteo," which made his name sound like a brand of air freshener.

He said hello to the man, who energetically introduced himself as Igor, but despite Szacki's inquiring look he didn't give his last name. Szacki shifted his gaze to Szarejna, in the hope of learning more.

Szarejna sighed and smiled radiantly.

"You've got such a great boss," said Igor.

Szacki waited.

"Mister . . ." Szarejna began, but he didn't let her finish.

"Igor, no mister, my dear Ewa, we agreed."

She laughed and stroked his hand.

"Igor . . . ," she said emphatically, looking the man in the eyes, and he nodded theatrically.

Szacki felt sick.

"Igor, if you could explain to Misterteo . . ."

Igor smoothed his blue jacket. Then he smoothed his hipster tie, which looked as if it had come from his rockabilly granddad's closet. They must have said in the papers, "It's worth highlighting your personality by introducing a zany touch into a classic outfit." Finally, he smoothed his fair hair and adjusted his glasses.

Szacki wanted to fucking kill him. One more neurotic gesture, and he was simply going to kill him, even if he turned out to be the new prosecutor general.

"So how do you think the general public perceives the prosecution service?" asked Igor.

Szacki sighed inwardly, wondering what strategy would work best for a quick getaway.

"They have no idea what we do. People think we're pencil pushers who waste time hovering between the police and the magistrates, obstructing their work. When in fact we don't obstruct them, we just cover up various scandals on the private instructions of politicians of all ranks, or else we make comments in front of the cameras, looking like jackasses and trying to camouflage our mistakes with incomprehensible legal jargon. That's it in a nutshell."

"And what can be done about it?"

What sort of a lousy academic conversation was this? Szacki did his best not to let his irritation show.

"I think it's a mistake to inform the public about our inquiries in the current style."

"I couldn't agree more," said Igor. "Any specific ideas?"

"Of course. We should stop communicating with the media."

Igor and Szarejna exchanged baffled looks.

"Why's that?"

"It's the logical choice." He found himself quoting Falk. "The public perceives us badly because that's the image of officialdom it sees in the papers. You can't subtract the public from this equation because it's there, whatever. And you can't subtract the prosecution service, because our activities are essential to the public. You have to cut the cancer out of this healthy organism. In other words, cut out the media, which is doubly harmful. Firstly, they mislead the public, and secondly, they obstruct us in our inquiries. In other words, they act to the public detriment."

"Misterteo, how are you going to inform the citizens about our actions without the media?"

"Directly. It's the twenty-first century. Let's post information about our major inquiries on the regional service website and leave it at that. They don't have to be terse messages. Have them written by someone who knows the Polish language. Have someone who's good at choosing the right tie to go with his jacket record his comments and post them on YouTube." He cast Igor a meaningful glance. "There's nothing to it. Let's make ourselves the sheriffs—nobody's gonna do it for us."

Igor smiled cryptically.

"Interesting that you should have mentioned sheriffs in particular."

"Interesting that so far you haven't given me any explanation for this meeting, just asked a few meaningless questions. On top of which, you didn't introduce yourself."

"My name's Igor."

In reply Szacki bestowed one of his iciest, most disdainful looks on him.

"Bikoz."

Szacki waited for him to continue. "Because what?" he finally asked.

"Bikoz. Just Bikoz."

Szacki hid his face in his hands. He felt very tired.

"Here, look."

Szacki looked. In front of him lay a business card. Igor Bikoz, CEO, Portfolio Communications Consulting.

He nodded, struggling to stifle his laughter.

"Our company has been commissioned by the national prosecution service to improve its public image. I admit, we quickly realized how disastrous the situation is. Sometimes I think it would be easier to convince people that Adolf Hitler merely conducted a mildly controversial foreign policy. I'll give a quick rundown of the remedial action to be taken. Number one, an evaluation of the current press spokesmen for the prosecution service at the regional and district levels. Number two, either retraining for the people dealing with communications until now, or appointment of new ones and training for them."

Szacki had a bad feeling about this. A fuck-awful feeling.

"No way," he said, just in case.

"Misterteo, that's exactly why people don't like us. Coming up with negatives right away, saying no right away, all stiff and starchy right away. Let's talk about it."

Igor Bikoz rapped a fingernail on his business card.

"This is my firm. I conceived it, founded it, and got it up and running. I've worked my butt off to get it to the stage where I can say that it's the most effective PR firm in Poland. Thirty of my people are in the process of touring all the prosecution services in the entire country. I should be sitting behind a desk at my head office in Warsaw counting the banknotes. Do you know why I bothered to come all the way to this backwater place?"

"I'm most terribly sorry," said Szarejna, bristling as if it were a joke, but her jaw had suddenly clenched. "I realize you're not here for long, Igor, but this is a very special place. Do you know that there are eleven lakes within the city limits? Eleven!"

Bikoz looked at her politely.

"Dear Ewa, do you really think that proves how metropolitan it is? The number of lakes, swamps, and impenetrable forests?"

Szarejna froze as if he had slapped her, while in Szacki's view it was a first-rate joke. He even felt a shadow of sympathy for this badly dressed man with the weird name and the ridiculous profession.

"This is why I bothered." Bikoz pulled an iPad in a burgundy cover out of his briefcase. "Because as soon as I realized we must make you the sheriffs"—at this he placed the tablet in front of Szacki—"I started searching to see if anyone had ever presented you that way. I tried looking for a movie, a TV series, or maybe a crime novel as a hook to start from. I typed 'sheriff prosecutor' into Google and found out I didn't need a crime novel, because such a person really does exist."

He switched on the tablet, and there Szacki saw the results of the search.

He knew those headlines. "Sheriff in a Suit Catches the Villain," "The Columbo of Kielce County," "The Sheriff and a Grain of Truth."

He knew those pictures. Of him, at a press conference. Of him, with Sandomierz Cathedral in the background, him in his gown in the Kielce courtroom. And, sadly for him, in women's magazines too. Once as the sexiest civil servant, and once as the best dressed. Yes, his list of reasons for disliking the media was almost infinite.

"No way," Szacki repeated.

"Misterteo!" said Szarejna, and it sounded like a prayer, an invocation to God. "We can't be a bunch of anonymous bureaucrats who turn our backs on people. There are reasons why the sheriff always wore a gold star. Pinned to his chest, visible from afar, announcing to all that in this place they stick to the law. You're going to be Olsztyn's gold star."

He clung to the hope that he was only expected to make a one-off appearance, a speech during Urban Safety Week, or the harvest festival, or whatever they had in this province. But he had to suppress this idea before it had had time to take shape in his mind.

"Officially speaking, from today you're the press spokesman for the Olsztyn Prosecution Service, in charge of communications and contact with the media."

"Congratulations," said Bikoz, smiling.

"I'm sure you've been told I hate the media. And I've never treated them well, by which I don't mean just lack of respect, but upfront contempt."

"Even so, they've always loved you. I think your no-nonsense, uncompromising attitude just adds to your charm, Misterteo."

"The law guarantees me independence," he lied in desperation.

Szarejna smiled her wonderful smile that everyone took to be an expression of warmth and empathy, but Szacki saw nothing but ice-cold triumph in it. He knew how satisfying it was to catch a lawyer in blatant ignorance of the law.

"Misterteo, of course the law guarantees you independence in conducting legal proceedings, meaning self-reliance in performing legal functions. Nevertheless, the law also says the prosecutor is obliged to carry out the orders, directives, and instructions of his supervisor."

He said nothing; there was nothing to say. Snapping her alligator teeth with joy above her velvet jumpsuit, Ewa Szarejna couldn't resist kicking him when he was already down:

"Article eight, paragraph two."

Igor Bikoz took out a wad of papers bound with red string. On the cover there was a five-pointed yellow star with each point ending in a large dot. In the middle of the page Szacki spotted the words "OPERATION SHERIFF" in a Western-style font.

He didn't even sigh.

10

Rage, frustration, and irritation had gotten him so worked up that after pacing his office for fifteen minutes, he decided to take off. He was afraid he'd blow a fuse or burst a blood vessel.

His first thought was simply to go for a walk, but the weather was so crappy that he decided to go for a drive instead.

Five hundred yards and fifteen minutes later, the car radio was blaring "Agadoo," which seemed oddly summery for the present weather conditions, and he was still trembling with rage. There was no traffic on Kościuszko Street, which had sunk into a coma; the time-space continuum was clearly trapped in quantum aspic—this corner of the universe was at a total standstill. Through the drizzle two hundred yards ahead, Szacki saw the lights changing at a regular pace: first they were red forever, then green for a second, followed by a yellow flash, and then red again. If three cars had time to drive into jammed-up Niepodległość Avenue it was a triumph. He gazed at the huddled pedestrians flitting along the sidewalk and imagined one of them was the Olsztyn traffic designer. He imagined inviting him into his car. The guy's pleasantly surprised, the weather's awful, he would never have expected such a kind gesture from a driver with Warsaw plates, thank you very much, and so on. *No problem, we really ought to help each other,* the whole works. He even lets him choose the radio station, unbutton his coat, relax, and admire the classy car. At the same time, Szacki quietly takes a Phillips-head screwdriver out of his side pocket. And once the traffic designer is relaxed, Szacki locks the car doors and sticks the screwdriver into the man's thigh with all his might, as deep as it'll go, twisting it relentlessly. Up ahead, he saw that this time, no car had managed to turn on green, and he smiled as he imagined the scream of pain, surprise, and horror. He hadn't realized his right hand was drilling a hole in the leather upholstery.

Twenty minutes later he was feeling a little better because he'd decided that instead of sitting in a traffic jam all the way to Jaroty, he would drive down to the Statoil station near KFC, stop for a cup of coffee, read the newspaper, and let off steam. He drove a hundred yards along the sidewalk to get to the entrance, and parked outside the gas station with a sigh of relief.

He sat down at a small table in the corner, between the brushes for sweeping off snow and some only partially concealed porn mags. With the *Olsztyn Gazette* and a large cup of black coffee. For some time he'd been drinking it black because he thought it manlier.

He felt OK at the checkout. He felt great at the espresso machine. He felt awesome as he strode to the table with his cup—he never covered it with a lid, just to let everyone know that tough guys aren't ashamed of their choice. But once at the table he felt crappy, because he hated the taste of black coffee. After two sips his stomach was churning, and there was a bitter taste in his mouth. But what could he do? Go back for creamer? Add sweetener?

He wanted to rest and unwind, but instead he looked through the *Olsztyn Gazette*, feeling annoyed. The main topic was insultingly low hourly rates of pay—in this region where unemployment was the highest in the country, the employers were mercilessly exploiting human misery and desperation. He skimmed the text; the just cause didn't concern him, and if they were devoting the front page to such a general issue, it meant there was absolutely no news to report. Of course he was right—it just got worse as it went on. In Szymany, the civil servants had put up a monument to their own megalomania in the form of a redundant airport. In Gołdap, people were afraid of wolves; some archaeological remains had been found under the Old Town. There was a poll for the best teacher, a poll for the best postman, and a poll for the best athlete—yawn, yawn, yawn.

He was just about to put the newspaper aside and take advantage of the fact that the place had emptied out—he could now sneak some milk into his coffee—when a familiar face looked out at him from the educational supplement. At first he couldn't fit the face to the situation; as he gazed into the pale-blue eyes of a young woman, the cogs in his brain stood still.

Then suddenly—click. Wiktoria Sendrowska, class 2E, "How to Survive in the Family"—he remembered the title of her essay because it had sounded so intriguing.

He pulled out the supplement and read the interview with the girl. She gave extremely smart answers to the pointless questions put to her by a journalist who spoke to her as if she were a child, to which she responded like a mature woman.

The journalist asked what had prompted her to write on such a serious topic.

The girl replied that she had never had personal experience of domestic violence—she came from a happy home, and her parents were in respectable professions. But she had known people who went home to absolute hell, who cowered when they heard footsteps in the hallway, and who were more afraid of going home than going out. She had known people who longed for someone to come and take them away to a children's home. And she thought she should write about it.

Luckily such extreme cases are very rare, aren't they, countered the journalist.

Szacki scowled as he read the question. Yet another citizen who's convinced everything happens to other people, and only very occasionally, so really there's nothing to get upset about. He skimmed the entire interview—the schoolgirl talked about violence within the family and had clearly put in a lot of effort to gather material for her essay.

Families vary, the journalist commented on the examples Wiktoria cited of pathologies among her school friends.

To which Wiktoria replied, "I refuse to use the word 'family' to describe a group where any kind of violence is applied, any attack on personal or sexual freedom. We're insulting the genuine families by giving that name to pathological setups that should be dismantled right away."

Journalist: "That sounds ominous. I'm starting to imagine children reporting their parents . . ."

Wiktoria: "What's ominous about that? Any parent who's an evil, harmful, aggressive psychopath should be reported right away. We should know we're not defenseless. At school we have numerous lectures warning us about fanciful dangers. We're told we're at risk of drug addiction, human trafficking, having our kidneys cut out, or being raped in a dark forest, but what are you supposed to do when a drunken uncle comes at you, your father's drinking away your pocket money, or your mother screams insults at you every day of the week? I've never heard a word about any of that in school. But that would be useful. Bullies should be aware that they can't get away with it."

What's true is true—Szacki, too, had a very low opinion of parents as a social group. He yawned and drank the coffee, which was cold by now. The girl gave the impression of being as belligerent as she was levelheaded. He sincerely hoped nobody would ruin her along the way, that her public-spirited passion wouldn't wane, and in a few years from now, he'd be able to vote for her.

"Good luck," he muttered, and tossed the paper in the trash can.

By now the traffic was minimal, and Szacki figured he could get to Jaroty without risking an apoplectic fit. Fifteen minutes later he turned into Wilczyński Street, one of the main roads through this residential suburb, passed a church so hideous that it could only have been built by the Society of Friends of Lucifer to put people off religion, then started looking around for the address. He parked outside a five-story block constructed in the 1990s, a sad decade when things were built quickly and without imagination, not to mention any sense of design. The building was horrid, bitter evidence that you only had to move away from the old German center to start wanting to avert your gaze from the omnipresent eyesores. In fact, Olsztyn was no different in this regard from any other city, and Szacki thought it a cruel fact—even if everything were to change in Poland, people were to start being nice to one another and the politicians become sensitive to human injustice, even if the freeways were finally completed and the trains were clean, even so, these people would still have to live in 120,000 square miles of urban-planning hell, littered with the ugliest architecture in all of Europe.

On the ground floor he found a row of stores and agencies. Najman's business, the Tauris Travel Bureau, was a tiny place, squeezed in between a veterinary clinic and a store selling mirrors. Contrary to his fears, the lights were on, and inside a female employee was near the back wall, shelving catalogs: palm trees on top, snowy peaks below. On the wall there were posters of azure seas and white sands. He had only once been on that sort of vacation; on one side he'd had a view of a power plant and on the other a freeway. There had been waves of pale cellulite pouring across the brown gravel beach, and he'd promised himself never to have that experience again.

He examined the ads in the front window. The Alps by plane. Slovakia by car. Exotic destinations. Italy, a tour of Rome including the Pope's tomb, already taking bookings for the canonization. No notice announcing a break, a vacation, or a temporary closure.

He stepped inside into an aroma of coffee, glossy paper, and musky incense. Quite a pleasant mixture. The woman turned around and smiled at him. He quickly introduced himself to stop her from trying to seduce him with palm trees and snowcapped mountains. She said yes, as if she'd been expecting this visit, and introduced herself as Joanna Parulska.

"Would you like coffee?"

He felt like breaking down and asking for milk and sugar but realized he was here on duty.

"Why not? Black."

If it did make an impression on her, she didn't let it show.

"The police have been to see me today!" she called from the back room.

"I know," he said. "I wanted to see the victim's workplace."

She didn't answer. She came back with two mugs of instant coffee, with milk for herself. The coffee smelled of rubber—there are few things as revolting as instant black coffee.

"I only have a few questions."

She nodded, folded her legs, and sipped her coffee. She had the energy of a woman who owns a small firm. A woman who has a successful married life, who likes to work, likes to cook and share a glass of wine with the same friends she's had for the past twenty years. Who dances well, exuberantly, and when she and her husband go away to a hotel for the weekend she packs lace stockings. Though she's coming up to fifty, they've probably always said of her that she has that "something." Despite her visible efforts, that "something" had grown older and disappeared, but probably when she closed the office on a November afternoon, the men still looked at her. Knee boots, shapely legs below her skirt, feminine curves, long black hair, makeup, cool glasses the turquoise color of the Caribbean. You might think she was a woman who was at peace with her age and her destiny, feeling good in her own skin. But Szacki was ready to bet that if she had a glass of wine on a Friday night, on Saturday morning, if it was a sunny day, she stood in front of the mirror, looked at that skin, and didn't feel remotely comfortable in it. He had felt that for himself all too often.

He had questioned too many people to be unaware that there were only about a dozen types, and that apart from some minor differences, within these categories, their characters and fortunes were usually very similar. He didn't have to ask to know that she had had no other connection with Najman apart from a professional one—even if he had tried to schmooze her, he'd soon have had a slap on the wrist. That while he was downing martinis in Tunisia, she was here, sorting out the invoices—even so, the clients preferred to do their business with her, not with the boss, who had seen in person the brightly colored fish darting around the coral reef.

One thing didn't fit. He'd often seen this type of woman before, and they weren't typically employees.

"How did you come to work for Najman?"

"I never worked for him. We're . . . we were partners. We opened travel agencies almost simultaneously on opposite sides of the same street. His was new, mine had moved out here from the center. Two years later we realized it was pointless staring at each other as if we were rivals, so we joined forces. One site, one set of accounts, and each of us brought our own clients. I do school trips and summer camps, he does families seeking the sun."

"Najman's wife referred to you as an employee."

She shrugged.

"I know he presented me as an employee—he even tried treating me that way for a while. A short while. He was a bit of a lord and master, but on the whole we got along well."

She glanced at the wall. Szacki followed her line of vision. Among the paradise beaches hung a comical picture of Najman and Parulska, taken in winter, at a Christmas fair in the Olsztyn marketplace, with ice sculptures of animals around them. Among the sculptures they had set up a thatched beach umbrella and two summer recliners on the snow, and were lying on them in winter jackets and sunglasses, drinking lurid-looking cocktails. Between them stood a sign with the travel agency's logo and website. They were smiling radiantly into the camera, looking happy.

"We thought it was a great idea for an ad. To show we could take people from the middle of the Polish winter to somewhere with palm trees."

"Is business all right?"

"It's in pretty good shape. Of course the market's unpredictable; one time they want to go on pilgrimages, another time it's sports. We had a year when about half the neighborhood went to top-class exotic destinations, the Caribbean or Mauritius. But it was generally doing better and better—we were actually thinking of opening another branch."

"What about the financial crisis?"

"It's baloney. It's a rumor put out by the big corporations so they wouldn't have to give any raises for ten years."

A prosperous business with plans for the future, money. He wondered if that was sufficient motive for murder. Not really—unless there were private debts, gambling, blackmail. Partner lends to partner, the trouble begins. One of them dies, and not only are the debts forgotten, the business is left behind too. He made a mental note of this hypothesis.

"How did you divide the work?"

"It varied. We did a lot of traveling, both business and personal, so sometimes there was only one of us at the office. But during peak periods we both stayed put. After years of practice, as soon as anyone came in, we both knew at once who should serve them. If it was a vigorous man in an overcoat, Piotr did it, with direct talk that says, 'I'm not going to mislead you, sir, I've seen some unusual things in Arab countries, but it's a really great place' and a joke about how a trip with your wife is really a business trip. I would take care of the young couples, showing that I understood they wanted as much sun-drenched happiness as possible for the lowest price. If it was two female friends over fifty, Piotr served them, of course. He had something of the life and soul of the party about him, and it worked."

"And who would have served me?"

"I would, definitely."

"Why definitely?"

Joanna Parulska smiled the smile of an experienced saleswoman.

"Because you don't like interacting with men, all that patting each other on the shoulder. I figure a trip to the DIY store or a car repair shop must be worse for you than a dental appointment."

"What do you stand to gain by Najman's death?" He refused to admit how accurately she'd analyzed him.

"Nothing. For the time being I'll have to run the business on my own and hope I don't lose Piotr's clients. His wife inherits his shares. At this point she says she's going to meet me halfway, but we'll see what happens once the estate is settled."

"Halfway, meaning?"

"She'll sell me her shares at a reasonable price."

"You two have already discussed it?"

"An hour ago. She was very nice. We even wondered about running the business jointly."

"Would you go for that?"

"Yes, I would. It won't give me anyone to charm old ladies into taking trips to Morocco, but generally it's good working with women."

Szacki wondered what this remark might mean—that it was bad working with a man, perhaps. He made a mental note of it.

"Last Monday he left home for work and never came back. Did you see him that day?"

"Yes. We saw each other that morning. He came in with a suitcase, checked his email, left me a few ongoing issues to deal with, above all a large ski camp in Slovakia, and took a cab at about noon to Kortowo, where he was catching the bus to Warsaw. Then he was going to fly with Balkan Tourist to Macedonia and Albania. Albania is being heavily promoted these days as a new destination. The country's getting back on its feet, the prices are low, and the Adriatic's lovely. The trip was supposed to be for ten days, and Piotr was going to call on his return to say if he was staying on in Warsaw for a briefing on some new destinations."

Szacki was sure he had heard the exact same words from Mrs. Najman. Both women were equally cool, equally devoid of emotion, and both only said what was necessary. And not a word more.

"Did you communicate?"

She shook her head.

"It's the middle of the low season, everyone's already bought their New Year's vacation in Egypt and their skiing holidays; the whole country's getting set for Christmas. I could close the business for two weeks and nobody would notice. It actually suited me that he was away because I could work in peace on the deals for the summer. We want to sell Ukraine well—after all, the agency's name obligates us. I hope the trouble there will be over soon."

Szacki stood up without a word and took his mug with him. Piotr Najman had been permanently involved with two people—his wife and his business partner. Neither of them was surprised by his disappearance, neither seemed bothered by his death. The only thing they had to say about it were the same three sentences, devoid of emotion, as if they'd learned them by heart.

He looked around the room, and only now did he notice a reproduction hanging by the door, on a smaller scale, of the classical genre painting he'd seen in the hall at Mickiewicz High School. He went up to the picture, in which a sad woman in a white dress was gazing at the sea as it crashed against the rocks. It blended in remarkably well with the glossy photos of beaches, seas, and blue skies.

"Is it possible to go there?" he asked, half joking, pointing his mug at the painting.

"Absolutely. That's Tauryda, in Latin it was called Tauris, hence the name of our agency."

"And where is it?"

"In Ukraine. Tauryda is the ancient name for Crimea."

He had no idea.

"And do these characters mean anything?"

"That's Iphigenia, daughter of Agamemnon. And behind her that's Orestes, her brother, and his friend Pylades."

It meant nothing to him. But he didn't want to compromise himself, so he just nodded.

"I've spent years staring at that picture, but I only read up on it fairly recently. Agamemnon was ready to sacrifice Iphigenia to the goddess Artemis in exchange for favorable winds for the Greek ships sailing to Troy. The goddess took pity and spared the girl by whisking her away to Tauris, but Agamemnon's wife didn't know their daughter had been saved."

"Electra?" offered Szacki, as something dimly returned to him from years ago.

"Clytemnestra. As a result, she murdered him when he came home. For which in turn she was murdered by her children, Iphigenia's siblings. Which was all part of a greater curse that caused each successive generation to murder members of their own family."

"The inheritance of violence," he said, more to himself than to her.

"Absolutely. Curiously, it stopped at Żenia."

He gave a start.

"Why Żenia?"

"Because Iphigenia is like the name Eugenia, which shortens to Żenia, so we started calling her that as a pet name—clients often ask, and we tell them the story."

"Not a very encouraging tale," he said. "It's a Greek tragedy—by the end they're all lying on the stage in a pool of blood."

"Actually, no. I mean, it looks as if that's what's going to happen, but Żenia persuades the others that they have to remove the curse to break away from evil. And she succeeds. Nobody dies."

"Not much of a tragedy."

"Maybe not, but you know what? I've always believed in happy endings."

He didn't believe in happy endings, or in happy middles or beginnings either, but he kept that to himself. An awkward silence fell, and he gestured to ask if he could go into the back room. She nodded and followed after him.

Beyond the area for receiving clients was a small hallway, off which there was a toilet and a small storeroom with a little window onto the courtyard. There was a cupboard in there with a kettle and a large jar of instant coffee, a small fridge, and a desk piled with papers and a computer. One corkboard had invoices, emergency phone numbers to insurance firms, and the addresses of Polish consulates pinned to it. On a second one, there were lots of photos of Najman's and Parulska's trips abroad, prints the size of postcards overlapping one another. Standard tourist scenes, such as portraits taken in front of the Eiffel Tower or the Egyptian pyramids, were mixed with photos from trade banquets featuring lots of alcohol-flushed cheeks and flash-induced red eyes. Parulska appeared in more winter scenes, and Najman turned up in some African or Australian wilderness. His Kojak features looked pretty good in the tropics—not a tourist, but a seasoned traveler, a veteran of the outback.

"He liked exotic places," said Szacki.

"He sure did. And he knew his stuff so well that the more honest people from other agencies often sent their clients to us. He knew how to advise whether Africa or South America was the right choice, which tour operators were suspect, and which were safe to travel with. His star turn was when he'd show his hand and say, 'You don't want to make the same mistake I did and choose a bad guide.' The client would go pale and ask what happened, and depending on how he was feeling, Piotr would say he'd had an encounter with a lion, a puma, or an infection caused by a scorpion sting. Jeez, I'm gonna miss him," she said, but as if ashamed of her words, she immediately added, "in my way."

"Did something really bite him?" asked Szacki, sensing that he was wasting time here.

"No way—he lost his fingers in a fire, but he liked to put on a show for the clients."

Szacki froze.

"What was that?"

"I don't know the details, I only asked him once, he said something about a fire, an electric shock perhaps. I realized it must be something embarrassing. He'd fallen asleep drunk by the fireside, or—"

"That's not what I meant. Did he have some sort of deformity, or were his fingers actually missing?"

She looked at him in surprise, as if all Olsztyn knew about it. *Plus eleven lakes and minus a finger or two, welcome to Warmia.*

"They were missing." She raised her right hand, and with the other she bent back two fingers so that they couldn't be seen. "He had no pinky and no ring finger on his right hand. He wore his wedding ring on the middle one."

She stared at him, clueless as to why this information had made such a strong impression on him. She couldn't know that as an apparent side effect of being dissolved in lye, Piotr Najman had regained his lost fingers. Because if Frankenstein was to be believed, the skeleton didn't have a single missing bone.

CHAPTER FOUR

Thursday, November 28, 2013

Albania, Mauretania, and Panama are celebrating their Independence Days. Agnieszka Holland and Ed Harris are celebrating their birthdays. It is the ninety-fifth anniversary of women being granted the right to vote in Poland. In Vilnius a summit meeting of the Eastern Partnership opens, pitiful and pointless because the Ukrainian dictator has declared that he won't sign the EU association agreement. Protests continue in Ukraine. In Egypt the military junta has twenty-one young girls sentenced to eleven years in jail for taking part in a peace demonstration. And in France the outgoing head of Peugeot resigns after a major uproar over his company pension of 310,000 euros a year. On the day of the premiere of the Russian war movie *Stalingrad,* the Polish deputy minister of defense resigns, suspected of favoritism toward one of the firms aiming to sell unmanned planes to Poland. In all the confusion nobody stops to ask why the hell Poland needs unmanned planes anyway. In Olsztyn the provincial administration announces a tender for the "Copernicus" bell for the cathedral; the authorities believe it will be an excellent Copernican advertisement for the city and a valuable heirloom for future generations. The names of the Pope, the archbishop, and the head of the provincial administration will be engraved on the bell. Apart from that, a new restaurant opens that's styled to look like Communist Poland, and a road hog gives himself up to the police after causing some officers to ram a councilman's car during a nighttime chase two weeks ago. The daytime temperature is about 45 degrees, it's totally overcast, with fog and rain, and in the evening, freezing drizzle.

The sun had risen long ago, and was shining down on cloud-covered Warmia, but despite shining with all its might, it couldn't get through to Równa Street. Here there was no light, and no air; the whole place was dark, dirty, and dreary. The ordinary woman's view through the kitchen window was sucking out the last of her strength. The longer she gazed at the black fog, and their mud-covered yard, which was supposed to be a vegetable garden, she felt even more fed up.

The little one was still asleep, the big one was off to work. For breakfast she'd made coffee, toast and cheese, and squeezed a little orange juice. He'd thanked her politely. She'd said he was absolutely welcome, while thinking she'd give ten years of her life to spend a month on the sort of vacation he enjoyed.

He'd go off in his car, listen to music, buy a chocolate bar for later. Then he'd sit in the office with his coworkers, tap at a keyboard, answer twenty important emails, and go out to lunch. He'd come back, do a bit of flirting, and swap a few jokes at a meeting. He'd call home to say he'd be an hour late, because he still had to "get his head around a project"—sounding pained and tired, to spell out the scale of his sacrifice and devotion.

She would go shopping, make dinner, do two loads of laundry, clean up two turds, soothe fifteen sorrows, stick on one Band-Aid, extract the kid five times from places that were out of bounds, wipe the floor three times and the table after his meal—she'd be on her feet nonstop, slightly out of breath, with a sweaty forehead, to the tune of the child's squawking, always wanting something different. If she were lucky, he'd nod off at home, and she'd be able to have a sandwich while stirring soup with the other hand. But usually he only fell asleep on a walk—he'd be wrapped in a blanket, protected from the wind and rain, pink and snoring. She'd be pushing the stroller, frozen to the core, breathless, and rain-soaked, because on the dirt road it was impossible to push the stroller and hold an umbrella.

She watched him eat his toast. He had the sad look of a man who devotes himself to his family, and she thought that if he had to do real work as she did, in a few weeks they'd be looking for a sanitarium where he could recover.

He finished breakfast, stretched, and got up, leaving crumbs, a coffee stain, and his plate and mug on the table. She tidied up without a word, stood with her coffee by the window, and mentally pushed him out of the house. There was a chance that if he left right away, and the little one slept a while longer, she'd have fifteen minutes to herself. A whole fifteen minutes! She needed that time to gather her thoughts, to think about how to play it, how to choose the best moment.

In the hall she could hear him pulling on his woolen coat, then zipping up his ankle boots, and the rap of his umbrella as he took it off the shelf and set it on the floor.

She closed her eyes, squeezing them tight, as she waited for the metallic sound of the lock. But she heard steps approaching. She mentally cursed—a compound, vulgar expletive. Even her father would have been shocked.

She stood leaning against the kitchen counter, facing the window; in the glass he could see the reflection of her face and her closed eyes. He smiled. He realized she was ashamed to go back to the warm bed while he was still bustling about the house, preparing to go out into the

November crap, pulling on his coat like an uncomfortable suit of armor or special overalls designed to protect him from the Warmian climate.

He didn't want to go. He'd rather stay here and revel in idle warmth, drink coffee in the kitchen, smell the aroma of dinner cooking, and watch his son playing on the rug, looking up from his building blocks only to smile at his parents. He felt warmth flooding him—the scene was so unreal. Outside there was gray hell, and in here paradise. The subtle light, the smell of mildly charred toast, the warm color of the beechwood kitchen furniture, his wife in a hoodie, with her eyes closed, good and quiet like the goddess of the domestic hearth in her still-sleeping kingdom, drawing strength from the harmony of the world.

He gently embraced her, nestling his head in her ruffled hair.

She sighed.

He knew he'd never tire of this harmony—that he could have more of it, lots and lots, as much as possible. The family was like a drug that he could never get enough of. The certainty filled him with joy and strength again.

He took her hand.

"You know what the good news is?" he asked softly.

She shook her head without opening her eyes. He breathed in her warmth and fragrance and thought of wet spring earth, of swollen buds, ready to burst into bloom.

"We're going to have a big family. People will laugh at us, they'll say we're running a preschool, but we'll be laughing at them, because we'll be so happy. Would you like that?"

She turned to face him. Her eyes were wide-open, but he couldn't see the domestic goddess in them, or fertile soil ready to procreate. He saw derision and determination.

"I very much . . ." she whispered, "I very much need to tell you something. Right now."

2

She squeezed him tight between her legs, put her arms around him, and pushed off. They managed to roll over without coming apart, and now she was on top. She straightened up, pressed down on him as tight as she could, and began to move rapidly to and fro, moaning—as he saw it—far louder than the situation demanded. He wondered if he should make noises, too, so she wouldn't tease him afterward, saying they'd had deaf-and-dumb sex again, but he realized that at this stage it was all the same to her anyway. So instead of that, he grabbed her hard, slender butt and squeezed it tight—she gave a loud scream, which aroused him so much that they soon came almost simultaneously. Wonderful.

Żenia moved on him a little longer, purring and laughing, and Szacki thought of how he envied women's orgasms. He took the opportunity to check the time and read a text from Dr. Frankenstein.

"I can see you," she muttered, without opening her eyes.

He wasn't sure what to say, so he put down the cell phone and mumbled in a way that he thought expressed sexual satisfaction. To make it clear: he felt immensely satisfied, but he couldn't understand why that should be a reason to be late for work.

Żenia sighed one last time and climbed off.

"I'd love to fuck you when you're wearing your lawyer's gown one day."

Her voice, always a bit throaty, was even huskier after sex.

"Best of all in the courtroom. I don't know why, but it gets me really hot. Do you think they'll let us in there after hours?"

He scowled at her and got up.

"Well? Don't make that face. It's not a cassock. In fact, they're both just bits of rag from a certain perspective. Besides, cassocks don't make me feel at all horny—yuck! They make me think of men who don't wear aftershave." She got up too. "Not that I have experience, but I've never noticed a priest smelling of anything when I've gone past one. Not that I've gone out of my way to sniff one. Are you listening to me?"

"Not that I've gone out of my way to sniff one. Are you listening to me?" he said, putting on his shirt. He always had three outfits in the closet ready to go. A pressed suit and shirt, a polished pair of shoes, a tie, and cuff links in a little plastic bag tied to the hanger. She made fun of that, but if he kept his cuff links in his jacket pocket, the material could lose its shape.

"And before that?"

"Smelling of anything when I've gone past one."

"I don't know how you do that—it's some kind of a trick, because you don't listen to me at all."

"To me at all."

"Ha, ha, thank you." She kissed him on the lips. "I've wanted to have a good scream for ages. Lately we've only had deaf-and-dumb sex, if at all."

"I'd rather not . . . you know . . ." He made a vague gesture.

"You're right, it would be terrible if your daughter found out her father has sex."

"Oh come on, don't talk about Hela and sex while we're standing here like this." He pointed at the naked Żenia, then at his penis, dangling under his shirt to the same rhythm as his tie.

She shook her head and went to the bathroom.

"You're even afraid of her when she's not here. It's pathological."

He felt his irritation rising. Something was wrong again.

"Here we go. You cannot be jealous of my daughter."

"You can't be talking about jealousy and your daughter while we're standing here like this," she mocked.

He counted down from five in his head. For some time he'd been promising himself to try calming techniques before exploding.

"If you think there's something wrong with our relationship," he said, "then maybe we should all sit down and talk about it."

"How do you imagine that? You'll say she's right before she even opens her mouth. And she'll be embarrassed by how easy it is to manipulate you. Besides, I've got no problem with Helena, she's great, she's a smart girl."

"So who do you have a problem with?"

She raised an eyebrow in her trademark way. Really high. He thought it must involve training the right muscles.

"I really don't know. What the fuck do you think?"

She started swearing very easily—he found it cute.

She turned to face the bedroom, put her hands on her hips, and aimed her small, pointed breasts at Szacki like additional arguments.

"You're doing her wrong, Teo. You treat her like a child because you have no idea how a mature father should relate to his mature daughter. She doesn't either, but she doesn't have to. She's confused and has no idea how to behave, so she takes advantage of your weakness. I don't blame her, just to be clear. I'm sorry to say it, Teo, but the time when she was a child who needed her daddy is over. I get it, you're sorry you had other things on your mind then, but it's been and gone."

He was trying not to explode, and he knew Żenia was right. What was he supposed to do? He loved Hela, he wanted everything to be the best for her. He accepted the idea that he spoiled his daughter as a way of appeasing his own pangs of conscience after splitting up with Weronika.

"And to be clear," added Żenia, "don't go thinking it has anything to do with your divorce, blah, blah, blah, all that psychological baloney for people who feel sorry for themselves. Bullshit! Your daughter is brave, modern, strong, and self-confident. You're doing her wrong by demanding nothing of her and treating her like your darling little girl. You're just doing the same as your sexist father and your sexist grandfather. You're afraid of strong women, and you're trying to push your daughter into a mold that's totally alien to her."

"How do you know my father and grandfather were sexist?"

She cast him a look and burst into husky laughter, even louder than her recent moaning.

3

He woke up the same as always. No tossing and turning, no sleeping in, no wondering whether to lie there a while longer or to get moving right away. He simply opened his eyes, confirmed that it was light now, and got up, as if he didn't want to miss a single second of the new day.

The bedroom was empty, which rarely occurred at this time of day, but sometimes did. He went into the hallway and looked around. The house was quiet—he couldn't hear anyone moving about, or the radio or television. He wanted to go to the bathroom, but instead he stopped at the top of the stairs and hesitated. He looked down them, wondering whether to call out or descend unnoticed and find out what was happening. The fifteen wooden steps were tempting. He decided to go down them quietly.

He sat on the highest stair and waited a few seconds. Nothing happened, so he slid down to the stair below. Once again, nothing happened. He looked around, but heard nothing. He decided to take advantage of this opportunity, and using the same technique, he slid on his little butt from one stair to the next, until he was at the bottom.

Earlier he'd had a plan to look inside the utility room, the most mysterious place in the house, but he was so excited from coming down the stairs that he forgot. Not only had the gate at the top of the stairs been open, so at last he could go down them on his own, but for the first time in his life he'd remembered how to do it. He felt proud of himself.

"*Momma*, I'm come alone!" he shouted. "Momma, daytime! I'm come down the stairs on my butt. Don't shout," he added, just in case it turned out he'd done something that wasn't allowed.

The house on Równa Street was quiet and deserted.

4

Even for Warmia this was going too far. He figured this was what a nuclear winter must look like—ominous and dark. A few minutes after nine the streetlamps were still on, and such a feeble glow was breaking through the clouds that he regretted not bringing a flashlight with him. He imagined that from a bird's-eye view, Olsztyn must look as if it were coated in a thick layer of dark-gray felt torn from the inside of a shabby rubber boot.

Szacki had never imagined the weather could be this bad.

He quickly ran a few paces to get inside the illuminated building as fast as he could, nodded to the desk clerk, and without slowing down reached the first floor, where he bumped into his boss in the hallway. He nodded, certain their meeting was a coincidence and that she'd just come out of the restroom. She was camouflaged in her beige suit, standing near the beige wall.

"My office, now," she said, pointing toward the front office.

He took off his coat and went in. This time she didn't play the warm and open boss; he had barely crossed the threshold when she shut the door.

"Misterteo! One question. Why is your junior, a jumped-up, weird little shit who recently coerced me into letting him work with you, now filling out a formal application for you to be reprimanded?"

Szacki adjusted his cuffs.

"Actually, I've changed my mind. I have no question. I don't want to hear the answer. I'll give you an hour to get it straight. Falk is expected to come see me by noon to withdraw the application, apologize for the misunderstanding, and run along."

Szacki stood up and straightened the coat hanging over his arm so it wouldn't get creased.

"I don't know if that's possible," he said.

"One hour. Then I'll write a request to the regional service for them to take over your investigation into the Najman case, considering its complexity. You'll be able to read about its progress in the *Olsztyn Gazette* while you're busy bringing all the force of your authority down on college kids smoking dope. Good-bye."

He turned without a word and left. He was just about to close the door behind him when he heard her chirp with merry optimism, "Misterteo, please leave the door open, I don't want anyone to think I'm not here."

5

Unlike his mom or dad, who were in some ways apostles of the ordinary, the little boy from Równa Street was rising above the average. It took him only about fifteen minutes to change the family home into a theme park. For starters, he got into the cat-litter tray, something he'd always dreamed of, behaving like a cat, scattering the pink granules in all directions. Then he took advantage of the open laundry-room door to overturn the vacuum cleaner, knock some of the mysterious liquids off the shelf, and press enough buttons on the washing machine to make the word *Error* light up.

Still placid, from the laundry room he went into the kitchen, where he saw a blue mineral-water bottle on the counter beside the stove. By holding on to the knobs for controlling the gas and the oven, he managed to knock the bottle off the counter. Finally he sat down on the kitchen floor with the bottle of water between his legs. He felt thirsty, but his mug was nowhere to be found. He grunted and groaned as he tried to unscrew the plastic cap, but he didn't have the strength. Besides, he wasn't sure if he was turning it the right way. He tried both directions, but even though he tensed his muscles as hard as he could, not just in his hands but in his entire body, the cap wouldn't budge.

"Can't do it!" he cried, but the deserted house gave no answer. "Help me, Momma, can't do it!"

Upset, he threw the bottle, hoping that would get it open, but it just bounced and rolled away. He got up and went after it, but as he was crossing the hall he caught sight of his three-wheel bike, and in a split second he'd lost interest in the bottle. Each successive activity engaged him totally—nothing that came before or after mattered.

He dragged the bike out from under the stairs and set it upright, which wasn't all that easy, pointing it toward the kitchen. He took off the helmet hanging over the handlebars, put it on back to front, and rode toward the kitchen and dining area. It looked like a game, but in fact he was carrying out a plan. His aim was to ride the bike to the refrigerator, stand on the seat, open the door, and take out the milk. Every morning he always got warm milk in his platypus mug with a blue-striped straw.

He gathered speed, went past the kitchen island, and turned right toward the corner of the room where the fridge stood.

Suddenly the bike ran into something and stopped. The child was thrown forward, hitting his belly against the handlebars as the badly secured helmet slipped over his face.

"No," he said, struggling with the helmet.

Once he'd finally pulled it off, he saw that the bike had stopped against Momma, who was lying across the dining area.

"Momma, you can't!" he cried. "I'm on my bike here."

He put the helmet on again, backed up, rode around the island the other way, and parked by the fridge. He took off the helmet and hung it on the handlebars, then climbed onto the seat and opened the fridge, only to discover that he couldn't reach the milk.

He stood on tiptoes, straightening his legs and stretching as far as he could, but he was still a couple of inches away from the shelf in the door of the fridge, where the milk was kept. His total engagement prevented him from calling for help, so instead he tried shifting his body into all sorts of different positions to reach higher; finally he managed to stand a foot on the back support of the seat, pull himself up, and grab hold of the shelf, on which there were two bottles, whole milk for him and skimmed for coffee.

The shelf couldn't take the strain. The plastic compartment broke free, the milk crashed to the floor, and he slipped, landing by pure luck on his butt on the seat. It didn't hurt, but it would have been enough of a surprise for him to burst into tears, if not for the sight of the white puddle. The glass bottle had smashed, and milk was flooding the kitchen.

The white pool grew bigger, and when it reached the red pool around his mother, it began to create incredible patterns, changing the gray kitchen floor into a fabulous carpet with oriental designs, woven with threads in every shade of pink and red.

He gazed at it spellbound, but only now did he feel anxiety. He had never gotten away with anything like this before.

"I wanted milk," he said quietly, foreseeing the fuss to come. His big brown eyes were glistening with tears—one tear, as round as in a cartoon, trickled down his cheek. "I wanted milk, Momma?"

Nothing happened, so he got off the bike, stepped into the puddle of milk and blood, and stood by his mother.

"Momma, it's daytime!" he cried. "Wakey, wakey! Get-up time!"

His mother didn't move, and he felt very much alone. He wanted his momma. He wanted her to cuddle and kiss him, so he'd feel safe and warm.

"I wanna do a poop," he said through his tears.

Nothing happened, so he ran to the bathroom, leaving a trail of wet pink footsteps. He opened the door, took off his pajamas and pissed-in diaper, and sat on the potty.

"No hard poop!" he shouted toward the kitchen, sharing the considerations that were always part of the potty ritual. "'Cos I didn't eat choclit. Just apple. And fruit does a soft poop."

"Ready!" he cried.

This tactic always worked in the morning. Even if Momma hadn't gotten up when he had, even if for some strange reason she hadn't reacted to the message about wanting to do a poop, at the word *ready* she came running with a handful of wet tissues.

"Mommaaa, reaaady!"

Nothing happened. He sat there a while longer, then got up, completely confused. He ran back into the kitchen, his little feet pattering against the floor.

"Momma, I done a poop. Get-up time!"

He slipped on the puddle of milk and blood, lost his balance and fell, hitting himself painfully. As usual he didn't feel the pain in just one spot—his entire body hurt, sending his brain a deafening siren signaling injury, danger, and the need for help. In the same nanosecond he started wailing, the alarm call that for tens of thousands of years the world over has invariably informed grown-ups that a little one needs help.

This time, nobody came to the little one's aid.

6

Szacki's phone call with Dr. Frankenstein was short and almost fruitless. The scientist informed him coldly that there are 206 bones in the human body, and if the prosecutor thought he could take samples from each one and do DNA tests on all of them in a single day, he must need a neurological examination himself. Which wasn't a problem, by the way—they had an excellent neurology and neurosurgery department, and they'd be happy to help. The only thing he did manage to confirm at high speed was that yes, the bones in two fingers of the right hand did not match Najman's DNA.

Next he got in touch with Bierut, and told him to draw up a list of people missing from the area over the past year and collect DNA samples from their relatives for comparison tests. Never in his career had he come up against a serial killer like something out of an American movie, a madman who plays weird games with the detectives—like wanting to complete the victim's skeleton to avoid spoiling the effect, for example.

He decided to put off looking into Najman's past. As for now, he had to deal with Falk. To his own surprise, he didn't really hold a grudge. Mainly because the young lawyer's reasoning had convinced him.

He thought for a while, as he gazed out of the window, at the lights of construction machinery moving about in the dark fog. And he realized he had no alternative other than to go see yesterday's "pseudo panda"—anyway, what on earth had induced him to use that phrase? He'd go there, inspect the scene, apologize, and tell her what the state could do for her.

He looked through the papers on his desk in search of the address, but he couldn't find yesterday's transcript anywhere. Had he written one? He must have. Then what had he done with it? He'd been in a hurry to get to the hospital on Warszawska. Maybe he'd taken it with him? No, that made no sense, he wouldn't have done that—his briefcase was in perfect order and he never kept anything in his pockets—they might as well not exist. In other words, he'd thrown it out.

He knelt down and pulled the wire wastebasket from under his desk. The plastic bag lining it was empty.

He sighed.

7

Every leash has two ends. Sea captain Tomasz Szulc had no desire to pull his other hand out of his warm pocket, so he used the one holding the leash to zip up his waterproof jacket and protect himself better from the weather. As he did it, he tugged at the neck of his stupid Labrador, who jumped about joyfully, causing Captain Szulc to slip and almost fall headlong into the river of churned-up mud that passed for Równa Street.

At the last moment his wife grabbed him by the elbow.

"Do you know what I'm thinking?" he asked.

"Sadly, I'm living in ignorance."

"I'm thinking how many places in the world we've been together."

"If our map is to be believed, twenty-eight different countries."

He nodded. He'd counted yesterday, and it had come out the same. Their map was a sort of secular altar—on a huge elliptical map of the world they'd marked every place they'd visited with colored pins. Red where they'd gone as a family with the children, orange if they'd gone as a couple, blue for her alone, and green for him. When the children had grown up and started to travel on their own, they'd added white for their daughter and yellow for their son. The six colors of the Rubik's Cube.

"Have we ever seen a place where they'd put up houses in the middle of a field? Where mansions clad in sandstone, with wrought-iron fences and granite driveways, stand along a river of mud?"

She said no, they hadn't.

"Tell me what's wrong with this goddamn country. What sort of a quagmireland is this, where they let people build houses and connect up the water and the power, while the road's always a decade behind? It must be some kind of plot! Do they take bribes from the companies that make off-road vehicles? Or suspension-repair shops? Car wash centers? Dry cleaners?"

"Don't forget the orthopedic surgeons."

"And what are we doing out in this sort of weather anyway?" Szulc found it hard to stop grumbling once he'd started.

"We have a dog."

True, they had a dog. And now they were wading through the mud on the ugliest, foulest, ghastliest day of the year. All because they had a dog—Bruno.

They walked away from the road. Tomasz let Bruno off the leash. Now they were in the new part of the village, as populated at this time of day as Pripyat. The residents were out trying to earn money to pay off the next loan installment, and if any children were left at home with mothers or grandmothers, they were probably well protected from the miserable climate.

Bruno raced through the muddy potholes, splashing in the puddles, changing his chocolate coat to cream, for that was the color of the mud in this part of Warmia. All of a sudden, the dog came to a halt and began to bark.

They stopped, too, and exchanged glances. Bruno very rarely barked. Once they had even asked the veterinarian if everything was all right with his vocal cords. The vet had laughed at them and said Labradors aren't really talkers.

But now he was standing by a fence, barking.

Tomasz went up and silenced the dog by patting him on the head. He looked at the small house on the other side of the fence. It was new, quite ordinary. It had a ground floor, a loft with skylights, and a carport. Of course, it was bigger than their old German shack.

The house had a classic layout—through a window next to the door he could see a kitchen that opened onto the dining area and the living room. Tomasz noticed that the fridge was open. There were lights on in the kitchen and in the bedroom upstairs.

He thought he could hear the monotonous wailing of a child.

"Do you hear that?" he asked.

"I can't hear a thing, my ears are frozen."

"Sounds like a child crying."

"In my experience that's mainly what children do. Come on, or I'll freeze to death."

"But it's crying and crying."

"Because its balloon burst, or it's got an earache, or Mom switched off the cartoons, or didn't give it a Snickers bar for breakfast. You're talking as if you never had kids."

He stroked Bruno. The dog was still gazing toward the house, but he wasn't barking anymore, or growling. Maybe he really was being oversensitive.

"I'll try ringing the bell," he said, putting a finger to the intercom button.

"Give it a break, that's all the woman needs." She gently took hold of his arm and pulled him away from the gate. "A howling brat and a nosy neighbor—for me that'd be too much in a day."

He thrust his hand into his pocket, along with his wife's hand, and thought maybe he really was being too sensitive. He had always been a bit of a protective dad—the whole family made fun of him. He'd thought of nothing but the kids.

They passed three more properties before they noticed that Bruno still hadn't moved from the spot. Tomasz had to whistle three times before the wayward dog ran after them.

8

This day was different from all the others on Równa Street, definitely unusual. A day when anything could begin, or end. And the more time went by, as she drifted in and out of consciousness, the more she reconciled herself to the fact that it was all irrevocably coming to an end. The first time she came round, she was still hoping for the best; she mainly felt rage toward that prick, who had, of course, turned out to be a wife-beater. Not only had he punched her in the face, he'd also pushed her, causing her to hit her head and lose consciousness.

The anger was soon replaced by fear when she found she couldn't move; something must have gone wrong in her brain or spine. She couldn't feel her body at all, not counting the dreadful, intense pain in her head. She'd managed to move her eyelids, but she couldn't make a sound.

She realized it was serious and passed out.

She came to again, feeling very weak, when the milk bottle landed near her head. A solid piece of glass, from the bottom, flew so close that it hit her eyebrow. She found herself looking at the world through it, as if through thick glasses—everything was distorted and out of focus. Her heart stopped in horror when she saw her son's chubby legs trotting through the pool of milk, among the shards of broken glass. Drops of milk splashed on her face. She realized that cretin had left her alone at home with the child, and a wave of terror ran through her. In a split second she remembered everything she had ever read or heard about domestic accidents. The wet floor in the bathroom. The staircase. Power sockets. The boiler in the utility room. The toolbox. The knife on the tabletop. The cleaning chemicals.

Had she poured cleaning fluid down the drain yesterday? Had she put the bottle back on the highest shelf? Had she screwed the cap on until she heard the click securing it? Had she put it away at all or left it beside the trash can?

"Reaaaady!" she heard him call from the bathroom.

She strained her entire will, but all she could manage was to blink her right eye. What would he do if she didn't come? He'd probably get up, try to wipe himself, smear a bit of poop on his butt, no great tragedy. He'd want to wash his hands. He liked to feel independent. He'd stand on the toilet seat to reach the sink. Would he put the lid down? If he didn't, would he fall in? And what if the soap were to fall into the toilet bowl? He'd lean in to try and get it out.

Her head was spinning. In panic, she looked in all directions. In the corner of her eye she noticed the oven—switched on at full blast; inside, the hot air shuddered and rose with the scent of yesterday's leftover sponge cake.

She drifted away again.

Then the sound of barking brought her back to consciousness. A large dog with a deep voice. It must be barking right by the gate, very near—nothing but barking and crying were getting through the fog surrounding her. The fog was making the world go dark and lose its contours, and the sounds were blurred, too. She felt as if everything were drifting away from her, but at least her head had stopped hurting.

Then the barking stopped, and she realized help wasn't coming.

She would never go to his preschool celebration or drop him off for his first day of high school, never catch him smoking, never meet the girl he brought home, never take the grandkids for the weekend to give him and his wife a break, and she'd never have the sort of Christmas she remembered from childhood, with four generations gathered at the table, all talking at once.

A shadow appeared in her field of vision. She managed to move her eyeball enough to see her child grab the handle of the heated oven to reach for the one-gallon carton of apple juice on the counter.

She realized that her death was not the worst thing that could happen that day. A day so different from every other that it didn't seem part of her life at all.

9

He felt like the ultimate moron. As he'd left the house, to be on the safe side he'd pulled the hood of his thick cotton sweatshirt over his head in case anybody recognized him. He set off at a rapid pace down Emilia Plater Street, without looking up at the prosecution service windows. When he reached the corner of the building, he looked around vigilantly like the spy in a comedy crime movie and turned toward the black-and-green hole. Which at this time of year was simply a black hole without a hint of green; against the gray fog the leafless branches looked like the set of a horror film, a weird spiderweb on an alien planet, waiting to catch the unsuspecting intruder. Actually, there was one green element here. The dumpster.

Szacki went up to the dumpster, looked around one more time, raised the lid, and jumped inside.

Of course the prosecution service had a special machine for shredding documents, but the regular trash collected from under the desks, in other words, apple cores, empty soda cans, used tissues, crumpled notes, and incomplete transcripts of interviews with freaking victims of domestic abuse all ended up in a regular dumpster.

He stood among identical black bags, tied at the top with identical knots, and wondered if there was any way to identify his own. By the volume? He'd tossed a few bits of paper in there yesterday, an empty tomato juice bottle, and an empty tub of cottage cheese.

He felt a few of the bags. In one he could feel a small bottle. He tore it open, and cautiously peeked inside. *An empty vodka miniature, hmm, interesting.*

He put it aside.

He felt out another bottle. He raised the bag, which was indeed tied at the top, but also torn at the bottom. The first thing to fall out onto his pants was an empty energy drink bottle, followed by a yogurt—unfortunately, only partly eaten, then a filter full of coffee grounds, a large blob of mayonnaise, and finally the remains of a triangular sandwich from the gas station. It bounced off his pants and landed on his shoes, mayonnaise side down, of course.

Szacki cursed aloud, wishing his colleagues would take better care of themselves.

"Get the fuck out of there or I'll call the police." Szacki shuddered as he heard a voice right by his ear.

He turned to face the security guard, who must have noticed him on the monitor inside and had come to restore order.

"Mr. Prosecutor! What are you doing here?"

"A legal experiment."

The security guard didn't seem convinced. He stood and stared suspiciously.

"Can I go back to work now?" asked Szacki, pointing at the mixture of discarded food scattered at his feet as if it were the files for an important case.

"Yeah, sure thing," said the security guard. "Good day, Mr. Prosecutor."

The guard walked away, and Szacki went back to groping the bags of trash. Among the interesting things he went on to find were a prayer book and a green-and-white Olsztyn volleyball team scarf. He was starting to get dangerously sucked in, when at last he found his tomato juice, and his heart began to race. Waiting for him in the cottage cheese tub was the interview transcript form, crumpled into a neat ball.

10

He passed a couple out for a walk with a muddy Labrador, and a few hundred yards farther down this road resembling a four-wheeler track, he found house number seventeen—the plate was in the style of Paris street signs, edged in green. In a semicircular field above it was written "Avenue Równa."

Szacki shifted into Park, but he kept the engine running. Firstly, he wasn't eager to get out into the land of ice and mud, and secondly, he needed to think about what to say. Above all, what to say if the woman was at home with her husband or if only the husband was there. "Excuse me, could you please pass on some information to your persecuted wife about the procedure for putting herself on the at-risk register? I'd be much obliged."

He sighed, buttoned his coat, and looked toward the house. There were lights on in the kitchen and the upstairs bedroom. He switched off the engine and got out of the car—he had to hold on to the door to avoid slipping.

He rang the bell.

Silence.

He waited a while and rang it again. He stood there for a few minutes, thinking she might be changing the baby or putting him down for an afternoon nap.

He walked along the fence, climbed on tiptoe, and peered into the kitchen. The fridge was wide-open and he could see the butter, pots of curd cheese, and yogurts in brightly colored tubs. He noticed that the compartment on the lower shelf had come loose, and was hanging from its clip like a broken arm.

He felt uneasy. And although he knew it was irrational and that soon he would awkwardly have to apologize, he climbed the fence, clumsily jumped down on the other side, and ran to the door. He didn't bother ringing or knocking, just immediately tugged at the door handle. It was unlocked. He went into a small entry, and slowly opened the door to the hall.

He could smell something burning.

"Hello? Ma'am, are you there? It's me, Prosecutor Szacki . . ." He broke off at the sight of the small dried footprints on the floor. The tracks of a child, imprinted in something pink—he had no idea what it was. Yogurt? Strawberry milk?

"We spoke yesterday," he said loudly, opening a door. "Can you hear me, ma'am?"

He hesitantly walked toward the kitchen and living room, with every cell of his body crying out that something was very wrong here.

And it was.

The corpse was lying on the floor; the pool of blood and milk had formed a two-tone halo around the victim's head. He felt himself come unstuck from reality, and the world went spinning. He would have passed out, if not for the sight of the little pink footprints that led him to the woman lying on the floor.

He looked around. A stream of smoke was seeping from the oven—
that was why he could smell burning. A little boy in a luridly turquoise
pajama top was squatting in a corner of the room, with his hunched
back turned this way. He was busy with something. Szacki went up and
squatted beside him. The child must have been about three years old.
He joined two pieces of a jigsaw puzzle, featuring a smiling figure from
a fairy tale or maybe a car. Then he separated the pieces and joined them
up again with the same automatic movement.

"Hello, can you hear me?" Szacki said gently, moving around so
the boy could see him. At first the child didn't react, then he looked at
Szacki with eyes devoid of emotion. The whole front of his pajama top
was covered in milk and blood.

"I'm going to pick you up, OK?" Szacki knelt down, smiled, and
held out his hands.

The boy with vacant eyes embraced his neck, nestled against his
coat collar, and was still.

Szacki slowly stood up and took the phone from his pocket.

And then he saw the woman blink.

11

He was standing outside the house on Równa Street, soaked to the bone
and frozen solid, watching the old Nissan in which the social welfare
people had come to fetch the little boy as the car bounced along the
potholes. Its brake lights shone through the fog, and then its turn signal
blinked as it turned onto the road toward Olsztyn and then disappeared. An ambulance had taken the boy's mother away fifteen minutes
ago. The forensic team was gathering evidence inside.

He had absolutely nothing to do here.

And yet he wasn't quite capable of getting in his car and driving off.
Bah, he couldn't even move.

He was just standing there.

He heard a car pull up behind him. The engine died and the door slammed.

Edmund Falk was standing in front of him; he had to crane his neck to look Szacki in the eyes.

"If she doesn't survive, I'll destroy you," he said.

Szacki didn't answer. It was the logical choice.

CHAPTER FIVE

Monday, December 2, 2013

International Day for the Abolition of Slavery. Nelly Furtado and Britney Spears are celebrating their birthdays. Exactly twenty-two years have passed since Poland became the first country in the world to recognize Ukraine's independence in 1991. Meanwhile, following the Eastern Partnership summit in Vilnius that ended in a fiasco, the protests continue non-stop in Kiev's Independence Square, as the opposition gains strength and people call for revolution. While the Ukrainians want to join the EU, the British want to leave it. Only 26 percent of Her Majesty's subjects rate the EU positively. Researchers announce that they have discovered the gene for alcoholism. Once their GABRB1 gene has been modified, mice—usually teetotal—take a liking to vodka. With time, these rodents will tackle some very tricky tasks just to get another fix of alcohol. The courts are doing a good job today: In Rawa Mazowiecka, a town in central Poland, a forty-nine-year-old priest is sentenced to eight and a half years in prison for pedophilia. In Strasburg a hearing into the case of some secret CIA prisoners held in Warmia continues all day. In Olsztyn it's the first day of the trial of members of the local housing cooperative, who organized a protest against irregularities in the way it was managed; the defendants include a woman of eighty-four. At night there's a mild frost, during the day it's 35 degrees, overcast, and of course there's fog and freezing drizzle.

This time the anatomy department at the Faculty of Medical Sciences didn't resemble a Shakespearean witches' cave. All the bubbling cauldrons had gone, and so had the distinctive smell of broth. PhD student Alicja Jagiełło had vanished too—only Professor Frankenstein was still there, and so was the victim, known until recently as Piotr Najman, entrepreneur in the tourist industry. Until recently, because since his skeleton had turned out to contain not just an endoprosthesis but somebody else's bones as well, the question of its identity had become rather complicated.

The bones had left the dissection table where they had been lying earlier, and were now on the floor, spread out on a large sheet. All separated, numbered, and labeled, they reminded Szacki of photographs from plane crash investigations, where all parts that are found are laid out in a hangar. Everyone in Poland would have exactly the same association—the Smolensk air disaster had educated the entire nation on the topic of aviation inquiries.

Najman and Co. had been treated in a similar way. A human shape had been drawn on the white sheet in black marker, unnaturally large, as if inflated—it must have been eight feet long. Inside the phantom, all the bones had been arranged properly, large and small; the pensive Frankenstein looked like a teacher, standing over the remains and wondering how to grade the work of students trying to earn credits in anatomy.

"Of course, 206 is simplifying things a bit," he said.

"Sorry?" Szacki didn't understand. Surely he wasn't suggesting the skeleton could consist of bones from 206 different victims. That would mean an investigation that dragged on all the way to retirement.

"I told you earlier that the human skeleton contains 206 bones. That's a bit of a simplification. A newborn baby has 270, an adult usually has 206, and a person of advanced age may have fewer, because with time the bones fuse together. You know, I've trained plenty of pathologists, truly excellent ones, but I myself have rarely conducted an autopsy as the basis for a legal opinion. And so I've never acquired the right mindset, the obsession with seeking signs of a crime everywhere."

Frankenstein folded his hands behind his back and straightened up.

"What are you getting at?" asked Szacki.

He didn't want to hustle the professor, but he was keen to move on to specifics.

"The fact that not a single piece of the jigsaw you sent me was missing should have set me thinking."

"Why's that? We established that somebody brought the bones in a bag shortly before they were found. There wasn't time for any rats or medical students to get to them."

"You're a layman, that's why you say that. You think of a skeleton, and you see a femur, a skull, ribs, vertebrae. But that's just a small part of the whole structure. You have to have a good deal of knowledge to notice, in some strange spot where murders are committed . . ."

"Now *you're* talking like a layman. Murders aren't committed under road bridges or in the cellars of abandoned houses. Quite the opposite, most of them take place in clean, well-lit interiors, in other words, the family home."

"Either way, they're not sterile spaces specially prepared for the purpose. But here someone has managed to commit a murder, dissolve the corpse, and then fish out all the bones from the remains. Some of them are very small, the phalanges for example, or the coccyx, and some are positively microscopic. Look at this."

Frankenstein squatted beside Najman's skull and gestured to Szacki to join him. He took a pencil from his pocket and pressed it against some tiny bones lying on the sheet at the height of the phantom's ear.

"These are the auditory ossicles. They transmit vibrations in the tympanic membrane to the inner ear, thanks to which you can hear what I'm saying. The malleus, the incus, and the stapes—a very interesting structure. As you probably know, these are the only bones in the human body that never change from birth onward. They are 100-percent formed during fetal life, and it happens in an unusual way, which is one of the proofs in support of the theory of evolution, because in fish and reptiles they have an identical—"

"Professor, please."

Frankenstein straightened up proudly. Even if he had a reply ready, he kept it to himself.

"This is the stapes. You see? It's the Latin word for a stirrup."

Szacki nodded. He knew that, and he'd always thought the name was symbolic, but in fact the tiny bone did look like a miniature stirrup, part of an elf's riding kit.

"This bone is less than an eighth of an inch long, and its limbs are only about a hundredth of an inch thick. Firstly, it's extremely unlikely that such a tiny structure could survive being treated with lye. Secondly, I don't believe it would be possible to pick out something of this size from the magma that would result from dissolving a corpse in sodium hydroxide."

Szacki listened carefully. He didn't like what he was hearing, thanks to his stapes, unchanged since birth. He didn't like it, because the professor's argument was tending toward confirmation of the theory that a crazy serial killer was at work.

"Professor, I understand what you're saying, but are these just theoretical digressions, or are we talking about this specific case?"

"Prosecutor," said Frankenstein, peering at him over his glasses, "neither I nor my team have slept for the past few days while analyzing and cross-analyzing the genetic data from all 206 bones on your instructions, but the only appreciation we're getting is your rising irritation. Would it be too much to ask for a few seconds of patience?"

Szacki should have shut up and smiled politely—after all, what difference would a two-minute lecture make? Unfortunately he always found it hard to be patient.

"Please understand that there are professions where time has meaning, and the aim is something other than publication in a scholarly periodical read by a handful of colleagues."

Frankenstein smiled subtly.

"Of course, justice, I almost forgot. *Misstraut allen Denen, die viel von ihrer Gerechtigkeit reden.*"

"I'm sorry, I'm from Poland."

"As the philosopher said, 'Mistrust all who talk much of their justice.'"

"I haven't said a word about justice."

The professor removed his glasses, took a cloth from his pocket, and wiped them carefully. Evidently the pause was his favorite rhetorical device.

"Somebody has gone to a lot of trouble to complete the perfect skeleton," he said. "To make sure nothing is missing. You'll be getting a detailed report from me, but the main findings are as follows: Most of the bones are Najman's. But not all. Some of the bones in both hands had another owner, a man."

"Can you establish the gender on the basis of DNA? What about the age? Or other data?"

"Eye color, hair color. Age only very, very approximately, I'm sorry to say, and only after complex tests. I can go on, or would you prefer some theoretical digression?"

This time Szacki shut up.

"Curiously, there are twelve more bones in the skeleton that don't belong to Najman, and not one of them has been treated with lye. Apart from gathering DNA, I had them do some chemical tests."

Szacki gave him an inquiring look.

"Six of them are the auditory ossicles. Two sets of three bones. One set belonged to a man, the other to a woman."

"To the owner of the hand?"

"No, they're three different people."

"And the remaining six?"

"It looks as if they're just stage props."

"Why?"

"They're several tiny bones from various places." Frankenstein put away his pencil and took out a telescopic pointer. "The coccyx, or the tailbone, at the very end of the spine. The xiphoid process, right here, at the very end of the breastbone. And the four smallest phalanges from various toes of both feet. All these bones are, first of all, genuinely old, secondly, have not been subjected to the effect of lye, and thirdly, they belonged to a woman."

Szacki analyzed this information for a while.

"In other words, after the murder, somebody put together a skeleton jigsaw, checked what was missing, and dug out the missing pieces from some old coffin."

"That's the hypothesis that suggests itself."

"Why?"

"Luckily, I don't have to look for the answer to that question."

Unluckily, Szacki did. Several theories ran through his head, each worse than the last. And each one featured a miserable psycho, lurking in the cellar of one of those Warmian Disney castles, surrounded by little heaps of bones sorted by type, and ticking off the missing items needed to complete his work. Screw that.

"So these are the bones of five different people?" he asked, to confirm it. "Our victim in the starring role, the bit players being the man who owned the hand, the man who owned one ear, the woman who owned the other, and in a walk-on role, the lady who kindly donated the missing parts."

Frankenstein gently nodded.

"Where's the neurosurgery department here?"

"In the new building, way over there, on the left, third floor."

Szacki offered the professor his hand in farewell and left the dissection room. Only in the hallways did it occur to him that somehow he should have said thank you. He almost turned back, but realized he didn't have time. Besides, assisting the judiciary was a civic duty—all they needed to do was send everyone flowers.

2

He left the anatomy department and looked around. "Way over there" must mean farther from the street, and there indeed was a new building, looming from behind a German block. Szacki headed toward it across the hospital yard. In summer it had been a pretty garden, but now it was a few small squares of mud and patchy grass, with paths crossing them and thick black tree trunks shooting out of them.

When he got to the new part of the development, he was pleased to find that the designers of this hospital were not just the first in the postwar history of the city to succeed in achieving more than just throwing up in a public space. They were also the first to succeed in coherently combining a typical redbrick German edifice with contemporary architecture. As a result the new development looked attractive, as well as modern and professional—the sort of hospital where you'd want to be a patient, if you had to be one.

He went through some sliding doors and an admissions ward, and took the elevator to the third floor. As in every hospital, the ground floor was noisy and chaotic, but upstairs in the wards there was peace and quiet; the halls were deserted, there was a smell of coffee and disinfectant, and a sound of whispers mixed with the murmur of medical equipment.

There was no one behind the reception desk. Szacki stood and waited. In reality he was trying to find an excuse to disappear, so he didn't seek eye contact with the female doctor who emerged from one of the rooms holding a file, walking at a rapid pace. He was sure she'd go straight past him, but she glanced at him, frowned, and stopped.

"Are you looking for someone?" she asked.

He took a look at her. A few years over forty, petite build, dark hair, glasses, bangs. The A-student type. She was holding her file protectively like a shield.

He gave the first and last names.

Instead of answering, the doctor tilted her head, as if thinking very hard about something. This characteristic gesture seemed familiar. Who did that? Żenia? His boss?

"And what relation are you to the patient?"

"I'm the prosecutor. Teodor Szacki."

The coolly professional doctor beamed.

"Well, I never. Prosecutor Szacki in person! I was wondering where I'd seen you before. I'm extremely pleased to have the chance to meet you. Do excuse me, I'd love to have a proper talk, but I'm already late for my meeting. Maybe next time?" She smiled.

He nodded, wondering what on earth had won him fame on the neurosurgical ward.

"Last door on the right!" she said, before getting on the elevator.

He thanked her, waited for the door to close, stood there a while longer, and finally realized he had to get this confrontation over with as soon as possible. He set off at a fast pace, passed several empty bays, or almost empty, and finally found himself in a room where a young woman lay on the only bed.

She looked quite ordinary.

3

Her consciousness keeps coming and going quite suddenly, as if someone were compulsively playing with her main switch, like repeatedly clicking a pen.

Click.

And the darkness is replaced with white absorbent cotton, which then changes into opaque glass, with various foggy blobs moving around behind it, gradually starting to gain focus. She tries hard to concentrate on them.

Click.

Darkness.

Click.

And as the darkness is replaced by white absorbent cotton again, a thought appears, fleeting, feeble, only sufficient to confirm that she is who she is, and to let her define herself as a conscious being. She focuses on this thought and builds more of them around it. Now that she knows who she is, she tries to remember where she is, and why. It feels as if she has to catch up with each thought. It's very tiring.

Click.

She's been fighting this battle for ages, but now she's having her first successes. Once or twice she manages to remain conscious long enough to understand that she is in the hospital, and that something has happened. One time she comes to the terrible conclusion that she may have been living in a coma for the past thirty years and no longer recognizes anyone. But at once she drifts away—click—and when she comes back, she's forgotten that conclusion.

Once or twice the world sharpens enough for her to see some unfamiliar faces. She tries to speak, but it's futile.

Click.

All of a sudden she remembers that she has a child. A little boy perhaps, but she's not sure. She can't find his name in her memory. But he's small. She can remember the sense of love and the sense of fear. Has something happened to him? Is he dying just as she is? Too much emotion.

Click.

For the first time, along with consciousness comes pain. She thinks it may be a good sign, and that if she can grab hold of the pain, she can remain conscious longer. She needs to do that, to extract more information from herself about her child, whom she loves so much and whom she's so worried about.

A boy. She's almost certain it's a boy. Dark hair. What about his eyes? She can see the image of a child, sleeping on his back, snoring, in pajamas with a motorcycle on the top. A blue motorcycle marked "Vrrooom!" He's asleep, so she can't see his eyes. She tries to summon some other image, but she can't do it.

Click.

She opens her eyes. This time instead of absorbent cotton, the opaque glass appears at once—progress. Learning from experience, she doesn't force her senses to work but waits calmly to see if she's going to switch off or not. Soon the image gains more focus, and she sees a man standing in front of her.

She'd like to reflect on who he is, but she has no control over her thoughts, and instead she wonders if it's possible that as a result . . . as a result of what has happened to her, whatever it was, she has lost her color vision. Because the man is monochrome. White hair, pale face, black coat, jacket, shirt, and tie in various shades of gray. He's standing in the doorway, then he comes up to her bed. He stands upright, with his hands dropped to either side of his body.

She has no idea who he is. She tries to identify the emotions that go with him.

Love? Friendship?

"I came to ask your forgiveness," says the man quietly. "But I realize I may never get it. Because you won't be able to give it to me, or more likely, you won't want to."

She can see that the man is saying something, but none of it gets through to her. She concentrates on the emotions—by now she knows that the easiest way to get to the facts, to the images, is through emotions.

Sorrow?

"But I'd like you to take note of my apology at least." He looks her in the eyes. He has a cold gaze—she doesn't like this man. "I've made lots of mistakes in my life, but this is the worst. I'll never stop being ashamed of it."

Regret?

"I promise you that the people to blame for what happened will be punished. Of course, there's your husband. We haven't caught him yet, but it's a matter of days or hours."

Hatred?

"I shall submit myself to disciplinary proceedings and leave the prosecution service. I promise nobody will ever suffer because of me again."

Rage. Yes, that was the right emotion.

With the emotion comes an image. Her son's back, leaning over something. A streak of smoke from somewhere. Tremendous fear. And then footsteps, the tails of a black coat flashing before her eyes. It's this man. He leans over and picks up the child. The boy trustingly nestles against his coat collar, speckled with drizzle. They both look at her. The man's icy gaze, and her child's brown, tearful eyes. Brown. What a relief!

Rage. She's decided to hold on to this emotion because so far it's the one that has had the most to offer her.

Click.

4

The cold wind sobered him up, but he still felt weak, so he sat on a bench outside the hospital to recuperate. He'd kind of known what he'd see in the hospital room, but it was one thing to know and another to see. He couldn't get rid of the image of the body lying in the hospital bed, more like a corpse than a living person. The face, disfigured by the slack muscles, the exposed teeth, visible behind the drooping lips. The eyes that were probably trying to show him some emotion. Had she been mentally screaming at him to get out of there? Hurling abuse? Rightly blaming him for everything that had happened?

The worst thing was the bruise under her eye. A huge black-and-purple bruise.

He'd said what he had to say, but he didn't feel any better. Partly because he hadn't told her the entire truth, just a few platitudes. He hadn't said what had really caused him to arrive on his white horse—that neither concern nor even common decency lay behind his action. It was nothing but bureaucratic fear, a desperate attempt to save his own ass. Which, moreover, he'd done reluctantly, out of obligation.

He felt ashamed he hadn't said that, and deluded himself into thinking he'd do it another time. There was no point in telling the woman, who had escaped death by a miracle, that if it weren't for a coincidence, one overzealous junior prosecutor, and a boss who wanted to put an end to the matter right away, right now her mother would be wondering how to dress her grandson for the funeral.

But going to see her had helped him make the most important decision he had ever made in his entire life to date. He'd been thinking about it for several days, but now in the hospital hallway the thought had changed into a cast-iron conviction.

He wouldn't be a prosecutor anymore. That stage in his life had come to an end. He'd devote a few more days or weeks, either to solving the Najman case, or passing it on to someone else. He'd make sure Falk was in charge of the case of the butcher of Równa Street. Those two inquiries would be the last he would ever deal with as a prosecutor.

He got up from the bench and decided to walk to the prosecution building across the Old Town. But halfway there he chickened out at the thought of an encounter with Falk and Szarejna. On impulse he turned off beside the Old Town Hall and went into SiSi, the café that lately had become his favorite. The style of the place gave it a very Warsaw feel, and Szacki felt at home there. Besides, they had excellent cakes—best of all were the meringues. Another reason he liked the place was that ever since he'd flashed his ID and meanly asked if they paid royalties, they'd switched off the music the moment he crossed the threshold. Freeing him from the horror of popular music, especially rap.

Fifteen minutes later, stimulated by sugar and caffeine, he was slogging over his notebook, trying to put his racing thoughts in order. Finding the little boy playing beside his battered mother had shaken him badly. The appalling, overwhelming sense of guilt had crushed him and wouldn't let him get back to his usual routine. And yet he had to pull himself together because Frankenstein's revelations meant that the case had ceased to be just a curious murder. It had become a priority investigation of national importance.

He wrote in the notebook, Równa—Falk 100%, poss. consultancy, apart from that, THE END.

OK, onward and upward. On the next page, he wrote *Minor league.* Underneath, he made a list of all his cases, checked his journal for the deadlines for arrests, the official dates when the investigations were due to end, and the days he had to be in court. It didn't look too bad—he had no court appearances until January, nor did he have to finish anything urgently. It would be easy to reallocate his duties when he announced his departure from the service. Right now he would ask Szarejna to reassign the three investigations in which several activities needed to be commissioned quickly. Nothing major, just expert

witnesses and one visit to a crime scene. Under this short list he added
THE END, then turned the page.

He hesitated for a while, wondering whether to write *Ton of shit* or
Pain in the ass. Finally he neatly wrote the word *Spokesman*, recognizing
that there was no point in surrendering to his emotions. Totally lying
his way out of it was impossible until he announced his decision to
leave. If they wanted him to put on a show in the course of his investigation, then naturally he'd do it. He could. If they wanted something
else, he'd try to be nice about it. And he'd promise to give it his full
attention in just a short while, but for now—*I'm sure you understand,
ladies and gentlemen, such an important investigation, a serial murderer—
I'm terribly sorry.*

Yes, quite—a serial murderer. He turned the page, folded the notebook back to keep it open, and wrote in block letters *NAJMAN* across
both pages.

"Close your eyes, dude, do it right away!" a man's voice roared in distorted English just overhead. Szacki jumped, and a bit of meringue fell
off his fork. *"Don't even think about the level of your fear."*

The sound of atrocious rap music vanished. The silence was filled
by rapid footsteps, and there stood the manager, with a terrified look
on his face.

"I'm so sorry, Mr. Prosecutor, the barista's new. I promise it won't
happen again. Coffee on the house, perhaps?"

He said no thank you. He was still working on a cup of fiendishly
strong black coffee. It was pretty good, but he was afraid that if he drank
all of it, he'd have palpitations.

On the left-hand page he jotted down what he knew. Not much,
considering almost a week had gone by since the corpse was identified. Thanks to recordings from various security cameras and witness
statements, they'd managed to confirm that on Monday morning Piotr
Najman had driven his Mazda to work. He'd left it at a repair shop on
Sikorski Avenue for servicing. Logical, if he was due to be away for

several days. Except that nothing else confirmed he was planning to go away for several days. According to the repair shop staff, he had no luggage. The tour operator in Warsaw knew nothing about a trip to the Balkans or about any briefing. None of the Olsztyn cab companies had had a booking to pick him up from the agency in Jaroty on Monday. He hadn't bought a ticket in his own name for the bus to Warsaw; he may have boarded it at the stop, but the bus company staff hadn't been able to confirm that.

Only his wife and his business partner had testified that he was supposed to be going away. And now there were two possibilities: one, they were both lying, or two, Najman had lied to both of them. The first supposition would mean the two women were involved in a conspiracy to commit murder, which seemed unlikely. Especially as the phone bills confirmed Teresa Najman's story. During the week of her husband's absence, she had tried to call him twice and had sent three text messages to say everything was fine at home. OK, maybe she wasn't the most caring wife, but that wasn't a crime. Or maybe she'd gotten used to her husband's constant trips, some of them exotic, and to the fact that she couldn't contact him.

In other words, the second version of events was more likely. The guy takes advantage of his job involving frequent travel to deceive his wife, deceive his partner, and spend a week with his lover in some Warmian hotel for adulterers. On the right-hand page, he wrote *lover*. He underlined it. If such a woman existed, then even if she had nothing to do with the murder, the guy had gone missing on his way to join her, or on his way back, or during a break in their lovemaking when he'd stepped out for a bottle of wine—either way, this could be their most important witness. They'd have to check Najman's computers and phone bills, interview his friends, and find the girl. Check his trips abroad—maybe they'd met on some exotic briefing trip.

He wrote down *lye*. He drew two arrows leading from it, and then two more words: *motive?* and *psycho?* Baldheaded Piotr Najman from

Stawiguda had not been murdered, like most of his compatriots, with a metal bar while drunk. He had been deprived of his life in a sophisticated way. Why? Perhaps he'd given someone reasons to hate him. Maybe he'd run someone over in the past on his way home from a party. Maybe he'd screwed someone else's wife (Szacki drew an arrow to the word *lover*). Maybe, as Falk had claimed, he'd rubbed someone the wrong way by giving them a room without a view. That meant the madman who'd dissolved Najman had had previous contact with him. Under *motive* he wrote the word *past* and realized that soon he and Bierut would have to set a limit for the scope of their research.

There was also an increasingly likely chance that Najman wasn't the most important element, and that the key person was the murderer—a serial killer who murdered and dissolved his victims for fun. The choice of victim was either secondary, or insignificant. Unfortunately there was more and more evidence in favor of this idea. Planting the skeleton in a weird place. Next to the word *psycho*, he wrote *Mariańska Street*. Completing it with other bones. He added *additional victims*, and next to that *missing persons/DNA*.

He thought for a while, sighed, added the name *Klejnocki*, and circled it several times. He didn't believe in psychological shamanism, and he wasn't wild about the freaky profiler from Kraków, but he had to bring Klejnocki in before they gave him some local expert who knew how many lakes there were in Olsztyn.

He decided to go see Bierut at the police station and immediately called a cab.

5

Bierut came back with two bottles of sparkling water and put one down in front of Szacki with a look on his face as if it were a chalice of cyanide. It occurred to Szacki that he had no luck when it came to colleagues—hadn't the boggy Warmian soil borne any sons full of joy and optimism? Falk was stiff enough to put a porn star to shame, while Bierut's gloomy nature was a fine advertisement for the Warmian climate, as if he were determined to make the atmosphere on this side of the window just as bleak.

The deputy commissioner sighed heavily, like a doctor before imparting bad news.

"I'll summarize," Bierut began. "Let's start with the fact that none of the doctors from the city hospital has disappeared or had a day off or gone on a business trip. One of the midwives has gone on vacation, but she'd had it planned for six months."

"Where did she purchase the trip?"

"Downtown. I called her in Egypt, and she'd been on package tours before, but never through Najman's or Parulska's agency. Not with anyone in Olsztyn, in fact, because she only moved here recently from Elbląg. Everyone moves out of Elbląg," he added in a tone that seemed to imply this migration was the effect of plague.

"Either way, let's not give up on the hospital idea," said Szacki. "Especially since it turned out that our lakeland vampire constructed Najman from several corpses. That takes medical knowledge. What's come of the DNA from the other bones? Have you put them through the database yet?"

"Nothing leaped out."

"That's bad. We need to check unexplained disappearances for the past—I don't know, the past two years, for a start. Collect samples from the families who haven't given any yet, and compare them."

Bierut raised an eyebrow.

"From the whole city?"

"From the whole region. This isn't New York, where every serial murderer can have his fill and still leave something for others. I'm actually wondering whether to expand it to cover the neighboring provinces, but let's start with the marshlands, and then we'll see. Maybe we'll get lucky."

Even if Bierut wanted to defend his homeland, he restrained himself.

"Please also send a question to national police headquarters to ask if there's an ongoing investigation anywhere in Poland into the case of a corpse without hands. It's crucial to identify the owners of the remaining bones, above all, the hands."

Szacki was thinking about it as a mathematical problem. He imagined each piece of circumstantial evidence and each bit of hard proof as a circle of a defined radius. These circles overlapped, and the murderer was standing in the common area: the logic was merciless. For the time being they were staring at a single circle, marked *Piotr Najman*. A large set, not infinite, but large. If they could identify the remaining bones, they could place other circles on top of Najman's and look for the common areas. That would considerably reduce the range of their search.

"And now I want to hear the Personal History, Adventures, and Experience of Piotr Najman," he said, drank the sparkling water, crossed his legs, adjusted the crease in his pants, and added, "The Elder, of Stawiguda, Which He Never Meant to Publish on Any Account."

He glanced at Bierut. Even if the policeman was fond of Dickens and recognized the quote, he didn't let it show. He just twitched his outdated mustache.

"Unfortunately, for a fifty-year-old he hasn't got much history. His parents are dead, the father long ago, the mother for several years. No siblings, he was an only child. We found an uncle at the other end of the country, but all he knows about his nephew is that he exists. Wife, five-year-old kid."

"We didn't learn much from the wife."

"Unfortunately. Do you think she's hiding something?"

"Possibly. But it's equally possible that something was being hidden from her. I'll tell you about that in a while. Any close friends?"

"The partner is just as reticent as the wife. Our colleagues in Warsaw questioned his business contacts from the tourist companies, but they didn't learn anything new. We've talked to the neighbors at his residence and his workplace. Nothing interesting. I spoke in person with two of his rivals. You know what it's like, some are inclined to denounce their competitors to the tax office to clean up the market, and they're often willing to spread gossip and slander. Not this time. What's more, they praised Najman, especially for his expertise on what they call 'the exotic.'"

Bierut scoured his notes.

"I also followed the medical lead. I thought since he'd had the operation on his toe in Warsaw, he may have sought help here first. And indeed he did have some consultations at the provincial hospital—I spoke to the orthopedic surgeon, who had nothing to say apart from medical details. Besides, he's seventy, so he seems unlikely to have committed a sophisticated crime involving packing an adult male into a cast-iron coffin."

"What about your databases?" Szacki asked.

"What do you mean? You know that nobody ever turns up in our databases."

True, Szacki did know that nothing ever came up in the official databases. The police had the National Police Information System. The prosecution service had its own system, Libra, because somehow no genius had ever had the bright idea that the law enforcement bodies should have a single information resource. Or rather, some genius had decided that the more systems and contracts were out there, the lower the probability that he'd end his term with empty pockets. On top of that, all these systems were bizarrely dismembered, incompatible, and disconnected. Which meant it was enough for a serial killer to move to a different province after each successive murder, and nobody would ever make the connection.

"So I wondered," said Bierut, "if maybe we should ease up on Najman's past. Lots of effort and resources, but it looks as if there's nothing there. He's an ordinary guy. He had a fairly interesting job, traveled a lot, his business was doing well. He found himself a wife, built a house out of town. He sat there, watched TV, and had a barbecue in the summer. Same as millions of others. Digging around in it is a dead end."

Szacki regretted that he didn't smoke. Maybe if he did, he'd have matches on him to prop up his drooping eyelids.

"I'm still going to write to the bank and the tax office," he said. "We can't drop the possibility that it could be Mafia score-settling. Maybe something will come out of his tax returns or his bank accounts." He broke off abruptly. One of the thoughts that were trying to push their way through his sleepy mind had gotten lost along the way. Just now he'd thought of yet another database. Which one was it? He couldn't remember, so instead he told Bierut about his theory that Najman had a lover. That would explain the lies he'd fed to his wife and partner.

"And you think she might have had something to do with it?"

"Not necessarily. But I do think it's an important lead."

Bierut cast him a weary, disheartened look.

"So what does that mean? Do we have to interview everyone over again, this time to ask them about the lover? If they didn't tell us the first time, they're not gonna do it the second time."

That would be the best thing to do, but Szacki realized it would be cruel to insist on it. Bierut would dig his heels in, and his bosses would start to make hell for Szacki's. He didn't need that.

"Parulska, the business partner, must have his trips written down. I don't mean his vacations, I mean the kind where the tourist agents are herded around the five-star hotels. Please get details of the last three and then lists of participants from the organizers. We'll check if any of the names are repeats. Exotic locations, hotels, alcohol—I'd be surprised if he'd found a lover anywhere else."

For a while they sat in silence. Szacki was trying to recover the thought that had previously escaped him. He'd almost got it when

Bierut asked, "Do you think this really is a serial killer? A real psycho? A madman who wants to play with us?"

"I hope so," muttered the furious Szacki.

"You hope so?"

"It's easier to catch that sort of asshole than a guy who strangles his wife in the bedroom and buries her in the neighbor's yard. When someone plays games like this, he's bound to make a mistake and leave too many clues. Besides, making stuff up is circumstantial evidence in itself. Just look how much we've got already. The bones of five people, a unique modus operandi that limits the number of possible crime sites, and we've identified the killing method. If he really is crazy, then I can't wait for him to start sending enigmatic letters written in the blood of brides."

That was it! Brides. It was something to do with brides. He wanted to check if . . .

Now he was smiling, pleased that at last he'd cornered his wayward thought, when someone knocked urgently at the door, and immediately opened it. It was Edmund Falk.

"We've got him," he said.

6

Szacki never referred to the prosecution service and the police as "we." "We" meant the prosecution service, "they" meant the police. A clear division of two institutions tasked with keeping law and order jointly, but not shoulder to shoulder. The prosecutors were the chiefs, in charge of the case from when the corpse was found, through the trial, and all the way to the convict's release after serving his sentence. The police carried out the duties assigned to them in the initial stage of the proceedings, which was meant to lead to catching the criminal. And that was the limit of their involvement.

But he understood why Falk had used the first person plural. Why, for all his practiced stiffness, the young prosecutor was not immune to the adrenaline kick that came with catching a criminal. Why he wanted to be a part of this triumph. If the judiciary were compared to the arts, the policemen played the role of rock stars, and the prosecutors were like the writers. The cops went out onstage, and if the performance went well, the excited audience carried them on their shoulders. They got an immediate response, a sense of fulfillment, a high like after taking drugs. Meanwhile, the prosecutor toiled away at establishing the proof for months or even years, and by the time he finally got his big reward in the form of a conviction, the case was already receding from everyone's memory. Of course it was satisfying, but it was hardly rock 'n' roll.

He had often envied the police that rush of adrenaline. And he'd very often been accused of behaving more like a CID officer than a prosecutor during his investigations—there were those who thought he pushed way too far into the front lines. But unlike Falk, he never used the first person plural.

Looking through a two-way mirror at the man sitting in the interview room, it occurred to him that this particular triumph was definitely not up to the standards of Hollywood. The guy had simply come back to his house on Równa Street, which had been under surveillance since Thursday. Apparently he'd gotten into the patrol car without resistance, showing neither surprise, nor fear, nor the typical anger of a wife-beater.

Since being detained he hadn't said a word. And it looked as if this state of affairs wasn't going to change.

"Am I to understand that you're exercising your right to refuse to give an explanation?" asked Falk yet again. To Szacki's satisfaction, despite the bizarre turn of events, the junior prosecutor's voice betrayed no emotion.

The man just went on staring into space.

"Allow me to explain your situation once more. You have been charged with the attempted murder of your wife. A charge that could change at any moment into a charge of murder, as your wife is in a critical condition. You are now being detained in custody, and a petition has been made to the court for your temporary arrest. Do you understand?"

No reaction.

Falk said the man's first and last name.

"Please nod to confirm your identity."

No reaction.

Falk sat up straight and adjusted his cuffs. He looked at the suspect and waited. A standard tactic—you didn't have to graduate from the FBI to know that few people can bear a prolonged silence. They all start to talk in the end.

But it looked as if the man sitting opposite Falk was totally impervious to all interrogation techniques, including the FBI's. He just sat there without moving. Like every wife-beater, he looked totally normal. No demonic Jack Nicholson smile, no glare of a hood from the suburbs, no look of a contract killer, no scar across the face, no broken tooth, not even bushy eyebrows. Just an ordinary guy, the kind that leaves the office at five with his tie in his briefcase, gets into his Skoda, and buys himself a hot dog at the gas station on the way home. If being average wanted to advertise itself, it would hire this guy to appear on its billboards.

"Enough of this game," said one of the policemen standing next to Szacki. "It's time to put the squeeze on this asshole."

Szacki rolled his eyes. He was allergic to flatfoot testosterone—any more and he'd start sneezing.

"The prosecutor supervising the proceedings is interviewing the suspect now," said Szacki, as the policeman grabbed the doorknob. "Go ahead and disturb him if you want major trouble."

The temperature in the room dropped several degrees. Szacki almost reeled, so strongly could he feel the wave of hatred being blasted at him by the policeman. But even so, the cop let go of the doorknob.

"I usually try to avoid this sort of reasoning," said Falk, as if it were his millionth interrogation, "but imagine you're driving a car, and you're gradually accelerating, watching the speedometer needle move in a clockwise direction as you gather speed. Do you see? Now imagine the numbers on the clock represent years rather than miles. From eight to infinity. With every moment of silence you're pressing on the gas. Eight years, twelve, fifteen, twenty-five. You're just coming up to a life sentence. You don't have to confess, you don't have to cooperate, it's all understandable, and legal. But playing dumb will harm you more than you might think."

No reaction. He didn't even sigh.

"I'll give you a while to think it over. I'll be right back."

Szacki went into the hallway. He realized that Falk wanted a tête-à-tête.

"Well, so, what now?" Szacki asked, knowing that battlefields are the best place to learn.

"Frankly I have grave doubts about whether or not bringing charges is the right approach. He's behaving as if he's catatonic and hasn't dropped the act for a second. Maybe he's faking, or maybe he really has tuned out. If so, he hasn't understood the charges or the information about the rights he's entitled to. Which means we can't lock him up."

"So what do you suggest?"

"Let's send him for psychiatric tests and have him kept under observation. They'll isolate him at the facility, we'll have eight weeks to gather evidence, and then we can proceed on the basis of an expert opinion."

Szacki nodded. It was the best possible decision—he'd thought of it as soon as the man had failed to answer the question about his first and last name. He'd seen a legion of these con artists before.

They established that Falk would go fill out the forms for the court, and Szacki would go to the interview room. Perhaps a new element would prompt the detainee to open up. Doubtful, but worth a try.

He went inside. The man was just staring into the mirror behind which the policemen were standing. He didn't react to the prosecutor's entrance, he didn't even twitch as Szacki walked up to the table, sat down, pulled up his chair, and placed his folded hands on the table.

At least five minutes of perfect silence went by, until finally the man turned his head toward Szacki. In a regular, mechanical way—there was nothing decisive about it. Szacki shuddered when the man's gaze finally met his. He realized that the man wasn't keeping silent as a strategy. He was keeping silent because he was frightened to death.

Szacki had never seen such fear in anybody's eyes before.

7

Olsztyn might not have been as quick off the mark as Warsaw, where the shopping malls started blasting Christmas carols before the All Saints' Day candles were out, but on Monday, the first day of December, the festive atmosphere was tangible. At the Staromiejska café the Christmas decorations were up, and outside in the marketplace half an artificial Christmas tree had already been erected. In the *Olsztyn Gazette* they'd eagerly noted that the most important tree in all of Warmia had been felled and would soon be adorning the square outside the Town Hall. As Szacki gazed out of the window he felt a tremendous, childish desire for it to snow—not out of nostalgia for his years of innocence, for a sled, snowballs, and a life without any cares, but because of his happy memories from last year. Olsztyn had still been new to him, Żenia was new, and he was filled with the euphoria of a new life. A mistaken euphoria—at the age of forty-three, illusions and illnesses can be new, but life can't be all that different anymore. At the time he hadn't felt that, of course. Euphoria leaves no room for common sense, and Olsztyn had given him a magical setting for his elation. Beautiful snow had fallen, and there had been a Christmas fair in the Old Town; it smelled of winter and mulled wine. Żenia had held his hand in his coat pocket, and they'd played with each other's fingers like teenagers, giggling as they strolled with the crowd among the ice sculptures and the brightly lit-up Old Town houses in the marketplace. Żenia had told him about her adventures in high school here in Olsztyn, and it had made him feel young, new, and happy.

He longed for it to snow again this year. Just for a little while.

"Oh, come on, Dad, if you wanted to just come here and think on your own, you really should have said so."

He looked at his daughter sitting across the table at the restaurant. It was on the tip of his tongue to say that he couldn't have guessed her phone's battery would run down, so she wouldn't be able to text non-stop and would suddenly insist on actually talking to her father for a change.

"I'm sorry. I was just thinking I wish it would snow."

"That would be dangerous around here. Yesterday I read that here-abouts the wolves come creeping up to human habitations and prey on the livestock. If it snowed, they'd come into town, and I'd be in terrible danger wading through snowdrifts to school, trying to dodge packs of wild beasts."

"Drop it, Żenia's not here."

She made a face that very clearly expressed that this was a unique situation, where for once she didn't have to share her father's time with his annoying girlfriend. He read the message correctly and reached for the menu, to do what he always did in these situations: change the subject, pretend everything was all right, and act as if he had no idea what she was thinking.

But then he remembered what Żenia had been telling him over and over again—that for him it meant nothing, but he was doing Hela a disservice by running away from every tricky topic, treating her either as an independent woman who didn't require respect or as a little girl, depending on which happened to suit him better and would allow him to avoid confrontation.

He put down the menu.

"Say it."

"Say what?"

"Instead of giving me those looks, say it in words. You must have heard of that form of communication."

"I don't get it. What am I supposed to say in words?"

"That although you're tremendously relieved that Żenia isn't here, you're not gonna let me forget that this is one of those exceptionally rare moments when I'm actually forcing myself to pay attention to you and you alone."

She chewed her lip.

"Jeez, you don't have to be so heavy."

"I'm not being heavy. I just want to make it easier for you to talk about something that interests you."

"I'm not interested in talking about that."

"But I am."

"Then talk to someone else about it. Talk to Żenia, or best of all a shrink."

Fuck the little brat, he thought—so much for taking her seriously.

"Have you ever been afraid of me?"

"What's that?"

"Have you ever been afraid I'd hit you? Push you, slap you, do you physical harm."

"Right now I'm afraid you've gone nuts."

"It's a serious question."

She looked at him. And for the first time in ages he felt that she was looking at him normally—not negatively, not with studied, fake normality, but truly normally, just like that, the way one friend looks at another during a conversation.

"Have you decided what you want?" The waitress was standing by their table with her notepad at the ready.

"Dumplings in broth for two?" asked Szacki, looking at his daughter.

Hela nodded. The waitress took the menus and disappeared.

"It's a serious question," he repeated. "I've got this case, I mean I'm supervising it, never mind the details. Imagine a normal family from out of town, on the road toward Gdańsk. You know what it's like—one of those developments out in the sticks, small square lots, new houses, a car in the driveway, a grill out back, and a trampoline for the kid, inside there's a plasma TV on the wall. A husband, a wife, and a three-year-old. She stays at home with the kid while he toils away in Olsztyn to pay off the mortgage. For their vacation they spend two weeks at the beach. It's all totally normal, one day's just like the next. Except that she's afraid. In theory nothing's wrong, but she's afraid anyway, more and more so with each passing day. He's probably the traditional type, a bit domineering, proud of the house he built, the tree he planted, and the son he fathered. But she's afraid. Finally she can't take it anymore, so she tells him. Cut. Some hours later I find them. He's not there. She's lying in a pool of blood and milk with a hole in her head. The kid's playing on the floor next to her, connecting the same two pieces of his puzzle over and over."

Hela was staring at him, speechless.

"Do you realize, that's the first time you've ever told me anything about your work?"

"Seriously?"

She nodded. Strange, it hadn't occurred to him. He'd always thought they talked about everything.

"And I wondered if I'm capable of something like that too. I wonder if every man displays his physical advantage, his readiness to be violent, a sort of unexpressed threat, as if to say everything's just dandy, but don't you forget who weighs sixty-five pounds more than you do, and who was made to have the more physically powerful muscles by nature. That's why I ask."

For a while she said nothing.

"But you won't do anything to me if I give the wrong answer, will you?"

"Very funny."

"I've never been afraid you'd hit me. Not even when you threw Bunny out the window."

"Don't say you remember that!"

"As if it were yesterday."

"I lost my temper, but I was half joking. I brought him right back, anyway."

"I know, I know. But that time I was afraid. Not that you'd hit me, just 'cos it was so awful. You were shouting and waving your hands around and all that."

He didn't know what to say. To him it was just a comical anecdote—he told it now and then to amuse his audience. He thought that was the end of it. He'd lied his way out of the one and only incident, and now he could breathe easy. But Hela had more to say.

"Sometimes I've been afraid you were gonna shout at me. You could say I'm always afraid of that."

"I've got a temper." He was trying to trivialize the matter.

"You don't know what it's like on the receiving end. When someone's leaning over you, looking huge, and making loud noises. A man's face looks so animal when he's angry. I remember you scowling at me late at night, so close I could see your stubble. And the sound of it. I remember not being able to hear words, just that sound, as if those noises were attacking me, holding on, refusing to let me get away." She said it calmly, dispassionately, and slightly pensively, as she carefully remembered. "That made me feel afraid. I sometimes used to wait for you to get home at night, and on the one hand, I'd be longing for you to get there, I'd be wanting us to do something together. Make those little pictures out of plastic beads, remember? But as soon as I heard the elevator doors open and your footsteps coming down the hall, I'd feel a touch of anxiety too. I used to wonder if you were going to be bad."

He said nothing.

"I mean, 'bad' is the wrong word. You're not bad, you're a very good man, you know? Really." She patted his hand. "But you're . . ." She paused, looking for the right definition. "What's the word I want? Not annoyed, not aggressive. Oh, I know—enraged. Maybe it has to do with your profession, but if I had to choose one feature that characterizes my father, I'd say it's rage."

Luckily, just then the waitress set down two steaming plates of broth with dumplings. Droplets of fat and shredded parsley were pushing their way to the surface, and there were so many piroshki in it that "dumplings in broth" seemed more justified than the traditional "broth with dumplings."

Hela started eating heartily, as if nothing had been said. But he was feeling totally crushed.

"I'm so sorry, I didn't know. I never meant it."

"Jeez, Dad, you look as if you're about to cry," she said with her mouth full. "You asked if I was ever afraid of you, so I told you. If you'd asked about cool stuff, I'd have told you cool stuff. Are you having a midlife crisis, or what? Maybe go find yourself someone younger. Then at least I'd have someone my own age at home—Żenia's older than me. Not much, but still."

In his mind, he couldn't help applauding her. First she'd softened him up, and then she'd gone straight for the jugular. Regretfully, he had to admit she hadn't gotten that from her mother. Those were his genes, no question. She'd gotten her fair share from her mother, too, and she'd be sure to cry at least once before the evening was over and try emotional blackmail again as well. Why hadn't they gone to the movies? They wouldn't have had to talk.

"You're being unfair."

She shrugged. For a while they ate in silence.

"One thing does make me wonder," he said at last. "I'm not asking out of spite. I don't want to argue, so don't take it as an attack. I'm not blind, I can see that you two get along quite well, and maybe you're even friends. Why is it that as soon as I appear, it's like stepping onto a battleground? Why do I always get that kind of treatment?"

"Eat up, cold broth is useless."

He shuddered—he'd heard the exact same words, uttered in exactly the same tone of voice, from the girl's mother a decade ago. *Eat up, cold broth is useless.*

"Since we're being honest," she began after a while, "I do like Żenia. I don't think she's pretty, and she's not particularly brilliant, but she's really smart and perceptive."

"So why the act?"

"It's not an act. I just can't stand seeing the two of you together. It's a physical reaction, like someone stroking me with barbed wire. I can't understand it. Don't ask me to explain."

He didn't.

"Sometimes the worst things are really small, just stupid little things."

He looked at her inquiringly.

"You're going to laugh."

"No, I won't."

"Whenever you watch *Friends* I feel like running away. Seriously, I wanna put on my coat, climb out the window, and run away."

This was unexpected.

"That old crap? We only watch it because it's Żenia's favorite show. She has the entire series on DVD, and I took them off the shelf as a joke. You shouldn't even know that ancient junk exists."

"Dad, I used to fall asleep to that music, didn't you know?"

He didn't.

"I used to fall asleep while you and Mom were watching TV. There must have been a million different shows, but that's the one I remember.

Not the show itself, not the people or the jokes, just the music. To me that music means my home, my childhood, my sense of security that my mom and my dad are right there, watching TV together, and everything's OK, and that's how it's always gonna be."

He started crooning the signature tune.

Hela dropped her head and began to cry.

"I'm sorry," she stammered, and ran to the restroom.

His heart sank. As he ate his food, he wondered what Hela was really missing so badly. Even if he was defined by rage, as he was inclined to agree, then the second pillar of his character was sadness at the transience of life. For as long as he could remember, from early childhood he had nurtured it in himself like a rare and beautiful plant that needed constant care. It looked as if he'd also passed on the gene for this unique, never entirely evaporating sorrow.

After that they talked for another hour. He realized this was a day to commemorate in future years—the day he'd had his first real conversation with the wonderful woman who had done him the honor of being his daughter. They sat there for such a long time that eventually they felt like ordering dessert. They didn't usually want any, because the sweet flavor clashed with the aftertaste of the dumplings.

"I'm sorry for all the fights," said Hela, once they were standing in the arcade outside the café. "You've never hit me and all that, but I still make a fuss."

He kissed her on the forehead.

"Quit talking nonsense. Better bundle up."

For once she obeyed. The temperature must have dropped below freezing; the thick fog had solidified on the sidewalk, coating it in a glistening sheen. In this sort of weather, even teenage girls buttoned up their coats.

"Sometimes I think I'll find a husband who's like you."

He thought about that sometimes, too. He sincerely hoped she wouldn't. But he figured it would be wrong to say that, and he wasn't entirely sure how to respond.

"You're a wonderful, clever woman. And I'm proud you're my daughter."

"Does that mean tomorrow I can . . . ?"

"No. Tuesdays are sacred. I'm expecting two courses and a dessert."

CHAPTER SIX

Tuesday, December 3, 2013

It's International Day of People with Disability, and in Poland it's Oil and Gas Workers Day. Birthday celebrations for Jean-Luc Godard (83) and Trina (35). It has been exactly twenty-one years since the first text message was sent. In Ukraine the opposition fails to force out the government, and the protests intensify. When Berkut special police units beat the demonstrators with batons, the number of people in Kiev's Independence Square increases. Poland has moved up on Transparency International's corruption index from forty-first to thirty-eighth place, ahead of countries including Spain and Greece. And Polish teenagers rank first in Europe in terms of numeracy and literacy in skills tests conducted by the OECD. In Olsztyn the Faculty of Medical Sciences at the University of Warmia and Masuria announces a call for professional patients to do simulations for the students—the requirements are good health and acting skills. It's cold, and the number of crimes committed in the region by people who want to spend the winter in a nice warm cell increases. One such desperado has set fire to the door of a convent in Szczytno. For technical reasons, decking Olsztyn's number one Christmas tree, on the square outside the Town Hall, is delayed. Apart from baubles and lights, there will be crocheted snowflakes hanging from it. There's no real snow, just fog and freezing drizzle.

1

Every city has its wrong side of the tracks—an area that's poorer, inferior, uglier, more parochial, usually hiding its complexes behind showily displayed pride in its otherness. Every place has its backyard, backstage, backwater, or backwoods, separated by a distinct border. Whose residents invariably say, as they head downtown, that they're "off to the city."

Olsztyn was divided by the railroad, and here the Polish name for the area on the other side of the tracks was Zatorze—literally "beyond the tracks"; clearly nobody had ever tried to think up a more romantic name for it.

Szacki left home by car at daybreak, though the sky was still as dark as in the middle of the night, battled his way through the city center, passed the Town Hall and the theater, and finally crossed the tracks, making use of the recently renovated viaduct.

He crossed several junctions and just before reaching a gloomy-looking park he turned into a small street that—if the map on his cell phone was to be believed—was called Radiowa Street. He was curious to see this place. He took a gentle curve, and on the right he passed a park with a large, frozen pond, and on the left a row of fabulous villas. Before the war this must have been an extremely beautiful district—the villas looked grand compared to the usual single-family housing the Germans had built.

A few hundred yards later, he reached the end of the street and his destination. The building clashed dramatically in this attractive district—it was a pseudo-modern glass-and-plastic nightmare, part blue, part red, and bizarrely asymmetrical, as if the architect were suffering from a rare combination of color blindness and astigmatism.

He parked and turned off the engine. He had no desire to get out of his Citroën. It was warm, cozy, and safe in there. On the radio some gal kept singing over and over that she was here to stay. Szacki thought it was a grim prophecy, as if fate were trying to confirm his suspicion that he'd spend the rest of his life in this city of eleven lakes, a thousand showers, and a million fogs.

"As we've just heard, Christina Aguilera isn't going anywhere, and that's awesome, 'cos we'd sure miss her," said the DJ, and Szacki snorted with laughter so abruptly that he spat all over the steering wheel. "Next up, the news, and then our guest will be Teodor Szacki, the one and only star of the legal system, recently appointed press spokesman for our local prosecution service."

"Oh, for fuck's sake."

2

Edmund Falk didn't like making changes to his routine. Not as the result of neurosis or obsessive-compulsive disorder. He simply knew himself well and was sure that as soon as he eased up once, he'd do it again, and soon there'd be nothing left of his routine. He'd been through it so often that finally he'd come to accept that he had to be his own sentry. Otherwise everything he undertook would end the same way as his dance career. He'd started young and talented, one of many in Olsztyn, which has a reputation for producing professional dancers, and then he had advanced to be a rising star and won some junior competitions, but then, between the partying and the love affairs, in a few months it had all been reduced to ruins.

Not that he regretted his dance career, quite the opposite, but there had been a time when he'd thought nothing worse could ever happen to him. And so he'd changed. People laughed at his obsessions, while in fact there was nothing obsessive about his behavior at all. Nothing but the logical choice.

And so now, just as he did every other day at this time, regardless of the weather, he was running through the woods with a steady pulse of 140 beats per minute. He'd already covered two miles and had another four to go.

He never listened to the radio or music while running, but this time he'd brought his phone with him and had put the buds in his ears. He wanted to hear what Szacki would say after the news on Radio Olsztyn.

For now they were still broadcasting music, and he was wondering whether or not he should meet up with Wanda. In theory he'd already made a date with her, but in practice he could call it off. In theory he'd done it for his father's sake, but in practice he was very curious to find out if there was anything left of what had once existed between them. And something really had existed.

In theory he understood that, in his case, commitment was impossible—that was the logical choice. But in practice he'd have latched on to any excuse to see her.

He ran out into Wojsko Polskie Avenue and decided that instead of cutting across the road as usual, he'd run along it for a while. He was feeling strangely anxious, and the lights of civilization seemed more tempting than the deserted paths in the wet woods.

As he ran in the direction of the city center, to his right were the park and the radio building, and to his left the mental hospital. He glanced at the hospital's illuminated windows. And then at his stopwatch. One hundred and sixty beats per minute.

He knew he shouldn't run past here.

3

Szacki took his seat in front of the Radio Olsztyn microphone feeling tense, worried that a badly conducted conversation on the topic of

Najman could lead to media hysteria. One incautious word, and the case of the Warmian serial killer would get out of hand.

Luckily the local radio station turned out to be just as uninterested in controversial topics as the local press. Szacki replied to a few general questions about the city's crime profile. When he was pinned to the wall on the issue of local patriotism, he got out of it by joking that he aimed to become a real Warmian as soon as winter let up and he could learn to sail, because for now instead of eleven lakes it had eleven ice rinks. He brushed off the political question about conflict at the top between the prosecutor general and the prime minister by explaining that as an ordinary investigator he had a different perspective.

He was pleased that his first official media encounter was going so smoothly, but he was pretty bored. The journalist had the low radio voice of a hypnotist, which, combined with the warmth of the cozy little studio, was making Szacki's eyelids droop. He needed coffee.

"The listeners are sending in live comments on our conversation," said the journalist, glancing at his computer screen during the break while a song was playing. "Some about how the system functions in general, critical rather than not. But there's also a joker here asking if there's a serial killer on the prowl in Olsztyn."

The journalist smiled, and Szacki smiled, too, nodding his head. He put as much amiable forbearance into this smile as he could summon, as long as he wouldn't have to answer that question. He couldn't lie, and to say that "at this stage I cannot provide any information on specific inquiries" would throw all Poland's media into a state of alarm.

"And there's also a call from a listener. May I?"

Szacki nodded. Someone was probably going to shower him in abuse because some colleague of his at the other end of Poland had let their town hold a pride march, but better that than having to talk about a serial killer.

All he could hear in the receiver was white noise, and as it crossed his mind that the connection might have been lost, he and all the Radio

Olsztyn listeners sitting in their cars in traffic heard the wavering voice of an old lady: "Good morning, I'm calling to let everyone know that not every prosecutor does nothing but sit at his desk shuffling documents. Mr. Szacki isn't going to say it himself, but a few days ago he saved a woman's life. Not just on paper, but in actual fact—he went into her house and saved her life. A wonderful life saved. Thank you very much, good-bye."

The journalist stared at him in amazement.

"Is that true, Prosecutor?"

Szacki hesitated. He imagined Szarejna and Bikoz at that moment, sitting by the radio, raising their hands in a gesture of triumph, giving each other a high-five or a fist bump. They were right, hurray, success, and more success, Prosecutor Teodor Szacki will be the new face of justice, the sheriff of a new generation, and every prosecutor will want to hang his portrait in their office next to the national emblem. All he had to do was confirm it.

"It's not true," he said. "It is a fact that on the morning of November the twenty-eighth I proceeded . . ." The journalist scowled at Szacki's formal tone, so he broke off abruptly. "In short, on Thursday morning I went to see a woman who the day before had sought my help. I found her dying, having been severely battered by her husband. There was a small child playing beside her. Five minutes later, and he'd have been playing beside his mother's corpse."

There was an awkward silence. The journalist stared at Szacki in astonishment. The producer in the control room started making desperate signs at them to say something.

"I can only congratulate you," said the journalist at last.

"Not necessarily. The woman is still in a critical state. If I weren't such a mindless pen pusher and had listened to that lady the day before, instead of ignoring her cry for help, there'd have been no need to save her. If I had behaved correctly, that woman, a victim of domestic violence, and her child would have been guaranteed legal and psychological help. She wouldn't have had to return to her husband, and she wouldn't have had to lie dying on the kitchen floor. I would like to take this opportunity to apologize in public to that lady, her son, and her family. I'm deeply ashamed, and I wish I could turn back time. I'm sorry."

"We all make mistakes," said the journalist sententiously, and he pointed at the clock to let Szacki know their time was almost up.

He had woken up now and felt his irritation rising. *Rage,* that's how Hela had put it. He liked that word—it gave his aggression a touch of grandeur and righteousness.

"Of course. But if you make a mistake, then a truck driver on his way to Augustów hears Beyoncé instead of Rihanna. If I make a mistake, if I fail to perceive a threat, or to eliminate a menace from society, someone's life could come to an end."

"I can see your point," said the journalist, adjusting his trendy glasses—at last he was taking an interest—"but there's a catch in that way of thinking. The human factor is the weakest, most accident-prone element in any system. But it's usually indispensable. If we accepted your way of thinking, fear of making a mistake could become so crippling that nobody would ever choose to become a prosecutor, a judge, or a neurosurgeon. We can't eliminate the errors, because we can't eliminate the human being."

"We can," said Szacki. "We only have to switch off the autopilot and carefully consider every single one of the decisions we make each day. That way we can avoid mistakes." Szacki smiled and decided to give his junior a present. "It's the logical choice."

The producer signaled that time was up.

"That was Prosecutor Teodor Szacki. We're just coming up to the regional news, and before that there's still time to hear something stirring for a change, so here on Radio Olsztyn it's Aerosmith—this one's for those of you who haven't quite woken up yet: 'Janie's Got a Gun'!"

The little red light went out, and Szacki put his headphones on the table as the unmistakable opening chords of the evergreen hit by the guy with the monster mouth resounded.

He quickly said good-bye and ran out of the radio station.

He didn't get far. On Wojsko Polskie Avenue he got stuck in a jam, and as he stared at the brake lights of the Nissan ahead of him, he thought what a small town Olsztyn is. And that sooner or later the paths of those responsible for organizing the traffic in this poor excuse for a provincial capital were bound to cross his. And then he, Prosecutor Teodor Szacki, would change into a terrible avenging angel.

4

Two hundred yards away, Angela Zemsta felt like taking a Xanax. She was desperate for it. She decided she would just take one without worrying about getting addicted. At her age, and with her experience, she knew perfectly well that if she was going to get hooked on anything it would have happened long ago. And although in her working environment it wasn't popular, but was actually considered a joke, she believed in the theory promoted by some research centers that to become an addict you had to have something special about you. Maybe it was a gene, or maybe a protein, maybe an extra fraction of a drop of one particular hormone. Angela Zemsta didn't have that special something. And so her life was under her control and hers alone. She didn't believe in God, she was sure love is a deep friendship between two people rather than some mystical merging of souls, and she made purely recreational use of a popular mind-altering substance with the chemical formula C_2H_5OH.

Only once in her life had her red light come on. Only once in her life had she felt fear that an emotion and a substance could take control of her life. The emotion was calm, and the substance was alprazolam, a psychotropic benzodiazepine prescribed for anxiety disorders, better known by its brand name Xanax. She had tried various drugs in her life for academic purposes, but the first time she took Xanax she felt like Saint Paul on the road to Damascus. She had a revelation, wanted to fall to her knees, burst into tears, and set out into the world to spread the good news, to teach people with the help of fancy metaphors that peace and happiness are within reach, that they come with a bitter taste in the shape of an oval pill. She could add a bit of sexism and xenophobia, without which no religion ever achieves success, and hallelujah—she could have been a prophet for the god Pfizer.

But after a brief period of fascination she had stopped taking Xanax, and in the past twenty years she had only turned to it a few times, when she was in a rare state of extreme stress. She was very proud of this achievement, because if anything was missing in the closets, drawers, and gowns here at the mental hospital, it certainly wasn't Xanax. They handed it out to the patients like candy, took it themselves, and prescribed it for their friends—there were truckloads of it here. In this hospital, it was harder to find a bottle of water than a tab of Xanax.

Now she realized she wasn't going to manage without one. She went to the consulting room, dug a blister pack of pills out of a drawer, swallowed a 0.25mg tablet, opened Minesweeper on her computer, and waited for the benzodiazepine to join up with her GABAA receptor, thanks to which her palms would stop sweating.

She flicked on the radio, heard Steven Tyler howling "Janie's Got a Gun," and instantly switched it off again. Why is it that whenever a rock musician takes up the topic of domestic violence, someone immediately grabs a six-shooter and hands out rough justice? Apparently that's the only course of events that suits a strident guitar solo.

What a good thing that as chief resident in charge of the department, nobody could hustle her. She opened the browser and found "Baby Can I Hold You" on YouTube. For a moment she hesitated, but finally she pressed Play. Bad move—tears sprang to her eyes. She'd been through it so many times before, her therapist must have been truly sick of the subject. If anything ever went wrong, she always picked at that scab, put salt in the wound, and poked it with a needle. But there was no helping it. For the rest of her life she'd be wondering, along with Tracy Chapman, if things would have been different if she'd found the right words to say. If she'd found a way to get through to him.

The song ended. Angela wiped her eyes, listened to a few more of Tracy's songs, and suddenly felt as if there were more room for air in her lungs. She took several deep breaths, and felt a wave of calm flow over her.

She picked up a file from the desk, hung a magnetic key card around her neck, and decided to start with the new patient, to get it over with as soon as possible. She knocked at the nurses' door.

"Marek," she said, "just in case, OK?"

Without a word, Marek put aside his breakfast and followed Angela. He was the antithesis of the typical image of a psychiatric nurse—not a tall, burly guy with a dumb grin whose mom makes him corned beef sandwiches to take to work, and who's only just on this side of the divide between patients and staff. Marek was intelligent and full of empathy, his personal life was in order, and he was fit. As an Israeli martial arts instructor, he didn't need the advantage of size to cope with the violent patients. Angela figured he'd make an excellent therapist or maybe even a doctor. But he came from such meager beginnings deep in the Warmian countryside that, despite major effort, he had only managed to clamber up to the post of staff nurse. Marek's career was conclusive proof for Angela that not everyone can forge their own destiny. And even if you can, a lot depends on whether you've got a good set of tools from the start or have to steal your first hammer.

They walked in silence down a long corridor; the isolation room was at the far end of the ward. Psychiatric observation of criminals was usually done in special wards at the custody jails. This was an exceptional situation, as the young prosecutor who looked like Peter Sellers had explained to her. It wasn't about the suspect's sanity. The point was to confirm whether or not the suspect had any idea of his own identity, his situation, and the charges against him.

"He seems to be functioning," said the prosecutor. "He drinks and goes to the toilet. He brushes his teeth and gets undressed at bedtime. But everything else is switched off."

That was the first time she felt the hairs on the back of her neck stand up. She asked for more details.

"He doesn't communicate at all. And when I say 'at all,' I mean it quite literally. It's as if he were in a space of his own. He hasn't said a word since he was detained. Not a peep."

Angela put a lot of effort into not letting it show how much this conversation cost her. She asked if they thought the man was faking.

"I hope so. Only then will we be able to isolate him from society."

She asked what he'd done.

"Wife-beater. He'd been harassing her, and when she made up her mind to leave, he almost killed her. He left her unconscious on the kitchen floor, alone with a three-year-old child. No one knows if she'll survive."

Angela felt weak at the knees. To keep up the appearance of a professional conversation, she said it was unheard of—perpetrators of domestic violence are usually proud of what they've done. She'd never heard of one having pangs of conscience, not to mention going mute.

The prosecutor had agreed. Despite his youth, he seemed well qualified.

She stopped at the door separating the last stretch of corridor from the rest of the ward.

"Doctor," said Marek, "would it be OK for me to bring in my daughter during your shift tomorrow evening?"

"Tonsils again?" she asked.

"It looks like it, but we want to see if her ears are all right. So we won't have the same problem as in the spring."

"Of course." She smiled. She didn't mind that plenty of people on the ward, including some of the patients' families, "exploited" her other specialty as a laryngologist. When she had her breakdown and dropped psychiatry, she'd taken a feel-good job at a family clinic, where she'd gained a fine reputation as an ear, nose, and throat specialist. Then she'd gone back to psychiatry because it really was her passion and vocation, but she still gave laryngological advice now and then, and enjoyed it too. Everyday infections that could be cured with a single antibiotic made a nice change from her usual occupation.

She pressed the key card against the reader.

5

Edmund Falk had not withdrawn his application for Szacki to be reprimanded. Moreover, rather than trying to make him change his mind, Szacki was backing him up. It was driving their boss crazy—she took it as a personal affront, and that day she had already had two pally conversations with "Edmund darling" and "dear Misterteo." Smiling warmly, appealing to professional solidarity, friendship, camaraderie, and empathy, she urged them to sort it out between them. Her speech was peppered with proverbs, Buddhist digressions about karma, and a Christian plea for mercy.

It all bounced off them. Falk believed he was doing the right thing, and Szacki thought so too. Paradoxically, though nobody else could understand it, their agreement on a matter that ought to be making them argue was causing a thread of sympathy to form between the two men.

"I must admit I find your decision a little disappointing," said Falk, stirring a cup of instant coffee.

They were sitting in Szacki's office, waiting for Chief Commissioner Jarosław Klejnocki to appear. The police psychologist who created psychological profiles of criminals had already arrived from Kraków, but apparently he absolutely had to go see Copernicus's medical incunabula at the castle museum first. Szacki didn't protest, he had come across innumerable eccentrics in his career, and in fact Klejnocki was a fairly ordinary example, compared with Dr. Frankenstein, for instance, or the junior prosecutor sitting in front of him.

"I'm sorry I've failed to live up to your high standards yet again. Anyway, I thought you'd be delighted. After all, it's your FBI gurus who came up with the whole idea of profiling and behavioral analysis."

Falk sipped his coffee and scowled—it was hard to tell whether it was because of the coffee or Szacki's words.

"Profiling seemed to me suspect from the start," said Falk. "Too good to be true. A guy reads the files, analyzes them, and then says, 'You'll find him in a bar, he'll be eating a hamburger with extra cheese, and reading the sports page, and he'll have a gift for his mother in his briefcase.' If something's so contrived that it sounds like it's out of a crime novel, it has to be suspicious. But I decided that rather than let myself be led by my emotions, I'd look into the matter."

"And?"

"I found out they'd done a series of tests designed to confirm the effectiveness of profiling. They gave the files from cases that had already been solved to some profilers, and at the same time they also gave them to students from various disciplines, regular police detectives, and psychologists. Each of them was asked to create a profile of the criminal on the basis of the files, which were then compared with the real culprit, who was well known to them, because as I've said, all the cases they used as examples had been solved long ago and the criminals convicted. So what was the result? None of the profiles produced by the professionals were any more accurate than the ones the others came up with, including the amateur criminologists. While significantly, the chemistry and biology students did extremely well."

"Significantly, but not surprisingly," said Szacki. "In the world of science there's a place for logic, common sense, drawing conclusions on the basis of hard evidence, and verifying those conclusions."

"Whereas profiling is a fraud. That's the conclusion I reached, and then I was sure I don't believe in it. It was the logical choice."

Falk stopped talking, and for a while they sat in silence.

"I refuse to believe that you believe in it."

"Of course I don't," said Szacki. "I regard psychology as a pseudo science, and psychological profiling of criminals is just a nice name for what a clairvoyant does. If someone repeats ten times that he can see a body in the woods, he must be right three times out of ten—after all, one-third of this country is forest, and it's easier to bury a corpse there than along the highway."

"In that case, why are we meeting with the profiler?"

"He's a smart guy. Weird, but really smart. And he's read more files than you'll ever set your eyes on. He talks about irrelevant bullshit, as they all do, but sometimes he says a thing or two that make sense."

"A thing or two?" Falk was unable to hide his contempt.

Szacki didn't comment. Falk was right, in his way, but there were some things he'd only understand after fifteen years on the job. For example, that an investigation is like a jigsaw puzzle, a really tricky one, a seascape of ocean waves at night, with ten thousand pieces. At some point you have all those pieces lying on the table, but they're damned hard to connect. And that's when you need someone who can take a look at them and say, "Hey, that's not the moon, just its reflection in the waves."

6

Thanks to the Xanax, she could actually enter the isolation room instead of quivering in fear outside it. But it couldn't switch off her emotions. The sorrow caused by her memories of the past competed with the physical repulsion she felt at the sight of the pale man sitting on the bed. She knew this sense of disgust was highly unprofessional, but she couldn't help it.

The man was making no effort to communicate. She soon realized it wasn't for lack of ability, but lack of desire. It wasn't that his brain had decided to log out of the world of its own accord, as in the case of most patients on this ward. It looked like a fully conscious decision. Observation would confirm that, and then it would be up to the prosecutors to decide what to do with him. She wasn't going to do the observation herself, but she would personally ensure that no court was in any doubt about the suspect's sanity.

She wondered what the cause of his lack of communication might be. In her view his cast-iron consistency indicated that there must be more to it than just ordinary fakery, a calculated tactic to avoid punishment. Pangs of conscience? It would be the first time she'd ever heard of some punch-drunk wife-beater acquiring a conscience. You could write an entire doctorate on that. Shock? More likely. Trauma? But what kind? Like all wife-beaters, he must have been a victim of violence during his childhood. Maybe the suppressed memory of some monstrous experience had surfaced.

Maybe they'd manage to find out, if they could get through to him.

As that last thought occurred, she was flooded by a wave of grief. She gathered all her willpower and thirty years' professional experience to stop herself from bursting into tears in front of the patient. She'd sat on a stool in just the same way then, she'd thought things through in just the same way, and tried to find a way to open up the patient.

She got a grip on herself.

"Please remember that we don't work for the police or the prosecution service," she said. "We're doctors, and regardless of why you've ended up in here, we want to help you. You're surrounded by people who care. We're going to come and ask questions, and we're not going to stop trying to communicate. But if you were to decide for yourself that you want to talk, we're here for you at any time of day or night. We're here to listen, with kindness and understanding, and we're here to help, in whatever way you wish. Whatever brings you relief and makes you feel better. We're your friends. Do you understand that?"

She was counting on the trick working. Combined with a positive message, her gentle, velvety voice of an experienced therapist would make him forget himself and nod his head. It would be a nice step toward total sanity, and a long stretch in a penal facility.

But he didn't move a muscle. She noticed that he was morbidly pale, as if he were suffering from anemia or had lost a lot of blood. She made a note to do a blood test.

She glanced toward the corridor. Marek was leaning against the wall, watching what was happening inside. Vigilantly, but patiently. She understood that he probably had something more urgent to do than just stare at a conversation with a man who didn't respond. She nodded to indicate that she'd be done in a moment.

"I'll be off now. I'll come back after my evening rounds, all right? Maybe you'll feel like a chat then. And not just food." She forced herself to smile and pointed at his breakfast tray. He'd drunk the hot chocolate, but the cheese sandwich was still there, untouched. "Please eat something, all right? You're a big guy, you won't get far on nothing but hot chocolate."

She stood up and was on her way to the door when the man was shaken by a short fit of coughing that he stifled by keeping his mouth shut. It sounded strange, a bit like a cough, and a bit like a gagging reflex. She turned around. He was sitting on the bed in the same position, with his gaze fixed on the wall, but his fingers were gripping the bedsheets. She could see that he was putting such a lot of effort into restraining his coughing fit that his eyes had glazed over.

She went closer. A wet bronchial cough, as if his lungs were trying to get rid of something. She'd heard it at the clinic hundreds of times.

Trying to suppress that sort of cough was pointless—the body so often knew best in the fight for health.

Panic appeared in the man's eyes. As if a stupid coughing fit were a threat. He was battling as hard as he could against his bronchial tubes, and if not for the circumstances, it would have been comical.

Shaken by spasms, he was starting to drop the act. He glanced at Angela with hysteria in his eyes, a fraction of a split second, but it was enough for her to confirm her conviction that there could be no question of insanity.

Finally the coughing eased, and once it stopped, the man breathed heavily through his nose.

Something wasn't right.

Angela nodded to Marek, who instantly came inside and gave her a questioning look.

"Please take the patient over to the window," she said.

Her tone of friendship and empathy had evaporated, and now she was the chief resident. And the laryngologist. She had no disposable gloves, no speculum or spatula, but she figured she could take a look at his throat anyway. There was something disturbing about that cough.

The man meekly got up from the bed as Marek took him by the arm. Only now did she notice that the bed had been made in a very strange way. The top end of it had been carefully covered with a blanket, so carefully that two feet of quilt and sheets were sticking out at the foot of it. Nobody makes a bed like that.

She went closer, and pulled off the blanket with a decisive tug. Nothing. The pillow was covered by the quilt. She raised the quilt, and once again found nothing. A pillow on a sheet. She was about to put the quilt back in place, but she peeked under the pillow too.

She gasped. The sheet underneath the pillow and the underside of the pillow were soaked in blood, as if the man had been bleeding into them all night long.

Something was very wrong indeed.

"Please open your mouth," she said, walking up to the window.

The man trembled and shook his head; there was a look of such extreme terror in his eyes that, in spite of it all, Angela felt sorry for him.

"Please, sir, this is no time for silly games. We all know there's nothing wrong with you and that I could just as well write my assessment today. I'm a doctor, I need to examine you. Please quit fooling around and open your mouth."

As she leaned forward, the man opened his mouth wide.

She peered into the bloody hole, and instantly regretted it.

7

Chief Commissioner Jarosław Klejnocki had transformed. The old Klejnocki, with glasses as thick as transparent armor, a beard, and a pipe, had been the textbook example of an eccentric intellectual whose statements can be divided into incisive, iconoclastic, and thought-provoking.

The 2013 model looked like a fifty-year-old academic, who after many years in a happy and passionate relationship with his bookshelves, has fallen in love with a busty student. He had shaved off his beard, swapped his glasses for contact lenses, his tweedy jacket for a hoodie, and his practical haircut for a gel-styled spiky look. And he was probably convinced these efforts took twenty years off him.

He was wrong.

He refused coffee, but took a bottle of water and a plastic container full of bean sprouts from his sports bag.

He made a gesture as if wanting to run his fingers through his hair, but must have remembered the gel at the last moment and withdrew his hand. Instead, he ate some sprouts, the typical compulsive behavior of someone who recently gave up smoking.

"Prosecutor Szacki, you're lucky I have some respect for you. Normally there would be no question of rattling about on the Polish railroad all day to get to this land of eternal fog and freezing drizzle."

Falk shifted nervously, and to his own amazement, Szacki felt offended.

"I thought a trip away from the land of smog, stale air, and petty bourgeois thinking would do you good. Even you people must sometimes have to breathe in something other than curtain dust and the smell of British vomit."

Klejnocki squinted in surprise.

"Eleven lakes within the city limits," said Szacki, unable to believe he had actually uttered those words. "Two months of fog is a small price to pay for living in a tourist resort, don't you think?"

"I think rheumatism is a terrible affliction. But you'll soon find out for yourself."

"Let's get down to business," said Falk.

Klejnocki pulled out an iPad. He delayed unblocking the screen long enough for them to see a picture of a chubby brunette in a halter top. Well, she wasn't exactly Lauren Bacall, but she was probably unrivaled when it came to filing and indexing.

"I've familiarized myself with all the material, and I have several theories that might help you. But I must ask a few additional questions."

For the next half hour Szacki specified in minute detail the findings of the investigation, sometimes supported by Falk, who was able to demonstrate his analytical mind to such an extent that Szacki felt envious that he hadn't been as brilliant at Falk's age.

When they were done, Klejnocki mulled it all over, while eating sprouts instead of lighting his pipe. He peeped into the near-empty box with the expression of a smoker who only has one cigarette left in the packet, and set aside the rest of his snack for later.

"My answer is the stake," he said.

They gave him quizzical looks.

"You, I understand, are a native of this locality as yet untouched by civilization?" he said, addressing Falk, who nodded, and then he continued. "Then your mom and dad will surely have shown you the castle at

Reszel—it's only forty miles from here in the direction of Kaliningrad. Did they?"

Falk confirmed that they had.

"So at this castle, in the early nineteenth century, the German powers, famous for their enlightenment, imprisoned a woman called Barbara Zdunk for four years in terrible conditions, apparently pimping her left and right to while away the time until there was a verdict in her case. This verdict was finally reached in Königsberg, where Germany's most enlightened judges condemned the woman to burn at the stake. Yes, my dear Warmian sir, the last time anyone was burned at the stake in Europe was in Holy Warmia." He dug a small sprout out of the box and ate it. "Why am I bringing this up? Because I think what happened to your victim is today's equivalent of the stake. A modern stake, a chemical one, without any smoke or fire. If we accept this hypothesis and take a look at the history of burning at the stake, we can, by analogy, draw some conclusions about your culprit. Do you follow me, gentlemen?"

"Yes," said Szacki.

"Which doesn't mean we agree with you," added Falk.

Klejnocki smiled.

"Well, I never, the Prince of Reason in person. You probably believe in hard evidence, DNA tests, indisputable statements, and fingerprints left on the doorframe. And you probably regard my field as shamanism, the ravings of a lunatic who didn't fancy working in a hospital and who's too nutty for private practice, so he had to find himself a niche. Am I right?"

Falk made a polite gesture implying that he could only agree.

"I don't mind, very few people think otherwise. But please allow me to finish, seeing the taxpayer has already shelled out for my journey from Kraków."

Szacki decided that if Falk provoked Klejnocki into digressive effusions again, he'd turn the little punk out.

"Treat this like an intellectual exercise," said the scientist, a little sourly; evidently his role was rarely questioned so blatantly. "That's all. It won't hurt, and it might mean you fall upon something that turns out to be important."

"Doctor," said Szacki, unable to stop himself, "please get on with it."

"I've found several analogies. The first is that those who burned others at the stake in Europe were convinced they were acting righteously. Of course they were deranged, murderous madmen, just like your culprit. But there was a form of logic in their madness—it had an ideological, legal, procedural foundation. The prosecutors and judges went to bed with a sense of having done their duty, and the next morning they felt pleased to be helping society, purging the world of the bane of witches."

"Like in *Seven*," said Falk.

"Exactly. But in this version, don't go looking for Hannibal Lecter and his ilk, who kill for the pleasure of inflicting suffering. Look for someone who believes he's the only righteous man alive. He'd rather be enjoying a quiet barbecue at home, but what choice does he have when the world needs purging?"

"So that means Najman paid for a crime he had committed?"

"Yes, but we cannot predict the extent of the Righteous One's mental disorder. Perhaps the victim illegally dumped toxic waste in the lake, and the killer is an eco-warrior? Please don't forget for an instant that we're dealing with a deranged mind. A seriously deranged mind."

Klejnocki reached for the sprouts—there were only a few left.

"The second analogy is the public arena. Even if the, uh, inquisition-style preparatory proceedings were conducted in a dungeon, the executions took place in public, to entertain and act as a warning to the crowd. And to advertise the executioners."

"That's not an analogy," said Falk, shrugging. "Najman most probably died in some godforsaken spot, and then his remains were hidden

in a long-forgotten bunker. And, unfortunately, the culprit isn't standing in the marketplace waiting for applause."

"I think you're wrong, Mr. Falk," said Klejnocki. "The remains
weren't hidden—you found them a few days later."

"By coincidence."

"Do you really believe in coincidence? You, a man of reason? But
let's skip the nasty jibes," he said, seeing Szacki's glare. "Even to begin
with, when you thought the bones belonged to a single person, it wasn't
very likely that anyone was trying to bury them there. And since you've
known that the skeleton was carefully composed from several people,
it has become totally unlikely. Nobody goes to such lengths without a
purpose. This skeleton was meant to be found. And quickly. If there
hadn't been roadwork in progress, the culprit would have found another
way."

"I can agree with that," said Falk, "but it still isn't analogous to a
public execution. The act was performed in secret, and hardly anybody
knows about it apart from us. You're wrong."

Szacki clenched his hands so hard under the table that his fingernails pressed painfully into the base of his thumb.

"Excuse me, but this is the twenty-first century, our latter-day
inquisitor has to act in secret because otherwise you'd have locked him
up at once. And then how would he deliver justice? But as for a public
execution, please give him a chance. It wouldn't take much for all the
media to leap on it, as you're perfectly well aware. These days it's harder
to steer a radio-controlled car than the media."

"So why hasn't he done it yet?" Falk refused to let up and finally ran
into Szacki's gaze. Addressing his supervisor, he added, "It isn't even a
theory, it's some sort of hallucination. I'm afraid we'll be taken in by it,
and get led down the wrong path."

"You could say the flames aren't high enough yet," Klejnocki continued. "The culprit wants his deeds to be noticed in all their glory. First
you found the remains. Later you discovered they're fresh. Then you

found out about the horrible death inflicted on the victim. Then that the remains are 'multiperson.' Soon you're sure to find something that makes his deed even more spectacular. And then it'll be running across the news ticker on every TV screen in the country. That's the best-case scenario."

"Best-case?"

"That you'll discover something that has already happened. The worst-case scenario is that he'll present you with another corpse, or several—he'll go for quantity, rather than quality. He's crazy, let's not forget."

Szacki didn't like the sound of Klejnocki's argument. He sincerely hoped the colorful hypothesis had nothing to do with reality.

"Third, he's not a lone hunter . . ."

"Bullshit!" said Falk. "The behavioral analysis is unambiguous—serial killers always act alone."

"You're insulting me by putting me on a par with those charlatans from the FBI who claim they're capable of predicting what tie he'll be wearing and which nostril he'll be picking when he's arrested." The scientist had lost his temper. "What I do is not behavioral analysis. It's an attempt to think in parallel, as a means of getting you out of a rut, opening your narrow prosecutor minds to something other than what you've already thought of."

"If this conversation costs you so much energy," said Szacki in an icy tone to Falk, "I would remind you that you're not actually involved in this investigation, and your presence is not compulsory."

For a moment Falk looked as if he might explode, but then he did up the top button of his jacket and nodded by way of apology.

"Third," repeated Klejnocki, "in this narrative, the culprit is not a lone hunter. The stakes were set alight because the force of an institution stood behind them. Also the law, as I have mentioned. Have you considered the existence of a sect?"

Szacki shook his head.

"I'm aware that it's a fantastical hypothesis. But we're living at a historical turning point. The financial crisis, social inequalities, relativism, a move away from religion, the insane Putin just across the border. These are traditionally the times when all sorts of psychics, prophets, and shamans come out to prey on human uncertainty. Besides, if we accept the idea that the culprit isn't acting alone, a lot of things about this case become easier to explain. For one person, a kidnap, an elaborate murder, and then dumping the corpse is a huge undertaking—only a genius could do all that alone. With several people to help, it wouldn't take a genius, just an efficient manager."

"I understand," said Falk with artificial calm, "but I'd like it on record that I don't agree with you. The killing of Najman and the others is the work of a lone madman, and it's impossible to share madness with others."

"Tell that to the Holy Inquisition and your Warmian forebears who joined the Hitler Youth."

"I object to that. I come from a long line of Warmian Poles who were persecuted by the Germans."

"I see," said Klejnocki, smiling wickedly.

Szacki counted down from five to stop himself from exploding.

"Gentlemen," he said very calmly, "as far as I'm concerned you can debate this for hours when we're done. But please, let's finish first."

"Fourth and last," said Klejnocki, holding up four splayed fingers. "This hypothesis assumes a motivation that we could call systematic. For the culprit, purging society is the overriding aim, and that's the key to his choice of victims. But in the process he's guided by some particular code, or the principles for specific and general deterrence as known to us from theories of law. In other words, he wants to punish a criminal or send out a message to potential criminals, to say that he and his code are on alert, and that they should watch out because his methods are much more stringent than those applied by the regular forces of law and order. This theory supposes that personal motives play no role at all. The avenging angel is not guided by such inferior motives as family injustices."

"That brings us back to the same point of doubt," said Szacki. "If the principle of general deterrence is going to apply, then the case has to be publicized. If society doesn't know about it, the action makes no sense."

"And it brings us back to the same answer. Perhaps the case is going to be publicized in a while. It's worth considering whether you'd prefer to publicize it sooner yourselves, on your own terms. An overtaking maneuver, putting a spoke in his wheel. This madman seems neurotically well organized—foiling their plans usually has a bad effect on that sort of person. Perhaps he'll make a mistake."

For a while Szacki considered this proposition. It made sense. The case was too unusual, and the way they were proceeding was too ordinary and predictable. Doing something unexpected could bring a positive result.

"Women were burned at the stake," said Falk. "But our victim is a man. Very masculine, too."

"Equality cuts both ways," said Klejnocki, shrugging.

"And what if you were tempted to produce the typical profile?" said Szacki. "To create a portrait of the culprit, according to the theory you've put forward. In this version he is, as you said, neurotically precise, planning it all very carefully, and he's convinced his actions are right. Anything else?"

The psychologist ate the last bean sprout. He thought for a while.

"Fair, shoulder-length hair," he said in a confident tone. "Two kids, the older one's astigmatic. His wife works for a paint-mixing service. He suffers from gephyrophobia, a rare psychological affliction manifesting itself in a pathological fear of crossing bridges. That's why all his victims will be found on the same side of the river."

Szacki and Falk stared at him in silence.

They didn't even blink.

"Jeez, you guys are so humorless!" said Klejnocki. "I've thought of two things that in practice would have to be present in the profile of this sort of culprit. One, he has definitely experienced personal injustice. But, *nota bene*, not just from another person, but from the system too—for some reason it didn't work for him. That's why he has decided to give the system a hand. And two, this sort of activity demands knowledge of people, of their lives and doings. He has to have a way of seeking out those who deserve to be punished. If it's not about polluting the lake or screwing someone on the side, but about punishable offenses, he has to know enough to get to that person before the law does."

"Who has that sort of knowledge?" asked Falk.

"A priest. A therapist. A policeman. A prosecutor—you don't have to look far. A doctor."

Szacki cast a watchful glance at Falk. But he was looking the other way, gazing out of the window.

"I can see that a doctor fits the bill for you." Klejnocki couldn't hide his satisfaction.

Before he could carry on, Falk's cell phone rang.

"Speaking of doctors," muttered Falk, looking at his phone, "I'm sorry, I've got to take this."

He left the room, closing the door behind him, but Szacki and Klejnocki hadn't had time to exchange a word before he was back. Szacki glanced at Falk and understood the meeting was over.

8

Dr. Angela Zemsta radiated calm. In a world of people who are agitated, hypersensitive, stressed out, and tense, she was like an oasis of natural serenity. Szacki felt very good in her company and was wondering if she owed her tranquility to therapy or meditation, or perhaps she had simply seen so much by now in her life as a clinical psychiatrist that even if she'd seen the *Hindenburg* bursting into flames outside the window, she'd have smiled sweetly and tossed a packet of popcorn into the microwave.

"I don't entirely understand," he said, after listening to her brief report. "So he can't speak, or he refuses to?"

"I'll put it another way. He doesn't want to communicate with you. If he did, he'd certainly find a way. He could use paper or tap something out on a cell phone. I can also provisionally say that his lack of communication is the result of a conscious decision, not a pathological state. But even if he did want to communicate with you he couldn't do it verbally, because his vocal organs have not just been removed, they've been devastated."

"Which parts in particular?" asked Falk.

"All of them. We need to do an ultrasound and an MRI to get a proper appraisal of the extent of the damage, but I've never seen anything like it. His teeth have been knocked out, his tongue has literally been torn out, and his vocal cords are in tatters."

"Severed?"

"I expect that as prosecutors you have some knowledge of anatomy. The vocal folds are not actually cords that can be severed, but delicate pieces of muscle fixed within the larynx, looking a bit like labia. They're very easily destroyed, which is why nature has hidden them."

Szacki glanced at Falk. He had questions, but he realized he was acting as supervisor, and Falk should be asking the questions in his own investigation.

"Do you have a theory about how these injuries were inflicted?"

"I do a lot of cycling," she said—it occurred to Szacki that maybe physical exercise was the source of her calm—"and I often stop at a crosswalk. You know what Olsztyn's like, the lights are always red. And to avoid having to get off my bike, I grab hold of the red-and-white post that stands in front of the crosswalk. And that was my first thought when I looked down that man's throat. That someone had taken one of those metal posts and used it to, forgive the expression, orally rape him."

They were silent. Outside the window, dusk was already falling, and beyond the dark patch of the park, Szacki could see the lights of the radio building where that very morning he had given an interview. He recognized it by the unusual windows, very tall and narrow.

"Could he have done it himself?" asked Falk. "Mutilated himself as a punishment for what he did to his wife? I've seen various things people were driven to by pangs of conscience."

"I've said this a hundred times to all sorts of people, and I'll say it to you: Wife-beaters don't have pangs of conscience, because in their world they don't do any wrong. They just take advantage of their sacred right to discipline others, to educate, to punish, and call to order. They manage their two-legged property in a way they regard as correct. They're usually proud of it, and pangs of conscience simply don't enter into it, nor does shame. Of course some of them acknowledge that the world has gone to shit, and these days they might get into trouble for beating their wives. But that doesn't change anything, they simply do the beating without leaving any marks, or else they replace physical violence with psychological, and instead of beating their wives, they find ways to humiliate them. Got it?"

They said yes.

"There's a specific dehumanization process at work here. I don't like to draw comparisons with Nazism, because it's always the ultimate argument, but discriminating against ethnic minorities and the sexism that's at the root of domestic abuse both carry the hallmarks of systematic violence, permitted as the result of ideological indoctrination. In killing the Jews, the Germans weren't committing murder, because the Jews weren't people, just Jews—so they were taught. And that freed them from responsibility. Perpetrators of domestic violence have also been taught that women aren't human, but a subspecies whose representatives are their property. That's why as a psychiatrist I can guarantee that self-mutilation is out of the question. But even if we accepted the fantastical assumption that he did it himself, it's doubtful he'd have dressed his own wounds."

"Dressed his own wounds? You said he's still hemorrhaging."

"Yes, he's bleeding, and there's blood collecting in his lungs, too, but compared with the scale of the injuries it's nothing, just a cut. Your client hasn't bled to death because the major blood vessels have been sewn up. Maybe not professionally enough for the person who did the stitches to find work as a plastic surgeon, but well enough for them to scrape through a college exam."

9

Six p.m.

Szacki went inside and hung up his coat, but, sadly, there was no delicious aroma of a hot meal to greet him. He went into the kitchen and dug out a carton of tomato juice from the fridge. He shook it. Full, or almost full. Damn, he couldn't remember if he'd opened it or not.

He put a glass on the kitchen counter and unscrewed the cap, only to find white, fluffy mold blossoming underneath. So he had opened it.

He poured the juice down the drain, poured himself some water, and sat down at the kitchen table.

Szacki felt hungry. As he'd learned from the lesson of the past week, he didn't start to shake with rage but checked to see if there were any text messages from his daughter about why there was nothing on the stove. Then he called Żenia. He found out the little brat had not checked in with her, hadn't made any excuses, or apologized. She'd done nothing.

Maybe that was for the best, he thought; this time she wouldn't escape the punitive hand of justice.

He started calling her, unable to get over the fact that in spite of it all, she had treated yesterday evening as an excuse to get out of her one and only chore. She'd asked directly, and he'd said no directly, but even so she'd made light of it. What was this about? Was she messed up in some way? Maybe she'd done something he didn't know about and was subconsciously doing everything she could to receive punishment and cause a fight? Or maybe her hormones were making her lose control of herself?

Of course she didn't answer. Incredible. He sent her a nasty text message and decided to make pasta with pesto, the fallback of everyone who isn't fond of cooking but doesn't like the idea of starving to death.

Seven p.m.

Żenia got home just before the news came on, which was a relief to him, because he was finding it hard to cope with his rising anxiety. Until then, he'd done some cleaning and cooking. He'd found a bunch of asparagus in the freezer, so he had steamed it, cut it up, and added it to the pasta. He'd also added some grated pecorino, which he rated higher than parmesan, extracted an emergency bottle of wine from the back of the pantry, and hey, presto! There was a first-rate supper.

"Call her, she can eat with us," said Żenia, sitting at table.

"There's only enough for two."

"Drop it, give her a call."

"No."

"Then at least find out if everything's OK."

"I tried calling, but she didn't pick up."

Of course her eyebrow shot up.

"Aha. And what do you think—why's that?"

He thought for a while, as he mixed the pasta. It wasn't exactly refined, but he liked it when a big spoonful of cheese melted into the noodles.

"Just a second, I'll try to remember some of the most typical lies. In Warsaw the usual reason she couldn't answer was that she just happened to be in the subway when I called—to a point where she was almost always in the subway, walking down the tunnels, no doubt! Here there isn't even a tramway, so that excuse is gone. Or else she says her battery ran out, or she switched her phone to silent like a good student and forgot to switch it on again, or she put it deep in her bag so thieves wouldn't attack her and steal her precious gizmo. There are frequent accidents, too. A popular excuse is to 'blame the drizzle.' If she calls from outside, something happens to make her lose the connection. Every time I hear that, it just makes me wonder."

"Well?"

"Doesn't she know what I do for a living? I've spent the past twenty years listening to all sorts of cutthroats and villains, so she should at least have enough respect for me to think up a more sophisticated lie. I think that's what hurts the most—the fact that she tries to deceive me with any old crap. It makes me feel she doesn't respect me as a prosecutor."

His cell phone rang. It was lying on the table next to him, and he glanced at the display. Not Hela, no one from his list of contacts, just an unfamiliar number.

"Well, here we go," he said, reaching for the phone. "I'll put it on speaker so you can hear her lying about how her battery ran down, she tried looking for the charger, but she couldn't find it, so now she's calling from a friend's phone, but she couldn't do that before because her friend only had a few minutes left. You'll see."

He answered.

"Yes?"

"Is this Prosecutor Szacki?" asked a woman's voice. Young, but not very young.

He gulped. The dreadful thought struck him that it was somebody from the police or the emergency room.

"Speaking."

"My name is Natasza Kwietniewska, I'm calling from *Debate* magazine. Please allow me to introduce myself because we're sure to be working together often—"

"I'm not working now."

"Sorry?"

"It's after seven. I'm at home having supper. I'm not at work," he said, and hung up.

Żenia was tapping her head.

Eight p.m.

The calories, alcohol, and Żenia's company, though perhaps not in that order, had lessened his anxiety. But he couldn't get back to his usual level of impatience, or as his daughter had put it so well yesterday, rage. He knew he was going to wait up for her to come home, just to chew her out, and then he'd go to bed.

"Do you think I should punish her?" he shouted to Żenia from the living room while she was soaking in the tub.

She couldn't hear him, so he picked up his wineglass and went into the bathroom.

"May I?"

"No."

"Why not? I want to look at you naked."

"Well, wouldn't you know, I'm not in the habit of smothering my tits in foam and waiting for my lusty young lover to appear every single time I get into the tub."

"What on earth can you be doing in there that's so private? The toilet's in a separate room."

"Can I help it if I like to shit in the tub now and then? Don't be dumb, I don't look very good right now. I'm in the middle of some cosmetic operations. No man can see me until I'm done."

He sat on the floor by the door.

"Do you think I should punish her?"

"Don't drag me into it."

"Seriously."

"Don't drag me into it—seriously."

He sighed. Punishment had never been his strong suit. He knew how that sounded, and that as a prosecutor it wasn't exactly the right cross-stitched motto to hang above his desk. Four times as a prosecutor he had demanded a life sentence without batting an eyelid. But he had no idea how to punish a sixteen-year-old girl. Should he ground her? She'd make fun of him, sitting in her room, spending all her time socializing via her computer and her phone. Take away her money? She'd pull a fast one and her mother would wire her money, or Żenia would give it to her.

"Think of something, you're the wicked stepmother, after all."

"Marry me and I'll be the wicked stepmother. For now I'm just the wicked live-in lover. Jesus, how awful that sounds, like something out of a police report."

"I'll try to get through to her again," he muttered, to avoid the subject.

Nine p.m.

By now they both knew it wasn't funny anymore. Despite the late hour, Szacki dug out the phone number for Hela's teacher, called him, and got the numbers for the parents of the children she hung out with. The teacher, who had made a fairly bland impression on Szacki at the parents' meetings, turned out to be very efficient, and, above all, helpful. He also asked to be sent a text message once Hela was found, however late it was. As a result, Szacki decided to change his mind about the teacher.

Ten p.m.

They divided up Hela's friends and called all of them, talking first to the parents, then the kids. Żenia was worried that, thanks to this hysterical action, her classmates would make fun of the poor girl later on.

How her prosecutor dad was stalking her, interrogating her friends at night. Szacki got mean satisfaction out of it—causing her embarrassment would be a fine punishment. All teenage girls are hypersensitive when it comes to their ego and status within the group.

Oh, yes, he thought, as he waited on the next call, there'll be another punishment too. Every day I'm going to wait for her outside the school. In white socks, sandals, a nerdy sweater, and a beret. And as soon as she appeared in the doorway he'd shout, "Hela! Hela! Over here!" Three days of this, and she'd superglue her phone to her cheek rather than ever miss a call from her beloved father again.

The conversations with her friends were fruitless. Some of them could only confirm that she had been at school. Two claimed that after classes the three of them had gone for frozen yogurt (according to one) or coffee (according to the other). Which probably meant they'd sat somewhere smoking cigarettes, drinking beer, or taking whichever drugs were in vogue. He pressed them, but both girls were adamant that they'd parted ways at around five p.m. outside the Town Hall, and that Hela had walked off in the direction of the post office, in other words, toward home.

He didn't like this piece of information. It meant that instead of taking the ever-so-slightly longer but populated and well-lit road around the Alfa shopping mall, she had chosen the shorter half-empty street between the back of the mall and the black-and-green hole. Suddenly he remembered all his old cases that had started with a pretty young girl walking past a deserted park at night. He quickly warded off those thoughts because they stopped him from thinking clearly. But at this point he suddenly felt real fear for Hela. For several seconds he couldn't catch his breath.

He also questioned the girls about Hela's boyfriend situation, and both of them denied she had one. Despite appearances, it wasn't good news. Going off somewhere with an admirer, a classmate, or a student from Kortowo would mean that his daughter hadn't come home and wasn't answering her phone because she was high on hormones, busy losing her virginity (assuming she still had it) in some dorm. In this optimistic scenario, poorer for the loss of her virginity but richer in life experience, she would then board the bus and come home, or else take a cab, or call her father.

It was harder to talk to the boys because they all had slow, slightly absent voices, as if they had just finished jacking off and the blood had not returned to their brains yet. They knew who Hela was, but that day they'd only seen her at school. They knew nothing about any boyfriends. But one boy named Marcin had sighed heavily. He must have fallen for Hela.

They'd ticked off the entire list and found out absolutely nothing.

Eleven p.m.

The hour between ten and eleven was extremely tense. As soon as they'd finished with Hela's friends, they checked to see if anything had happened in the city that Hela could have been caught up in. Szacki called Bierut and told him to use all the police channels, especially the traffic cops. Żenia used her old medical contacts and found a friend on call at the provincial hospital who promised to check the ER and all the other admissions and emergency wards.

Teodor Szacki the father was feeling bad. He was forcing himself to think rationally and precisely, but he couldn't stop his thoughts from racing, or curtail the images that his overheated brain was producing. The rush of adrenaline made everything seem extremely vivid—he wasn't so much thinking about events as seeing them. Cursed be the profession that had caused him to spend a large part of his life looking at the sort of images he was now associating with his daughter.

Helena Szacka, run down by a drunken driver. Lying in the bushes, her shoes cast aside, her legs broken, bent at impossible angles in places where there aren't any joints. Her skull crushed, her mandible exposed, her mouth foaming with a mixture of blood and saliva.

Helena Szacka in the emergency room, the doctors exchanging helpless glances; thanks to the collision with a tree there's no breastbone to press down on to revive her.

Helena Szacka in intensive care, intubated, entwined in cables and tubes. He, her father, sitting beside her, staring at an organ-donation consent form, unable to believe he's got to make the decision to switch off the machines. Hela is still alive, maybe she can hear him telling her over and over that she's the greatest daughter in the world. Just one signature, and he'll be saying the same words at her graveside.

Helena Szacka and her funeral. He's surprised the coffin is so big and adult—after all, his daughter's still a child.

It's easier for him to imagine her dead than as a victim of rape. Dragged to some apartment, thrown on an old couch or a designer sofa. Probably by a schoolmate, an acquaintance, who smiled nicely and invited her in for a glass of wine. That could seem better than being hit by a speeding van, certainly better than death. But Szacki had conducted a large number of rape cases, and he knew what happened to the victims. If someone's car gets stolen, they pull themselves together and buy a new one. Someone who's attacked in a dark alley is afraid to walk around after dark for a long time, but eventually life goes back to normal. Even victims of attempted murder get back on their feet, with the aid of a furious desire for revenge.

Rape victims don't recover. He was familiar with the theory. He knew it had been described as post-traumatic stress disorder, that it often happened, and that the trauma excluded the victim from family, social, and professional life. They fairly often ended up in psychiatric wards, where they were given the same treatment as soldiers returning from a war zone who had seen their pals ripped to shreds by IEDs.

He had never heard of any woman who'd suffered rape, then led a normal life and forgotten about it. Every life-threatening and health-endangering crime leaves its mark, but rape, the most brutal personal invasion, the violation of privacy and freedom at every level, reducing its victim to a lump of warm flesh into which someone can thrust his dick, was like being branded with burning metal. Continuously. The echo of the event kept coming back to the victim, not just once in a while, not now and then, but nonstop. Someone was always holding a red-hot piece of metal to the woman's soul. Perhaps you could get used to it, but there's no way you could cease to feel it.

Bierut was the first to call back. Nothing had happened. A patrol had explored the black-and-green hole with a thermo-visual camera, but they hadn't found anything. Another team was going to search the terrain at daybreak.

Then Żenia's friend called. Szacki watched her face intently as she listened.

"She's not anywhere," she said after the call. "They haven't got her or anyone who could be a rough match. Basia's on ER duty until morning; she promised to check regularly."

He nodded.

"What now?" she asked.

"That's it," he said. "We just wait. It's too early to report her missing, and definitely too soon to start a search. She's not a four-year-old. The statistics are on our side. By morning at the latest she should be knocking at the door, hungover and remorseful—that's how teenage disappearances usually end."

"And if not?"

"If not, the best coordinated search for a missing person in the entire history of Poland will begin."

Midnight.

They were sitting quietly at the kitchen table. Szacki caught himself listening for a noise in the driveway, the gentle creak of the old gate, and his daughter's familiar footsteps. But outside total silence reigned.

"Could she possibly have run away?" asked Żenia.

He shrugged. He knew how very naive it is of parents to insist they know their own children.

"I doubt it, but if we take an objective look at her situation, she does have her reasons. She's at a difficult age, she's been removed from Warsaw against her will, torn away from her usual environment. Forced to live with her father's new partner and to build new relationships from scratch with kids at school. We thought she was coping, but maybe it was an act. And suddenly something happened to make her crack."

"Would she have told her mom?"

"I don't know. If she isn't found by eight, I'll call her. I'll call others in the family, too. I'll get a hold of her friends in Warsaw."

"Why not now?"

"Now it's pointless. If she's been the victim of a crime or an accident, nobody in the family will know anything about it. They'll just go apeshit if I call them in the middle of the night. And if she's with someone she knows, she's safe. Better talk to people in the daytime than at this hour."

They went on sitting in silence. And that was why Szacki jumped when the phone on the table buzzed. He glanced at the display and felt physical relief, as if a miraculous drug had suddenly relaxed all his agonizingly tensed muscles.

"It's from Hela," he said.

Żenia squeezed his arm tight, and he could tell she was about to burst into tears.

"So where will I have to go and fetch the little brat from?" he muttered, unable to stop his voice from trembling.

He opened the message. No text, just a picture. Weird, almost monochrome. At the center of the picture was a rusty ring. The area outside the ring was gray, and the space inside it was totally black. It looked like a postcard from a modern art museum.

"Is it a joke?" asked Żenia. "Some secret code of yours?"

"I have to go to work," he said very calmly.

He put the phone in his pocket and stood up. He took his jacket from the back of the chair, put it on, and did up the top button.

"Teo, what's in that picture?"

"I really can't say now. I'll tell you everything later. I'll be across the road. Trust me."

His darling Żenia had fear in her eyes, but he couldn't deal with her right now.

He knew exactly what was in the fuzzy gray-and-brown picture.

It was the open end of a cast-iron pipe.

CHAPTER SEVEN

Wednesday, December 4, 2013

Saint Barbara's Day. All the Barbaras are drinking, and all the miners, too, in honor of their patron saint. Maybe Jay Z and Cassandra Wilson are drinking, too, because it's their birthday. The protests continue in Ukraine. President Yanukovych has gone to China, and is hoping the issue will resolve itself in his absence. In Croatia the results of a referendum are announced, in which the majority of citizens have declared themselves in favor of adding a clause to the constitution stating that marriage is purely "a union between a man and a woman." A Polish emotional statistic: only 16 percent of those polled think of the father as a close friend; 8 percent of those polled associate sex with intimacy. An economic statistic: 57 percent of Poles spend all the money they earn. In Olsztyn the national railroad company is trying to combat a plague of traction equipment theft (five miles of it has already gone missing), and the first operation is performed in a new building at the hospital. A slipped lumbar disc was fixed, and the patient is feeling fine. A PE teacher from a suburban high school is feeling fine, too, after coming first in a poll for Olsztyn's best teacher. He wins the title "SuperProf 2013" and a stay at a spa. Nature abhors a vacuum, so a new poll was immediately announced for the funniest photo of someone in a Father Christmas hat. The Christmas tree outside the Town Hall has been decked, and the lights are on. It's 35 degrees, the smell of winter is here, and people keep glancing skyward, anticipating snow. It's going to fall soon, but for now it's a day like any other: fog and freezing drizzle.

One a.m.

At last he was feeling calm. He shouldn't have been—after all, he had just found out that his daughter could be dying a horrible death, dissolved by a maniac in a cast-iron pipe with the help of a few bucketfuls of drain cleaner. But at least he hadn't received a picture of a heap of bones floating in alkaline gloop, just the blurry end of a pipe. That meant an invitation to play the game, and in any game you can win—even if the cards are marked and one side dictates the rules, you can still win. So now he had no choice but to think. And then come out the victor.

It was the logical choice.

He tidied his desk, made a large mug of steaming coffee, placed the files for the Najman case in front of him, and started to think.

Two a.m.

It was very hard to conquer the desire to take instant action. After each thought he wanted to grab the phone and drag Bierut, Falk, and Frankenstein out of bed. Talk to them, hand out duties, give orders in a firm tone. Every time it took an almost physical effort to persuade himself not to do it, to work it all out in his head first, draw up a plan, go through it at least four times, and only then put it into action. He had to strategize quickly—he had four or five hours at most.

First and foremost, he assumed he would have to write his own rules for the game. Cheat, and by that he meant win. Like in the famous scene from *Indiana Jones and the Raiders of the Lost Ark*, when his enemy is brandishing a saber, 100-percent sure he's going to cut the archaeologist to ribbons, whereupon Indiana Jones pulls out a pistol and takes care of him with a single shot. His situation was analogous. His opponent was twirling a jewel-encrusted saber, pirouetting, and showing off all the swordsmanship he'd spent years mastering, planning how in the next few moves and cuts he would humiliate Szacki and prove his supremacy—but he was going to get a bullet between the eyes. Bang.

That was Szacki's strategy: bang.

It meant he had to act in an unpredictable way, almost irrationally. Totally contrary to what his opponent was assuming. That was the only way to stick a wrench in the works, foil the killer's plans, and force him to make a mistake.

Once he had come to this conclusion, he realized that if he wanted to act this way, he would have to make the most difficult decision of his life. Not just professional, but life in general. The killer must be expecting Szacki to use his position as a celebrity prosecutor to whip up a campaign that would become huge news, not just in Poland, but the world over. Experts would analyze the photograph of the pipe, and IT specialists would track down which base transceiver station the message was sent from. Every recording from every security camera on the route between Hela's school and home would be examined and analyzed. Sniffer dogs would be put to work. The entire police force would be mobilized to interrogate everyone unlucky enough to appear downtown that day who could have seen something. The normal procedure for a kidnapping case would be publicized out of all proportion: pictures of Hela would be shown around the clock on every TV channel, and there'd be live reports from outside her school.

He had a strong desire to act in the classic way, every neuron in his head was screaming for him to go ahead and do it. Every neuron? Almost. But a handful were still holding out, telling him the criminal was bound to have foreseen that sort of typical response. More than that—he must be expecting it. And that was why Szacki had to act in the opposite way. Hide the kidnapping from the world, not inform anyone, solve the riddle himself, and only then strike.

He thought about Falk's argument with Klejnocki. Falk had said you couldn't compare this situation to burning at the stake—a murder committed in a cabin in the woods wasn't analogous with a public execution that would draw in the crowds and let them know what was and wasn't allowed. Klejnocki had argued that maybe the whole case was only meant to go public when the criminal found it appropriate. And it looked as if he was right. They had prematurely mistaken building a pyre for an execution.

The flame was only meant to catch light when the public was suitably worked up and suitably prepared. That made sense. The pyre was going to be lit as soon as the crowd had filled the marketplace, and the fire wouldn't go out until they'd been given their dose of blood and horror. What right-minded person would quietly burn a witch without any advertisement, leaving most of the city thinking a small fire had broken out downtown but must have been quickly doused?

The question was, how would the criminal react when he saw that, contrary to his expectations, no major hysteria had been whipped up in connection with the disappearance of the prosecutor's daughter?

Yes, that was a good question. Szacki got up and started walking around his desk. Outside, it was total darkness. There were no little yellow construction machinery lights twinkling in the black-and-green hole, and the cathedral illuminations had been switched off long ago. Nothing but pitch-black night.

So how would the madman react?

At first he would probably wait. He'd sip his yerba mate, or whatever deranged people drink, something healthy probably, stare at the news on TV, listen to Radio Olsztyn, and refresh the main page of the local news website every thirty seconds. Until noon he'd be calm. After noon he'd start to wonder what was going on, and by the evening he'd realize that Szacki's and the police department's behavior must be part of a strategy. If, as Klejnocki suspected, he had any connection with the police or the prosecution service, he'd try to find out what this strategy was. If he couldn't, he'd start to feel anxious.

And then he might realize that he'd have to alter his plan. And that it was better to carry it out before a reduced audience than not carry it out at all.

Szacki came to this conclusion, returned to his desk, and sat down.

His inner conviction tallied with the result of logical deduction: if he wanted to rescue Hela, he had to do it today, and he had to do it alone. Acquainting anyone whatsoever with his situation and his intentions was too risky.

He had about thirteen or fourteen hours. Maybe less, definitely not more.

Three a.m.

The choice of relevant factors seemed crucial. He could assume the most obvious solutions had been foreseen by his opponent and would bring no result. In other words, seizing Najman's wife and partner by the throat made no sense. There was a hope that Bierut would manage to find a phantom lover, but he couldn't allow himself that hope now. Of course, it would help if he found her, but for now he had to believe it wouldn't happen.

What could he do, what hadn't he done, and what was imperceptible enough for that goddamn maniac to have failed to foresee it?

For a long while he considered the theory that the case of the wife-beater from Równa Street and the Najman case were connected, that the guy without vocal cords should be added to the same list of victims as Najman and the owners of the finger bones and auditory ossicles. Instinct told him he was wasting time; nobody had dissolved the guy from Równa Street, nobody had even attempted to, someone had simply given him a serious hammering for bullying his wife, not the first such instance, and surely not the last. Probably the victim's family, a brother or brother-in-law. But it wasn't a regular hammering. He'd been severely mutilated, and yet someone had gone to the trouble of making sure he didn't die.

Why?

Maybe because his wife hadn't died either.

Szacki tapped his pen against the sheet of paper that lay in front of him.

"OK," he said; his hoarse voice had an unpleasant ring to it in the empty, silent office. He flinched, as if he had discovered someone standing behind him. "Let's give it a try."

He decided to consider the theory that some fanatical champion of justice was inflicting punishment on perpetrators of domestic violence. And aimed to put things to rights not in the courts but by setting stakes on fire. Chemical stakes, where the flames would be replaced by sodium hydroxide.

But as he believed in justice, he didn't murder them at random, but inflicted fair punishments. So he'd mutilated the guy from Równa Street, ensuring that he didn't die. Lord knows why he'd done it in that way—maybe he knew something that they, as the investigators, did not. Mental abuse, verbal humiliation, aggression, shouting, persuading the woman that she's worthless. His organs of speech had been removed, so he'd never be able to harm anyone verbally ever again.

Szacki scowled.

What a fanciful idea.

Except that then Najman's death had to be a punishment for someone else's death. He shrugged. Najman's wife was alive, and doing fairly well. So was his child and his business partner too. Neither woman had mentioned any strange events from his past, and once he was dead, neither of them had any reason to be afraid to speak up. Najman wasn't to be found in any database either; not only had he never had any convictions, but he hadn't been charged or accused of anything.

Suddenly a thought occurred to him. He reached for the shelf but realized he hadn't yet received a copy of the updated penal code. He soon found the right document in his computer instead.

Mr. Looney Tunes wouldn't be expecting this.

2

There was no way she could tell him out loud, but she hadn't felt this good in years. She ran a hand over his ridiculously furry chest. The black hairs were very curly, and as she combed her fingers through them, they straightened out, and then coiled again like little springs. In the days when they'd danced, he'd always had a smooth, depilated chest.

She put her index finger to his Adam's apple and drew a snaking line across his hirsute breastbone, around his navel (he couldn't bear to be touched there), over his pubic bone, and along his penis, still warm and wet from being inside her.

She was hoping he'd surrender to her touch, but instead he gave her a tame kiss, got up, and went over to the window. He had a boyish build—he was slender in the typical way of those who've done intensive physical training in their youth.

"I've missed you," she said.

Edmund Falk nodded, but didn't turn around to face her.

"Are we going to do something with this?"

"Meaning?"

"Meaning that since we're living in the same city, it'd be quite easy for us to miss each other less."

She got up and went over to him. She lived on the top floor of a block in Jaroty, with a fabulous view of the city. All the more fabulous for not being blighted by this particular apartment block.

"I've thought about it," he said; the softness brought about by sex had vanished from his voice. "I've considered it at length. And it doesn't make sense, for many reasons."

"Is celibacy compulsory within the prosecution service these days?" she asked scornfully, trying not to betray how much his words had hurt her.

"You know that's not the point. I'm still a junior, but once I pass my qualifying exam I might be staying here, or I might get sent to the other end of Poland. In my case, making permanent plans wouldn't be logical. Getting attached to someone would be cruel. Besides, there's what I do. I feel as if it's changing me. More than I thought. I don't want it to change others, too, especially you."

"You're talking crap."

"It's the logical choice."

She didn't reply. Maybe because before there had been determination in his voice. But in this last comment, there was nothing but sadness.

3

Four a.m.

As he stared at the word *BONES* underlined several times, he wondered whether there was any way of fitting the individual bones into the overall plan of the Warmian Inquisitor (the media would like that nickname) and if it were possible to identify those remains. Perhaps there was a key that would allow him to narrow down the group of people whose DNA should be compared.

Two male hands. One interpretation did suggest itself. Maybe a wife-beater had ended up on the inquisitor's blacklist and had soon lost his favorite tools. Was that all, or had he lost his life too? Impossible to say. So far they'd assumed every victim had lost his life—presumably the handless man had died in the same way as Najman, dissolved alive in lye, as indicated by the marks on the fingers, proof that he'd been trying to get out of a cast-iron pipe at any cost.

This idea implied that he was dead. Up to this point, Szacki had managed not to think about Hela, or about the sort of situation she was in. He was afraid of going into hysterics, which would make him lose time. But now, as he thought about the cast-iron pipe, suddenly he imagined his daughter, with him since the moment she was born, shut in a thing like that; his throat went tight and tears sprang to his eyes.

It was a little while before he calmed down again.

You won't help her by panicking, he kept telling himself, you won't help her by panicking.

He realized that if the owner of the hand had been killed, establishing his identity was practically impossible. But what if he had only been deprived of his hands, maybe after being kept in the pipe for some time? That would explain why he'd tried to get out of it in paroxysms of terror, reducing his fingers to that state. This theory gave him hope. The surgical wards and the prosthesis suppliers should remember a guy who had suddenly lost both hands.

And the ossicles. That was a real puzzle. A male set and a female set. He couldn't understand how the organ of hearing could be involved in violence. Someone had failed to listen properly? Was deaf to his wife's emotional problems? It made no sense, and anyway, one set was a woman's. Maybe it had to do with children? Parents who hadn't listened to their children because they preferred to throw barbecues. Szacki couldn't force himself to go down that track.

He got up and stood by the window. The darkness was still total, but the city was gradually coming to life; he'd noticed long ago that people got up earlier here and finished work earlier too. He told himself off for letting his thoughts wander to things that didn't matter.

Someone dies because he caused someone else's death.

Someone loses his voice because he humiliated someone.

Someone loses his hands because he hit someone.

All clear.

Someone loses his hearing because . . . ?

He turned away from the window and began to pace the room, did a few rings around his desk, sat down, and nervously arranged the transcripts he'd removed from the files in an even row.

And then it occurred to him.

Evidently the owners of the ossicles hadn't reacted in time. The truth had come out, and the Warmian Inquisitor had decided they deserved to be punished. Painfully, but not very, because they had only lost the hearing in one ear.

Szacki latched on to the thought that if his assumptions were correct, then perhaps he could try to understand the deranged criminal's motives. Bah, a tiny part of him even sympathized with those motives. Witnesses of violence who stood and picked their noses instead of informing the police that something bad was happening were not culpable in the eyes of the law—the duty weighing on them to report it was a moral one, and nobody ever gives a shit about that kind of duty. Of course, Szacki would have been happy to add to the penal code at least a fine for failing to react, but as no such fines existed . . . well, mutilation might seem extreme, but if someone's passivity led to a death . . .

Frankly, he could just about agree with it.

But how do you find someone who's been deprived of hearing? Get someone to call around to every ear, nose, and throat department in the region?

"Fuck," he said.

How could he have failed to notice that? He figured he must be getting old.

Five a.m.

He realized he needed an ally, even if he didn't let the ally in on everything. He couldn't singlehandedly implement the plan he had worked out in his head.

For a while he hesitated, turning the phone in his hand. Finally he made a decision, and called Bierut.

4

Awareness of our own mortality is not innate, it's acquired. We gain it at about thirty, sometimes sooner if we produce children and suddenly start to fear we might not always be there for them. Of course, intellectually a childless sixteen-year-old understands and accepts the fact that sooner or later she'll have to die, but emotionally she's not capable of getting upset about it. Maybe a little, in the same way as we're upset about the war in Syria when we watch the news. Well, yes, it's terrible and all that, those children being killed, and the refugees, but I've got to go check the lasagna in the oven—the guests will be here soon. And so, after an initial stage of disorientation and terror, Helena Szacka scarfed down the McDonald's breakfast brought to her by her kidnappers. She usually avoided that sort of food, but she figured this time she was 100-percent absolved. So she ate the weird breakfast sandwiches, drank a huge chocolate shake, and flopped down on the bunk bed with a large mug of milky coffee.

She tried to think logically. All her life she'd heard her dad say, "First we think, then we act." Usually, either she didn't remember that or she couldn't care less, but now she realized that if anyone's advice could be useful in her situation, it was the advice of an experienced prosecutor.

She couldn't remember being kidnapped. She'd been on her way home past the park on the river, and must have been rendered unconscious somehow, because the next thing she remembered was waking up in the middle of the night in this room. With a hangover and an unpleasant taste in her mouth, which must mean some chemical substance had been used. She had no wounds, no marks implying brutality, no impressions made by ropes, and no bruises. Luckily nobody had sexually abused her either—that was the first panic-stricken thought that had filled her mind.

In all, a positive balance for the victim of a kidnapping.

She didn't wear a watch, and they'd taken her phone away. But from the time she woke up until dawn, about three hours must have gone by. Which meant that from her being kidnapped to waking, about eight or nine hours had elapsed. And that meant she could be anywhere—just outside Olsztyn, twenty miles away, or two hundred miles away. Most likely in Poland, because all the furniture in her cell seemed to have been made there or by common Polish companies.

The room was on the ground floor of a single-family house, not an old one, but not brand-new either. It smelled as if it wasn't lived in. Outside the barred window she could see a scrap of neglected lawn and a wall of mixed woodlands. It must be a remote place because she could slightly open the window, which wouldn't be allowed if a scream could alert the neighbors.

So she didn't bother to scream. Besides being a waste of energy, it might upset her captor or captors.

She hadn't seen anyone. She had no idea whether she'd been abducted by just one person or a whole gang. She'd gotten the food after a little light on the door lock had changed from red to green. For a while she'd stared at it, and then finally she'd pulled on the doorknob. On the other side of the door there was a small gap. A solid door, this time with no handle or lights, separated her area from the rest of the house. She guessed that both doors were controlled from the other side, making the gap a sort of air lock, and meaning she had no contact with her kidnappers. At least not until they wanted it.

Despite these precautions and her total lack of contact with the kidnappers, she suspected she'd been kidnapped by a woman, or that there was a woman in the gang. The evidence of this was the toiletries provided. Soap, toothpaste, a toothbrush—anyone would think of those. Tampons and sanitary napkins would take slightly more considerate men. And her dad was always saying criminals were morons. After all, there was a reason why they were criminals and not chairmen of the board. But it was hard for her to believe that a man would have thought of makeup remover. You'd have to be a woman to know that was the most important item in the toiletry bag, apart from tampons and a toothbrush.

The room was clean and tidy, its furnishings very modest. It looked more like a monk's cell than a hotel room. A bed, a mattress, and bedding from Ikea, the cheapest kind, brand-new sheets, with square creases from being kept in their packaging. A little table and a chair, both of them shabby, secondhand. On the table there was a small lamp, the kind you buy at the home improvement store for ten zloty. She thought perhaps they'd made somebody do some work here or maybe write something.

She was surprised to see a small Samsung television fixed to the wall. She couldn't see a remote anywhere.

In the tiny bathroom there was a toilet, a sink, and a mirror set into the wall. No bathtub or shower. For a while she wondered if that was a good sign or a bad one. On the one hand it was good—anyone who remembered about makeup remover wasn't likely to keep her for weeks on end in a room without a shower. But was it definitely a good sign? Maybe this was just a midpoint before she ended up on an operating table or in a Turkish brothel.

For once her own jokes didn't amuse her.

Closer inspection confirmed that she wasn't the first tenant of this cell. After moving the bed aside, just above the baseboard she found the word *HELP* scratched in the plaster.

She should have been upset, but she just sighed, recognizing that the previous inmate had been an idiot. Carving that sort of hysterical nonsense was totally pointless. Unless it brought someone relief. She wondered what to use as a tool, then finally pulled the tag off the zipper of her jeans and carved *HELA 12.04.13, 6 a.m. +1.*

If anyone discovered this place after she'd been taken away, they'd find out she was here today at about seven o'clock. She was going to keep adding another "one" to mark more or less each hour, as a way of recording the passage of time. This information could be crucial for someone trying to set a range for their search.

Because she was in no doubt that someone would be looking for her, and that this someone would be her father. This thought comforted her most—the thought that in their unfortunate situation, very few kidnap victims were lucky enough to be the daughter of the Sherlock Holmes of the prosecution service, as she sometimes jokingly called him.

She loved him, and she was also very proud of him. Proud of the fact that he was on the right side of the barricade and that his work ensured the triumph of justice. And of the fact that he really did have the adventures of a fictional detective. He knew how to solve unusual riddles and get to the truth when nobody else could. She had never discussed it with him, nor did he tell her about his work, but she was very familiar with all the press reports about him.

It occurred to her that, nevertheless, there was a chance, possibly a big one, that she would never see him again.

And for the first time since the kidnapping she felt genuinely sad.

5

It crossed Szacki's mind that Hela's definition of him as characterized by rage was probably far too polite. Rage sounded grand and dignified, while he just went off the deep end very easily. It may not have sounded quite so good, but it was a far better reflection of Szacki's emotional state, right now, for example.

Right now he was so angry that he felt like grabbing the head of the man sitting across from him and banging it against the oak table until blood was dripping onto the floor. He felt as if nothing else would bring him relief.

So just in case, he drew back his chair.

"I'm very sorry, but I can't help you, sir," said Witold Kiwit for the millionth time.

Szacki shook his head. He glanced at the fancy clock hanging above the fireplace. Half past nine. For half an hour he'd been sitting in a small prewar house, trying to get Witold Kiwit to tell him who had partially deprived him of hearing. To no effect. Even though on the way here he'd been quite convinced it would be just a formality.

Four hours before Szacki's arrival, Witold Kiwit, aged fifty-two, was brushing his teeth when Bierut knocked at his door. The sad policeman with the outdated mustache didn't want to talk. He had introduced himself and gone into the bathroom, where the light was still on and the water was still running. Ignoring Kiwit's protests, he had told him to rinse his mouth out, and then he'd dug around in it with a cotton swab on a long stick—which for Kiwit had very unpleasant associations with having something stuck in his ear. And then he'd left without a word.

Twenty minutes later Kiwit's DNA sample had arrived at Professor Frankenstein's lab on Warszawska Avenue. An hour and a half later, at about seven, the scientist had called Szacki and told him that Witold Kiwit's DNA matched the DNA of the male set of auditory ossicles belonging to their skeleton.

This was how Szacki had carried off his first victory of the day. He had confirmed that Kiwit's case, one of dozens of minor cases conducted by the prosecution service, was connected with his investigation. By pure coincidence, the case of the entrepreneur who had lost his hearing had been conducted by Falk, who had to inform Szacki about all his work. Otherwise he would have had no idea and wouldn't have realized that the man's mysterious injury was linked with the equally mysterious appearance of the auditory ossicles in Najman's skeleton.

Szacki had a foothold. And he had a witness he must press hard. And then he could start to take action.

First of all, he got Kiwit to agree to talk to him, threatening him with criminal charges when the man tried to protest.

Secondly, he equipped Bierut with the necessary papers, and then sent him off to the court and to Stawiguda to organize a legal experiment—one that would give him a second victory and the next foothold.

Thirdly, through Ewa Szarejna he had demanded a patrol car. He had no time or strength to drive or to sit in traffic jams. When she had expressed surprise, he'd won her over by spinning stories about his plans for his role as press spokesman, telling her he'd thought it through and realized communication could sometimes be the most important element in an investigation. Because a satisfied public was a helpful public. He had managed not to throw up as he told these lies and was very pleased with this minor victory.

Finally, taking advantage of his position as Falk's supervisor, he had demanded the file for Kiwit's case. He had soon remembered it: Two weeks ago Witold Kiwit—fifty-two years old, wife, two sons, owner of a firm that made tarpaulin—had been brought to the hospital by ambulance. The serious injury to his ear implied the involvement of third parties, so the hospital had informed the police, and at the prosecution service, Falk had taken on the case. Contrary to common sense, the injured man had claimed to have done it himself by accident and refused to identify those responsible. There was nothing to be learned from the interview transcript—Kiwit had stubbornly stuck to his version of events.

Sitting in the back of the patrol car on the way to Kiwit's house, Szacki was sure that as an experienced investigator, additionally equipped with proof in the form of the DNA analysis, he would have no problem prompting Kiwit to tell the truth.

But after half an hour he felt as if nobody could ever have been so badly mistaken. It would be easier to extract his own intestines through his nose than get anything out of Kiwit.

"I think you're wrong, and you definitely can help," he said calmly, "but you're not yet aware of it."

Behind Kiwit stood a bourgeois dresser with such crystal-clear glass that it looked as if it were cleaned three times a day. Szacki caught his own reflection and adjusted his slightly crooked tie.

"Well, quite, it was a bad injury of course. It was slippery, and I was walking—"

"Of course. I heard you. OK, you refuse to tell the truth. Your public responsibility doesn't appeal to you. Now please listen to the consequences. I will find the people who did this to you. Sooner or later. These people have more on their conscience than just your ear . . ." A shadow of fear crossed Kiwit's face, identical to the one Szacki had seen the day before in the eyes of the wife-beater from Równa Street.

"So it's going to be a major case, highly publicized, with long sentences. In this sort of investigation there's always some collateral damage along the way. I promise you'll be part of the fallout. You'll be officially involved in the case, within the range of interest of the law enforcement agencies, and I will have you charged with withholding information about a crime, and there will be several lesser charges too. It will probably end in a suspended sentence, but you know what it's like if you have a conviction. The bank withdraws its loans, the tax office takes an interest, and clients head for the hills. In less than a year, you'll have no company, no prospects, and maybe no family. You'll be in debt, and you'll be throwing heart medication down your throat by the handful. Maybe at that point you'll think it couldn't possibly get any worse. But you'll be wrong. Because that's when I'll really crank it up. Do you ever read the papers? Ever read about the civil servants who can destroy a man and get away with it, have you?"

Kiwit said yes, he had.

"Well, I'm one of them."

Kiwit shrugged. He looked around the living room to see if his wife was within hearing range, leaned over the table, and nodded for Szacki to lean toward him. The prosecutor moved forward, until there were only a few inches between their faces. It was the regular face of a fifty-year-old Pole who couldn't deal with his own weight gain—pale, rather puffy, pockmarked, and shiny. Freshly shaved too. In a few spots under the nose and on the chin where the stubble is hardest, Szacki could see the dark red traces of microscopic razor cuts. He looked into Kiwit's colorless eyes and waited.

"I don't give a fuck," he said, shrouding Szacki in the smell of digested meat and minty toothpaste. "I don't give a fuck, because there's fuck-all you can do to me. I'd sooner take you by the hand, go into the bathroom, and slash my own wrists than tell you a single word. Is that clear?"

Szacki was opening his mouth to respond when Kiwit's wife interrupted him.

"Stop tormenting my husband! He's been through enough already. Do you want to cause him a heart attack?"

"I'll be happy to stop," said Szacki, straightening up in his chair. "I'll be happy to stop when he finally stops lying and tells the truth. I promise that as soon as he does, I'll be out of here and you'll never see me again."

Kiwit's wife, a thin fifty-year-old with the look and hairstyle of Danuta Wałęsa, glanced at her husband. She probably wasn't expecting him to tell the truth but to get rid of this pest instead.

"I will be lodging an official complaint," said Kiwit.

"Please listen," said Szacki, addressing both of them. "I'm sure you know this, but for you, ma'am, this information will be new. Your husband was attacked and mutilated because he heard something. The findings of this investigation imply that he must have been a witness to domestic violence. He failed to react, someone was hurt, and as a result a madman decided to punish him. Not just any old madman." He raised a finger. "A genuine first-class madman, capable of the most monstrous crimes. Who is running around our streets because your husband is a fucking coward. Who not only failed to report that someone was being harmed, but is now obstructing the investigation and will go to jail for it. You'd better check which buses run to the penitentiary in Barczewo. The car will go toward fines and lawyers."

He got up and buttoned his jacket. He didn't let it show how disappointed he was. This couldn't be a blind alley, it just wasn't possible.

Out of the corner of his eye he noticed a movement, a shadow. He looked around, and there in the reflection of the dresser, he saw a skinny teenager standing in the kitchen door, the sort of boy the teachers discuss in the staff room as bright enough but far too sensitive to have an easy life ahead of him. Taller than Szacki, thin, with very fair hair. He had a gentle look in his eyes, and Szacki wouldn't have minded in the least if Hela had a boyfriend like him.

He felt every muscle in his body tense the moment his mind produced an image of what might be happening to Hela. Doped senseless, lying on a stinking mattress, as the gangsters line up to fuck the new girl—he didn't have the luxury of ignorance, he'd conducted several cases involving the white slave trade.

He couldn't leave here empty-handed. He would go to whatever lengths were necessary.

"Would you please leave us a little longer? Just a minute, I promise. Then I'll go."

Kiwit's wife glared, but she left the room, and the son trotted after her. The door slammed.

"In a way I understand you," he said mildly. "They've proved what dreadful things they're capable of doing. And I'm just an official, armed with rubber stamps and legal clauses. I can cause you trouble, but let's face it, you'll only have to lodge a couple of appeals and you'll be back on your feet in no time."

Kiwit fixed him with a confused and attentive look; he clearly had no idea where Szacki was going.

"But apart from being an official, I'm also a very bad man. A bad man who won't stop at anything, because he has a personal motive. If you don't help me, I'll take my revenge. I won't do anything to you, or your wife either, because I'm sure you don't give a shit about her—a wife isn't family, is she? But I'm not going to leave your sons alone."

"You can't do anything to them."

"I can't. But others can."

"You'll hire some kind of thugs to beat them up? You're ridiculous."

"I could. But I have better methods."

He leaned toward Kiwit and described in detail the dreadful fate that could befall his sons.

Kiwit stared at him in horror.

"You're a real shit," he said. "But all right, so be it. I have a plant that makes tarpaulin and advertising banners, too, as I'm sure you know. In the Barczewo suburbs. On one side of it there's a copse with little pine trees, and on the other there's a house on a large lot. A regular single-family house with little columns at the front. A normal family."

It's always the same, thought Szacki, feeling weary. They all think of themselves as unique, the only ones of their kind, but when it comes to seeing the individual qualities in others, it's always seemingly "a normal family."

"And?" Szacki glanced at his watch. Unfortunately time hadn't stopped; on the contrary, the hands seemed to be moving at high speed.

"Six months ago there was an accident, in the spring. He went to work, and she was left with the child, a toddler. The boiler went kaput, carbon monoxide. A tragedy, they're still writing about it in the papers, saying it's a silent killer. Afterward, the local gossips said it wasn't an accident and that things hadn't been going too well there."

"She sought your help, didn't she?"

Kiwit fell silent and stared out of the window, as if the answers were hidden in the gray fog.

"I was with my older boy." He nodded toward the hall, indicating that he meant the teenager Szacki had seen a little earlier. "He got upset, I told him not to interfere. It was a family matter, why go to the police or the prosecutors, nothing but trouble later on. My son wouldn't listen. He went over to their place to talk to the guy. But he just laughed at him, and then there was that accident with the boiler, such a strange coincidence." Kiwit cleared his throat. "Ordinary people, nothing unusual about them. A slide for the kid in the yard, a trampoline, a kiddie pool, just a small one. Normal house. I talked to the man a few times over the fence, the usual stuff, about cars, or mowing the grass, I don't remember. Totally normal guy. You get the picture?"

Szacki didn't want to say yes. He was still waiting for a piece of information that would help him—he didn't give a damn about anyone else's tragedy.

"Who would normally believe that in a situation like that the lady wouldn't simply take the kids and be out the door? I'm sorry, but it's always the same with that sort of story—as I'm sure you'll agree, she only had herself to blame. It's not as if he had her locked up in the utility room. It's true, I sometimes heard shouting, when I was up at night to get the bookkeeping done. But you tell me, who doesn't fight? What husband and wife don't fight?"

"Do you know what happened to him?"

"They say he's gonna appear in court in Suwałki—he lives there at his mother's place now," said Kiwit. "His mother cares for him since his accident—a drunk driver ran him down and he's in a wheelchair. He'll be pissing into a bag for the rest of his life."

He said it quite casually, *Oh dear, accidents happen, too bad,* but Szacki realized there was no point in asking if the driver had been caught.

"Mr. Prosecutor," Kiwit continued, suddenly fifteen years older. "I have no idea who it was or where they kept me. Not for long, less than a day. I didn't talk to anyone—nobody said a word to me."

"Where?"

"A house in the woods—there are millions of them in Poland. Not new, not old, just a house. I couldn't say if it was near here or sixty miles north or south of here. I'm sorry."

"Any identifying features?"

"A TV on the wall," he said so quietly that Szacki wasn't sure he'd heard.

"What on the wall?"

"A TV. And an operating theater."

Automatically, Kiwit touched his right ear.

6

She was lying on her back, with her hands behind her head, when suddenly it occurred to her that they might be watching her through cameras, so she switched to the position of a kidnap victim. Legs drawn up to her chin, embracing her knees, head dropped. She didn't want some maniac to see her lying on the bed and get stupid thoughts in his head. What she feared most of all was rape.

She was so scared of being raped that she couldn't even think about it—all such thoughts simply fell apart without leading to any mental images or sounds. Instead they just flew around her brain, crashing against her skull; whenever one of them did manage to latch on to her neurons she felt paralyzed, incapable of any action or other thought.

She'd read the papers and watched television. She knew that rape could mean being treated as a piece of meat by a large number of people for a long time. People who would do her harm, and she'd never be the same again. She was amazed to find herself thinking it easier to imagine death. Death was like a passage into the unknown—it undoubtedly meant the end, but it could also be a surprise. Where rape was concerned, there was no surprise. She would simply have to carry on living, maybe not for long, maybe for ages and ages, and she'd go through the rest of her life as a woman who had started her adulthood as a piece of meat.

She decided that if anything like that happened, she'd try to hold out for a while, and then provoke them into killing her.

7

He wasn't really wrong. He was sure Teresa Najman would be waiting for him in the hall, but she was nervously pacing the sidewalk. He scrambled out of the patrol car, and there she was, right next to him. She waited for him to shut the door and then let loose: "You're gonna regret this."

There was a cold wind blowing, but it was different from before, dry and frosty, the sort of wind that heralds the start of winter. He buttoned his coat, cast a glance at Teresa Najman and then at the gray building behind her; rather neglected, it looked just right for a social assistance center or an addiction therapy unit. And in fact it housed both, along with several other facilities whose clientele were neither healthy, wealthy, nor happy.

He understood Mrs. Najman's anger. He had left her no choice when he'd sent Bierut to tell her that either she would have to agree as a matter of urgency to let them question her five-year-old, or Szacki would no longer take her statement at face value. He would demand preventive measures, report the case to the family court, and then she'd have to persuade the probation officers whether, as someone under police supervision, she was fit to guarantee the child suitable living conditions. He wrote it all down for Bierut to read out to her—he was afraid the policeman would be too soft to blackmail the mother effectively by using the state to take away her child.

So he understood the woman, but he didn't give a damn about her. He had to act differently from usual—it was his only chance. And as he had failed to extract anything from Mrs. Najman, he'd get it out of her child. Preschoolers were usually much worse at hiding the truth than their moms.

"You've had your chance. You should have told the truth," he said.

For a moment he looked at her in the hope that she would change her mind and tell him everything. He could tell she was thinking about it. She must have been wondering whether the child knew anything that could incriminate her. Finally she stepped aside and let Szacki enter the building.

He walked down a dark corridor, decorated with depressing posters warning against addiction, above all to alcohol ("Moonshine causes blindness"), because the building also housed the therapy unit. It occurred to him that this was not how the route to a friendly interview room should look. Unless it was a deliberate ploy. Once the kid has seen the victims of home-brewed hooch, the interview would be like his favorite activity at preschool.

At the end of the corridor another woman was waiting for him, no less angry.

"If it weren't for Żenia . . ." She wagged an accusing finger at him. "If I hadn't spent several years at the same school with her, grinding away at anatomy . . ."

"How lovely to see you, too, my dear Adela," he said, feigning sincerity. It never worked.

"Do me a favor—don't even bother. I'm supposed to have two weeks to prepare for this kind of interview, not two hours. If it weren't for Żenia, I'd laugh you out of here, or report you for suggesting it at all."

But she had clearly agreed because she had heard something in her old friend's voice that worried her.

"You have no idea . . ." he began to thank her, but she cut him off.

"Give it a break. Let's get it over with. Do you have any questions beyond what your miserable flunky passed on to me?"

He did.

The friendly interview room consisted of two spaces. The first, where the actual interviewing was done, was furnished like a child's playroom. Pastel colors, child-sized furniture, soft animals, toys, and crayons. The cameras and microphones recording the interviews were hidden. There was no bed and no closet, but there was an extra, unusual item—a huge mirror that took up half the wall.

Behind the mirror was a technical room, where the recording of the interview was monitored, and the psychologist's conversation with the child was observed by those involved in the proceedings. In this case, Deputy Commissioner Jan Paweł Bierut, Teresa Najman, Prosecutor Teodor Szacki, and Judge Justyna Grabowska. The judge had to be present because according to the latest rules, a child could only be interviewed once, and the point was for the interview to have the force of trial evidence.

Szacki paid scant attention to Adela's casual chat with little Piotruś Najman (currently on the topic of cartoons). With one ear he listened to some crap about a patchwork elephant, without taking his eyes off the monitor, which showed a sequence of views from various cameras: a general view, the two in profile, a close-up on Adela, and a close-up on Piotruś. Above the monitor, a digital clock measured out the time to one-hundredth of a second, the two final figures flashing by so fast that they merged into a steady shimmer, reminding Szacki that every flicker brought Hela's death closer.

11:23:42—shimmer.

Meanwhile, the patchwork elephant was visiting his auntie; it must have been a funny story, because the speakers above their heads were ringing with laughter, both Adela's and the child's. He wanted to go in there and calm them down. Of course, he knew the theory for interviewing children. You had to introduce narrative techniques, relax the child as much as possible and clarify the situation, explaining that it's OK if he doesn't know the answers to the questions, casting yourself in the role of an adult who needs the kid's help to understand things. He knew the theory, but even so the lengthy procedure was driving him up the wall.

"But I don't know what your house looks like," said Adela, spreading her hands comically, and the little boy laughed. "Will you tell me what the place where you play is like?"

"I play in my room. I've got toys there and books and puzzles. And a rug that's like the road so you can race cars on it. And I've got a lamp with bubbles swimming in it."

"Colored ones?"

"Yes, they're like sapphire."

"Bravo! What difficult words you know. Any other colors?"

"Crimson."

Adela all but sighed in admiration, and the boy blushed with pride. Meanwhile, Szacki noticed that the little heir to the tourist business was more like his father than his mother, physically, as far as he could tell from Najman's photographs. Wide face, dark eyes, dark hair, well-defined eyebrows. He couldn't see any similarity to the mother. Maybe just the shape of the lips. If she'd said she'd adopted him, nobody would have doubted it.

"And do you like playing with toys at home more, or at preschool?"

"At preschool."

"And why is that?"

All the questions had to be open; you couldn't ask questions to which the child could answer *yes* or *no*. There was no guarantee that the little witness had understood the question, and anyway, in stressful situations, kids have a tendency to say yes to adults when they don't understand what they're being asked. Or to say no if they're asked about unpleasant things.

"At preschool we can bring our own toys, but only on Monday. And then me and Igor fight 'cos we want to play with each other's toys, and when we shout we get a rain cloud."

Like most small children, Piotruś Najman couldn't keep a narrative going for more than a few sentences.

"I see, you get a rain cloud as a punishment. And what do you get as a reward?"

"A smiley sun."

"And are there punishments and rewards at home?"

"I don't like it when Mommy shouts at me. Then I give her a rain cloud."

At the back of the small dark room Mrs. Najman cleared her throat.

"And your daddy?"

"My daddy's gone away, and we don't know when he's coming home."

Mrs. Najman coughed again, but this time she said, "I haven't told him his father's dead yet. I'm preparing him for it gradually. We have no idea when the funeral's going to happen or when you're going to give my husband's body back. It's a scandal. I will be making a complaint."

Nobody commented.

"And tell me, do you often give your mom and dad rain clouds and smiley suns?"

"They get rain clouds."

"So you do that when they're naughty. And what do Mommy and Daddy do when they're being naughty?"

"They shout."

"And how does it make you feel?"

"It makes me mad!"

"And what do you do?"

"I never shout 'cos shouting's not allowed. I've gotta be good and quiet."

"And what happens when you can't help yourself, and you're not quiet?"

"Then I get a punishment."

Piotruś became sad. He let his head droop and got off his little chair onto the rug.

"Can I sit down next to you?" asked Adela gently.

The boy nodded, and she joined him on the rug.

"You must put your legs in a bow." He showed her how to sit cross-legged.

Adela sat as he showed her.

"Very good," said the boy.

"Nobody likes getting a punishment, do they?"

The boy shook his head.

"Tell me, what's your very worst punishment?"

In the technical room everyone held their breath.

Piotruś took a sheet of paper and started to draw something on it with crayons. Adela picked up a yellow crayon and added a sun to his picture.

"I don't like being alone," he finally muttered.

"And what does that mean, being alone?"

"I have to be in my room, and me and Mommy can't go outside. When I've gotten a punishment."

"I don't understand. Are you trying to say that when you've gotten a punishment you have to stay in your room with your mom?"

The boy huffed, impatient with Adela for not understanding him.

"You don't understand anything. I have to stay alone in my room when I've gotten a punishment."

Szacki clenched his fists. Please, he thought, let this be leading somewhere. Let him give me a reason to put the screws on Mrs. Najman and get the truth out of her.

"That's why I'm asking, to understand. I wonder where your mom is when you're in your room alone."

"She's in the house." The boy shrugged, busy with his drawing.

It occurred to Szacki that children are all alike. When Hela was little she'd called their living room "the house" as well.

"But when she's gotten a punishment she stays in her room too. Except she's got a TV in her room and I haven't. I can't watch cartoons like 'Franklin's Afraid of the Dark.'"

"And why does Mommy get a punishment?"

"Daddy gives her a rain cloud."

"And what happens then?"

"She has to stay in her room, I told you."

"And what do you do then?"

"I play with Daddy."

"And what do you and Daddy play?"

"Do you like it?"

Piotruś showed Adela his drawing. An ordinary kid's drawing, no black holes or red clouds, or men with huge dicks, or terrifying faces, such as the victims of pedophilia and violence usually draw. Just a family in front of a house, orange clouds, and a yellow sun.

"That's beautiful! I love your orange clouds."

"I like orange. I like blue too," said the boy happily. "There's a parrot in a movie, and he's blue."

Szacki rolled his eyes. *Christ, give me strength, or I'll rip the little brat to pieces.*

11:47:18—shimmer.

"I know that movie. It's *Rio*, isn't it?"

"Yes, *Rio*. I went to the movie theater with Daddy."

Because Mommy had a rain cloud, figured Szacki, and glanced at Mrs. Najman. She didn't seem unsettled by the interview.

"Tell me what else you play with Daddy."

"We read books about Elmer."

"The patchwork elephant."

"And Wilbur. Wilbur's got patches but not color."

"And what else do you do?"

"Play-Doh people. Or we watch cartoons. But I can't watch them when it's the news."

"And what do you like best of all?"

"When I go to the pool with Daddy on my bike and Daddy fools around, puts on the jet engines, and does a rally."

"And is there any game with Daddy that you don't like?"

"Daddy's awesome," said Piotruś.

Adela glanced toward the mirror. Her look said: We're wasting time. A normal boy, a normal family. The parents don't seem to get along particularly well, but there's nothing abnormal about it. Besides, maybe the boy sees their arguments the wrong way and says his mom has a punishment when the woman's just annoyed and shuts herself in her room.

"Does Mom go to the pool with you?"

"Mommy doesn't like getting wet."

The technician working the computer sniggered and then immediately gave them an apologetic look.

"Does she often get a punishment and have to stay in her room?"

"I don't know."

He was drawing more and more vigorously. Szacki could remember what small children are like, and he knew it wasn't a sign of stress. The child was simply distracting himself—he couldn't pay attention for such a long time and was feeling antsy.

"We'll be done in a few minutes, OK?" Adela interpreted the child's body language correctly. "Just three more questions, about your mommy and daddy, and you can run. All right?"

"All right."

"Does Mommy get any other punishments besides staying in her room like you?"

"When she's very naughty she has to go in the attic. There's no TV in there."

Szacki and Bierut exchanged glances. To be searched as soon as possible.

"And what's it like in the attic?"

"It's smelly and there's dust."

Not good, thought Szacki. If it was really bad they wouldn't let him go up there.

"And do you know why Mommy gets rain clouds from your dad?"

"'Cos she's naughty, I guess. You've gotta be good."

Szacki turned so he could see the scene beyond the two-way mirror and also Teresa Najman, who was standing behind him. She was relaxed and unruffled, even smiling a bit. And to his horror Szacki realized they were asking the wrong questions. At first she'd been tense, because she knew something might come to light. But now she was calm, because they hadn't touched on it.

Fuck the updated penal code. There'd be no second chance to interview him. Never. Mentally he let out a howl.

"And when Mom's naughty, what happens then?"

"I don't like shouting."

"Does anything else happen when your mom and dad are upset? Something you don't like?"

"Shouting makes me sad."

"Is there anything else you don't like?"

"Biting and pushing. Marek's always pushing me at preschool."

"And does anyone push you at home?"

"When I push Daddy, he says you shouldn't push."

"And do Mommy and Daddy push each other?"

"You're funny!" The little boy laughed. "They're grown-ups, they don't push."

Adela glanced toward the mirror. Interview over.

Szacki swore hideous oaths to himself.

"Can I take him home now please, Prosecutor?" said Teresa Najman in a firm, confident tone—how very different from the one he'd heard during their first encounter. "Or do you intend to lock him up for the next three months to extract valuable information?"

11:59:48—shimmer.

The technician stopped recording a moment later, on the stroke of twelve, and switched on the light. The judge picked up her purse to show she regarded the session as over. Szacki did nothing. He had no idea what to do. He felt as if there were too little oxygen in the air.

"In fact," said Mrs. Najman, unable to restrain herself, "I sincerely hope you have some other way of catching my husband's killer than persecuting a five-year-old fatherless child. Do you, Prosecutor?"

Adela's entrance saved him. Without a word he turned to face the friendly room where little Piotruś was trying to sharpen a broken crayon. For a while he struggled with the awkward device, but finally he got the better of it, and went back to his drawing.

Once Mrs. Najman had taken the boy away, Szacki found himself standing in the corridor, desperate for oxygen. With no better idea, he went into the interview room. The stuffy little space smelled of dusty carpet tiles, the five-year-old's sweat, and Adela's subtle flowery scent, too subtle for her tough personality as well as the time of year.

He felt weak, as if he were going to faint. He sat down on the little blue chair and started examining the little boy's drawings, which Adela had picked up off the floor and left on the table.

A little house, clouds, a sun, a happy family. How badly he'd misfired.

A happy family. Huh, something he might never have again.

His head was heavy, so he put his elbows on the table and rested his forehead in his hands. A big guy, in a gray suit and a black overcoat, hunched as if he'd almost snapped in two, squeezed into a little plastic chair for preschoolers. He realized how it looked, but he didn't have the strength to get up.

Just under his nose lay Piotruś Najman's drawing, quite joyful in its pastel colors. Adela's sun was nice and symmetrical, while the other elements were typical of preschool artwork. The orange clouds were more like puddles than clouds. The trees consisted equally of brown trunks and green crowns, two-tone rectangles. The house, wide and squat, was exactly like the Najmans' Stawiguda property. Outside it stood the entire family: the mommy, the daddy, and their little boy.

And one other woman, holding the child by the hand.

He sat up abruptly.

The five-year-old Najman was already capable of capturing the figures' main features. He himself had brown eyes and brown hair. And a blue top, maybe a favorite T-shirt. Next to him stood his parents. Szacki recognized the deceased Najman by his bald head, black eyebrows, and the fact that his hand was missing two fingers. For the child it must have been an important feature. Najman was holding a bizarre angular dog on a leash; it was red, and it had no head. Szacki stared at this monster for a while before realizing it was a suitcase on wheels. Daddy the traveler, of course. Mommy Najman was slender, with light-brown hair, wearing a green dress and holding a bunch of flowers. Maybe she liked flowers? Maybe she liked messing around in the garden? The boy had even caught the fact that his mom was a shade taller than his dad.

Mr. and Mrs. Najman weren't holding hands, but just standing next to each other. Mommy and Daddy. The father wasn't holding the boy's hand, and although he was standing next to him, they were divided by the red suitcase. Standing to the right of it, Piotruś was holding hands with a woman, clearly an adult, though not as tall as his mother. This woman had long hair drawn with a black crayon, and dark blue eyes, exaggeratedly large—in fact the eyes took up her entire face. It produced quite a creepy effect. She was wearing a long dress drawn in the same color.

Szacki spread the drawings on the table. Mom and Dad weren't in all of them. But every single one showed the little boy holding hands with the black-haired woman with huge blue eyes.

He gathered the drawings and ran toward the exit.

Teresa Najman was trying to join the stream of traffic on Wojsko Polskie Avenue, heading toward the center, when Szacki appeared in front of her hood, blocking her way.

She rolled down the window.

"Aren't you going a bit far? This isn't the Soviet Union where you can go around persecuting people and get away with it."

"Who is this woman?" he asked, showing her the drawings.

Piotruś Najman was asleep in his little seat, tired out by his adventures in the land of law and order.

"How should I know?"

"Your son drew her. Is she an aunt? A babysitter? Grandmother?"

He spoke deliberately loud in the hope of waking the kid, but he was fast asleep.

"Number one, don't yell. Number two, I have no idea. Number three, I couldn't give a shit. And finally, please get out of my way before I run you down."

"She's in every picture. She's the only one holding his hand. It has to mean something. Just tell me who she is!"

She smiled at him, coldly and sweetly all at once.

"You've had your chance," she said. "You should have asked the right questions."

She drove off abruptly, splashing Szacki with black winter mud that had gathered in the parking lot, unevenly surfaced with old paving stones. The Skoda's brake lights blinked at him, and zoomed into the traffic just in front of a city bus; two seconds later it was out of sight.

He stood in a rippling puddle, covered in mud spots from head to toe, clutching the child's drawings. The splashes of color looked surreal against Szacki, the sidewalk, the mud, the social assistance building, and the whole wintry urban landscape.

He had no idea what to do. He decided to let himself weep. Just then someone put a hand on his arm.

Jan Paweł Bierut. As sad as ever. It couldn't be good news.

"We've found the guy with no hands," he said.

8

The little light by the door changed to red. Hela sat quietly, but she couldn't hear any sounds from the other side; it was hard to say if someone had taken away her breakfast leftovers or not. Maybe they'd done it silently—maybe the door was soundproof. She shuddered—she couldn't bear to think what the kidnappers might need soundproof rooms for.

Half an hour had passed since she'd drawn the line marking noon, and she was planning to take a nap, when for the first time since breakfast something changed.

The television came on.

There was black-and-white interference on the screen.

Then the interference disappeared and was replaced by the image of a room. A room like any other—it looked like the unfinished ground floor of a single-family house, yet to be supplied with interior fittings:

walls made of cinder blocks, a concrete slab floor, roof beams visible on the ceiling. The room had been lit up by several strong lamps.

In the middle stood a sort of pipe, a thick one, made of metal. Possibly a sewage pipe. Or maybe it was a sort of column?

Set against the column was a painter's ladder, the kind with a platform at the top.

The camera angle changed, and now she could see into the pipe.

She felt a nasty shudder.

Stuck inside the pipe was a naked man. Maybe asleep, maybe unconscious, maybe dead. His head was slumped to one shoulder, so that all she could see was an ear, part of a cheek with dark stubble, and the top of a bald head.

She gazed for a while at this unusual, disturbing image. But there was nothing happening. She wanted to go and pee, but she realized she'd better not move, or she might miss something. But nothing was happening, and she couldn't hold it, so she quickly ran to the toilet, and came back without washing her hands.

There was still nothing happening.

She was starting to suspect some madman had recorded a decaying corpse and was now making her watch it for the next two weeks so she'd know what lay ahead. She couldn't restrain the thought that if she was going to spend those two weeks sitting in a six-foot-square room eating McDonald's, there was no way she wouldn't gain weight.

Suddenly there was audio. Nothing special—background noise. Footsteps, a text message notification, somebody putting something down, somebody shifting something, somebody slamming a door.

Then the angle changed for a few minutes, showing a general view: the cinder blocks, the pipe, the lamps. A shadow, as if someone had walked behind the camera. And then back to the close-up on the body.

The image was very high quality. In the well-lit room she could clearly see that the man's ear was very slightly misshapen. At first she wondered if it was the first stage of decomposition, but she soon came to the conclusion that it was a scar, as if from a burn.

And just then, when she had almost set her nose against the television screen to take a closer look at the scar, the corpse moved.

Hela screamed and jumped away from the TV.

"Oh fuck, just like a horror movie!" she said out loud to give herself courage, and automatically went back to her safe place on the couch.

It took the man a while to regain consciousness. He coughed, looked around, and craned his neck, staring at the camera, and thus straight into Hela's eyes.

A man with an ordinary face, neither ugly nor handsome. Square, masculine in a caveman sort of way, which always put Hela off—she thought men like that sweated more and stank. He had thick black eyebrows that looked almost fake.

For a while the man's eyes moved in all directions; he must have been trying to see where he was, but from Hela's point of view it looked comical, as if he were inspecting her cell. His initial amazement was soon replaced by fury, and his face twisted into a nasty scowl.

"Have you gone completely crazy?" he shouted. "What's this dumbass show about?"

Nobody answered him, but nobody stopped working either. The whole time Hela could hear the noises of something in the background that made Hela think for the first time of preparations for an execution. A shiver went down her spine.

The man thrashed about violently, as if trying to overturn his prison. His hands were tied at the front, and he could touch the wall of the pipe with his fingers. He laid his palms flat and tried to rock it, but to no effect—it didn't move an inch.

She noticed that he had two fingers missing on one hand.

"You'll be sorry!" he yelled.

He was tired of squirming. He went quiet and tried to calm his breathing; drops of sweat broke out on his forehead.

"You fucking bitch, you'll be sorry, you can be sure of that," he muttered to himself. "I can fucking guarantee you."

A shadow appeared on the man's face. Evidently someone was standing on the ladder, blocking the light.

The man gave a crooked smile.

"What will you gain from this? What are you trying to achieve? Well? Are you going to drown me in here? Kill me? Get rid of me? What will that change?"

A broad stream of small white granules began to flow into the pipe. They looked like polystyrene beads. Hela arched her eyebrows in amazement. Strange, very strange.

The granules were soon up to the man's knees.

"You're going to bury me in Styrofoam? For real?"

He sniffed, as if smelling a nasty odor. He stared at the little grains burying his body at a rapid pace. His eyes said something was wrong. He frowned, and twitched like someone bitten by a mosquito, or who's got an itch in a place where it's impossible to scratch.

He glanced at the camera, and for the first time the aggression on his face was replaced, first by anxiety, then fear.

The white granules were up to his waist.

"Hey, but we loved each other, didn't we?" he said gently. "We still can. Seriously, the world is made for love. We've only got one life, why waste it on hatred?"

"You haven't got one anymore," replied a female voice softly. So softly that Hela could hardly hear it; perhaps the microphone was picking up the sound badly. The gush of plastic beads was also drowning out almost everything except for the man's deep voice.

"What do you mean?" he asked, scowling and twitching violently.

"You haven't got a life," said the voice. Softly, calmly, without hatred, and without sorrow. Hela shuddered. The voice seemed familiar.

The granules had buried the man up to his neck.

"OK, I get it," he said with difficulty. "It hurts, it stings, I've had my lesson in suffering. What's the point?"

His face had gone red, and drops of sweat were gathering on his nose, dripping onto the granules. Hela noticed that they were behaving as if they'd been dropped into a hot frying pan, and from the spot where the sweat fell, faint smoke was rising.

Hela froze. She realized that whatever fate had been prepared for the man in the pipe, it must be terrible. In theory she knew that it wasn't going to leap out of the television, but terror was getting the better of her. The man let out his first scream—not of fury but pain, the scream of a wounded animal. Hela covered her ears to block out the sound, but she couldn't tear her eyes away from the screen.

Then something unexpected happened. The prisoner started to thrash about in all directions, shaking his head desperately—it looked as if, contrary to logic, he was trying to crawl out of the pipe. In the course of all the struggling, panting, and screaming, he made a big mistake: he immersed his face in the mysterious granules. He must have breathed some of them in, because suddenly he started to choke, spit, and yell at the top of his lungs. In paroxysms of pain he threw his head back, banging it against the metal pipe, and Hela saw that the inside of his mouth was a bleeding cavity—the white granules were smoking and foaming in there. Clearly some chemical reaction made them change into a corrosive substance.

Suddenly the screaming stopped. She thought the sound had been switched off, but it hadn't. She heard the hiss of the chemical reaction, the rustle of the granules as the man wriggled about in them, and the dull thuds as he banged his head against the pipe. As she stared at his gaping mouth, she realized that he was still screaming. Except that the acid, or whatever it was, must have eaten through his vocal cords.

His scream had become silent.

It was the most horrifying thing she had ever seen. Worse than his bleeding mouth. Worse than the collar of blood that had appeared around his neck, at the top of the white granules, where they were slowly dissolving his flesh. Worse than the eye into which a granule must have fallen, and which was now going cloudy, bleeding and starting to cave in, as if sinking inside his skull.

The image changed, and she saw the pipe and the room from another angle. On the platform of the ladder stood the woman. She was bending low, almost with her head in the pipe, as if she didn't want to miss a single second of his suffering.

Long black hair shielded her face from view.

9

The clock in the patrol car showed almost one p.m. as the driver parked outside the bakery on Mickiewicz Street.

"Is it here?" Szacki asked Bierut.

"Opposite," he said, pointing at a tenement house on the corner across the street.

The building must have once been the pride of Olsztyn. Half a century of Polish administration had reduced this beautiful Secession-style mansion to a council slum. The plaster was flaking off the building, and for some strange reason the drainpipes ran crosswise, disfiguring the front. Three recessed balconies on the left-hand side were each painted a different garish color. The three on the right were each enclosed in a different way. The picture of misery and despair, an advertisement for Polish aesthetics.

"I used to go to the children's library here," said Bierut as they were crossing the street.

"Where?"

"In here—it's the local member of parliament's office now." He pointed to a sign hanging on the building.

"*O tempora, o mores,*" said Szacki, at which Bierut nodded with his characteristic sorrow.

"It's a fine house, isn't it?" The policeman sighed as he stopped at the door and gazed up at the grand, ornate facade.

"It used to be," muttered Szacki, and pushed open the front door—the old, original one, decorated with soft Secession details, obvious despite the peeling layers of paint. He stepped inside, into damp, cellar-like mustiness, the unmistakable smell of rotting wood. He flicked on the light and couldn't restrain a heavy sigh.

There was an old joke in which the devil catches a Pole, a Russki, and a German. He gives each of them two metal balls and a week to learn to do tricks with them. Whoever does the best tricks will be let go. After a week the German's balancing both balls on his nose, and the Russki's juggling, but the Pole has ruined one ball and lost the other.

The same thing had happened to this building. The Pole had ruined the facade and lost the inside. To call the stairwell "neglected" would fail to reflect the scale of devastation, all the more acute because, from under the effects of Polish housekeeping, from under the grime, filth, chipped plaster, and layer upon layer of paint in the most hideous browns and yellows, its former beauty still came through: the joinery of the banister and doors, the decorative ceiling, the plaster moldings, and ornate windowpanes with soft art deco lines. Halfway down the hallway, above a lightly vaulted doorway, the wall was decorated with a subtle, shallow relief, depicting the face of a boy in a frame of botanical elements. Szacki shuddered; not only did the pale stucco face look ghostly in this interior, but the subtly smiling boy looked frighteningly like Piotruś Najman. The same chubby, square face, the same thick, slightly wavy hair.

"Which floor?" he asked hoarsely, to get away from his own thoughts.

"Fourth, I'm afraid," said Bierut.

A few dozen creaking wooden steps later, the two men were standing at a brown wooden door, in the hope that someone would open it. Szacki was wondering what the locks were like in the home of a man with no hands. Was there some sort of special equipment for sliding bolts with your mouth?

"Who's there?" asked a woman's voice.

"Police," answered Bierut in a sepulchral tone, holding his badge up to the peephole. "It's nothing serious, we just want to ask you some questions."

Szacki knew they said that even when they were going to throw tear gas inside, and several commandos from a special unit were close behind.

A bolt rattled. The door opened, and there stood a woman of about fifty, who waved them in. Neat, thin, and subdued, she had graying shoulder-length hair, a gray turtleneck, and black pants. She looked like a college professor. And more like one from the Sorbonne than the University of Warmia and Masuria (or "wormier and misery" as it was meanly called).

Szacki hesitated because everything seemed wrong. He'd been expecting a guy with no hands, hanging out in a filthy dive in a dirty undershirt. But here was a classy-looking woman with a complete set of limbs, an educated homeowner. From the hallway he could already see that if anything was missing in this home, it was room for all the books.

"Prosecutor Teodor Szacki," he introduced himself. "This is Deputy Commissioner Jan Paweł Bierut. We're looking for Artur Ganderski."

"In other words, my former husband," said the woman.

"Do you know where he's residing at present?"

"Of course. Nine B Poprzeczna Street, apartment twenty-one."

"Thank you." Szacki bowed and turned to run down the stairs, when Bierut grabbed him by the arm.

"That's the address of the local cemetery," he said.

The woman smiled and curtsied girlishly.

"I hope you can forgive me. My husband's not here, and, luckily, he won't be back. But if I can help you in any way, please come in and have a cup of tea. Especially if you're looking for him in connection with an unexpected inheritance or something of the kind. I'd be more than happy to oblige."

They disabused her of this mistake and accepted her invitation.

10

The tea was delicious, prepared in the oriental style, brewed with sugar and fresh mint in a brass pot. Probably the best tea Szacki had ever drunk. First, Jadwiga Korfel told them the story of how her husband had lost his hands eighteen months ago in a hunting accident, and had been so distressed by the fact that he would never again wipe his own ass or pull a trigger without help that he had decided to end his own life. For obvious reasons he hadn't been able to shoot himself, so he'd drowned in the river while drunk.

Szacki had little time and asked her point-blank whether she had been the victim of domestic violence. Without hesitation she answered yes; the hands that were lost out hunting had beaten her up so many times that after fifteen years of marriage, she'd lost count. Asked for the details, she told a classic textbook story. The cycle was always the same. First, the tension rose. From day to day there'd be rising fear in her, and rising aggression, malice, and irritation in him. Finally the first fuse would blow, and she would be subjected to verbal aggression, insults, and threats. Then the second fuse would blow, and she'd get a beating. A first-rate thrashing, she said in admiration, claiming that even if her late husband wasn't the national champion, he was certainly the provincial number one in this particular discipline. Sometimes he got drunk, sometimes he abused her when he was hammered. But whenever he avoided alcohol, even liqueur chocolates, for a few days, she knew the day was approaching. He always beat her when he was sober and well rested, as if he were taking part in a competition to cause her as much pain as he could while leaving as few marks as possible. Then he would vanish for two days and come back with a bunch of flowers, gold jewelry, tickets for a trip abroad, and promises never to do it again. She would believe him, accept the flowers, go on the trip, and enjoy her new happiness, until one day she'd come home and sense that the atmosphere was more strained than usual.

"How did he lose his hands hunting?" asked Szacki.

"An accident. He tripped and fell in such an unfortunate way that he hit his hands against a trap set by poachers. It was summer, he was only wearing a light shirt. He was thin, skinny in fact. Trip, trap, snap! No more hands."

Bierut and Szacki exchanged looks.

"And how come they couldn't sew his hands back on?" asked Szacki, out of curiosity.

"Animals took them. The Warmian forest can be a wild place, you know."

She sipped her tea.

Szacki looked around the room. Books everywhere. Plenty of fiction, but above all, academic books. History, archaeology, art. Most of them in German, the rest in Polish and English. On the only wall without any bookshelves, there was an old political map of the Middle East.

"Are you an archaeologist?" he asked.

"When I was young and beautiful. I studied under Professor Michałowski, and I used to go to the digs with him. Now I teach history and art history."

"Where?"

"Mainly at the university, but I moonlight at high schools, too."

Szacki felt hungry. He scarfed down a few of the chocolate chip cookies lying on a small plate.

"We're conducting an investigation under great time pressure, and so I'm going to be frank with you. We all know the hunting story is garbage. And we're all aware that your husband was punished for wife-beating. But only we know that the perpetrator's insanity has gotten out of control. First, from a phase of mutilation, he smoothly shifted into a phase of killings, and then from the stage of murdering wife-beaters to a higher level, murdering anyone who falls into his hands. We've got to find him."

Jadwiga Korfel sipped her tea, ate a cookie, and ran her eyes around the room, as if for the first time.

"I understand. And please believe me, I'd be more than willing to help. But I have no idea who my benefactor is. And I'll tell you right away that you don't have to play good cop, bad cop with me. Regardless of the fact that I'm pleased about what happened to my husband, I'm a normal person and a normal citizen. I know it's wrong to take the law into your own hands—it's the road to perdition. I'd tell you every-thing—eventually I'd say a few warm words about the perpetrator in court to reduce his sentence a little, but that's as far as I'd go. Am I making myself clear?"

Szacki said yes.

"Did you tell anyone about your troubles before the accident? Did anyone question you? Or come to see you?"

She thought for a while. Finally she said no.

"Please think very carefully. Did you go to the doctor at the time? A male or female doctor who might have guessed you were the victim of abuse? Maybe somebody gave you first aid. Especially at the city hospital?"

This time she was even quicker to deny it.

"Artur was a pro. It hurt like hell, but never enough for the wounds to need dressing or to have any bones set. I rarely had any bruises. He'd beat me on the heels, for instance. I'd cry with pain as I walked for a week, but it wouldn't even go red. A punch in the stomach—no marks. A piece of elastic behind the knees, ditto. But it hurt as badly as if I'd torn a ligament skiing. You wouldn't believe what miracles can be performed by hitting someone on the head through a pillow, or by whacking them anywhere through a pillow. Sometimes he knocked me around so badly that I had to take time off because I couldn't tell which way was up. But I looked like I'd been to the beauty parlor. Glowing with health. Pardon my French, but he really did fuck me up, there's no other way of saying it."

She must have noticed their astonished looks, because she added, "Please don't think I'm crazy. My therapist has taught me to unburden myself. Talking about it has become pretty natural for me. So natural that suddenly I lost all my friends."

"A good doctor must have noticed something," said Szacki, who chose not to respond to her last comment. "Please think. Maybe a regular checkup, or a routine consultation."

She sighed.

"I'll get my journal from last year and check."

She got up and went over to a writing desk, a very fine piece of furniture, ideally suited to this bourgeois interior. She was refined, tranquil, self-confident, not hiding her age, attractive in her own way. If there was anything Szacki couldn't imagine, it was her lying on the couch, covering her head with a pillow, and letting some troglodyte hit her with a stool.

"Three months," she said, clearing her throat, "before the hunting accident I went to the dentist. And I'll preempt your question now—I go to the dentist in another town, because a very old friend sees me there, and it was during one of our honeymoon periods. I wanted to have a nagging cavity filled before a long weekend in Prague."

The clock in the hall struck two. Szacki closed his eyes and slowly turned his head in an attempt to relieve the stiffness in his neck, which was tense to a point of pain. It crossed his mind that fate had it in for him. Every time he thought he was getting somewhere, just as he was gathering speed to move into the final stretch, he'd turn the corner. But instead of a nice smooth run ahead of him, he'd smash into a concrete wall.

"Do you know a woman with long black hair and strikingly blue eyes?" he asked.

"Prosecutor, I work at a college. Half of my students look like that. They're the ones who used to be blonde but dyed their hair. The other half are the ones God punished with dark hair, and as a result they've dyed it blonde. And these days, colored contacts are so trendy that almost every one of them has eyes like a Japanese cartoon character."

"But is one of your students closer to you than the rest? More talented, perhaps? Maybe you've become friends? Maybe she's been here for tea?"

She spread her hands helplessly. She really did want to help.

"Of course, some of them are more talented, I rate them more highly, and I like talking to them. But I do my best not to let those relationships gain any social footing."

Suddenly a shadow crossed her face, and she paused in midflow, as if a thought had leaped into her mind.

"Yes?" Szacki correctly picked up on it.

"There was a strange thing that happened." She paused for a moment. "I picked up the landline, and a woman asked me if I needed help. I said no, I didn't need a new phone or anything new at all. I was sure it was one of those dumb sales calls. She said she wasn't selling anything, she was just worried about me and wanted to know if I needed help. To which I replied that she must have called the wrong number. And she said I should say no, if I didn't need or want help."

Jadwiga Korfel broke off. Szacki thought it was a pause and didn't press her. But the woman just sat in silence.

"And what did you do?"

"I hung up," she said.

"Right away?"

She chewed her lip and gazed at Szacki with the look of an intelligent, experienced woman.

"No. A little later."

"Did the voice remind you of anything? Was the woman old? Young? Any speech impediment? Did she sound upset? Or use any unusual phrases?"

She shook her head.

"It was an ordinary woman, speaking standard Polish. I'm sorry. Not an old woman, that's all I can say."

All three were silent. Jadwiga Korfel because she had said what there was to say. Jan Paweł Bierut because he was like that. Prosecutor Teodor Szacki because he was thinking hard. He had to find the woman with long black hair and blue eyes. Probably with black hair and blue eyes, because nowadays you could change those features in a couple of hours. In fact the only certainty in her description was that she wasn't old. How feeble it sounded: "The police are looking for a woman up to seventy years old." He felt like crying. He had no foothold at all, nothing. His daughter had been kidnapped and was either just about to die, or was already dead, and every trail led nowhere. Each time he thought about it, he felt even more hysterical. His thoughts were scattered, and he couldn't get back to the process of logical reasoning, which was making him feel even greater panic.

"I'm sorry, but looking at you there's something I have to ask you," said Bierut. "Why did you let it happen?"

"Because I'm an educated, intelligent, well-read woman of the world, right?" She smiled.

Bierut made a gesture to say yes, that was what he was thinking.

"I call it a virus. You know, gentlemen, there's one thing that emerges from the research: Not every person who has experienced violence as a child is bound to become a victim or a perpetrator later on. But everyone who starts doing harm in adult life, or who lets themselves be harmed, was a victim or witness in childhood. One hundred percent. Which means we carry a virus that doesn't have to become active, but in favorable conditions is all too willing. That's what happened to me."

Szacki tried to fake a concerned look, but he couldn't care less. He felt angry with Bierut for prompting the woman to make confessions.

"And there's another thing. I rarely talk about it because I'm ashamed. You know, everyone likes to feel special sometimes, one of a kind. I used to have that experience, too, during our honeymoon periods. It's not usually like that in a marriage. At first, people want to seduce each other, so they make an effort. But then everyday life takes over, the usual routine. But I was regularly conquered all over again, seduced, won over, and showered in imaginative presents. I'd walk down the street knowing he was thinking about me the whole time, wondering how to surprise me, how to give me pleasure, what to do to make me happy."

"Wondering whether he could go into IKEA and change his brand of pillow for one that let him whack you with a lead pipe for a change," said Szacki in the same refined tone.

That rendered her speechless; for a while she stared at Szacki with her eyes wide-open, and then burst out laughing.

"That's a good one. Dark humor is my favorite."

Szacki stood up. He was sick of all these confessions.

"Let's go," he said, though he had no idea where.

Bierut drank his tea, and they walked toward the door, escorted by their hostess.

"Are you really called Jan Paweł Bierut, or is it a stage name?"

"Do I look as if I've ever been on stage?" said Bierut.

"Oh yes. In commedia dell'arte."

Bierut glanced at Szacki, but he just shrugged to show he didn't care if Bierut responded or not. He just tapped his watch, though even if time were running out, he had no idea what to do next.

"Nobody chooses their last name, but my father didn't want to change it, because it's a family with a long tradition. Of course, we're not related to the Communist leader. My parents had the idea of balancing out the weight of it, so they named me Jan Paweł after the Pope.

I was born on the day he held the famous mass in Warsaw. I have a sister, too, whose name is Maria Magdalena."

"Why don't you change it? As part of my therapy I've gone back to my maiden name. One trip to the registry office and it's done. I never expected it to be so easy."

Szacki took hold of the doorknob. He wanted to leave, and at the same time he didn't; he felt a flood of weariness and wanted to give up, switch off. Lie down somewhere, go to sleep, wake up in another world or another time. Hela was probably dead by now anyway—it was all pointless. For the first time the thought of suicide occurred to him. Just end it, find out what happens next. Not have to live without her, not have to deal with searching for her body, not have to go to the funeral, not have to tell Weronika. Not wait for another nightfall. Not have to fall asleep in the deplorable certainty that he'd instantly wake up again. Not have to carry on with this work, in which he neither prevented evil nor righted any wrongs, but just swept up the broken pieces.

Not have to do anything at all. Nothing.

"Is there anything else you want to ask, Prosecutor?" Bierut asked.

Szacki woke up. He must have been standing there, holding the doorknob for quite a while; the other two were behind him, gazing at him expectantly.

11

After leaving the slum on Mickiewicz Avenue, in an act of desperation Szacki sent Bierut off with a warrant to search the Najmans' house, with instructions to focus on the attic, but he wasn't expecting much to come of it. In fact, he wasn't expecting anything. He called Żenia to find out if Hela had made contact or turned up at any hospital. He called Weronika to tell her the whole story. She went into hysterics, accused him of being careless, and left for the airport to get back to Poland as fast as she could. He returned a call from Hela's teacher, but they had no news to share. He didn't return a call from Szarejna, or several from Falk. He didn't believe the junior prosecutor could help him and had no wish to explain why he had suddenly taken off to interview Kiwit.

He didn't know what to do. Bierut had taken the car, so Szacki roamed the city aimlessly. Finally he came to Piłsudski Avenue, Olsztyn's backbone. The Town Hall, the shopping mall, the custody cells, the provincial administration, the sports center, the planetarium, the new water park, the stadium—they were all on the same long street. He stopped, wondering whether to walk toward the Town Hall or the planetarium, and after lengthy deliberation he turned toward the Town Hall. He decided to go to the Old Town and maybe sit in a café—he should eat something, whatever. As he crossed the junction with Emilia Plater Street he glanced to the left; he was only about two hundred yards from home, and the same distance from his office. But he didn't turn off or even slow down.

He passed the shopping mall, and suddenly felt so faint that he had to grab hold of a lamppost to keep from collapsing. The blood was pounding in his ears, his legs were giving way, there was a stabbing pain in his chest, and his hands were going numb. He took short gulps of air, feeling as if his lungs had suddenly constricted. He rested his brow against the cold lamppost to wake himself, to avoid losing consciousness or falling into a puddle.

He managed to get enough of a grip on himself to wobble his way from one lamppost to the next, and from one patch of grass to the next, until finally he trudged into KFC, which was buzzing at this time of day. He bought a coffee, which he had no intention of drinking, sat down by the window, sent Żenia a text, and laid his head on the table.

There must have been something he'd overlooked. Something obvious. Somewhere in this case there was at least one piece of information, maybe more, to which he hadn't paid due attention.

A woman with black hair.

Rage

He raised his head. At the next table, directly opposite him, was a woman with a huge soda. Young, probably a student. Of course, she had long black hair, and of course she had huge dark blue eyes. He stared at her so insistently that finally she gave him a flirtatious smile. Rather than return it, he quickly shifted his gaze outside the window.

A teenage couple was holding hands.

A woman with black hair holding hands with a child. The child liked it. He wanted to draw her holding his hand. That's someone close to him.

The door banged and Żenia sat down at his table, out of breath. The image of his languid neighbor with black hair was replaced by the image of his agitated girlfriend. With black hair too. Żenia looked at him with concern and took a device for measuring blood pressure out of her purse. The classic kind, with a bulb.

"You must be crazy—you're not going to test my blood pressure in KFC."

She leaned forward. The eyebrow rose so high that it looked as if someone had shaved off the old one and drawn a new one on her forehead in an impossible position.

"You're forty-four years old, you live under constant pressure, you're going through unimaginable stress, and you're feeling faint. Of course I'm going to test you in KFC, since you refuse to come home."

He tried to protest, but she was right. It wouldn't do anybody much good if he croaked in here. At most, it would bring him relief. He took off his jacket and held out an arm. It caused a bit of a stir in the restaurant; the shift manager kept an eye on them from behind the counter, possibly suspecting it was some sort of protest by health-food fanatics.

"You're not even qualified," said Szacki.

"But I took the courses. Believe me, I know enough to measure blood pressure."

She spoke without taking her eyes off the gauge.

"No big deal," she said, quoting a book they'd both read recently, "but no big shame either."

She put away the device and looked at him inquiringly.

"I know nothing at all. Absolutely nothing."

"Why is the media so quiet about it?" she whispered. "Shouldn't she be the world's most wanted teenager by now?"

He made a vague gesture. He both couldn't, and didn't want to, answer.

Żenia was surprised.

"It's no ordinary kidnapping," he said. "It has to do with the investigation I'm conducting. Someone's kidnapped Hela as a way of playing games with me."

She looked shocked.

"But how? What for? Have they demanded anything? A ransom? Do they want you to drop the case? Resign?"

He shook his head.

"Shouldn't you make it public?"

"I wanted to outsmart them. But I will go public soon. I have no other option now."

"Is there any way I can help?"

"Who's really close to a five-year-old? Close enough for him to want to draw himself with that person, rather than with his parents?"

Żenia gave him a shocked look.

"Seriously—who could it be? Someone from the family?"

He scanned KFC in search of families. Children. Whose hand were they holding? At this time of day it looked as if only high school kids were wolfing down fried chicken, too young and dumb to think about their health or the harmful effects of carcinogenic substances.

In one corner sat a father with his daughter, who looked about eight years old. There was another dad by the cash register, with twin sons. One boy was trying to knock his brother's hat off and trouble was brewing.

Then a mother came in with three children. She was quite heavy, evidently not steering clear of deep-fried chicken. She was either sparing her children the same fate, or else they'd inherited their metabolism from their father, who came in after them. He was small, thin as a rail, and tired. She wasn't pretty and he wasn't handsome, but the children were all right. A boy and two little girls, aged from five to ten, judging by appearance.

"I'm going to the restroom," said the man in a weary voice. "Stick with your mom, OK?"

The man disappeared, and the woman stared at the menu, as if she'd never seen it before.

"Teo, that's the simplest question under the sun. You really are an incorrigible only child if you have to ask that. A brother or sister."

Szacki froze. He gazed at the two small children standing by their mother, and saw one of the most beautiful gestures to have accompanied mankind since the dawn of time. A gesture of trust, kinship, and security. Performed automatically, without a second thought, a unique symbol of love and friendship. The gesture of a child's hand reaching for the hand of an older sibling.

It's not possible. He couldn't possibly have made such a simple error.

The only official database he hadn't checked. The only one, but in this case the most important from the start, obviously so crucial.

Family. Brother. Sister. Vengeance.

He glanced at his watch, leapt from behind the table, spilling the cup of coffee, and ran out of the restaurant.

It was nearly half past three. The sun had gone down five minutes earlier.

12

It was pitch-black outside and the same inside. So it must have been between three and four. She ought to get up and carve another line, but she didn't want to. She could have gotten up and turned on the light, but she didn't want to do that either. The darkness made her feel safe, it enveloped her, and the more she thought about it, the more she felt the lack of light to be like a soft fabric that she could wrap around her like a blanket.

Unfortunately it turned out she wasn't the only one who could switch on the light. When the room suddenly filled with brightness, she squeezed her eyelids shut and lay there without moving, staring at the afterglow beneath her eyelids, wandering patches in various shades of gray.

The lock rattled. She froze with horror, holding her breath and tensing all her muscles.

Nobody came in. The lock just rattled.

She waited a while longer, but nobody came in.

She raised her head. The diode by the door had changed from red to green.

She waited a while, got up, went over to the door, and found a large bag from McDonald's behind it.

She thought it through. She was sure to die. That was bad news. She was sure to die in agony. That was very bad news. But—maybe—she wasn't going to be raped. That—maybe—was good news.

None of it sounded great, but she saw no reason to be tortured and raped on an empty stomach. She picked up the bag, took the food out, then looked around the room and said aloud, "If you tell anyone that Helena Szacka ate a Filet-O-Fish from McDonald's for her final meal I'll come back and fuck you up bad, you junk-food homicidal maniacs."

She felt a little better—after all, what did she have left apart from her innate sense of dark humor? She started with a shake, while it was still cold, figuring kidnap victims have every right to start their meals with dessert.

13

Several famous people had been born on the same day as Myślimir Szcząchor, December the fourth. Rainer Maria Rilke, for instance, shared his birthday. He wasn't wild about Rilke—not only had he died prematurely of leukemia, but Hitler had been a psychofan of his. Speaking of dictators, General Franco was born on the same day too. At least he'd lived to a ripe old age. And exactly nineteen years to the day before Myślimir, Marisa Tomei had been born; he thought of her as a real soul sister, above all because she was extremely sexy. Seriously, he thought she was the sexiest woman on earth, and he was always defensive when they laughed at him, saying she was an old hag at fifty. Apart from anything it wasn't true—Marisa was only going to be forty-nine today.

He sighed heavily, took the phone out of his bag, and placed it next to the keyboard. It rang at exactly twenty-four minutes past three. As usual.

He answered.

"Happy birthday, Son!" his parents roared in unison through the receiver. "You're thirty years old! Congratulations!"

"Thank you, I love you," he mumbled, always rather embarrassed by their eagerness.

While he was waiting for the call, he'd thought up some middle-class birthday wishes: he'd like to have Momma's Black Forest cake (to please his mother) and a Kindle (so his father would know what to buy him), and to meet a girl with a kind heart (to give them both the hope of a wedding and grandchildren). Because they would never understand if he admitted to them that his greatest dream was for a real adventure to come knocking at his door. An adventure with a capital A. An adventure that needed a symphony orchestra and a full choir.

Myślimir Szcząchor believed that one day it was bound to happen. The fact that he was an ordinary civil servant at the Public Records Office, and not an explorer, an archaeologist, or a scientist in search of a cancer vaccine in the Amazon was actually in his favor. Isn't that what all the books and movies were about, after all? At the beginning, these ordinary people are defensive. They refuse, they beg to be left in peace—but eventually they're sucked into a whirlwind of events, action, plot twists, love, friendship, and a battle for the highest stakes.

The clock on his computer showed that in two minutes it would be three thirty, which meant nobody was likely to want his services again today. It also meant that he could close up shop and go home. Or instead he'd go to the movies. After all, it was his birthday.

He'd go on his own. It wasn't very festive, but then what woman would understand a guy wanting to celebrate his thirtieth birthday by watching Disney cartoons? He smiled. He went to see just about everything except Polish movies, which always put him in a gloomy mood. And it was ages since anything had pinned him to his seat as much as *Frozen*, the animated film about the Snow Queen, cursed by her own gift. He had no idea why. Maybe it was a fabulous cry for freedom? Or maybe because for once it wasn't about romance, but the power of love between siblings. As he'd watched it, he'd swallowed tears, feeling that he should have been ashamed, but my God, what a great adventure.

He started packing his bag, with a song from *Frozen* playing at full blast on the computer to put him in the mood.

The lyrical ballad filled the reception room. Myślimir hummed along to it as he crawled under the desk to grab his phone charger.

The office door suddenly slammed, but Myślimir was up to his ears in cables and didn't notice.

He loved the stuff of fiction. He loved adventure so much. He wondered why it never came his way.

As the vocalist drew out the last bar, Myślimir crawled out from under the desk and saw a ghost in front of him. The ghost was tall, thin, and deathly pale, positively blue with tiredness and the chill of December. His face blended in a single pale shape with his snow-white hair, quite unnatural for a man of his age. And the white face contrasted with his long black coat, his graphite-gray suit, and his pale-gray shirt, buttoned up to the collar. A plain tie, perfectly knotted, with a subtle silver pattern that blended in—a shade darker than the shirt, a shade lighter than the jacket.

"It's after hours," said Myślimir, slightly alarmed by the madness in the stranger's eyes.

"It's a matter of life and death," rasped the stranger in a metallic voice.

"You don't understand, I could lose my job," said Myślimir once he'd heard more, finding it hard to conceal his excitement at having the chance to deliver such a cinematic line.

The prosecutor drummed his fingers on the desk. He was clearly trying to control himself, but furious impatience radiated from him.

"You can't, because there's a law requiring the Public Records Office to provide information to the prosecution service. I'll send you all the necessary paperwork afterward."

"But there are procedures, and the law on data protection—there really can be serious consequences as a result of backdating documents."

For a moment the white-haired prosecutor looked as if he was about to make threats that would prompt this pencil pusher to cooperate, but suddenly his tense face relaxed, and the fire in his eyes dimmed.

"I'll tell you the truth," said Szacki quietly, "because I've reached a point in life where I have no more desire to lie. Last night my daughter was kidnapped, and every trail I've followed in a state of total hysteria since the day began has proved a dead end. I'm banging my head against a brick wall, while somewhere out there my little girl is probably dead. I could seek out regulations that would formally force you to cooperate. I could make all sorts of elaborate threats—prosecutors, of all people, know how to make life uncomfortable. But I beg you, as a human being, please enter these names in your system and let's see what comes up, OK?"

Without a word he switched on the computer and logged into the database.

"What's the name?"

"Piotr Najman."

He typed it in, the program thought for a second, and then brought up a list of over a dozen people.

"Do you know the date of birth?"

"The early 1960s."

"There's one here, born on November the nineteenth, 1963."

"That's the one. What do you have in his file?"

"A birth certificate and two marriage certificates."

Hearing this, the white-haired prosecutor took a very deep breath, raised his head, and with his gaze fixed on the ceiling exhaled again, smiling.

"Perfect. You're actually helping to expose a very dangerous criminal who will stop at nothing. Would you please give me the name of the bride from Mr. Najman's first marriage certificate?"

He clicked.

"Of course. Beata, maiden name Wiertel, born in Reszel."

"I need her national identification number."

"Six, eight, zero, two, zero, two, zero, zero, one, eight, five."

"When was the wedding?"

"September 1990."

"And the divorce?"

"The marriage ended in November 2003."

He waited until the prosecutor had made a note and added, "But not as the result of divorce."

"Sorry?"

"The marriage didn't end in divorce—the wife died."

This information, though perfectly ordinary from the viewpoint of a public records official—marriages and deaths were what their job was all about—had an electrifying effect on the prosecutor. He reeled, as if about to lose consciousness and fall off his chair.

"It's not possible," he said. "She's got to be alive. The lady with long black hair just has to be alive. Otherwise none of it makes sense."

"I'm sorry."

For the first time, Myślimir was frightened. Until now he had felt a bit uneasy, but the excitement prompted by this unusual situation had muted his anxiety. But at this point he was scared. The stranger did have a prosecutor's ID, but there were screwballs among the prosecutors, too, maybe even dangerous ones. The bizarre remark about the lady with long black hair could be an indication that the man had lost touch with reality.

"Please check again, would you? You must have spelled it wrong. You must have made a mistake. You probably looked at the wrong entry. That's criminal incompetence!"

A hysterical note had appeared in the prosecutor's voice, but this time Myślimir didn't feel fear—he felt offended. Nobody was going to accuse him of incompetence.

"Look, sir, maintaining the public records may not be rocket science, but it's not simple either. You could say it's the cornerstone of the state, monitoring how the population rises and falls. We do our job very thoroughly, and we know how to read the data."

Though it hadn't seemed possible, the prosecutor went even paler.

"Please show me her death certificate."

He opened the document and moved the monitor, staring at the boxes on the form himself out of curiosity. It occurred to him that as he was the public records official, he knew their secrets. In this scene the prosecutor was the hero, and he was an eccentric, slightly crazy expert, whose knowledge would allow him to solve the riddle.

"It doesn't look like a death certificate."

"It doesn't look like the ones issued at the registry. Because what you get there is actually a copy of the death certificate, in most cases abridged. What you see here is the full death certificate, the official state document."

"OK, I get it. Can you decipher this for me?"

It crossed Myślimir's mind that the prosecutor was like a one-man impatience factory—he could sell the surplus in jars and make a good living out of it. Not that anyone in Poland was suffering from a shortage of impatience, but who knew? There was a demand for dumber things than that.

"Of course." He started off calmly, knowing well that to begin with the conversation would be ordinary, nothing shocking, and a little later there'd be some minor revelations, but even so, the flash of inspiration would only strike the hero very suddenly once it was all over. Fiction had its rules. "Here are the official signatures, the name of the registry, and the certificate number, but that won't interest you. Then the decedent's details. Beata Najman, maiden name Wiertel, born 1968 in Reszel, last place of residence Naglady."

"Where is that?"

"A village outside Gietrzwałd. The place where the Virgin Mary revealed Herself."

The prosecutor gave him a strange look.

"She died in Naglady, too."

"When?"

Myślimir felt a tremor of emotion.

"The precise details are unknown, because she died under tragic circumstances. Look at this: the date and time of death should be recorded here. We usually get this information from the hospital or the doctor confirming the death. But in other instances, they record the place, date, and time when the remains were found."

"And?"

"And in this case Mrs. Najman's remains were found on November the third, 2003, at six thirty a.m."

"Go on."

"Husband's details: Piotr Najman. And the decedent's parents' details: Paweł Wiertel and Alicja, maiden name Hertel. Finally the details of the facility reporting the death, usually this is the hospital, but in this case, we received the information from the city police headquarters."

"Are there any circumstances or cause of death?"

He shook his head. The prosecutor stood up and began to pace the room, the tails of his coat flapping behind him like a cape. He was clearly thinking very hard.

"Earlier I asked what there was in Piotr Najman's file. You said a birth certificate and two marriage certificates. Najman is dead, but as I understand it, the police probably haven't sent you the forms yet. How long do they have, officially?"

"Two weeks from identification."

"Right. But Piotr Najman has a five-year-old son, too. Why doesn't his file show a connection with the child?"

"From the point of view of the state, the child is a separate citizen. He has his own file, which includes his birth certificate, and to which his marriage certificate and death certificate will eventually be added."

"Meaning that parents' files don't ever include a record of their children's birth?" The prosecutor raised his eyebrows in surprise. "Is that some kind of a goddamn joke? Doesn't this fucking country have a database that tracks what happens to its goddamn citizens?"

Myślimir shrugged.

"To tell you the truth, I thought you guys had something like that."

"You guys?"

"The police, the prosecutors. You put in a name, and it all comes up on the screen."

The prosecutor sat down heavily.

"It comes up on the screen. We can check the penal register, which only lists those who've been convicted by force of law. Can you show me a list of people with the last name Najman who were born between 1988 and 2003?"

"Are you looking for children from that marriage?"

The prosecutor nodded.

He typed the information, and three records came up.

"First this one." The prosecutor pointed at the name Paweł Najman. "Named after his grandfather."

He opened the file.

"Bingo," he said. "Paweł Najman, son of Piotr and Beata, maiden name Wiertel, born April the second, 1998."

For a while he was pleased he'd managed to find something important, but as he ran his gaze down the items in the file he gulped. He hated being the bearer of bad news—his family had always laughed at him for running and hiding whenever he had to deliver anything other than good news.

"Unfortunately he's dead too."

The prosecutor didn't react.

"I'll show you the death certificate, OK?"

He opened the relevant document.

"He died on November the seventeenth, 2003."

"Which date?" Szacki's eyes grew wide with amazement.

"November the seventeenth."

"Ten years. Exactly ten years to the day," whispered Szacki. "So there is something. Was he killed in an accident too?"

"No, he died in the hospital. Hmm, that's curious."

"What?"

"Usually the kids recorded here have died at the children's hospital."

"And?"

"The death was reported by Dr. Angela Zemsta at the Provincial Psychiatric Clinic."

14

She was reveling in being alone. Some people take advantage of solitude to listen to loud music, dance around the room, or watch TV at full volume. She always used the opportunity to switch off everything—radios, telephones, the TV, even the boiler, so she wouldn't hear hissing and bubbling in the pipes.

No washing machine, no dishwasher, no computer with a wailing fan and a buzzing hard drive. Even the plug to the fridge. The first time she did it, she was amazed to find how many domestic appliances make a noise of some kind. Even her desk lamp. There must have been something wrong with it. When it was on it just shone, but when it was off it let out a weird, low murmur.

By now she was a pro at this, and it only took five minutes to get rid of all the noises in the house. Afterward she always sat still for a while, listening to her own breathing, her pulse, the gurgling in her stomach—all those sounds made by the human factory.

Then she'd walk around the house, noticing all the noises we're not usually aware of, because they're drowned out by hundreds of other more insistent ones. For instance, the sound of our thighs brushing each other when we're walking. If she was wearing pants or panty hose it had sounded artificial, so she had conducted her ritual of silence naked. Depending on the time of year, her thighs brushed as softly as the pages of a book being turned, or made a slightly wet noise, like someone licking their lips.

It was very sensual.

Now she was standing naked in front of the huge bedroom mirror, brushing her long, black, shimmering hair. The sound of brushing her freshly washed hair had a squeaky quality, a bit like running a wet finger down a crystal wineglass.

She used to have even longer hair, but she'd trimmed it for comfort because the summer had been so hot. Now she regretted it.

She put down the brush, took hold of her hair on either side of her part, and straightened her arms.

Now it looked like a raven's wings.

She let go of it. The hair fell with a gentle rustle and clung to her naked body.

It was a shame about her hair. A shame about her body. A shame about everything.

15

The public records official was annoying him beyond belief, but Szacki was making every effort not to let it show. The chubby man, who had childlike energy, though he must have been about thirty, never ceased to smile, or make meaningful faces and squint like an actor at a provincial theater who has no idea how to perform with dramatic tension. Of course, Szacki didn't expect all that much from someone who listened to children's songs at the Public Records Office, and besides, he realized he was in Myślimir's debt.

But those faces were driving him up the wall.

This research into the public records was becoming such an emotional ride that he could feel every beat of his heart and was seriously afraid of being struck down by a heart attack before he had the chance to make use of the information.

He almost leaped out of his seat when it came to light that Najman had a first wife. At once he'd imagined a forty-five-year-old woman with black hair, taking revenge on her ex for his past crimes. The theory held water for a whole ten seconds, until he discovered that she was even deader than her husband.

It was like being hit below the belt. Physical pain.

Then it turned out Najman had a son. A son who may have witnessed his mother's death—perfect material for an avenger. A bit young, but the right motive can work wonders. Too bad. The son hadn't outlived the mother for long. Another miss. But this time he'd gotten a consolation prize—he turned out to have been in the care of Dr. Zemsta, whom Szacki already knew. At least that gave him a foothold.

He glanced at Myślimir, looked at his computer screen, and for the first time that day felt that something might work out.

He thought about what he'd seen at KFC. He thought about the small boy who saw his dad going off to the restroom and automatically held out his hand, without even looking to see if someone was there. Because the little fellow knew his paw would instantly be grabbed by his older sibling. That was how it had always worked, still works, and will continue to work, because the tie between siblings is one of the strongest and most unbreakable. Spouses are unrelated people who have chosen to spend their lives together. It matters, but not as much. Children must eventually break away from their parents in order to become real people. And parents have to let them sever the tie that was once the cornerstone of their existence.

The tie between siblings never has to be broken. Of course it may be stronger, or weaker. But being in such close contact at the time in life when the world is new means no people on earth can be closer than siblings.

That was why the little boy had so trustingly held out his hand, and why it had instantly been seized. Pure instinct, prompted by unconditional love.

"Please check the two remaining entries," he said.

"Do you think they're siblings?" asked the official.

"I don't think so, I'm certain," he said, eager to find out the killer's national ID number. "I'd bet everything I've got."

In fact he didn't have much, and he wasn't too worried about property. But if Myślimir had taken the bet, the prosecutor would have lost all his possessions.

Neither Paulina Najman, born in 1990, nor Albert Najman, born in 1994, were in any way related to Piotr Najman and his wife. They weren't even siblings—they were both from a place called Dubeninki, which, judging by the name, must have been close to the Lithuanian border.

"It's not possible," said Szacki. "Please check again a few years earlier—maybe they had a child before they got married."

Myślimir checked. They found Maria Najman, born in Gietrzwałd in 1982, but she wasn't related. It was a very long shot anyway—Najman's first wife was only seventeen at the time. Old enough to have a child, but 1980s Poland wasn't twenty-first-century Britain, with teenagers multiplying like rabbits.

"It's not possible," Szacki repeated, wanting to bewitch reality. "I can't explain it to you, but there has to be a sibling, otherwise none of it makes sense. Otherwise nothing fits. Could a child have been born somewhere else, in another province?"

"Of course. Each hospital always reports births to its own local Public Records Office. Even if the parents register the child's birth in the place where they live as well, the registration form will be sent to the office in the place where the hospital is located, and the birth certificate will be kept there."

Szacki cursed, colorfully, and at length. Myślimir made no comment, but his eyes flashed with excitement.

"There is one more possibility," he said.

Hearing this, Szacki stared at the official in anticipation.

"The child was adopted."

"And what then?"

"Then, in the case of full adoption, a new birth certificate is prepared. The date and place stay the same, but the child is given a new last name, sometimes a new first name, and a new national identification number. The adoptive parents are added to the certificate as the biological parents."

"And what happens to the old birth certificate?"

"It becomes classified. It doesn't come up in the database—only the manager has access to it."

Szacki wondered if this lead was worth following.

"I doubt it," said Szacki. "It's small children that are adopted, right?"

"You'd be surprised. As far as I know, of course people would like to adopt children an hour after they're extracted from the womb, but it's rarely possible. Children are taken away from their parents at all sorts of ages, and it's usually a few years before the parental rights are removed and the decision becomes legally binding. People who want to adopt have a choice: either take a child that's a few years old, or go on being childless. Besides, you'd be surprised how many people adopt children that are virtually grown up, teenagers. They're often mature couples who've raised their own children and want not so much to raise them as help them enter adult life. My manager once made out a new birth certificate for a young woman a week before her eighteenth birthday."

Szacki thought. The Najmans had been married since 1988. Supposing the first Mrs. Najman had given birth at roughly the same time, the child would have been a teenager when it went through the death of its mother and brother. Today that person would be twenty-something at most. Meaning what? Was his pool of suspects suddenly limited to people under the age of thirty? Was he banging his head against a brick wall again?

"Who can see the original birth certificate?"

"Almost no one. A court can demand access, but only in exceptional, justified circumstances—if it can prove in its application that it's essential to the case. Of course neither the biological nor the adoptive parents can get anywhere near the certificate. In fact the only person who can see it is the child concerned, who gains that right on reaching the age of eighteen."

Suddenly it all snapped into place.

There was just one thing he needed.

He leaned toward Myślimir and smiled. He didn't realize how awful he looked and that the ghastly grimace sent shivers down the official's spine.

"Only the manager has access to those files?"

"Of course. For all sorts of reasons, that personal data is bound to be the most highly confidential."

"I understand. But let's face it. I'm a public servant, and so are you. We both know exactly what it means when only the manager has access to something. Right?"

"When only the manager has access to something?"

"In theory. Under the law. But in practice there's no little golden key to the secret safe handcuffed to the manager's wrist. The manager's role is to delegate. He hangs the key in a closet somewhere, and when it turns out he can't get the job done because the law insists that he's 'the only one allowed,' he recognizes that a trusted employee is just as good as he is."

Myślimir didn't comment.

"I think you're just that kind of trusted employee. And that you have access to the classified files."

Myślimir sighed. Szacki couldn't understand why the hesitation in his eyes was mixed with pride.

Finally Myślimir stood up.

"A matter of life and death, huh?"

16

For two hours Hela hadn't marked the passage of time above the baseboard, because she'd been fast asleep. She didn't look like a kidnap victim terrified to the point of brutalization. She wasn't sleeping with one eye open, or sitting bolt upright now and then, she wasn't tossing and turning, and she wasn't curled into a ball, sniveling in her sleep.

She was just a sleeping teenager—lying on her stomach with one arm trapped beneath her body, and the other hanging over the side of the bed. She was snoring gently, as if she'd crashed after a long day of strenuous activity. This good, solid sleep was entirely false, induced by the drugs that had been hidden in the shake. The kidnappers had rightly guessed that in no situation will a sixteen-year-old fail to consume a chocolate dessert.

The dose had been adjusted to her weight and calculated to make her regain consciousness a few hours later.

This gave them enough time to make careful preparations, to be sure that at the right moment, Prosecutor Teodor Szacki would be able to watch his daughter die.

17

It was fifteen after five, and by now Dr. Angela Zemsta should have been on her way home to Jonkowo, where, after she'd fed the cat, she'd wait for her husband to make her a yellow curry with spinach, which she'd been looking forward to since Monday. Unlike her, Mr. Zemsta, a notary by profession, was a superb cook, and whenever possible she encouraged him to practice his favorite hobby. What worked best was flattery, or appealing to his better nature, especially after ward duty. Although she never let him know it, on these occasions she always removed her makeup before leaving the hospital so she'd look like a zombie when she got home. Then he'd immediately ask if she fancied something good to eat. And what do you know, she always did. She felt a little guilty, but she told herself that manipulating people was in fact an art that a good psychiatrist ought to practice.

She sent her husband a text to say she'd be late. She switched off the phone, shut her office door, returned to her desk, and gazed into her visitor's steel-gray eyes. The picture of misery and despair, the man was so wasted and exhausted that her husband would have made him a three-course dinner with zabaglione for dessert.

"Most adults don't even know there's such a thing as a children's ward at a psychiatric hospital," she said. "Quite naturally, there are various disorders that we associate with adults alone. A woman who can't get out of bed. A man who walks around the house because he's afraid to go inside and die alone. Someone who's in a manic state and pays the deposit to buy a different property every day. Someone who thinks he's Christ, or who spends day after day counting the tiles in the bathroom. We all know they're crazy. Sometimes when I ask people, they think a children's psychiatric clinic is just a sort of repository for teenagers who are disappointed in love and have slashed their wrists in the bathtub or started making themselves throw up after meals."

The prosecutor looked as if he didn't have the strength for conversation.

"But in fact, children's brains are not free of ailments. Depression, neuroses, bipolar disorders, psychoses—it happens to people at any age. Can you imagine a four-year-old who has to be put in a straitjacket and tied to the bed because he's found creative ways to harm himself?"

The man didn't react.

"I've seen that. That and other things. When I took up my specialty, I thought I'd be helping children with their problems, or some such optimistic crap. But I became a warder in hell. I was less than thirty when I found out a five-year-old girl can put the fear of God into you. I had to go into her room with two male nurses so she wouldn't hurt me. Have you seen *The Exorcist?* There were days when I dreamed of having a nice quiet job like Father Merrin's."

"I'm sorry," said the prosecutor at last, purely in order to say something. "How do you treat those children?"

"I should say that we apply a combination of modern techniques depending on the case, but in fact we stuff them with antipsychotics like fattened geese to stop them from harming themselves. And we hope they'll grow out of it in time."

"Do they?"

"Sometimes. Sometimes not."

"Was that what happened to the Najman boy?"

She gave a deep sigh. And was happy to find that her drugs were still working. She'd run to the john to take a double dose of Xanax as soon as she heard what the prosecutor had come to see her about.

"Paweł Najman's case destroyed me. I dropped psychiatry and became a family doctor for several years. I was in charge of his case, I felt responsible."

The man really did look as if speaking required an effort way beyond his present state. He just looked at her searchingly.

"I remember it as if it were yesterday. It was my twenty-second hour on call, it was almost four in the morning, the worst shift of all. A policeman called to say he was bringing in a five-year-old who'd been through a tragedy—a house fire somewhere in the province, the mother had been killed, the father was injured, and the boy was in a stupor. Ten minutes later they were on my ward. The boy smelled of burning, not smoke, but a choking stink, just like when people burn trash in a furnace. He was in his pajamas, wrapped in a dun-colored blanket, with muddy little feet. Such a lovely boy—there are some children all the moms look at in the street, wishing they were theirs. Very nice-looking, fine, delicate features. Black hair in a pageboy cut and highly intelligent eyes. The eyes of a good and clever person. The kind who'll have the power to change the world. You may laugh, but I could see it at once."

The prosecutor didn't laugh. He didn't even blink. He just listened.

"Once in a while an exceptional child is born, and I regard it as an exceptionally nasty twist of fate that they're born at random to just any old family. I mean I know in theory people inherit genes. But science doesn't touch on anything to do with the soul. I never touch on it myself, I'm an atheist. But I've had a ringside view of people who deviate from the norm. And sometimes I can't help thinking that once the parents' genes have blended together, something magical happens, and each of us gets something extra. It could be something ordinary, or ugly, or it could be very beautiful. This boy had received something very beautiful, something unique. He was five years old, but if he'd suddenly started to gather disciples around him, I'm sure he'd have found plenty. I saw that quality in him and realized I had to help him. After all, it was for that sort of moment that I chose this specialty—to help innocent creatures with beautiful souls. In those days I was still in the optimistic crap stage. It's ancient history now."

"I understand it didn't work," said the prosecutor. Not coldly, not spitefully.

"No, it didn't. Though I did everything in my power. For two weeks I never left the hospital. Literally—that's not a metaphor. I ate here, showered here, and slept here. My husband brought me a regular change of clothes. I wanted to be right there for Paweł all the time, or at least nearby, to seize the moment when I'd be able to get through to him, when he'd suddenly show me a small crack I could get a toe through before it slammed shut again. Or, I'd notice something that would let me find the key to him, the way to open him up."

"What was the official diagnosis?"

"Reactive psychosis. But you know, in psychiatry the names don't mean much. A kidney stone is a kidney stone, a throat infection is a throat infection—physical conditions are all very much alike. But when it comes to mental problems, there's usually a set of identifying features that allows us to give each one a particular name, but it can be very symbolic—there are really as many different forms of schizophrenia as there are sufferers."

"And what would you call what happened to Paweł? I don't mean the medical term. How would you describe it in your own words?"

She thought for a while. She'd thought about it so often, lived through it over and over, analyzing it from new angles, and adding perspectives every time. But the prosecutor's question threw her off-balance. Could she simply put a name to it? Was it Camus who said the toughest challenge in life is to call things by their proper name?

"He switched off," she said at last.

"In what sense? Did he commit suicide?"

"No, he just stopped living."

"I don't understand."

"The human being is a complicated piece of machinery. More like a factory working on three shifts, without a moment's respite. There are chemical, physical, and electrical processes going on in it. At the level of systems, organs, and individual cells there's something happening the whole time. That's why we wear out so quickly. Even so, it's a miracle that we're capable of getting to eighty. Can you imagine any kind of machine that functions for several decades without a single break? We understand the workings of the individual subassemblies quite well by now, but the unit in charge"—she tapped her head—"is still a mystery. And don't you believe the charlatans who tell you otherwise. All we know is that it's in charge, and where the physiology of the rest of the body is concerned, it has unlimited power. Paweł Najman pressed the right buttons on his control panel, made use of that unlimited power, and switched off his body. He just stopped living."

"You mean he starved himself?"

"You're not listening. He did nothing that fits the definition of suicide. He simply stopped living. He switched off each subassembly in turn. We were helpless. Of course we gave him psychotropic drugs, intravenous substances to assist his failing organism, and finally we revived him. But all for naught—none of our knowledge was a match for his determined five-year-old brain. We felt ashamed of what we were doing. I could see in his eyes that we were causing him distress. He wasn't angry, but it distressed him."

The Xanax was good, but not that good. Her hands were moist, her throat was dry, and she had to use the restroom. She could tell she was starting to fall apart. A few seconds more and she'd start to tremble—she knew the stages of her own neurosis all too well. She wanted to end this and go home.

"Did you get through to him at all?"

"Verbally? No. Right at the end I was coming apart. We were alone, I began to weep in front of him. Very unprofessionally I begged him not to do it, but to wait a little longer. I told him he could still have a wonderful life, his father would recover, and why miss out on the world? And then he said one sentence. I thought at the time, and I still think he did it for me—he felt sorry for me being in such a state, and he wanted to help me."

"What did he say?"

"He said, and I quote: 'I know, but I don't want to live without Monna.' A five-year-old's a bit like a foreigner learning the language, don't you think? At least once every day I can hear him making that funny mistake, 'Monna' instead of 'Momma.'"

Her body couldn't cope with the emotional overload. She badly needed to go.

"I'm sorry, but I have to go to the restroom. Will you wait?"

He shook his head.

"I have an appointment just across the park. I must run. Thank you for telling me about it. I must admit I understand your pain, but . . ." He paused. It worried her that the look on his face suggested he was wondering whether to spare her grief or not.

"But?" she asked, in spite of herself.

"But for all my sympathy for you, you've managed to prove to me yet again that psychology and psychiatry are nothing but pseudosciences divorced from reality. You think you've got all the solutions here, in these sterile spaces, between the couch and the medicine cabinet. But actually the answers as well as the solutions are right there outside, in the real world."

"What are you trying to say?"

"Paweł wasn't talking about his momma. When he said he couldn't live without 'Monna' he wasn't garbling the word—what he said was Monia, short for Monika, his older sister."

She had just been talking about the brain as the omnipotent unit in charge. Her own brain was evidently the exception to the rule because it took a long time to process the information the prosecutor had provided. As soon as Dr. Zemsta had absorbed its meaning, black and white spots began to dance before her eyes. Alarm bells began to ring, and a voice was calling through a loudspeaker: *Faint, faint, lose consciousness, don't try to think about it!*

"You don't mean to say . . ."

"That's just what I mean to say. That if you'd gone into the real world and found his sister, you'd have saved not just that beautiful boy, but lots of other creatures, too, including my daughter."

He stood up, put on his black overcoat, and buttoned it neatly.

"I hope you'll think about it every day for the rest of your life," he said in a weary tone, and was gone.

18

At moments like this, eminent Olsztyn neurosurgeon Agnieszka Sendrowska was grateful to her late mother for endlessly repeating that every decent home should be ready to receive an unexpected guest.

So here she was, putting the coffee cups on a tray, the sliced sponge cake, some squares of Wedel's new nut-flavored chocolate, and some of their plain variety, too. She glanced at herself in the kitchen window to make sure she looked all right for the unexpected visit. Not bad. Once again, her middle-class upbringing helped by never allowing her to parade around in pajamas in the middle of the day, messy, and without makeup. Even when she didn't have to go to work and had nothing to do.

She smoothed her long black hair, pulled down her simple navy-blue dress so it didn't pucker between her bust and thin waist, and went into the living room.

After their encounter at the hospital, when she had bumped into Prosecutor Teodor Szacki by accident, she hadn't been able to forgive herself for not inviting him over for tea, and for not even introducing herself. She'd been worried he'd take her for some wacko who accosts strangers. But it was just that she'd heard and read so much about him that she felt as if she already knew him. She'd even seen videos of him on YouTube, speaking at various press conferences.

And all because her child had a thing about law and justice.

She put the tray on a low table next to the corner couch, where the teapot and coffeepot were already standing.

She smiled at the prosecutor, thinking he didn't look too well. If that was the price of fighting crime and misdemeanors, she'd rather Wiktoria didn't opt for that sort of career.

"Thank you very much for calling, and for accepting my invitation to tea," she said. "I don't know if you're aware, but it meant a great deal to Wiktoria to receive her diploma from you, of all people."

"Really?" Szacki politely expressed surprise as he put a square of bitter chocolate into his mouth.

"Oh God, I hope I don't come across as a psychofan," said Wiktoria, blushing and laughing nervously. Her mother felt parental pride. What girlish charm she had! Such charisma! "It's just that I'm really interested in law—I'd like to study it, so I check out various things. Oh dear, I'm getting all mixed up. In a way I knew you long before you started to work here. I read about the National School of Judiciary and Public Prosecution, and about the prosecutor's training program, then out of sheer naïveté I entered the term 'prosecutor' on YouTube, and you popped up."

"And how did I do?"

"Honestly?" Wiktoria made a funny face, squinting. A child who's not sure of her own maturity, as if slightly embarrassed.

"Of course. A future prosecutor can't tell lies."

"I was stunned by how you looked. That suit!"

"Wika!" her mother cut in; she didn't want any sexual undercurrents.

"Calm down, Mom." The girl said it in such a farcical tone that they all laughed. "What I mean is that on Mr. Szacki, his suit looked like a uniform. More than that—like a superhero's costume. Every superhero has a costume, right? A cape, or a catsuit, or something like that."

"Wika, dear, you're making me blush."

"But, Mom, what I'm saying is good. What I mean is that Mr. Szacki didn't look like a public official. He looked better than that. Like someone who's on the good side."

"I think you should talk to my junior prosecutor, Miss Sendrowska," said Szacki to Wika, and Mrs. Sendrowska could tell that her daughter was flattered by being addressed like an adult. "He recently graduated from the National School, I think you'd like him. He's much more like a superhero than I am. He always wears a suit, he's always formal, always on duty. Sometimes I think his conscience has been replaced with the penal code. He's not interested in motives or extenuating circumstances, personal entanglements or traumatic childhood experiences. He won't rest if someone somewhere has broken the law."

"That sounds rather cold," she said.

"I think a cold attitude is an aid to justice," he said. "Emotions obscure the case and prevent you from appraising the situation objectively."

"Do you work in pairs, like policemen?" asked Wiktoria.

"No, not officially, but we work in the same room, and we help each other. For instance, I work very closely with Edmund Falk, my junior prosecutor. We tell each other everything. Sometimes I get the feeling he knows not just exactly what I'm working on, but he knows where I am, too, and what I'm thinking." The prosecutor laughed, as if ashamed of his intimacy with his colleague. "Sometimes I catch myself treating him not as a junior but a friend, like a younger brother. Have you got any siblings, Wiktoria?"

Mrs. Sendrowska froze. They never talked about it at home. It took her so much by surprise that she couldn't think how to change the subject. She quickly put her cup on its saucer, spilling a little of the pale, milky coffee. Her mind was a complete void, but she really ought to say something—the silence was becoming more and more palpable.

"What are you working on now?" Wiktoria finally asked.

"A kidnapping."

"That's interesting. Is it difficult?"

"Kidnappings are always difficult. We never know if we're still investigating a kidnapping, or eventually a homicide."

"That uncertainty must be awful. You have no influence on what the kidnappers are going to do. You must be imagining the kidnapped person is somewhere out there, at the mercy of God knows who. Especially if it's a woman, the worst possible scenarios come into play. And knowing that one incautious move on your part could change everything."

Szacki nodded, seriously engaged in this theoretical conversation. Mrs. Sendrowska was proud that her daughter, who had only just ceased to be a minor, was capable of talking to an experienced lawyer in such a mature way. Maybe she really was destined to go into law. Even so, she'd prefer her to be a counselor or a notary—there was so much talk about violence toward female prosecutors. Assaults, acid attacks—she refused to think about it.

"You're right. Obviously we're more like the police in this case, aiming to find and rescue the person being held captive. But if a crime has already been committed, we'll do everything in our power to administer justice."

"Are you successful?"

"Almost always. The criminals underestimate us. They watch too many movies—they think it's easy to put pressure on someone, to blackmail them, and then just disappear, dissolve into the mist. They think all it takes is a bit of cunning and common sense. But we never ease up. Especially in the case of kidnappings. We keep searching to the bitter end. And we find them. The more the case matters to us, the more effective we are."

"Revenge?"

"With the full sanction of the law."

"And have you ever been tempted to act outside the law?"

She decided to react.

"Wiktoria! My dear child, don't forget you wanted to go stay over at Luiza's tonight."

The girl was startled and turned her head so abruptly that her long ponytail almost whipped the guest in the face.

"But, Mom, we're not in court, we're just having a chat and a piece of cake."

"My dear child . . ." She turned to Szacki. "Would you please excuse me for a moment?" And then back to her daughter. "It's Mr. Szacki's first visit to our home, and as far as I know his work does not involve operating outside the law, quite the contrary. So if you could . . ."

"If you could not tell me off in front of guests I'd be grateful," said Wika, proudly raising her head.

Mrs. Sendrowska bit her lip but didn't say anything. She was ashamed to find herself thinking that blood is thicker than water—she would not have spoken to her mother like that. Never. There were moments when Wiktoria's genes, and the first few years of her childhood before she came to them, were apparent.

"Please don't argue, dear ladies." The prosecutor was trying to ease the situation. "I don't think any questions are too difficult or inappropriate. At worst I just won't answer, but if I could put in a plea, I'd ask you to drop the fight against your daughter's curiosity. Curiosity and a desire to know the truth are the mainstays of a good investigator. He or she won't get far without them."

She didn't think this statement particularly sharp, but she nodded, as if it were the wisest thing she'd heard in years.

"I'm happy to answer because Wiktoria has brought up the greatest ethical dilemma we encounter in our work. It's true, we're often helpless. We conduct an investigation, we gather irrefutable proof, but because of some tiny detail, often a formality, all our efforts are in vain. Not only do we have to let a man go free when we know he's guilty—and we've even got the proof—we also have to take it on the chin from society."

Taking advantage of the prosecutor's lengthy speech—what a pretentious, flowery way he had of expressing himself—she discreetly wiped the coffee from her saucer with a napkin. She was tempted to tip it back into her cup but was afraid her mother would return from the world beyond to scold her in front of the company.

"Then we do fantasize that justice should be done, or that at least something should be done. To punish, or hurt the criminal. Let's face it, the organs of state have plenty of ways to harm a citizen. And none of those organs will refuse a prosecutor in a rightful case. Problems with taxes, passports, visas, permits, licenses, practicing their profession, interrogations, summonses, explanations. Sometimes, I must tell you, Wiktoria, power on that scale can be intimidating. If I insisted, I could hurt you, not just you, but your entire family to the fifth degree of kinship so badly they'd never get back on their feet again."

She cleared her throat. The prosecutor stopped talking and looked at her; there was a strange shadow in his eyes, and it crossed her mind that Teodor Szacki was not necessarily a good man. There was something about him—what was the right word? she wondered. Not hatred, not frustration, not aggression . . . it was on the tip of her tongue. *Rage*, that was it. A rather outdated word, it sounded quite biblical. But it suited him well.

"You said 'you.'"

"What's that?"

"I'm sure it was a slip of the tongue." She laughed unnaturally. "You said you could hurt my daughter."

"Did I really? Do forgive me, it's late, and it's been a long day. Of course, that's no excuse, I'm very sorry. I guess it's a sign that I must be going."

Wiktoria jumped to her feet in a childlike way and picked up her phone, which was lying in its usual place among the apples on the dresser, hooked up to the charger. A really good phone, an eighteenth-birthday present. She was pleased Wiktoria was looking after it—she kept it in a red-and-white-striped cover she'd crocheted herself.

"I'll send you a text, OK? Anything, so you have my number. It would be great to see you again."

Mrs. Sendrowska smiled. She may have been big, she may have come of age, she may have expressed herself in an adult way.

But in fact her darling daughter was still a little cutie.

19

He took the phone from his pocket, waiting for the message to arrive. And wondered what next. Whether to keep playing, like so far, according to the rules of the clever high school student Wiktoria Sendrowska, or go on the attack. He may not have been in peak form, but hatred was giving him the extra strength to smash in the fucking heads of both these goddamn women against the snobby oak dresser or the vintage ceramic radiators. It would have been enough for him to rip dear Mrs. Sendrowska to shreds in front of her adopted daughter. For the little brat to see what it feels like when someone you love is suffering. Then he'd wonder what to do next.

He imagined her skull striking the radiator. He imagined the skin splitting, the bone being crushed into the brain. Blood pouring from her broken head, steam and hot water gushing from the cracked radiator, Mrs. Sendrowska still conscious, too surprised to react, not aware of what's happening. He tightens his grip on her black hair, twists it around his wrist, and slams her against the radiator again. More steam, more blood—the shards of bone lying on the floor look just the same as the shards of ceramic. It's easy to spot the gray jelly-like bits of brain against them. Now her dear little daughter can see for herself what her mommy's gray matter looks like. Right now at the closedown stage.

Mrs. Sendrowska smiled at him over her coffee cup. He smiled back.

Rage was filling every fiber of his being, turning every single action into an effort beyond his strength. He was trying to conduct a normal conversation, but he felt paralyzed. He was hiding behind words to avoid doing anything stupid. That was why he was rambling like a half-wit, as if giving a lecture on law, understanding only every third word of it himself. But drawing out his words, carefully selecting them, focusing on the inflections, as if talking in a foreign language—all that was allowing him to preserve relative calm.

He got a text, which read `Telno1`.

Just as she'd said: I'll send you anything. "Telno1," as if to say "telephone number one," a stupid little joke from a smart high school student. She'd just tapped out whatever came into her head so he'd have her number.

In reality the message was totally legible. *Tell no one*, or your daughter will burn at the chemical stake erected by the fucked-up Warmian inquisition.

He stood up, politely said good-bye, and allowed Mrs. Sendrowska to show him into the hall. On the way he courteously admired the swanky house. In all honesty. The part of his consciousness that was managing to keep up the conversation genuinely admired the effort the Sendrowskis had put into restoring the splendor of this old German villa, successfully combining elements of the original architecture with modern Scandinavian design.

He put on his coat and left without shaking hands with anyone. He was afraid that if he felt Wiktoria's touch he wouldn't be capable of containing his rage, but would kill her on the spot.

He walked across the small garden, opened the gate, emerged onto the sidewalk of Radiowa Street, and took a deep breath. The air was different from before. Cold, crisp, promising snow. The frost had chased away the damp smell and dispersed the fog, and Olsztyn seemed in sharper focus than usual. Szacki often felt as if he were looking at the world through a misted lens here, as if everything were faintly blurred. Now for a change it looked as if the image had been put through a sharpening filter.

He couldn't kill her. For a while there was nothing he had wanted more, but he couldn't do it. Because as well as rage, he was filled with an equal degree of unreasonable hope that Hela was still alive and he could still save her. If the price was to play the game according to Wiktoria Sendrowska's rules, he was ready for it. If the price was to be his own death, he was ready for that, too. He was ready for anything.

He received another text message from Wiktoria: o h .

And it was all clear. He was to be there at zero hour—midnight.

He hadn't the least doubt where.

20

She'd been going up the mountain trail for a while now, and she'd worked up quite a sweat before she noticed there was a glitch in the Matrix. First of all, the weather was never like this in the Tatras. Well, perhaps it was, but she'd never seen weather like this on any expedition. Whether skiing with her mom or trekking with her dad, or taking a boring hike on a school trip—in these mountains she had only seen wet rocks, fog, and rain (or snow) clouds at eye level.

This time she was walking along a stony path on top of a ridge, with scenes on either side that looked as if someone had pumped the air out so it wouldn't obstruct the view. She'd had no idea there were so many mountains in the wet Tatras—she'd never seen farther than a hundred yards ahead before. What a fabulous experience.

Suddenly she came to a steep wall with steps hewn out of it. It didn't look safe, but was still more like a tourist trail than a climbing route. Especially as there was a massive, rusty chain attached to the rock alongside the steps.

She pulled on it. It held.

She grabbed the cold iron and began to climb. At first she felt wonderful, but the more air there was between her butt and the path below, the more anxiety crept into her mind, and the more she saw images of an inert body falling and crashing against boulders sticking out of the wall of rock before finally shattering on the stones below.

Nervously she tightened her grip on the chain. Suddenly it sagged in her hand, as if made of rubber. She stared at the chain in amazement. She squeezed it again. It really was behaving like a rubber toy.

She sniffed the chain. It smelled strongly of rusty metal.

She shook it violently. Instead of rattling against the granite, it sounded like a rubber ball, bouncing off the wall.

And that was when she realized she was dreaming. She looked at the world around her, repeated to herself three times that it was all in her head, jumped off the rock, and flew. Fast and decisively, not like Mary Poppins but like Robert Downey Jr.

"*Wheeeeee!*" she shouted, gazing at the rapidly retreating mountains; from this perspective the granite ridge between two valleys was like the spikes on a gigantic green dinosaur's spine.

Her plan was to fly to Kraków, when suddenly she caught the strong smell of rusty iron again. She glanced at her hands and noticed to her amazement that she was still holding the rubber chain. Still attached to the mountains far in the distance, the chain was stretched to its limits, its links now as thin as fishing line.

It would have been a funny sight, if not for the fact that suddenly the stretched chain began to pull her back with great force. She couldn't let go of it, and now she was falling down, faster and faster, at high velocity and with a whistling in her ears, as the mountains came toward her at the speed of light. Now she could see the steps carved out of the wall, so she rolled into a ball and squeezed her eyes shut before impact.

And that was when she awoke. Her muscles were tense and aching, her eyes were shut, and there was still a strong smell of rust.

She took a deep breath, sniggered at the memory of her dream, opened her eyes, and felt tightness in her throat.

Instantly she knew where she was. There was enough light in the room for her to recognize the texture of the rusted metal. She glanced down. Luckily her fears were unfounded—there were no remains, no teeth or fingernails swimming in gunk.

The inside of the pipe was clean and dry, well maintained. To her surprise, she found that she had her shoes and clothes on. Unlike the guy in the video who'd died naked.

She knew she was going to die, but at least they hadn't raped her.

At the height of her rib cage the rust was grooved, scored with vertical lines. Hela shuddered when she realized how they got there. Someone had been so crazed with pain that they'd tried scratching their way out. Would she try to do the same?

She glanced at her hands, tied in front with a thin rope.

She probably would. As soon as the rope was snapped by the acid they were going to pour on her, she'd try to scratch through the iron, like everyone before her.

She forced herself to tear her gaze from the marks and looked up.

Straight into the eye of a camera.

21

Szacki opened the Citroën window, letting in frosty air that carried a strong scent of pine. The road to Ostróda meandered gently between wooded hillocks. It was wide, smooth, fairly new—in normal circumstances he loved driving out here. There was almost no traffic. He was alone with the forest, with winter hanging in the air. A few miles on, the forest ended, replaced by undulating meadows. A little farther, to the right he could see the lights of Gietrzwałd. To the left, the village of Naglady nestled between the hills. Closer to the road there were some old buildings, and closer to the forest there were some nouveau riche villas. It was actually quite an attractive place.

He slowed down at a crossroads, but rather than turning toward the village, he went in the opposite direction, where there were no lights, just a meadow and a black wall of forest.

The paved road soon changed into a graveled dirt road. But once he had passed a new development, that ended too. Farther on, it was just an ordinary Warmian cart track, bumpy ruts on either side of a ridge of withered grass that scraped against the oil pan.

He stopped on a stretch that looked dry and used his hydropneumatic suspension to raise his gas-guzzler a few inches.

For once in his life, this goddamn gadget had come in handy.

He drove on.

The road quickly disappeared into the forest. If he hadn't checked the lot number in the cadastral survey before leaving, he probably would have turned back, convinced it couldn't possibly be leading anywhere.

A few hundred yards along, he came to another clearing, where there were two new shacks, totally identical. Roofed building shells for some hideous cabins, teleported from an American subdivision. Someone had probably decided to become a developer in the days of plenty by building a "luxury woodland oasis for the discerning home-owner." And had wound up like all the rest.

He switched on his high beams and saw a huge, glaring banner reading "For Sale."

He passed the banner, passed the houses, and drove into the forest again. The road reached a new level of difficulty, and even his monster, which could usually cope with potholes, was mercilessly swaying in all directions, as if trying to turn on its side.

Two hundred yards on, he drove into another clearing and stopped the car.

The green figures on the dash showed 23:52. He figured showing up a few minutes early wouldn't be taken as an affront, so he switched off the engine and got out of the car.

At first it seemed pitch-dark as he fumbled his way toward the house. But his eyes soon adjusted to the gloom, and then he found that the visibility was surprisingly good, as it always is when snow clouds hang overhead with their unusual capacity to reflect the least bit of light from the ground and bounce it back.

He stopped in the spot where there must once have been a gate. Now there was just a gap in the fence.

So this was the place.

He thought of Hela. It came to him with difficulty. All day long she'd been in his mind, but after the conversation with Wiktoria Sendrowska, something had happened. His brain had cut off the steady flow of images prompted by his paternal imagination. Just as it cuts off consciousness when physical pain becomes unbearable. He realized that he was probably going to find her corpse in there. But this realization was deeply buried, foggy, and unreal. Like our imagination of a place we only know from mythology.

He walked through the gap in the fence.

He thought about little Paweł Najman, the boy who had decided to stop living. He thought about Piotruś Najman and his drawings. He thought about the child doing the jigsaw puzzle while his mother lay there in a pool of blood.

He thought about a child who has to hide from those he loves. He does everything other children do. He makes towers out of building blocks, crashes toy cars together, has his teddy bears hold conversations, and paints houses under a smiling sun. A kid like any other. But fear makes everything look different. The towers never tumble. The car crashes are more like gentle bumps than major collisions. The teddy bears converse in whispers. And the water in the paint jar rapidly turns to dirty gray sludge. The child is afraid to go change the water, and eventually all the paints are smeared with sludge. Every little house, every smiling sun, and every little tree comes out the same nasty black and blue.

That was the color of the Warmian landscape tonight.

NOW

Prosecutor Teodor Szacki felt calm because he knew that one way or another, here in this house, it would all come to an end. The number of possible variants was finite, and although logic was telling him to assume that in almost all of them his daughter would die, and so would he, even so, he still held on to the thought that somehow he was going to triumph. That he'd think of something. Something would happen that he hadn't yet foreseen. Or it would all turn out to be a monstrous joke.

It was a stupid hope. His experience as a prosecutor had taught him that nothing in life ever turns out to be a joke—it's always deadly serious. Things were not improved by the fact that the crazy avenger was a girl of only eighteen. At that age, people are inclined to be solemn, to have fixed, intransigent beliefs and radical views that only a decade later would seem comical to them. Which meant that however twisted a plan had developed in her homicidal mind, either she'd already carried it out, or she definitely would.

Unless something happened. After all, something unexpected can always happen.

He walked across the lot and stopped at the front door. The area between the fence and the house, which might once have been a yard or a garden, was like an experimental nursery for weeds, now withered, rotten, and dead, ominously black in the winter night.

Up close, the house didn't look quite so bad. From a distance it looked like a German cottage built in the early twentieth century, a forestry lodge perhaps, which had had a hundred years to fall apart. Now Szacki could see from the architecture and the building materials that it was from the 1990s, and its poor state was the result of the fire from ten years ago. He could see that the fire had raged on the right-hand side of the house, where there weren't any window frames. They must have burned up, and the roof had collapsed when the truss was engulfed in flames.

He was surprised that all the windows were tightly secured by wrought-iron bars. He wondered if they'd been installed when the property was vacated after the fire, to protect it from thieves and vagrants, or had been put in earlier. More likely the latter. Nobody would add fancy metalwork to a gutted property; they'd block the gaping holes with rebar, or board them up.

He glanced at his watch. Midnight.

He opened the front door and went inside, hoping he wouldn't stumble over his daughter's corpse.

He didn't. He was greeted instead by feeble light and an intense aroma of strong, freshly brewed coffee. He followed his nose and found himself in an empty room that must once have been the living room.

An almost empty room. In the middle stood the sort of camping table that folds into a neat little carry case, and on it a portable gas lamp, screwed onto a small cylinder, a thermos, and two thermal cups. And on either side of the table were camping chairs—two pieces of green canvas stretched on an aluminum frame. One chair was empty, and on the other sat Wiktoria Sendrowska. Young, beautiful, serene. With her hair loose for once. The long black strands fell to her waist, and combined with her pale face in the flickering lamplight, it made her look like a character from a Japanese horror movie.

"Good evening, Prosecutor," she said, pointing to his chair.

He sat down, crossed his legs, and adjusted the crease in his pants.

"Hello, Monia."

"Don't call me that."

He shrugged.

"Where's my daughter?"

"You'll find out. I promise. Coffee?"

He nodded and looked around. The lamp didn't produce much light, so the corners and walls were lost in the dark. Someone could be lurking there or standing behind the door. Someone could be aiming a gun at him or clutching an iron bar. Everything implied that this really could be the last conversation he was ever going to have. And yet, suddenly, he felt weary—he desperately wanted to sleep.

She pushed a cup of coffee toward him.

"Any questions?"

He sipped the coffee. Strong, black, and delicious. He could drink it every day. He thought about what she'd just said. For all her rare qualities, Wiktoria Sendrowska wasn't free of the megalomania typical of criminals. She was tapping her little feet like a preschooler, eager to be admired for her cunning.

"No," he said. "I already know the answers. I want to get my daughter and go home."

"Well, I never, what a smart prosecutor you are. So what are those answers?"

Jesus Christ, he really didn't want to do this. He forced himself, thinking that maybe, if he could satisfy her crazy ego, the whole thing might end better than he had figured.

"The abridged version, all right? You were born Monika Najman, you lived"—he gestured to indicate their surroundings—"in this charming house of horror with your parents and younger brother.

You were probably the victim of domestic violence or sexual abuse, or maybe just the witness to what happened to your mother. Ten years ago there was a fire. Your mother was killed, your brother died soon after at the mental hospital, and something went screwy in your head. A bright, pretty child, you were soon adopted by the Sendrowskis, who didn't notice, or refused to notice, your flaw. I don't know why your father lost custody rights, I haven't got to the files at the family court, only the documents at the Public Records Office. From what I've seen and heard, your adoptive parents guaranteed you ideal conditions to develop, thanks to which you grew to be a clever and beautiful young woman—endlessly burning with desire for revenge. On your father in particular, and on those guilty of violence in general. You waited until your eighteenth birthday, because only then could you gain access to the adoption records and the files relating to your father's loss of custody rights."

"You underestimate me. I've had those files for the past three years."

He was very tired, yet in his prosecutor's mind, the lie detector was going off. Something wasn't right. He had no idea what, but it was the first moment when he thought he must have incorrectly connected the facts. Unfortunately, drained and exhausted, he couldn't pursue that thought.

"I waited until I was eighteen because it seemed symbolic, apart from which I was observing him. I considered the idea that maybe he had changed and would guarantee Piotruś what Paweł never had."

"Well, yes, Piotruś." He didn't let her crank up the drama, because he wanted to get this summary over and done with. "You befriended the Najman family, above all Piotruś—you may even have been his baby-sitter. Despite appearances, it was a safe solution. Najman was always away on trips, and his wife needed someone to help out. You managed to avoid your father—you probably never met face-to-face until the very last moment."

Wiktoria nodded.

"The little boy took to you. It's understandable, you treated him like a brother, which in fact he was. I suppose that, one day, either before the kidnapping or just after, you told Teresa Najman your tale of woe. She believed you and didn't lift a finger when it came to her husband's fate. On the one hand, she may already have known what sort of a man he was—her child told us in his interview that she was sent to the attic as a punishment. On the other, there's something about you that makes people believe you and want to do what you tell them. Evidently a family trait. Right, Wiktoria?"

She nodded, taking the compliment with a smile.

"After which you dissolved your dear daddy in caustic soda, prepared a fine theatrical prop for us out of his bones and those of other perpetrators of domestic abuse, and planted it in the city center. It's curious that from the start I was swayed by the fact that the underground tunnel led to the hospital. I thought the solution was there. Knowledge of anatomy and all that. Meanwhile, the other end leads to the dorm."

"And what could be more natural in a dorm than an eighteen-year-old?" she added, smiling.

"Quite. Regrettably, only today did it dawn on me in detail. And that's it, really. For several days I've suspected all this is just preparation for something really big. My daughter and I are part of this plan. I suppose I'm going to be punished as a symbol of the incompetent, heartless legal system. Excuse me for saying this—I realize you're acting in good faith, but can't you tell how weird all this is? Aren't you too smart for this charade?"

She regally tossed her hair over her shoulder.

"That's exactly how I think of the legal system," she said. "They seem to have the right answers, but it's all dry, bland, devoid of emotion."

He shrugged. It occurred to him that if he made that gesture once more, he'd be left with a tic for the rest of his life. Not that he was planning to live to a hundred—right now even his forty-fifth birthday seemed out of reach. But a new defect right at the end? The inane spitefulness of fate.

"I wasn't abused, nobody ever hit me. Or Paweł either, just for the record. My mother was a different case. She was weak, she let anything be done to her. She was a little country mouse who never imagined things could be different. I don't have an ounce of pity for her. Nature shouldn't let people multiply if they're too weak to take care of their young."

Suddenly he understood.

"The female bones in your stage-prop skeleton?"

"That's right. She didn't deserve to rest in peace. She let the whole house be filled with fear. Constant fear, day after day."

"But you said . . ."

"Yes, I said he never touched us. But we were sure one day that would change. Rising tension all the time, a sense of threat strong enough to drive you mad."

"The fire?"

"Yes. She was too stupid to get out, just take the children and run. She had to announce it with such drama. And when he realized she meant it, he locked her in the same room as usual, and then set the house on fire. Did you see the bars to the right of the entrance?"

He nodded.

"She died up against those bars. She smashed the window—because as I've said already, she was pretty dumb—and she didn't know that an extra blast of air intensifies a fire rather than putting it out. Then she hung on those bars and fried there. Paweł and I stood by the gate, watching the whole thing happen. Now, of course, I know I shouldn't have let him see it, but I was eight years old, frozen to the spot."

She paused.

"But I'm going to pay for it too," she said quietly, as a shadow of fear and regret crossed her beautiful face. "You know, Teodor . . . You're not angry with me for calling you that, are you? Great. Everyone always adored my father. He really was the kind of guy everyone wanted to befriend, listen to, and hang out with. He could wrap people around his little finger. The salesman type. But then he did work in a service industry—he wouldn't have gotten far if he'd been an off-putting, dreary kind of guy. As a result he knew a huge number of people; he had lots of contacts. So after the fire, it all moved very quickly. He was the great victim of the tragedy—nobody would listen to me. They separated me from Paweł, and I was taken to a children's home because our father pretended to be too grief-stricken to take care of us. As a daughter I didn't matter to him anyway—all these assholes despise women of any age, they've got the mentality of medieval peasants. When Paweł died, our father quickly got rid of me, used his contacts to have his custody rights revoked, and had it all arranged really fast. Would you believe I was only told about my brother's death a month after the funeral? That was when I swore I'd get revenge. I'd make sure he suffered more than our mother, more than Paweł, more than me."

She paused for a moment, staring into the darkness.

"That lye works pretty well, wouldn't you say?"

He agreed. What else could he do?

"Yes, I know you don't believe in vigilante justice and so on, you've got your penal code and your suit, blah, blah, blah, boring." Her eyes were shining. "I was this close to his face when he died, you know?" She held her hand in front of her. "Until I felt faint from the fumes—my throat stung for several days. But I couldn't miss a single second. I was afraid he would soon pass out, but it took him a good fifteen minutes to dissolve. I could see his teeth through his cheeks, and he was still squirming. Unfortunately he didn't scream, because he'd swallowed that crap too soon. But it just heightened the drama."

He knew that encouraging her to be effusive was a mistake; regardless how unimaginable her losses and sufferings, she was just a lunatic. But one question really did interest him.

"How many of you are there?"

She cast him a hesitant look. He should have read that gesture correctly then. As the gesture of a person suddenly thrown off-balance and starting to lose their way. But he was so tired. And he'd gotten so many things wrong that night.

"Well, of course, I couldn't have done it all on my own. I knew from the start I'd need allies. Allies with a mission. Some . . ." She hesitated, as if there were certain things she wasn't allowed to betray.

"Some of them I've known for a long time. Some I found. You wouldn't believe how easy it is to find people with the right motivation—how widespread evil is, how ordinary, how universal."

She paused again.

"I soon came to the conclusion that vengeance doesn't solve anything. Afterward you're left with a void—Dumas described it in detail. And as I needed people, I decided to give them a purpose: to reform the world. I've always suspected that all those dicks are just cowards. And that's the truth. I don't want to deprive you of your illusions about the effects of your work, but the fact is, just one real pounding is worth a hundred times more than a three-year suspended sentence, a fine, or putting someone away for a time. Anyway, you've seen the effects of our work. They literally shat themselves. I bet they were afraid to tell you anything after that."

He confirmed it. He felt grief. In spite of it all, he felt sorry for this crazy, injured girl.

"We've seen the effects, too, and it only confirms our belief that we're doing the right thing. We really are changing the world for the better. We react faster and more forcefully than the state authorities, and we do our best to take action before a tragedy occurs."

"We, meaning who?"

She hesitated.

"Various people."

He thought about what he'd heard that afternoon from the merry widow on Mickiewicz Avenue. A virus. Everyone who's a victim or a perpetrator in adulthood experienced violence during childhood. One hundred percent. And who is Wiktoria Sendrowska? Who are her friends? Definitely not victims, that was for sure. But could they be equated with the perpetrators? Yes, in a way—after all, they had allowed the virus to become active and force them to inflict terror on others. Only this time, the terror wasn't aimed at the vulnerable, but at the offenders. A bit like the superheroes in movies who have to choose whether to use their special powers for good or evil. Legally the cause was obvious: these people were criminals, and they should be locked up before they got too full of themselves and started cutting people's feet off for the deadly sin of jaywalking.

"Did you form the group yourself?"

"There's something about me that makes people do what I say."

"What a wonderful gift." He couldn't conceal his malice. "So what's my part in all this? And what role is my daughter playing?"

"As I'm sure you've guessed, a prosecutor did play a major role in this story. A lady prosecutor, to be precise. The first person my mother eventually went to for help. Too little, too late. I'm sure you know what's coming next; it's often described in the papers. This prosecutor was no different from the norm—well-meaning, but instead of enforcing the law, she persuaded my mother to come to terms with her husband, to settle out of court. My mother had a fit, at which the stupid bitch lawyer started threatening to send her for psychiatric tests. Her, not my father, in case she was nuts and was making it all up. My mother wasn't smart, but she had the wits to know that during a divorce case, tests like those could be used as evidence against her. So she backed down."

"And what happened to that prosecutor?"

More hesitation.

"She died in an accident. I almost believed in a higher power when I heard about it."

Force of habit prompted Szacki to make a mental note that Sendrowska must have access to the legal authorities, either at the police or the prosecution service.

"My mother believed the system would help her. But the system just told her to fuck off."

Suddenly he realized what Wiktoria was telling him between the lines, and he couldn't believe it.

"So what? Am I supposed to be some substitute victim? To pay for the mistakes of the incompetent, heartless legal system? Are you completely out of your mind?"

She didn't answer. She didn't react. She just gazed at him in silence, a sad creature. Perhaps if he weren't so weary and emotionally drained, he would have sensed the falsity of the scene and the whole situation. At least that was how he explained it to himself afterward. But he was very tired. The instinct that would normally have kicked him in this situation barely gave him a prod. Szacki felt nothing but a mosquito bite, and he ignored it.

Unfortunately.

"At first sight you seem exceptional," he said coldly. "But in actual fact you're no different from all the little fucks I've been interrogating for the past twenty years. You like death, pain, and suffering because something's come loose in your brain. And you tack on an ideology that changes you in your own eyes into an evil genius, an avenger from a B movie. But you're just a nasty, spoiled little brat who'll spend the rest of her life in jail. After a week in there you'll understand there's nothing romantic about it. Just confinement, bad food, and a nasty smell. And most of all, stultifying, infinite boredom."

He yawned ostentatiously.

"As opposed to you, I hand out justice," she said, and sparks flared in her eyes.

"Of course. Are there any adults here I could speak to?"

"Your daughter's life is in my hands. Are you aware of that?"

"I am. But I've just realized I have no influence on what you're going to do in your madness. I'm sorry, but you're too far from normal for an ordinary person to be able to come to terms with you. Let's put an end to this farce. My proposal is simple. If my daughter is alive, let her go, then you can keep me here and dissolve me at will. If she's not alive, just own up to it."

"And then what?"

"Then I'll kill you."

He was surprised how easily those words tripped off his tongue. He was absolutely sure that if Hela was dead he would kill Sendrowska with his bare hands without batting an eye. For the first time he realized what the criminals he'd interrogated had meant when they kept saying over and over that at the moment they did it, they were sure they had no alternative. He'd always thought it was a stupid lie. But now he knew they were speaking God's honest truth.

"Well, I never. It's as if I were hearing my father again."

"Once a nasty little brat, always a nasty little brat."

The light in the room, warm and yellow until now, underwent a change. He looked around. To his right a television had come on, invisible until now. For a short while Szacki saw only interference, and then he saw the top of his daughter's head, stuck inside a cast-iron pipe. The image was of such high quality that he could see flecks of dandruff on her black turtleneck.

That was when he should have understood it all. But he was so tired.

Szacki stood up and took a few steps toward the screen. Hela craned her neck. Her lovely eyes were wide with terror, but there was no sign of tears or panic, just a look of resignation.

Sound came on. He could hear her rapid breathing.

He clenched his fists. He felt a movement and turned around. Wiktoria was standing right behind him. Like the statue of a beautiful goddess of revenge, a porcelain face with classic features, framed with black hair.

"You've got one last chance to stop this madness," he rasped.

"She's been in the same place all day, easy to find, guarded by just one person. You could have saved your daughter. I gave you a chance you didn't take, because you're incompetent, like all you people. And now you're going to feel what sort of pain the incompetent legal system causes. Watch this."

A murmur came from the television.

Szacki looked around, and saw a shadow on his daughter's face—someone had blocked the source of light. All her muscles tensed in a grimace of horror, which momentarily made her pretty face lose its humanity, changing it into the snout of a little creature that knows for sure it's about to die, knows it can't fight back, and has nothing left inside apart from terror. He'd never seen a grimace like that on a living person's face before. But he could remember corpses being found with the same expression.

He didn't pass out, but something strange happened to him, as if he'd become detached from himself. For the next few seconds he felt as if he were viewing the scene rather than starring in it. That was how he remembered it.

He seemed to be watching from one side. To the left stood the table with the thermos and the lamp. Then Wiktoria, slender, proud, head held high, hands folded on her chest, and black hair flowing. Then himself, his black coat a splash against the black wall, and only the white stain of his face and hair visible, hovering in midair. To the right was the large television set, with Hela's contorted face filling the entire screen.

And then a nasty rustling noise, a stream of little white spheres spilling into the cast-iron pipe, and his daughter's terrible, animal scream, combined with a dull thudding sound as her body convulsively began to defend itself in panic, despair, and pain.

As the white granules of sodium hydroxide filled the inside of the pipe at lightning speed, burying Hela up to her neck and higher, she was trying her hardest not to swallow them, stretching her neck and tipping her head back, breathing rapidly through her nose. He could see her nostrils flaring, and he could see her terrified, inhuman eyes. Then he saw her part her lips in spite of herself, and her wild scream changed into coughing as the first body-dissolving granules fell inside her mouth.

At that moment he turned and put his hands around Wiktoria Sendrowska's throat.

A LITTLE LATER

By the gate he turned back and looked at the house of horror. Its contours were melting into the darkness, a monstrous scene painted in shades of black. The pitch-black house with black gaping windows, set against the gray-and-black wall of forest. Suddenly something disturbed this festival of blackness, twinkling in his field of vision. He shuddered, sure they were coming for him. He would be next, the third creature to cross the border from life to death in under fifteen minutes.

He had no objection. Quite the opposite. He didn't want to be alive. He had no greater wish right now than to stop living.

But there was nobody behind the twinkling, no flashlight, no flare of a gunshot, or flash of a blade. Soon more sparks twinkled in the blackness around him, and he realized it was the first snow. Bigger and bigger flakes were falling more and more boldly from the sky, settling on the frozen, muddy earth, on the house of horror, and on Szacki's black overcoat.

He touched a large snowflake on his collar, as if to take a closer look at it, but it instantly dissolved, changing into a drop of cold water.

He looked at the drop, and a strange thought appeared in his mind. At first it was just a shadow, a mirage, almost imperceptible. He could tell who he was, he knew where he was, and what had happened. He realized he must get in the car and drive away, but on the other hand, all his thoughts and emotions were whirling behind a wall of smoky glass. There was something going on. He could hear muffled voices, shouts, he could see faint, hazy images—but it was all beyond him, at a safe distance, without access to his consciousness.

Apart from one insistent thought that was beating on the glass in one particular spot, screaming the same thing over and over, demanding to be noticed and heard.

"Impossible," he whispered aloud when he finally grasped the meaning of this thought. "Impossible."

When he stood up from the girl's corpse, the television was off. He couldn't remember when it had been switched off, but nothing had distracted him for the entire duration of the struggle. That was one thing. And then, it made absolutely no sense, apart from decency, for them to have put Hela into the pipe with her clothes on. The more he let this thought get through to him, the more he realized that as soon as he saw the dandruff on Hela's turtleneck, he should have seen through the whole thing. Except that at that point, the truth would have seemed even more implausible than all this insanity.

But what for? To what purpose? Why?

In the first instance he took the movement to his left to be the snowstorm, snowflakes dancing in the wind. But when he looked that way, he saw part of the darkness moving toward him—over there the snowflakes were coming together to form a human shape.

He started walking toward it, at first more slowly, then faster and faster.

And soon he came face-to-face with his daughter, shivering with cold and shock, but as alive as alive can be.

He grabbed her by the arms to be sure he wasn't hallucinating.

"Ow," said the hallucination. "Please tell me you drove here."

He nodded, incapable of uttering a word.

"Great. Let's go find the old wreck and get out of here. You have no idea what I've been through."

With his arms around her, he stroked her hair, and his hand was wet with snowflakes. As he glanced at his own palm, he saw that one of the snowflakes hadn't melted but was resting in the dip between his life line and his head line, as if heat-resistant. A new kind of snowflake, imported from China so the shopping malls could control the magic of Christmas more easily?

He looked at his daughter's hair; meanwhile she was gradually regaining her original, slightly sulky expression that said, "OK, but what's the point?" She had more artificial snowflakes in her hair, and on her black turtleneck too. He picked one of them off, held it between his thumb and index finger, and squeezed.

The penny dropped.

"Dad? Is everything OK? 'Cos I really want to get in where it's warm."

A polystyrene bead.

He flicked it away, and they walked toward the car without looking back.

LATER

CHAPTER EIGHT

Thursday, December 5, 2013

International Volunteer Day. Birthday celebrations for Józef Piłsudski (146), Walt Disney (112), and the Internet. Nelson Mandela dies at the age of ninety-five. Another legendary world leader, Lech Wałęsa, is bubbling with life. He attends the premiere of a movie about himself at the Capitol in Washington, and after the screening he comments that he can't wait to see how other filmmakers will portray his life. The European Commission blocks the construction of a new gas pipeline that would cross the Black Sea and bypass Ukraine. The Vatican appoints a committee to combat pedophilia among priests. Meanwhile in Poland curious things are happening. In Poznań a university debate on gender studies ends in a fight and requires police intervention. Pomerania is attacked by Cyclone Xaver blowing in from Germany. Warmia is under a blanket of snow. In Olsztyn it's the first day of winter. The whole city is stuck in traffic jams. Firstly because of the snow, and secondly because of a sudden decision to reschedule roadwork at the pivotal Bem Square roundabout to peak hours. Drivers are swooning with fury, and the mayor is talking about a public transport administration center, predicting that when the golden era of the tramway sets in, special cameras will control the lights. The passengers are rejoicing and so are the students, because the university announces that a ski lift will be built on the campus hill.

1

Poland is ugly. Not all of it, of course—no place is entirely ugly. But on average, Poland is uglier than any other country in Europe. Our most beautiful mountains are no lovelier than the ones in the Czech Republic or Slovakia, not to mention the Alps. Our lake district is a remote shadow of the Scandinavian ones. The beaches of the icy Baltic Sea are a joke to anyone who has ever been to the Mediterranean. The rivers don't attract visitors the way the Rhine, the Seine, or the Loire do. The rest is flat, boring terrain, partly covered in forests, but compared with the wildernesses of Norway or the Alpine countries, we come out rather pale.

There are no miracles of nature likely to grace the covers of a family travel album. It's nobody's fault, we simply happened to settle on boring, agriculturally promising land, that's all. What looked like a good idea in the days of crop rotation is not quite so obvious in the era of mass tourism.

Nor are there any entirely attractive cities. There's no Siena, no Bruges, no Besançon, Basel, or even Pardubice. There are cities in our country, though, where if you look carefully, without turning your head too much, or God forbid going one block too far, you can see the nice part.

No one's to blame. That's just the way it is.

But there are moments when Poland is the most beautiful place on earth. Those days in May following a storm, when the foliage is lush and fresh, the sidewalks wet and shiny, and we take off our coats for the first time in six months, and feel moved by the power of nature.

Those August evenings, refreshingly crisp after a long, hot day, when we fill the streets and gardens to drink in the air, catch the tail end of summer, and watch for a falling star.

But best of all is that first real winter morning, when we rise with the day after an all-night blizzard to find that the outside world has been transformed into a fairy-tale scene. All the minor defects have been covered up, the bigger ones are veiled, and the worst eyesores have gained a shining white frame, striking in its simplicity.

Jan Paweł Bierut was sitting on a bench in the children's section at the communal cemetery on Poprzeczna Street. He took in a deep breath of frosty air and reveled in the winter morning, which had changed the gloomy necropolis into a fantastical landscape, a sea of crosses protruding from immaculate white fluff, like the masts of ships sailing across clouds.

Not wanting to spoil this, he only swept enough snow off the little gravestone to be able to read the name of not-quite-two-year-old Olga Dymecka. He lit a memorial candle, crossed himself, said a prayer for the dead, and added a few words of his own, asking the celestial powers as usual to be sure to provide a proper playground. If those kiddies didn't grow after death, they'd be bored in the company of adults deep in prayer, and surely an awesome slide and a merry-go-round couldn't possibly offend the divinities.

The policeman was not related to little Olga, nor was she close to him in any other way. Just like the dozen other children whose graves he regularly visited on the anniversary of their deaths.

He knew people either laughed at him or were surprised that absolutely nothing ever shocked him. Usually the rookies in CID puked their guts out at the sight of their first bloated victims of drowning, or the old guys that had melted into the folding couch, found after decomposing for three weeks in the heat of July. There were corpses that made even the veteran detectives go pale and leave the room for a cigarette. But not Bierut. He was just as capable of functioning at the site of a death as at the site of a cell phone theft. The job was to carry out some defined duties, and that's what he did. Even the grisly tale of Piotr Najman being dissolved alive had failed to rattle him. He realized it was a particularly hideous crime, but he didn't spend weeks feeling upset, lose his appetite, or feel his heart beat faster.

In fact, Jan Paweł Bierut had spent ten years working as a traffic cop; he knew he would never see anything worse than the sights he'd already witnessed on the Polish roads. He'd seen families on vacation, tangled up with toys, provisions, and air mattresses, as if someone had thrown them all into a blender. He remembered a father and two sons on a cycling trip, all three dragged several hundred yards along the road—it had taken them two days to pick up the pieces. He'd seen children's safety seats with only parts of the passenger left in them. He had once mistaken a child's head, severed by a badly installed seat belt, for a football. He had seen death equalize the passengers in used Skodas and brand-new BMWs. It was always the same blood, the same white bones puncturing the air bag in exactly the same way.

Raised Catholic, and a genuine believer, after his first summer as a traffic cop he had lost his faith entirely. A world allowing that sort of thing to happen couldn't possibly have a guardian—no truth had ever been so plain to Bierut. With no regret or pangs of conscience, he had turned his back on God and the Church with the cold certainty of someone who knows.

A few years later he had suddenly had a conversion—not a return to Catholicism, but he had come to believe in a higher power. He realized that the circumstances of some road tragedies were too far-fetched to be the result of accident alone. The reality was slightly different from the media image: bravado plus alcohol plus a speed unsuited to the driving conditions. For there were some strange, inexplicable deaths.

The corpses at CID made far more sense. Someone had had a drink, someone had lost his cool, someone had grabbed a knife. A woman had found her lover's wife obstructing her happiness, or a wife had found her husband's lover obstructing hers. These incidents were typified by warped, homicidal logic, and yet you could still call it logic.

On the roads, that logic was missing. Two cars driving in opposite directions, in the summer, on a dry road, at a reasonable speed, crash head-on. The survivors can't explain it, nor can the witnesses. All of them were sober, well rested, and responsible. A higher power.

Read in today's paper: A couple is driving along in a car, it starts to skid, and ends up in a ditch. It's OK, the car's dented, that's all. She gets out on the shoulder to call for help, and she's hit by another car. Killed on the spot. A higher power.

Read a few days ago: A driver picks up a hitchhiker, a few hundred yards farther on he drives off the road and hits a tree. Nothing happens to the driver, but the hitchhiker is killed instantly. A higher power.

Read some time ago: A driver spots a man kneeling in the middle of the road. He stops, puts on his hazard lights, and gets out to see what's up. Another car drives up, tries to pass them, and hits the thoughtful driver. Killed on the spot. The man on his knees goes on kneeling. A higher power.

In Bierut's years as a traffic cop, so many of these incidents had accumulated that finally he had come to believe in a higher power. One of the results of his conversion were his visits to the graves of children whose deaths he had dealt with on the job. He was surprised to find how many of them were buried here, in Olsztyn. As if the parents or family had rejected them after death, refusing to take them home to their family gravesite. So the little graves were only visited once a year on All Saints' Day, in some cases not even then. They were neglected, apart from the occasional memorial candle lit out of pity. But Bierut preserved the memory of these little victims in a systematic way. He recorded the dates in his journal, and the day before each anniversary he consulted his notes to remind himself of the accident, and imagined how the child's fortunes might have gotten better since. Only then did he go to the cemetery.

On the sixth anniversary of her death, Olga Dymecka would have been almost eight, she'd have been in her fourth month in second grade, and would probably have been looking forward to Christmas by now, trying to guess what Santa would bring her. Do eight-year-olds still believe in Santa Claus? Bierut had no idea—he had no kids of his own, and no plans to have any. He was afraid of the higher power. He had a perfect memory of the day when he'd found the Passat wrapped around a tree, and little Olga Dymecka.

That was why nothing ever shocked him. So there at the cemetery, when he answered his phone and was told that a high school girl had been found dead in a house outside Gietrzwałd, he didn't bat an eye.

He genuflected and followed his own footsteps back to the car parked at the cemetery gates, feeling pleased about the snow. It hadn't been cleared away yet, and the roads were slippery as hell, so everyone would drive more carefully today, dragging along like tortoises. It was easy to have small crashes in those conditions, but not fatal collisions.

At least as long as no higher power was at work.

2

It took him forty-five minutes to reach the exit road for Ostróda, and as he drove into the forest he slowed down to admire the view of the pine trees covered in snow. Warmia was exceptionally beautiful that afternoon.

He double-checked over the radio how to get to the crime scene, and just before Gietrzwałd, when the tower of the Marian sanctuary came into sight, he turned off into the forest. On the way he picked up the forensics guys, who didn't have a Nissan Patrol and had gotten stuck in the snow and mud as soon as the fairly decent road had ended.

Yet someone had managed to drive through before him—the white expanse was bisected by black tire tracks. Probably from a four-by-four, a big one, because the snow between the tracks was untouched.

When he got to the place, he was surprised to find it was Szacki's ancient vehicle that had coped with the winter conditions.

"Goddamn, I don't believe it," said the head of the forensics team. "My off-road Kia couldn't cope, and that pile of junk got through?"

"Maybe because your Kia is as good off-road as my Astra is at flying," said Lopez, the technician in charge of biological and micro evidence.

Bierut said nothing. Luckily his reputation as a gloomy bastard meant he didn't have to take part in socializing. He valued this state of affairs highly.

He parked next to the Citroën. Everyone got out and slowly headed for the ruined cabin; no one was in a hurry to see the corpse. Only Bierut quickly strode after the two pairs of footprints leading into the house, thinking that whatever had occurred there in the night must have happened before the snow fell. He knew his colleagues were exchanging looks behind him.

He opened the door. Inside, the cold was just as sharp. The house had no furnishings, the floors were warped, there was mold climbing the walls, and the ends of electric cables were sticking out in places where thieves had dismantled the sockets and light switches. Nobody had lived here for years.

He walked through the hall and found himself in a spacious living room with a large window looking onto the forest. There was enough light coming through to examine the murder site before the technicians set up their lamps.

There wasn't much to examine—the contents of the room could be listed on a business card: one camping table, two camping chairs, one corpse, and two prosecutors.

Edmund Falk was kneeling beside the body of a girl, keeping the right distance to avoid contaminating the evidence. Teodor Szacki stood facing away from them, hands folded behind his back, his gaze fixed on the blank wall as if a gripping film were playing there.

"Which of you gentlemen is conducting the investigation?" Bierut asked.

"Prosecutor Falk," said Szacki. "Under my supervision, of course. Did you find the forensics men in a snowdrift on your way here, Commissioner?"

Bierut didn't have to answer, because just then the forensics team came in.

"Jeez, they must have whacked the president's wife—the whole prosecution service is here," said Lopez, putting his bag of equipment on the floor. "Well, look who it is—the Prince of Darkness and the Lord of the Night in person."

Szacki and Falk turned to face him. Above their perfectly knotted ties, their stony faces expressed the same standoffish disapproval. Bierut knew that they'd have laid into anyone else, but Lopez was just too good at his job. His superiors always let him get away with it.

He glanced at Falk inquiringly.

"A nice change after what we've had to deal with lately," said the junior prosecutor. "I mean it's a shame about the girl, but this time there's no mystery. Wiktoria Sendrowska, eighteen years old, a student at the Mickiewicz High School. A classic case of strangling. If there's anything else, the autopsy will show it."

"I saw the girl yesterday afternoon, I visited her family at about six on Radiowa Street," said Szacki. "I'll be making a statement, but briefly put it was because she had won an essay competition on crime prevention, and part of her reward was to ask me questions about the work of a prosecutor."

"And there you are," said Lopez, laughing as he kneeled over the corpse, "we have our first suspect."

"From what she told her mother, she was going to stay over with a friend named Luiza," said Szacki, ignoring the taunt.

"That's the first lead," said Falk. "Had she really arranged to see Luiza, or someone else? After leaving home, did she ever get to her friend's house, what does the friend know, and what do the parents know? Plus an examination of the site, plus an autopsy. Unfortunately the snow has deprived us of evidence outside."

Bierut nodded, scanning the crime scene. Something didn't seem to fit.

"Strange," he said. "I'd swear I smelled coffee in here."

Behind him one of the technicians snorted with laughter. Bierut was nuts. He could smell coffee at a murder scene.

They'd finished setting up the lamps, outside a small generator was purring away, and the room was flooded with garish white light. Suddenly everything became uncomfortably visible, above all, the youth and beauty of the corpse on the floor. If not for the mottled bruises on her neck, shimmering in shades of navy and magenta, she could have been the victim of an illness, not murder. Her porcelain face was at peace, her eyes were closed, and her black hair spilled across the floor as she lay there in her nice brown coat.

Lopez took out something resembling a small paint gun and started to spray a substance on the cadaver's neck. Bierut suddenly felt like a rookie. He was trying to remember what he'd learned about finger-printing. Could you take fingerprints from a dead body? Yes, perhaps you could in some cases, with the help of a special epoxy resin. He was ashamed to ask.

"The second lead is this house of evil," said Lopez, leaning over the victim's face, as if about to try reviving her. "I was here ten years ago, in the winter, too, or maybe it was late fall. Take a left turn off the hallway and you'll find a gutted room. There's a window with bars in there, probably installed for security. There was a fire, and a woman burned to death because of those bars, she had no way out. I'll never forget it. We scraped her off those bars, like charred meat off the barbecue. It's a house of evil, I tell you."

Nobody responded. They stood in silence, listening to the hiss of the spray gun and the rumble of the generator. They shuddered, when just outside a loud and piercing scream rang out.

3

Falk headed for the door, but Szacki signaled to him to stay put. Someone had to oversee the technicians and supervise the investigation. He guessed who had screamed and realized it was his duty to talk to Wiktoria's parents.

He glanced at the corpse, and his palms began to sweat as the memory of the previous night came back to him. He stuck his hands in his coat pockets and wiped them on the lining. A pointless gesture, as if anyone could see from a distance that his palms were sweating. He was amazed to perceive in himself the typical behavior of criminals. He'd always thought they were weak, not very intelligent, slow-witted. Hence all the hysterical, illogical moves that pushed them straight into prison cells, contributing just as much to an indictment as a confession.

And wouldn't you know, in the end he turned out to be no different.

Szacki went outside and squinted. Even though the sun had not emerged from behind the clouds, the light reflecting off the snow was dazzlingly bright for eyes that had spent the past few weeks in semidarkness.

By the gate, Agnieszka Sendrowska was kneeling in the snow, with her husband leaning forward, awkwardly embracing her, as if to help her to her feet. She stared in Szacki's direction, not with pain, but with reproach in her eyes. He took a few steps toward her and realized that her static gaze wasn't fixed on him, but on the ruined house behind him.

"It's not possible," she said. "It couldn't have happened here. What a curse this is. The man's not alive, it makes no sense. It can't be Wika, it has to be a mistake."

"I'm so sorry," he said.

Only now did she look at him, and a grimace of despair appeared on her face as she realized that if he had already been inside, there couldn't have been a mistake.

"Do you know what happened?" her husband asked in a hollow tone.

Szacki could see that he was trying to give the impression of being stronger than his wife, but there was an alarming void in his eyes, the look of someone who's ready to end it all. Seeing it made Szacki suddenly aware that Wiktoria might not be the final victim at all. It was a terrible realization; he staggered, almost falling to his knees beside Mrs. Sendrowska. He grabbed hold of a metal post, a remnant of the fence.

It crossed his mind that the father's bond with his adopted child could be stronger than the mother's. Motherhood is forged from day zero, when a couple falls back on the pillows, weary from making love. And it's a very biological relationship, as old as time, a little parasitic, written in blood, inaccessible to men, and as a result, unique and mysterious. But for the father every child is, in a way, adopted, alien to him; whether he watched his wife give birth to the creature that she promises contains some of his genes, too, or left a children's home holding a girl by the hand, he has to make the effort to fall in love with this little stranger.

In Sendrowski's eyes he saw exactly the same feelings as he'd had yesterday, watching Helena Szacka die. The man had lost his little girl, and there was nothing left of him. Just a body functioning to no purpose, its cells going through the motions, though no one expects them to.

"We have no idea," Szacki finally said, feeling as though someone else were talking. "My colleague is conducting the inquiry. I'm sorry, I know this sounds awful, but he must talk to you as soon as possible."

Sendrowski nodded, and then fixed his lifeless gaze on Szacki. The prosecutor put all his willpower into not retreating from that stare.

"You know what? She shone," he said. "It's hard to put it any other way. I know every parent always says his children are special and different, but let's face it, few of them ever are. But she really was extraordinary, everyone will tell you. What sort of person do you have to be, what sort of devil, to put out that light? How can it be possible for so much evil to have accumulated in a single person?"

Szacki didn't answer.

"Just you catch him, all right? Not for justice—in this situation, 'justice' is an empty word. But so that I can look him in the eyes, and find out for myself what the face of evil is like."

Szacki only nodded.

4

He'd gotten as far as the main road, where he hesitated for a while; finally, instead of turning left toward Olsztyn he turned right, toward Gietrzwałd. He drove a few hundred yards and, taking advantage of the lack of traffic, broke the rules by crossing the double line and drove into the gas station on the other side of the highway.

He parked next to a sign advertising new Bavarian hot dogs, got himself an extra-large cup of coffee from the self-service espresso machine, paid, and went outside. Behind the building were two wooden tables with benches; he swept aside the snow with a sleeve and sat down. When he put the paper cup down on the snow-coated tabletop, the snow around it melted so fast that it was like watching an animation.

Szacki was more aware of everything than usual, every little detail, as if wanting to get his fill before he said good-bye to the world of small, comical things that we don't usually notice because we're too preoccupied, too infuriated, or too busy procrastinating.

He had to admit it was beyond doubt. The graceful, obvious solution that released him from all dilemmas. He'd built his life on respecting the law, and that meant he must confess his guilt. Simple things are simple.

He sighed. Not because he would lose his liberty. Punishment for the crime he had committed seemed to him the most natural thing in the world. He sighed, because after conducting hundreds of investigations in his working life, now he'd have to end his career just as the one and only investigation had appeared for which he would have sacrificed everything: a case involving a screwed-up sect that had succeeded in forcing Teodor Szacki to commit murder.

He had never felt any romantic respect or admiration for exceptionally clever criminals, but this time he couldn't restrain a sort of recognition for those responsible for yesterday's events. It had all required preparation, it must have been planned to the highest degree, it must have meant taking care that the details didn't give away the theatrical set. A thousand things could have gone wrong, yet it had worked.

Result? Whoever they were, they had achieved everything they wanted.

He'd worked out his conclusions in the night, after hearing Hela's story. As he'd foreseen, her kidnapping was aimed at him. She'd been treated like a prisoner and shown a film of Najman being dissolved, so that at the critical moment, her terror of dying horribly would look convincing. But she said the fear had only lasted seconds. When the first granules fell into her mouth and she started to spit them out, she almost died of shock, but immediately she realized that—for want of a better word—it was a joke. The beads were very light, and they smelled and sounded like polystyrene.

"Suddenly I began to laugh like mad. Like I was hysterical. I just couldn't stop laughing, it went on for about ten minutes. I was afraid I'd hurt myself laughing," Hela had told him on the ride home.

Which meant that if he had held out a few seconds longer, if he hadn't instantly grabbed Wiktoria Sendrowska by the throat, their entire daring plan would have failed.

But it hadn't.

A little later the kidnappers had put a bag over his daughter's head and seated her in a car. As far as she could tell, she had spent about two hours there, which meant Szacki hadn't been watching a live broadcast, just a recording especially prepared for him. The car had been in motion the whole time, but it wasn't clear whether that meant the place where Hela was kept and Najman was murdered was two hours' drive away, or the kidnappers had simply driven around in circles to confuse her. Finally they'd pushed her out of the car, cut her bonds, and driven away. When she took off the bag she'd found herself alone on a road in the forest, in the middle of the night. For lack of a better plan, she'd started walking.

And soon after that she'd found her father.

Szacki had come up with several theories to explain the entire production, all similar in some ways. It looked as if they really did want to reform the world, hand out justice, and punish perpetrators of domestic violence. Wiktoria being in charge of them was a crude smokescreen, he could see that now. But it didn't matter anymore. Szacki assumed Klejnocki had been right about burning at the stake. Dissolving Najman, filming his death, planting the skeleton—it was all meant to lead to a grand finale, a climactic moment when every man who beat his wife or his child would find out who was hounding him.

But at what point had this plan changed into hounding Szacki?

It didn't really matter when. What did matter was that this way they had guaranteed themselves security. Szacki might not like felons, but whoever had thought this up must have been nothing short of a criminal genius.

Altogether, none of this was of much significance, nor was the interesting but irrelevant question of whether anyone he knew was mixed up in it. Irrelevant, because even so, soon he'd be saying goodbye to everyone he knew.

One single fact was critical: he, Prosecutor Teodor Szacki, was guilty of murder. Of course they'd done everything to provoke him into it, but let's face it, every killer he'd ever interrogated had stuck to the same old tune: "She had me up against the wall, I saw red, what else could I have done?"

He'd always given them a scornful look, just as he was now looking at himself. A man has the freedom to choose, and he'd had it, too. He could have controlled himself, called Bierut, summoned people, announced a breakthrough in the inquiry, locked up Wiktoria, caught the rest of the gang of maniacs, and convicted them all. He'd had a choice. And he'd chosen murder.

He hadn't killed in self-defense, he hadn't killed to save anyone else's life, and in this case it was even hard to plead extreme agitation prompted by the circumstances. He had killed because he wanted to. As an act of revenge and personal justice. And as a killer, he had to be punished.

Whoever was behind it all, they must have been watching to see what Szacki would do next. Would he exploit his position to machinate, so that even if the case came to light he'd be able to wriggle out of it? Or would he start to scheme like the typical criminal, in an attempt to evade justice? Or would he doggedly try to solve the case on his own?

The last option sounded tempting, but he knew it was a trap. The delay to this point was already reprehensible, and dragging it out, endlessly postponing the moment when he confessed—there was no other justification for it apart from cowardice. He must confess as soon as possible, to end this monstrous game, and also because otherwise he'd be exposing all his loved ones to risk. Hela had already been abducted. Lord knows what else they might think up.

He sighed heavily.

He was ashamed of it, but he had decided that, unless circumstances forced him to, he wasn't going to confess until Monday. As a result, Falk, Bierut, and the rest of them would just have to carry on with this farce all weekend, while he already knew the details of both murders and the victims, Najman as well as Wiktoria. He felt guilty in the extreme.

But that was the only solution that guaranteed him one last weekend with his daughter. An ordinary weekend—they'd go to the movies, go to the Staromiejska café for dumplings, dammit, they might even get to go skiing for a while, if the snow lasted. In the evening they'd watch TV, or she'd go see friends, and he'd come get her after midnight and pretend to take her carefully articulated speech at face value. On Sunday he'd nag her to do her homework to make up for the days she'd missed at school. An ordinary weekend for a father and teenage daughter.

On Monday he'd confess, he'd be arrested, then he'd go to jail for years and years, and his life would be over. Even if he survived as a man, that day would be his last as a prosecutor, and, above all, as a father. He wouldn't let her visit him, he wouldn't let her think about her dad in the slammer. He'd tell her to change her name and get herself a new life. Maybe he'd go see her when he came out. He'd be at retirement age, and she'd be a grown woman of over thirty. They'd go out for dinner together, without much to say to each other, and that would be that.

With Żenia, things were simpler. They hadn't known each other long, they had no formal ties, and no children. He'd forbid her to visit him, too. She'd forget him sooner. He loved her. In his way he was glad this had happened at an early enough stage in their relationship for her to be able to get over it and move on.

He sipped the coffee. His favorite, extra-large, with lots of milk and a double shot of vanilla syrup. The next time he drank one, he'd be sixty. If everything went OK. Probably older, because he wasn't going to pull any tricks to get his sentence reduced. A strange thought, but in today's world, fifteen years was no time at all. Would there still be any Statoil stations in Poland then? Would the ex-prosecutor know how to work the espresso machines of the future?

The thought of jail didn't frighten him. He knew the reality of Polish penal facilities; contrary to popular belief they weren't like third-world prisons, or the hellholes from American movies, where gangs of black men lined up to rape the new guy in a Gothic cellar. It was just a compulsory dorm for men in slippers who stank of sweat. They'd probably give him a bit of a hard time for being a prosecutor, but he was more likely to cause a sensation as an expert on the procedures. Who could possibly be better at writing appeals against the prosecutors' decisions for his fellow inmates?

The thought made him snort with laughter. He hadn't collected his uniform at the gate yet, and here he was writing the screenplay, like something out of *The Shawshank Redemption*. Huh, what an old fart, and a fantasist too.

At least he'd have time to read some books; he'd finally read all of Mann. He drank the coffee, savoring the sweet syrup that had settled at the bottom, and tossed the cup in the trash.

The sun peeked out timidly, illuminating the snow like an operatic set made of tiny diamonds. He looked around, scanning the hilly landscape of Warmia, bisected by the national road. He gazed at the soaring tower of the church in Gietrzwałd, at the forest on the horizon, and the red roofs of the houses in Naglady, protruding above the snow.

How pretty it was.

CHAPTER NINE

Monday, December 9, 2013

International Anti-Corruption Day. Kirk Douglas, John Malkovich, and former Polish *Playboy* Playmate of the Month Dorota Gawron are celebrating their birthdays. After a statue of Lenin was toppled on Sunday by protestors in Kiev, the Ukrainian authorities are starting to drop hints about round-table talks, but at the same time the militia are being increasingly confrontational. In the USA the leading technology companies write an open letter to the president demanding sweeping changes to US surveillance laws to help preserve the public's "trust in the Internet." On Mars a puddle is found, in which life may have thrived 3.5 billion years ago. In Poland politicians of all stripes parade with white ribbons on their lapels to combat violence against women, but at the same time no one is in a hurry to ratify the European convention that introduces legal provisions to facilitate effective measures against violence. In Szczytno a woman is jailed for harassing her ninety-three-year-old mother. She already has a previous conviction for the same crime. In Olsztyn, following a dispute, the head of the provincial administration withdraws his name from the new cathedral bell. Following another dispute, the mayor finds more money for culture in Olsztyn. Knowing the holiday period is on its way, everyone's gearing up for the rapidly approaching Christmas fair, although the winter magic hasn't lasted. There are melting snowdrifts everywhere after an entire weekend of snowfall. The weather is foul and cloudy, but thanks to a temperature of 37 degrees, Olsztyn is knee-deep in slush.

1

Prosecutor Teodor Szacki turned up at work before everyone else; it wasn't six o'clock yet. Earlier he'd walked around the sleeping city, taking advantage of his last few moments of freedom. After only three paces his shoes and pants were soaked, but he didn't care. He was glad about the slush, the bad weather, and his wet socks slipping in his loafers. He thought it a wonderful sensation.

He'd just wanted to get some fresh air, but he'd sunk into deep thoughts and ended up taking a very long walk. He'd reached Niepodległość Avenue, then the main crossroads near the fire station, and had stopped at the gas station for a large coffee to go and a copy of the *Olsztyn Gazette*. He'd come back a different way, between the Old Town and the neo-Gothic Main Post Office building, and then taken a roundabout way; instead of going along the edge of the black-and-green hole, he'd chosen a walk around the Town Hall and the shopping mall. At the mall he had stopped and looked up at the holding cells on the other side of the street. There was an 80-percent chance of his ending up in there today—they'd have him close by, at least to begin with, but he'd be surprised if the inquiry weren't taken over by another regional prosecution service, probably the one based in Gdańsk.

The turn-of-the-century building, redbrick of course, had been put up right in the center because in German times, Olsztyn was a garrison town. The point was the psychological effect: any soldiers loitering on passes could see where they might end up if they got stupid ideas into their heads.

And wouldn't you know, the psychological effect still worked. Here he was at the heart of Olsztyn, with the Town Hall within reach, the

Old Town a stone's throw away, the epitome of Olsztyn's architectural bad taste, in other words, the shopping mall flaunting itself behind him, and here in front of him stood the jail, only separated from the street by a high stone wall plastered with advertisements. The nearest one promised "the gentlest method of liposuction"—no doubt aimed at clients of the shopping mall rather than the inmates.

The jail had an interesting detail that caught his eye. The cell windows were covered by blinds consisting of a row of parallel metal strips set at a forty-five-degree angle, which meant that the prisoners could look up at the sky, the clouds, and the sun, but not down at the street and life going on outside.

He felt sorry about that. It would be great to see what was new at the Helios movie theater and the Empik bookstore, and the new collections in H&M heralding a change of fashions and seasons.

He smiled sadly and walked to work. Freedom was freedom, but his wet feet were making him shiver by now.

Once in the office, he took off his shoes, hung his socks on the radiator, and lounged behind his desk, finishing his now very lukewarm coffee as he browsed the newspaper. He was doing his best to put off the moment when he'd have to sort out his cases and leave detailed notes for those who would replace him. There was no point in causing his colleagues extra trouble. Once the whole thing came out, everyone here would be flooded in a river of shit anyway. A major scandal, a media sensation, extremely negative PR. Maybe it would help them a bit that this Szacki guy was an outsider, from Warsaw.

The front-page news in the *Olsztyn Gazette* was the winter weather, of course—what else would anyone expect? In the doom-laden tone typical of the media. The road services had been taken by surprise, there'd been crash after crash, the sidewalks hadn't been cleared, and to sum up: be afraid, people, be very afraid, because not only will it snow some more on Wednesday, there'll be freezing drizzle, too.

He had no complaints. For him, this first weekend of winter had been one of the best ever. On Friday he'd met up with Weronika, all in a state of nerves after flying home from the other side of the world in an effort to save her daughter. It gave him a chance to say good-bye to the most important woman in his life. She was the only person to whom he told the whole truth about recent events. As Hela's mother, Weronika had to know because, although the girl didn't seem traumatized, she could fall apart when her father ended up in jail. Or she could fall apart at any other moment when the emotional impact hit her. And it was important for someone to be there for her who knew the whole truth and would understand. Regrettably it couldn't be him. He managed to persuade his ex-wife to leave Hela with him for the weekend because he wanted to say good-bye to her.

Weronika had wept, and at first he had fought it off, then finally he had burst into tears, too. You're only young once, you only have each first-time experience once—falling in love, having a child, growing disenchanted, going through hell, and getting divorced. For him, Weronika was and would remain at the center of those first, most important times. However his life had worked out, even if he weren't going to end up behind bars.

Then he'd spent the weekend with Hela. They'd walked around wintry, snow-coated Olsztyn, more magical than ever. Of course they'd had dumplings at the Staromiejska café. And pavlovas at the SiSi. But the unexpected highlight had been the ancient *Star Wars* movies. There was a special Christmas showing at the Olsztyn planetarium, and they'd watched all six parts on a huge screen in the main auditorium, wandering the hallways in the intervals among storm troopers from the Empire, models of spaceships (advertised as "the biggest of their kind in Poland"), and screaming kids. They'd had the best time ever. Szacki only shuddered once, when in *The Empire Strikes Back,* Han Solo was forced into a sort of metal pipe and frozen solid.

But it had made no impression on Hela.

He thought about his daughter, how this morning for the last time he'd gone into her room to kiss her sleeping brow, just as he'd done since the day she was born, and tears sprang to his eyes.

He leafed through the newspaper to steer his thoughts elsewhere. Sheer boredom, just as ever in the *Gazette.* Sheer boredom that suddenly seemed attractive. A poll for Man of the Year, with the requisite ass-kissing for the mayor and the head of the provincial administration; the elder in a village called Dubeninki was warning about a further string of wolf attacks, and there was a heated debate on the topic of the orbital road, under the headline "Junction Jammed."

At least he'd be done with their hick-town traffic problems for good. Then there was a knock at the door and someone entered. Szacki quickly hid his feet under the desk to conceal the fact that he was barefoot.

A man of about sixty, who looked like a municipal clerk, greeted him and sat down on the other side of the desk.

"My dear sir," he said, "my name is Tadeusz Smaczek, I'm the deputy head of the Municipal Department for Communications, in charge of road-traffic operations here in Olsztyn. And I would like to report a crime that comes under Article 212 of the penal code."

Szacki froze. His first thought was that he was about to go to jail for one murder anyway. Would a second make much difference? He had him, he had the man right in front of him, face-to-face, suspecting nothing, defenseless. And by now he'd had some practice at strangling, too.

"And whose personal interests did you violate?" he asked.

"I'm sorry?"

"Article 212 of the penal code relates to violation of personal interests, in other words, insulting conduct. Whom did you insult?"

"You're joking. I'm the insulted party."

Szacki smiled. He couldn't imagine any abuse sophisticated enough to insult Mr. Smaczek as much as he deserved.

"How were you insulted?" Szacki asked, unable to conceal his curiosity.

The man took a file from his briefcase, on which the word *LAWSUIT* had been so carefully inscribed in capital letters that it would seem to refer to Jarndyce versus Jarndyce at the very least.

"My boss, the mayor, has received a letter from a certain citizen, who, fortunately, signed it with his first and last name, which should make your task easier. I'm submitting the letter in its entirety but shall take the liberty of quoting to you the more offensive passages concerning my person."

Smaczek peered at him over his spectacles. Szacki made an encouraging gesture, unable to believe all this was really happening. And so this was to be his swan song after twenty years in the prosecution service—mind-blowing.

"I quote: 'I see that you employ in this post'—meaning mine—'an ignoramus, and so I suggest appointing a sensible person to streamline the traffic in our fair city.'"

Szacki was impressed.

He never would have guessed a letter on this particular topic could be written so politely. He'd have started with a colorful insult, then added a list of recommended tortures, and finished with threats of violence. Meanwhile, the author of the letter to the mayor came across as the Warmian equivalent of the Dalai Lama, a Zen master of good citizenship.

"'I think that any moderately intelligent driver with experience of driving in our city would be capable of devising a better and more efficient way to regulate the traffic, especially the lights, which are posted where they're needed, and also where they're not, and that it's not necessary to employ'"—at this point he made a dramatic pause, raised an accusatory finger, and then continued in a higher pitch—"'a pseudo professional who creates obstacle after obstacle to make driving worse for us by the year.'"

Smaczek put the paper away.

"As I've said, those are merely excerpts."

Szacki could simply have thrown him out, but then he thought about all the times his own blood had curdled at Olsztyn's innumerable junctions.

"Does Concrete Man pass all his correspondence on to you?"

"I'm sorry? I'm afraid I don't quite understand."

"Concrete Man. Like Spiderman, or Batman. That's what we call your boss around here."

"You are insulting our democratically elected mayor."

"No way! I'm sure he's a great guy; I wish him the best of health, happiness, and good fortune. I'm just insulting his competence and taste. I'm insulting his faith in concrete, cement, asphalt, and paving bricks. I'm just an outsider, I don't really give a damn, and besides"— he hesitated—"I'm leaving soon. But I do feel sorry for the people here. Ever since the war, this city has been consistently ruined and disfigured, reduced to an architectural disaster area. But you guys take the cake."

Smaczek was slightly winded, but kept his bureaucratic chin up.

"Are you refusing to acknowledge my notification that a crime has been committed?"

"Absolutely. Acknowledging it would mean enabling yet another phase of your officious insanity. It would mean agreeing to cross the line between authority that is clearly stupid and incompetent, and authority that's evil, persecuting and terrorizing its citizens like in the Soviet Union. What will you think up next? Penal servitude in exile to the Warmian forest?"

The director touched his file but didn't pick it up yet.

"I'm sorry to say that I shall not be leaving it at that. I will be lodging a complaint about your decision. And about your attitude, too. I see I have two lawsuits ahead of me."

And a good thing too. It'd be a nice distraction from the prison routine when they took Szacki off to the hearings.

"I was counting on you. I was afraid the local prosecutors wouldn't take an objective view of this matter. But you're from outside Olsztyn, you're worldly-wise, you should have a broader perspective."

Szacki was saved by the phone. He picked it up.

"Good morning, Prosecutor." He heard a woman's voice. "This is Monika Fabiańczyk. Remember me?"

He frowned. The deep voice and its slightly irreverent tone seemed familiar, prompting a sense of affection and nostalgia. But he was sure he'd never crossed paths with anyone named Fabiańczyk.

She laughed, and then he recognized her. He quickly hurried Smaczek out of his office.

"Good morning to you, Editor," he said, thinking it really was a time for good-byes.

"I couldn't resist calling when I read that you're the press spokesman. It's like making Hannibal Lecter the head chef in a vegetarian restaurant."

He laughed heartily, though the joke wasn't that great. He asked about her change of name, and whether to congratulate her on getting married. As he listened to her chatter away, he thought how symbolic it was that she of all people had called him now. How long had it been? Eight years. A little longer. He was taken back to that blazing June in Warsaw, and his affair with the young journalist from *Rzeczpospolita*, which now seemed comical, the typical symptom of a midlife crisis. But it had caused his marriage to fall apart, which was why he'd left Warsaw soon after, broken his ties with the capital, and eventually ended up in Olsztyn.

Would he be heading for prison today if he'd behaved decently eight years ago—he had been married, after all—and hadn't gone to meet her at the café on the corner of Nowy Świat and Foksal Streets? He remembered wanting meringue but choosing a slice of cheesecake instead for fear that the meringue would leave crumbs all over him.

"But anyway, I heard an interview with you on Radio Olsztyn in which you admitted to making mistakes. I talked to some people about it afterward, and they were a little disappointed."

"Why?" He was genuinely surprised.

"I don't know, in the world of investigative journalists and crime reporters, you're a bit of a reference point—don't ask how my husband feels about it. You're the sheriff, the symbol of justice."

"Then surely it's a good thing I'm honest."

"Honesty and justice are two different things. We don't expect a sheriff to be admitting his mistakes. What we expect is security. A steadfast approach to guarantee law and order, to have evil punished, good rewarded, and to make the world a better place."

They talked for a while longer. After that he called Edmund Falk and arranged to meet him in the dissection room at the hospital on Warszawska Avenue.

2

Szacki parked outside the beer center as usual, and wincing with every step in his cold, wet shoes, he crossed the few dozen yards of slush separating him from the anatomy department. He'd been hoping to get there first, but ran into Falk on the steps.

The two men shook hands and went inside, shoulder to shoulder.

The hallway was quiet and empty, maybe because it was early in the day, so the students weren't there yet. Or maybe they had the day off.

They entered the dissection room, which was deserted. Although there was an odor of carrion in the air, there was no corpse, no Frankenstein, or anyone else.

Falk looked around in surprise.

"I thought we'd be meeting someone here."

Szacki walked over to the cold chamber. They took up more space at the average morgue—every cadaver found in the city had to be kept in there. The one here served didactic purposes, which was why it only had two shelves. Szacki pressed down a chrome handle, opened the door, and cold air and death came wafting out.

He pulled on the grip, and one of the metal beds slid out silently. A new piece of equipment, state-of-the-art. The Hilton for corpses, as Frankenstein had put it.

There on the stainless steel shelf lay Wiktoria Sendrowska. Blue, with a livid purple neck. She'd had her autopsy, as could be seen by the crude seam on her torso, a huge Y shape, the arms of which started near her collarbones and joined at her sternum, and the leg of which ran down to her mons pubis.

"Why are you showing me this?" asked Falk. "I was here for the procedure. I'm the prosecutor in charge of the case."

Szacki moved away from the cold chamber, sat down on the high dissection table, and looked at Falk, standing over the girl's body.

"I was going to leave it to the others, but I couldn't stop myself. I realized that after what's happened we have to sort it out between us. And anyway, I wanted to give you the chance to say good-bye to your old friend and victim. After all, she must have been like a sister to you for years."

Falk took off his coat, looked around, and carefully hung it over the back of one of the lecture-hall chairs. Then he looked at Szacki expectantly.

Szacki wasn't in a hurry. He suspected Falk was assuming he'd make a long speech, presenting him with his line of reasoning, but he was too tired for that. Apart from anything else, there was nothing to boast about. Not much brilliant reasoning à la Sherlock Holmes, just a lot of prosecutor's intuition. Earlier on, something in the back of his mind had been wondering why a stickler like Falk hadn't been through all the necessary procedures in Kiwit's case, why in spite of Szacki's instructions, he hadn't pressed the family. There was also his defiance toward Klejnocki, who had guessed the motives of Najman's killers. But above all, it was sheer intuition.

"I could ask you hundreds of questions," Szacki said. "But I'm only going to ask two. Weren't you sorry for her? Is the cause really that important?"

"Very sorry. But it was the logical choice," said Falk. "Wiktoria had been considering it for a very long time anyway—she was prepared for it. You ought to know she had tried to kill herself many times before. I saved her from one attempt myself. But this was the only way her"—he paused, looking at Szacki with a faint smirk—"sacrifice wouldn't be in vain. I don't think I have to explain to you what great significance it has."

Szacki agreed. That same night, on the way home, he had understood the significance of Wiktoria's death. The girl had not been motivated by social justice. Her revenge had a personal motive, thanks to which, sooner or later, sooner more likely, by checking the various databases, they would eventually have caught her and locked her up. Which was a threat to the whole enterprise.

In practice, her death made it impossible to explain the Najman case. And Falk was right, it was the logical choice. He had probably explained it to the girl so thoroughly that she believed it beyond a doubt. Just as he had provided her with her family's files at an earlier point and had skillfully fueled her hatred and thirst for revenge. How many years in advance does a criminal genius start planning? How many combinations of moves on a chessboard can he see ahead? Surely a good many.

"Why me?" asked Szacki.

Falk rolled his eyes.

"You know that," said Falk. "Because you could have discovered the truth. Getting rid of you was a pretty demanding task, I admit. Murder would be impossible to justify. You are, were, one of the most upright people I've ever met. Bribery was out of the question. You're too smart to manipulate or deceive for years on end—we could have been found out by a stupid mistake. But like this? We have a recording of Najman's death that will perform its educational task for decades, when shown to the relevant people. With Wiktoria's death, the only trail leading to us has disappeared. You as her killer are destroyed as a man, finished as a prosecutor, and stripped of all credibility as a witness. It's the perfect solution."

He nodded.

All that was true.

"Will you understand if I tell you that the aim of the theatrical production was not actually to eliminate you from the game?"

Szacki looked at him in amazement.

"It's the logical choice," continued Falk. "We need somebody truly exceptional. Upright, just, charismatic, uncompromising. And an experienced investigator."

"We need them for what?"

"To be our leader."

Szacki sighed. "Didn't it occur to you to ask?"

"And what would you have said?"

"I wouldn't have agreed, then I'd have started an investigation, broken up the whole ridiculous gang, and put you behind bars as a warning to any other screwballs with vigilante tendencies."

"And now what would you say?"

"Now I just won't agree," he lied.

Falk walked past the drawer with the corpse pulled out of the wall, came closer, and stood facing Szacki.

"Let's get the ugly part over and done with, agreed? Of course I have a detailed recording of what happened on Wednesday night. Not as a blackmail tool, but as an insurance policy. We're not planning to use it, but we'll change our minds if we feel threatened. By now, you're probably thinking you don't give a shit, you're going to make a confession anyway. But nobody lives in a void. Going public would brand everyone who's close to you for life. I'd like you to remember that, but at the same time to consider my proposal and agree for moral reasons."

"Says the blackmailer," said Szacki, snorting.

"You've been on the side of the law for twenty years now. A long list of successes looks good on paper. But we know what isn't on paper. Cases so weak in terms of proof that you didn't even launch them. Or else you did, but immediately dismissed them. Culprits who slipped through a legal loophole. Incompetent colleagues who've made us into the most despised institution in Poland, who, thanks to their mistakes and desistance, have not only failed to improve the world, but have made it worse. And the main thing missing from that list is your immense regret that you were supposed to be fighting for a better future. But the best you've ever managed to do is to mop up the spilled milk."

Szacki gazed at the sermonizing junior prosecutor. His face expressed nothing.

"But you can stop evil. Break the chain of violence. Save not just one family, but countless families in the future. Make sure that instead of repeating a social ill, people build good relationships with good children. So they won't end up being fathers or bosses who prompt terror. So they'll build a positive society. And in a positive society, there's less evil. It's exactly the same with cities. In an ugly district, everyone scrawls on the walls and pisses in the alleys. But if a beautiful apartment building suddenly appears there, a few properties down in each direction everything suddenly becomes cleaner too. The same principle applies to families."

Szacki jumped off the dissection table. He scowled as his socks made a wet squelching noise.

"You're too smart to believe in what you're saying. That sort of experiment is bound to get out of control. Today you're slapping evil husbands, tomorrow you'll get so drunk on righteousness you'll decide to start straightening out paid-off politicians, drivers who break traffic rules, and students who play hooky. Then someone else will come along who'll say such lenient measures are ineffective, you've got to beat harder and tougher. Then there'll be someone for whom anonymous tips will be enough to go on, and he'll start sternly repeating that you can't make an omelet without breaking eggs. And so on. Are you really incapable of seeing that?"

Falk went up to Wiktoria Sendrowska; even after death and an autopsy, she was still a beautiful girl. A real Sleeping Beauty.

"Only and exclusively 207. Nothing else. Ever. Just one category of crime, just that article. A narrow specialty."

"I thought you wanted to work in organized crime." He couldn't hold back the jibe.

"I lied. It grieves me to state that my colleagues from school are morons, getting all worked up at the thought of organized crime. Long, laborious, usually fruitless investigations that aim to punish one Russki mafioso for doing the world a service by bumping off another gangster in the woods. Waste of time."

Szacki frowned.

"It has always bothered me that the prosecution service only comes into play once the milk has already been spilled. Do you understand what I'm talking about? In a way, prosecuting the perpetrators of crime is the bitterest of professions. Someone has been injured, beaten up, raped, or murdered. They don't really care if the culprit is caught or not. The damage has already been done, and we can't undo it. But there is one kind of crime where we can take preventative action. Punish the perpetrator, isolate him from the victims and potential victims, free someone from danger. We can stop the violence before something irreversible happens. We can cut off the inheritance of evil." He paused, as if searching for the right words. "Two hundred and seven is the only article in the legal code where we really can change the world for the better and not just wipe up the blood and pretend nothing has happened. Working on that is the logical choice. I'm really surprised anyone would want to focus on anything else."

Szacki smiled to himself sadly, unable to tear his gaze from the corpse. It's always the same old story with revolutionaries. The line between saintly madmen and regular madmen is extremely thin.

"I've talked to Frankenstein," said Szacki. "He told me that it looks as if she actually wanted someone to strangle her. He said her body shows no signs of a struggle. She didn't scratch or bite or fight for her life. As if she wanted to die."

Falk made no comment.

"You know what, I once conducted a case where a major role was played by a specific form of psychotherapy."

"The Telak case. I wrote a term paper on it."

"The man who invented that therapy believed that family ties are stronger than death, and that even if people die, their close attachments pass on to their nearest relatives. He was convinced that emotions are passed down from one generation to the next, and so are crimes and injustices. If you believe that theory, Wiktoria did what she did to join her brother and mother because she couldn't forgive herself for their deaths."

"Psychology is a pseudoscience," said Falk. "Each of us has choices to make in life. And we have to bear responsibility for those choices."

Szacki smiled. He slid the drawer back into the cold chamber.

"I'm glad you said that. Because regardless of what Wiktoria did, and what you've all done, I made a choice, and I must pay for it. So let's do it this way: I'll go to the slammer, and you can go on fighting whatever you want to fight. Of course your fun and games will end badly, but if a wife-beater or two takes a good whipping along the way, I'm not going to cry over it. I mean it."

It cost him a lot of effort to utter this lie with a stony face. But he knew he had to stay in character if he was going to see through the plan that had started to form in his head the moment he had put his arms around his daughter outside that house, as Wiktoria Sendrowska's body lay cooling inside it.

Falk clenched his hands into fists.

"It can't be anyone with a personal motive," he said. "It has to be someone who'll guarantee justice."

Szacki shrugged.

"What I'm suggesting is supportive action. For a transition period. Please don't think as a prosecutor, in terms of penalizing and administering justice. Think about prevention, about saving people, about taking action that will make revenge unnecessary. Please think about . . . let's call it an early warning system equipped with combat functions."

Szacki said nothing.

"Apart from that, who knows better than you what we're fighting against?"

Szacki looked at Falk quizzically.

"Do you think some other gene prompted you to tighten your hands around that young woman's slender throat? A nobler gene than the one that causes a wife to be thrown onto the bed? A mother to be pushed away, a daughter hit? I'm afraid not. It's a male gene of readiness to inflict violence on weaker creatures."

Szacki buttoned up his coat. He suddenly felt very cold, and he was shivering—he must have caught a chill from the crappy weather and wearing wet shoes. He was truly sick of it all.

"I must serve my sentence," he said quietly.

Falk came up and stood so close to him that their noses would have touched if the junior prosecutor hadn't been six inches smaller.

"Fifteen years. That's probably what you'll get, right? You can turn yourself in today and start spending them in jail. Everyone loses, nobody gains. Or maybe instead of that you can resign from your job and devote the next fifteen years to making sure the fewest possible Najmans create the fewest possible Wiktorias."

"You're talking as if I had a choice."

"We always have a choice."

CHAPTER TEN

Wednesday, January 1, 2014

New Year's Day. The birthday of King Sigismund I, Stepan Bandera, and Grandmaster Flash. Latvia enters the Eurozone. Five towns in Poland gain city status, but none of the new cities are in the province of Warmia. There's nothing whatsoever going on—in the world of the Gregorian calendar everyone is asleep. Later they start on their New Year's resolutions, which most of them break that evening, with the first glass of wine. In Kiev's Independence Square half a million people sang the Ukrainian national anthem at midnight, as they saw in the new, landmark year. In Garmisch-Partenkirchen Polish ski jumper Kamil Stoch comes in seventh and loses his chance of a place on the podium in the Four Hills Tournament. In Warsaw Prime Minister Donald Tusk gives a New Year's interview via Twitter. In Iława a man attending a New Year's party went out onto the balcony for a cigarette, fell from the fourth floor, and suffered no injuries. In Olsztyn all's quiet—the only fact worth mentioning is that the former mayor of Olsztyn (now a councilman), who was accused of sexual harassment, is top of the ranking for Man of the Year 2013. Well-known clairvoyant Krzysztof Jackowski doesn't have the best predictions for Warmia. "It's going to be a tough year," he says. As a consolation he adds that the winter will be short. For now it's cloudy, the temperature is around 32, and there's fog and freezing drizzle.

1

Jan Paweł Bierut had never been especially fond of alcohol and regarded the national tradition of poisoning your system as unnecessary and boring; an all-day hangover seemed to him an exorbitant price to pay for a few moments of drunken euphoria. So he had no great trouble allowing the alarm clock to wake him before eight.

He got up and opened the window wide, taking pleasure in letting in the silence, which is only ever heard in the city on January the first at eight in the morning.

After that he stretched and went into the kitchen to make himself breakfast and some sandwiches to take to work.

Anyone else would have cursed like a sailor at having to go to work on New Year's Day. But Bierut was in seventh heaven. The fact that the phone hadn't rung once all night meant that nobody had slugged anyone else during the champagne-fueled fun, and if it had been a normal day at work for him, he'd have had peace and quiet until the time when people started to wake and some of them noticed that their partner had spent the night in the wrong bed.

2

Teodor Szacki slid out from under the sheets carefully to avoid waking Żenia. For a while he gazed at his sleeping girlfriend, who had been taking advantage of Hela's absence to parade around naked almost nonstop. Now she was asleep like that, too, at an angle across the bed, snoring, with her arms and legs spread wide. He had never seen any woman sleeping like that in a rom-com.

He gave her a quick kiss on the lips, kissed her on the nipple, and went to get dressed.

For the first time in as long as he could remember, the question "What should I put on today?" had meaning for him. For this reason he had spent the days between Christmas and New Year's with Żenia and Hela in deserted stores, adding to his wardrobe. They'd torn everything gray and black from his hands, claiming that twenty years of gloom and doom was already more than anyone could bear. And that at his new job, he should start with a new style, as his new self: beige, pastel colors, casual, self-confident.

So he put on a pair of thick light-blue jeans, brown ankle boots, a shirt with subtle colored stripes, and a cream sweater with a red edge to the neck. Of course he automatically buttoned the shirt all the way up, which made him look like a pedophile. He undid the top button and loosened the collar.

He took a critical look at himself in the mirror. Now he looked like a pedophile trying to hide the fact that he was a pedophile. He realized it was because of the sweater and swapped it for a dark-blue hoodie.

What a tragedy. An old guy with white hair trying to look younger, just to have his way with the head accountant after a few drinks.

He changed the top for a brown sports jacket made of a material he couldn't name.

Better. Now he looked like the author of a novel, off to meet the public at a provincial library to talk about creative torment after the age of forty.

He didn't like any of these styles, though when they were in the changing room he'd gone "ooh" and "aah" at everything, just to please the girls, and so they'd finally let him leave the dreadful place. He realized why he didn't like any of them. They made him look like an ordinary guy—not too dapper, pushing fifty, prematurely gray, already severely drained by life, with visible wrinkles, dark rings around his eyes, and thin, slightly drooping lips.

He took it all off, went to the closet, and dressed his usual way.

He drove down the empty streets of Olsztyn, heading southwest. With the radio off and the window open, he inhaled the scent of the Warmian winter, breathing it deep into his lungs. He passed the university campus and drove out of the city, then a few hundred yards down he turned left toward the village of Ruś.

The road was awful—steep, narrow, and full of holes; it must have had more victims to its name than the Boston Strangler. He slowed down to twenty and somehow reached the end of the road, then trundled into a hamlet stretching picturesquely along the River Łyna. Part of it was on the riverbank, the rest on a high embankment. He drove up it and wandered for a while—he had only received a text from Falk with the address the night before, but finally he found the right place, and stopped at a gate where there were several cars.

He smiled. He'd been expecting something unusual, the secret headquarters of a clandestine organization. A modern villa hidden deep in the forest behind seven gates. Or perhaps a neo-Gothic castle, with towers and terraces, located on a headland jutting far into a lake. Meanwhile it was an ordinary house, respectable, fairly new, its architecture and brick walls drawing on local tradition. Nothing to be ashamed about.

He sent a text, switched off the engine, and got out of the car, taking care not to brush his black coat or the pants of his favorite dark-gray suit against the dirty door. He knew he couldn't show any hesitation, so he shut the door, drew himself up straight, and walked steadily toward the entrance.

Fifteen years. Like the hero of a fairy tale, he had chosen fifteen years of servitude to atone for his misdeeds. What he did and said now would determine the next decade and a half. So far he hadn't given up his perfectly cut uniform, but what next?

Here was his unique chance to drop the formality, to renounce his stiff, cold, distant manner. To start a new life as a warm person, which in fact he was, empathetic, inclined to be humorous and friendly. Building relationships on the basis of partnership and mutual understanding, rather than being dazzlingly superior and inaccessible.

He figured it would make a nice change. He figured the people behind the green door would be expecting it. Thanks to Falk he knew all about them—who they were, why they were doing this, what their strengths and weaknesses were. He was impressed. People from a variety of professions and backgrounds, altogether an effective investigative team that could gather information fast, check up on it fast, and take swift action. Today he was going to meet them for the first time. Without knocking he went inside, and was met by a welcoming aroma of coffee and yeast cake.

He hung up his coat, took a handkerchief from his pocket, and gently wiped the tops of his loafers to make them spotless. He felt slightly tense—after all, in a few moments his old life would be over, and a completely new and unfamiliar stage would start. A stage that would be counted not in days, and not in months, but in years.

Falk came into the hall wearing jeans and a gray hooded top. He looked like a teenager. He came up to Szacki.

"Would you like a drink, Teo?" he asked.

Szacki glanced at him and adjusted his cuffs. His cuff links, tiepin, and eyes were all the same color of stainless steel, as used in operating theaters.

They faced each other in silence. Szacki listened for the familiar sound that would wipe the friendly smirk off Falk's face. And then he heard it. The gradually rising, steady wail of patrol cars with their sirens on. Not just one patrol car, but an entire cavalcade, carrying out a raid like the cavalry.

Only then did he smile, with a look that said, "Game over," and turned back the front of his jacket to show Falk his inside pocket, and the oddly colorful toothbrush sticking out of it. He couldn't resist this little joke at the very end. He deserved something for having spent the whole of December making all the right faces and seeing to every last detail, so Falk would believe he really intended to become the righteous head of his band of righteous citizens. And to bring about this meeting, when all these—for want of a better word—"righteous" people would gather in one room, and could all be nabbed at once, in the name of true righteousness, in the name of the official codes and laws, and not bizarre summary justice. He was relieved it was finally over. And felt a shade of satisfaction that at least he was going to have clean teeth on his first night in custody.

"Mr. Szacki," he said, and buttoned his jacket. "I'd prefer us to remain on formal terms."

"All right, if that's what you want, sir." Falk looked amused as never before.

Suddenly Szacki sensed something wasn't right. There were five cars outside, but he couldn't hear a buzz of voices, cups or forks chinking. And then he realized. He realized he'd lost the game.

For the past two weeks he'd been sure he was playing Falk, that he was moving things to a point where here, in this place, before he went to prison for killing that girl, he'd deliver justice one last time, by locking up the whole gang of maniacs determined to fix the world with their vigilante law.

But he was the one who'd been played. There he stood like a dummy, waiting for the cavalry—it was too late to call them off, though he wished he could, to spare himself humiliation. The saintly Falk, god-damn champion of justice and criminal genius rolled into one, would deny everything. And Szacki had nothing on him. In spite of himself he couldn't help thinking his protégé was good. Very good indeed.

"Did you really think I'd make such a schoolboy mistake?" said Falk, apparently unperturbed by the sirens wailing ever louder.

"You people always make mistakes."

Falk smiled. He stuck his hands deeper into the pockets of his cotton top, clearly letting it be understood they weren't empty, just in case it entered Szacki's head to resolve matters by force. A superfluous precaution.

"I don't. It's the logical choice."

His look left Szacki in no doubt that now it was his turn to make the logical choice.

3

Jan Paweł Bierut was in the second car in the column of five vehicles. As the officer in charge of the operation he should have been sitting in the first, but in these cases he always insisted on being in the second. The statistics were on his side—if the column of cars was involved in a collision, the first or last cars were the ones that got damaged.

Of course, there was always that higher power somewhere out there, making its plans, but Bierut held the view that it should be given as little room to maneuver as possible.

The entire operation had been meticulously planned by Szacki long ago, and Bierut had been brought in on it before the Christmas break began. He was the only policeman from Olsztyn taking part—Szacki had drafted the rest from Warsaw. They were the trusted colleagues of his old buddy with a Russian name.

At first Bierut hadn't understood Szacki's paranoid suspicion, but when he finally learned the details of the case, he agreed with him 100 percent. At least concerning the plan for carrying out the arrest. Because when it came to the idea of detaining them at all—although frankly he was ashamed to admit it even to himself—from a logical point of view, these people were doing entirely necessary work.

He explained to himself that maybe that was at the heart of the difference between the police and the prosecutors.

On January the first he had had breakfast, gone to the agreed rendezvous point, and waited for the signal from Szacki. A signal meaning that it had worked, he'd gained their confidence, they were all in one place, they would be able to arrest them all and put an end to the matter. The signal was a message generated by a special program in Szacki's phone, giving his GPS coordinates.

Five minutes later all roads leading to Ruś had been cordoned off. Seven minutes later Bierut's unmarked patrol car had pulled up alongside Szacki's wine-red Citroën XM, the most characteristic vehicle in Olsztyn's entire legal service.

Parked so cleverly that none of the other cars outside the property could possibly get out.

Bierut went up to the door and knocked.

No answer.

"Police!" he shouted. "We just want to ask a few questions."

Silence.

Meanwhile the men from the anti-terrorist squad had surrounded the house.

"Open up!"

Silence.

He gave the signal and stood aside. Invisible under their helmets, balaclavas, and goggles, the special forces unit lined up by the door. But before battering it down they tried the handle—and it opened.

They exchanged coded signals and rushed inside.

Bierut went in after them, waiting a sensible thirty seconds, in case it came to gunfire.

Once he got the all-clear, he went into the living room. There was a New Year's atmosphere, an aroma of coffee and cake, and pleasant warmth emanating from the fireplace. The whole room invited him to sit down on the soft beige couch, pick up a book, and spend a few hours oblivious to the real world outside.

In the middle of the room, standing straight as a post, was just one man: Prosecutor Teodor Szacki. He glanced at the policeman, took off his watch, and adjusted his tie. He held his wrists out toward Bierut. His cuff links, tiepin, and eyes were all the same color of stainless steel, as used in operating theaters.

As Bierut reached for the handcuffs, it crossed his mind that the prosecutor clashed completely with this warm and cozy interior.

AUTHOR'S NOTE

My sincere thanks to everyone who gave me their time and patiently answered all sorts of questions while I was working on this novel. First and foremost, the prosecutors and magistrates in Olsztyn, whom I won't mention by name in view of the nature of their work. Special thanks are due to Joanna Piotrowska of the Feminoteka foundation, who in a single conversation and by recommending two excellent sources of information (Jackson Katz, *The Macho Paradox: Why Some Men Hurt Women and How All Men Can Help* and Joanna Piotrowska and Alina Synakiewicz, *Dość milczenia. Przemoc seksualna wobec kobiet i problem gwałtu w Polsce* ["Enough Silence: Sexual Violence Toward Women and the Problem of Rape in Poland"]) opened my eyes to the widespread problem of violence toward women, and the problem of sexism in general. My thanks also to Professor Mariusz Majewski for providing me with a small fraction of his medical knowledge, and for his astonishingly vivid criminal imagination.

I apologize for occasionally twisting your words, misrepresenting the information you gave me, and showing it in the crooked mirror of a crime novel. I hope you won't hold it against me. I can assure the readers that if there's anything wrong with this book, all complaints should be addressed to the author.

As ever, I owe an inexpressible debt of thanks to Filip Modrzejewski, who is not just the best, but also the most patient of editors. Thank you also to my longstanding regular team of first readers: Marta, Marcin

Mastalerz, and Wojtek Miłoszewski. I know all the arguing was very good for the book, but personally I found it very tough. My wife, Marta; my daughter, Maja; and my son, Karol, deserve medals, as usual, for putting up with this raving madman throughout the writing process. Maja gets a second medal to allay her suspicions that she has been portrayed in the character of Szacki's daughter. It's just that every sixteen-year-old girl is fiercely uncompromising and has plenty of cast-iron excuses for not answering calls from her father.

I'd also like to take the opportunity to express my special thanks to all the wonderful people and excellent doctors who restored my father to health with great care and professional skill at the hospital on Warszawska Avenue described in this novel. My sincere thanks to Dr. Monika Barczewska and Professor Wojciech Maksymowicz.

Finally, I beg all of Olsztyn's local patriots to forgive me if their love of their city and its eleven lakes has been wounded. There's nothing I can do about the fact that Teodor Szacki is such a sarcastic Warsaw grouch. I can assure them that I myself am deeply in love with my wife's native city, although I must admit that in spite of that, or maybe because of it, its minor defects rankle all the more.

The adventures of Prosecutor Teodor Szacki are at an end. Thank you to everyone who has come this far.

Zygmunt Miłoszewski
Warsaw–Radziejowice, 2013–2014

AUTHOR'S NOTE TO THE ENGLISH EDITION

As every European crime writer knows, it's much easier to commit the perfect crime than to find a publisher in the United States. And so I bow low to my agent, Adam Chromy, who didn't just resolve to do the impossible, but also achieved it. And above all I'd like to thank my wonderful friend Antonia Lloyd-Jones, who translated this novel. Readers often think translators simply change foreign words into English ones, but there's far more to it than that. The translator writes the book, just as the author would have written it in that language if he or she were able. The better a writer the translator is, the better the book. Sometimes when I say my novels are better in English than in Polish, the readers think I'm joking. Well, not entirely.

Zygmunt Miłoszewski
London, 2015

ABOUT THE AUTHOR

Photo © 2014 Tisha Minö

Zygmunt Miłoszewski is an award-winning Polish novelist and screenwriter. His first two mysteries featuring prosecutor Teodor Szacki, *Entanglement* and *A Grain of Truth*, have received international recognition, making him the #1 bestselling author in Poland and one of the world's best-known contemporary Polish writers.

Miłoszewski has won the Polityka Passport for Polish literature. He's also twice won the High Calibre Award for the best Polish crime novel and earned two nominations to the French Prix du Polar Européen for the best European crime novel.

ABOUT THE TRANSLATOR

Antonia Lloyd-Jones is a full-time translator of Polish literature and twice winner of the Found in Translation award. She has translated works by several of Poland's leading contemporary novelists including Paweł Huelle, Olga Tokarczuk, and Jacek Dehnel, and by authors of reportage including Mariusz Szczygieł, Wojciech Jagielski, and Witold Szabłowski. She also translates poetry, essays, and books for children (including rhymes by Julian Tuwim, fiction by Janusz Korczak, and illustrated books such as *Maps* by Aleksandra and Daniel Mizieliński). She is a mentor for the Emerging Translators' Mentorship Programme run by Writer's Centre Norwich and currently co-chair of the UK Translators Association.

31901059831372